DOORWAY TO TIME

Dennis Caracciolo

ISBN: 978-1-71697-806-7 (sc)
ISBN: 978-1-71695-962-2 (e)

Cover Image Credit: NASA/JPL-Caltech/T. Pyle (SSC).

Source: Scientific Frontline.

With very special thanks to **Heidi-Ann Kennedy-Fourkiller**.

"An event can never cease to be an event. It can never get out of any time series in which it once is." -
John Ellis McTaggert

Scripture quotations are taken from the Jerusalem Bible. copyright © 1966, 1967 and 1968 by Darton, Longman & Todd, Ltd and Doubleday, a division of Random House, Inc. Used by permission

Lulu Publishing Services rev. date: 07/07/2020

This book is dedicated to my mother who
always supported my writing.

Contents

Doorway To Time

John Decker negotiated the farm tractor over his Iowa wheat field under a light rain that had just begun to fall. He braked his equipment, reached behind for his baseball cap, and, as he tucked it snugly on his head, noted something curious on the ground below. Off to his right, a book protruded upright from the freshly tilled soil. He blinked: a soft, golden glow shone from the volume and sprayed a pleasant halo of light. Decker jumped down from his tractor, pulled the book from the dirt, and read the black, strangely embossed letters:

THE BOOK OF TIME

He turned back the cover: His eyes widened when he read the chilling chapter title that followed:

The Assassination of President John F. Kennedy
35th President of the United States of America
November 22, 1963AD

Bewildered, Decker rifled through the book trying to locate the source of the golden glow. Drops of rain fell on the page he was reading, yet it retained no moisture. Who planted this thing in my wheat field? He asked himself. Decker snapped the book shut, climbed to the seat of his tractor, swung the vehicle around, and lumbered back to the farmhouse under a cloudburst. A moment before he reached the front door, he turned. Just beyond the small apple orchard, inside the barn, Decker's horses stirred and kicked restlessly in their stalls. That's not like them at all, he thought.

Once in the house, he removed his cap and unzipped his windbreaker, then he set the book down on the dining room table next to that morning's Des Moines Register. A headline near the bottom of the paper's second section jumped out at him: Kennedy to Visit Dallas Tomorrow.

John Decker was a tenacious man in his early 30's who possessed a probing, intelligent mien. Sturdily built with a narrow jaw, shock of black, curly hair, chiseled cheekbones, and muscular arms and wrists hewn from 15-hour workdays on his farm, Decker's dream since high school was to enter law school, pass the state bar, and devote his entire working life to trial law. But the burden of debt on the Decker farm buried his hopes and led to more than a decade in which Decker and his wife Elizabeth slaved to pay off the bank's loans. Then, as the couple finally saw light in their financial hardship, Elizabeth contracted tuberculosis and died nine months later. Crushed by his young wife's death, Decker declined into a bitter cynicism that erased whatever belief he had left in the goodness of life. Only one positive light remained for him: his passion for law.

Every evening Decker found comfort in the legal books that lined his dining room shelves. With an Oxford dictionary at his side, he treasured the great Supreme Court decisions of Oliver Wendall Holmes, Louis Brandeis, and Charles Evans Hughes. I will never be a lawyer, he reasoned, but I can revel in the wisdom of these three men who comprised some of the greatest thinking in American history.

Lightning lit up the house's interior and seconds later a roll of thunder slugged the sky above the farm. Decker poured himself a cup of black coffee, then shoved newspaper underneath tree branches curled in the living room fireplace. He fed a lit match to the paper, tossed his brown windbreaker on the couch, and rolled up the sleeves of his red, flannel shirt. Picking up *The Book of Time,* he sat down in the gray sitting chair next to the living room picture window and pondered the significance of the title. Staring again in awe at the pleasant glow from the book, he then searched in vain for an author, publisher, or page numbers. Mystified, Decker rested back and began to read *The Book of Time* from cover to cover.

The gruesome accounts of John Kennedy's killing, the Vice-President's chaotic succession, and the somber funeral in Arlington Cemetery in Washington on Monday, November 25, were written in a terse, incisive syle that Decker found strangely engrossing. People, places, and precise times were recorded as fact without any opinion whatsoever. The assassination described here occurs on November 22, 1963. That is tomorrow, he knew. Why would anyone fictionalize such a morbid thing as the murder of the President and describe it point by point in such awful detail? Decker flipped back through the pages. His amazed eyes re-read key, intermittent lines:

At 12:44 p.m. On November 22, 1963AD, Dr. Malcolm Perry opened a hole in the President's throat at Parkland Hospital in Dallas, Texas attempting to save John Kennedy's life...

...At 1 p.m., Dr. Kemp Clark pronounced the President dead to Mrs. Jacqueline Kennedy, the President's wife.

...At 2:32p.m Vice-President Lyndon Baines Johnson was sworn in as the thirty-sixth President of the United States of America on Air Force 1 at Love Field in Dallas, Texas by Federal Judge Sarah Tilghman Hughes ...

...At 1:55 p.m Lee Harvey Oswald, an employee of the Texas School Book Depository in Dallas, was arrested in a movie theatre for the murder of Dallas police officer Jefferson Davis Tippit at 1:11 p.m....

...At 11:28 p.m Lee Harvey Oswald was charged with the assassination of President John F. Kennedy...

...At 11:21 a.m on Sunday, November 24, 1963AD Oswald was shot by Jack Rubenstein while in police custody and died at Parkland Hospital in Dallas, Texas at 1:07 p.m...

Decker was dumbfounded. *The Book of Time* was the most sickening thing he had ever read. Why did "AD" follow the dates of some events, as though the accounts were coming from a future

3

century? As the volume dropped to his lap, his eyes drifted to the picture of his late wife Elizabeth framed in black crepe on the fireplace mantel. After a few moments of trying to come to grips with the book's accounts, Decker went into the dining room. Another framed picture hung on the wall between shelves of his law books: the official Presidential portrait of John F. Kennedy. He had been in the crowd when Senator Kennedy passed through Des Moines during the 1960 campaign. The President looked straight at him and Decker remembered thinking how the Massachusets senator struck him as being much taller than he had appeared on television and how the man exuded an extremely charismatic aura.

Decker studied *The Book of Time* in his hands and continued to be baffled by its strange composition. The texture seemed as firm as oak, yet it was strangely soft to the touch. The black print was unlike any print Decker had ever seen published on any page. Moreover, he couldn't pinpoint the source of pleasant, golden light that shone from the volume. Remembering the book had remained dry in the rain, he walked into the kitchen and turned on the faucet. Decker placed the book under the water and stared in amazement as he watched drops fall to the cover, then dissolve. He turned the valve up and allowed a gush of water to spill over the surface. It was as if the water hadn't made contact with the book at all. He lit a match and set the flame to the tip of the first page. The flame went out as soon as it touched paper. Finally, he picked up a ballpoint pen and tried to scribble a line in the margin of a paragraph. Not a speck of ink could be transferred. This just isn't possible, Decker said to himself.

Sifting back through pages, he returned to the paragraph describing the rifle fire that struck Kennedy's head, how the force of the shots threw the man to the left violently and sent blood and tissue in all directions. Then he pinpointed the precise location where the President's limousine would pass at the time of the shooting: Dealey Plaza, Dallas, Texas. The irony knifed through him: my sister works in that plaza. I met her there two years ago.

Decker reached for the telephone. "Operator, I want to make

a station to station call to Dallas, Texas. Miss Katherine Decker, 214-6789."

Decker's sister picked up the phone after two rings. "Katherine? Listen to me carefully," he said in an anxious voice. "You work in a legal building in downtown Dallas, right?"

"Yes, the Dallas Courts Building."

"Do you know of another building in that area of town with several stories that's a warehouse or a book something or other building?"

"Yes. The school book building across the street."

"*Across the street*?!" Decker shouted into the mouthpiece.

"Yes. Why do you ask, John?"

"The President is coming through Dallas tomorrow, isn't he?"

"I believe so, yes. They printed the parade map in the local paper."

"And he's passing right by the courts building, isn't he?"

"Suppose to pass here through Dealey plaza, I think. John, you sound funny. What's this about?"

Staring at the ashen sky through the pane of his kitchen window, he said: "Katherine, you don't know how bad I wish I knew the answer to that question."

The crash of thunder nearly tore the roof off Decker's farmhouse. Books fell from shelves and dishes rattled in the kitchen cabinets.

"The....floor...*John...is*....."

The line went dead.

"*Katherine!*" Decker stabbed the telephone key repeatedly. "*Operator! I've been dis—hello*?!" He tried dialing his sister several times, but the connection was severed. Then he put the phone down and turned to the last foreboding page in *The Book of Time*:

...After the administration of John F. Kennedy, the next two Presidents expanded a war in Southeast Asia that would continue until 1975AD resulting in 58,220 United States military fatalities...

This book is a depressing, sadistic work of fiction, Decker

5

thought. What is the point of publishing such a ghoulish thing as *The Book of Time*? But he kept coming back to the description of the President's limousine passing near the courts building where his sister worked. It coincided with the map of the parade route published in the local papers, according to Katherine. Decker grew increasingly uneasy. Mac and Jackie need to see this insane thing.

Throwing on his cap, windbreaker, and raincoat, Decker climbed into his Ford pick-up and fought rain and wrenching winds over the pot-holed road winding toward the Kellerman farmhouse. Glancing at the book lying on the seat next to him, he wondered what his two good friends would say when they read what he had read. By then, telephone power might be restored and he'd call Katherine again from the Kellerman's.

Bitter chunks of hail hit the pick-up's windshield like bullets as the wipers struggled hard to move from left to right. Suddenly, the brakes locked solid and the truck fishtailed, careened off to the road's shoulder, broke through the cross posts of Mac Kellerman's fence, and landed in an embankment. The rain slashed against Decker as he jumped out and stared at a flat, soggy rear tire. The spare, he remembered, had been left in the barn after hauling hay in the truck the day before. *Damn it!*

After tightening his cap and fastening his raincoat collar up to his ears, Decker sloshed in his rubber boots through the punishing rainstorm. He kept thinking of the unnerving parallels between his life and the life of President Kennedy as he hiked over the narrow, mud-strewn road: not only does my sister work in the plaza where Kennedy is supposed to be shot, the book described the President being pronounced dead at Parkland Hospital. I was at Parkland Hospital two years ago when I fractured my wrist helping Katherine move into her house in the Oak Cliff section of Dallas. When he finally reached the Kellerman front porch, he wiped his rubber boots on the mat and pushed the door open.

"Mac! Jackie!"

Stepping into the kitchen, he picked up the phone and cursed when he detected dead air again. Decker went into the dining room and, through the bay window, caught Mac's Dodge truck pulling in on the right toward the house's detached garage.

"John," Mac said, bursting into the livingroom, "I saw your truck and the blow-out. A hell of a time to—"

Decker stopped him cold and said, "Listen carefully to what I'm about to tell you, Mac."

He told Mac everything. His good friend listened with an oddly patient expression as he gazed out the window.

"It was the specifics of it, Mac," Decker continued emphatically. "The names, events, timelines. It was the weirdest, scariest damn thing I ever read. And that strange glow it gave off was *crazy*."

"John," Mac began gently, "can I say something as a good friend? Since Elizabeth passed, Jackie and I have watched ya' sink deeper and deeper into a very unhealthy isolation. I say this to help you: we don't think ya' ever recovered from Liz's passing the way you should have. Understand that kind of loss takes a very heavy toll on the emotions, John."

Decker exhaled. "So you think I'm having a mental breakdown and I'm imagining that book. Is that about it, Mac?"

Mac shrugged.

"I actually don't blame you for reacting this way. But we've got a book out there sitting in my truck that proves what I'm saying, don't we? How'd it get there? Unless, of course, you're implying I wrote that Godforsaken thing myself."

"John, when ya' lose your wife, live a life of 15-hour workdays, never give yourself any rest or leisure time off, emotions go haywire. And we know your admiration for the President, don't we? Please let me drive ya' over to Mercy General. Maybe they can give ya' some medication that will—"

"No offense, Mac," Decker said cutting him off, "but at the moment, I really don't give a damn what you think. Just drive me back to the pick-up and let me show you the most amazing thing you've ever read. You know, my sister works in the very plaza where the book said Kennedy will be assassinated."

"And what do you think that proves, John?" Mac shrugged. "All right, show me this crazy thing."

Twenty minutes later the two men pulled in behind Decker's washed-out, Ford flatbed on the narrow road's shoulder. Decker jumped out of Mac's Dodge under a cloudburst and threw the door of his truck open. His eyes bulged: the keys sagged in the ignition, but The Des Moines Register was all that lay on the front seat. *The Book of Time* was gone.

"It doesn't add up, Mac," Decker said, searching the interior frantically. "I left that book right here on top of the Register!"

Mac removed a jack and a spare tire from his Dodge in the heavy rain. "Let me fix the flat, John."

"That book was real, Mac! I held it in these hands! I read it with my own eyes!"

Mac loosened the lug nuts on the pick-up's rear wheel. Decker shouted in the pouring rain over his friend's stooped figure: "How'd I know the parade was going down Main Street in Dallas and then through the plaza? Explain that to me, Mac!"

Mac said nothing as he threw the deflated tire onto his friend's truck. But Decker screamed into the storm: "*I said I called my sister, Mac! What about all the coincidences? Explain them!*"

Mac wiped his face with a handkerchief. "Do you seriously believe someone wanted to steal a book more than they wanted to steal the truck? Who comes along here on this desolate road in a rainstorm like this? And even if somebody did happen by, they would have passed me and I saw nobody. You're saying somebody took a book, but not the truck with the keys left in the ignition? The assassination of the President? Listen to what you're telling me, John. *Listen to your words.*"

The two trucks pulled into Decker's farm as the ugly, black sky released a torrential downpour. A police car parked in front of the house and an officer in plastic rain gear had just lifted a hand to knock at Decker's front door.

"Mr. John Decker?"

"Yes."

"We received a call from your sister in Dallas who said she was concerned about you and requested we swing by and check to see if you were OK."

"I'm fine, Officer. Are the telephone lines still down?"

"Power is out everywhere. Police are working off emergency circuits right now. Worst storm I've ever seen in this county."

"When you get a chance, would you call my sister on those circuits and tell her I'm all right?"

"I will. But I do have other stops to make. Not sure when I'll pull back into the station."

The officer drove off in his patrol car. Mac and Decker stepped inside the house.

"John, I'm gonna' say it again: I really do think you need to see somebody at Mercy."

"Tell you what, Mac, let's wait 24 hours. By then we'll know for sure if I need a psychiatrist, won't we? But I'm not leaving here till the power comes back on."

"At least stay at my place tonight. Will ya' at least do that, John?"

"No, thanks," Decker stated, poking the fire with a long, iron stoker, then tossing in more tree limbs. "I'm stayin' right here till power's restored. Then I'll call Katherine."

"And tell here what? John, if ya' do reach your sister, I think it best not to tell her—everything. Might just scare the livin' daylights out of here."

"Thanks for the advice, Mac. And thanks for fixing the flat. I appreciate it."

Mac left Decker standing in front of the fire warming his freezing hands. Above the mantel, Elizabeth's portrait stared at him with poignant, caring eyes. "Everything's for a reason, Liz," he remembered assuaging her comfortingly as she lay weak and pale in the last hours of her life. Then his wife uttered words that were as clear to him as if she were in the room speaking them at that moment: *John, I pray that one day you'll come to think again*

9

and again about what you're saying now." The next morning, just after dawn, Elizabeth left him.

Two days later Decker crept away from his young wife's internment in a cold, bloodless state of mind and said to Mac: "Those who believe in the existence of a loving God and spout their empty religious words have the brains of an ass. Man invented religion to cushion us all from the curse of hell on earth." Time had stopped for John Decker. He answered his wife's death with 16- hour workdays caring only for his livestock, wheat fields, and orchards. As time collected, his brooding isolation deepened. Except for reading law books in the evening, the farm was all that mattered in John Decker's darkened world.

Dazed, Decker sagged in the chair next to the picture window and wondered if Mac had been right. Am I in the midst of a breakdown? Was finding that book a hallucination, the product of a run-down, battered mind? Then Katherine's employment in the Dallas plaza loomed up again. She works in the courts building on the very street where the book said Kennedy will be gunned down. What are the odds of those two facts parallelling one another? Does a sick mind create that kind of twisted connection?

The journalistic style in which the book was written also continued to gnaw at Decker. It was the unambiguous, succinct style of a front page newspaper story and not really like that of a fiction novel. The references to doctors, law enforcement officials, and politicians—so precisely described—with events told in chronological order to the minute. And if some madman wrote the book, why didn't he leave it near my front door where I'd be sure to find it? How could anyone possibly know I'd be on the tractor plowing that specific area of my wheat field this morning when I didn't decide to plow it until just before breakfast? But the book's disappearance from his truck's cabin unsettled Decker most of all. He knew he left it on the front seat. No one will ever convince me I put it anywhere else, he swore.

Decker's thoughts began to drift toward the irrational. What if the President's death described a *possible* future—a warning of what could happen if action wasn't taken? Insane, he reasoned. That would mean the book came from—impossible! Doctors working frantically on the body of the President of the United States at Parkland Hospital tomorrow is science fiction trash pure and simple. Decker cursed himself for considering such garbage.

He went into the kitchen and picked up the phone, listened again to a dead line, then slammed the receiver down in frustration. Over unrelenting wind and rain, the ominous whinnying and stomping of his horses in the barn reached his ears. Decker knew his animals well. Something more than the storm was aggravating them.

Putting on his cap and buttoning his raincoat to the neck over his Pendleton, Decker sloshed through the mud across the house's front yard. This is rain from Hell, he thought, as he threw back the barn door latch. Inside, the animals stomped wildly as if trying to break down their stalls and tear loose. My horses never behaved this way. Not in a hundred storms.

Decker tossed blankets over his horses and ran his comforting hands across their brows. He studied the frightened eyes and sensed his horses saw something he did not see. All at once a plank tore loose from the roof near the rear of the barn. Water sprayed through the opening and flooded in on hay bales and sacks of oats. Nearly dislocating his back, he shoved the bales into a dry area frantically as thunder and lightning broke overhead again. The barn's creaky walls rattled, the horses kicked and snorted in their stalls, but Decker worked fast and nailed plywood sheets into place under the torn plank. When he had plugged the leak, he collapsed on one of the bales. A haunting, whistling wind shot through a space in the boards he had just nailed and it sounded like a raving howl coming from the center of the Earth. These horses sense something I'm not sensing, Decker thought

As he wiped the rain and beads of sweat from his face, Decker sat on a bale trying to collect himself. A sunny, summer day in 1960 came back to him. Senator John Kennedy was touring Des Moines and Decker and Liz stood on the sidewalk in front of the Grange Auditorium waiting for the President to come out after a labor speech. Kennedy appeared, turned left with his entourage, and moved in the couple's direction. He was working his way along the crowded sidewalk, shaking hands, beaming from ear to ear.

"He's coming straight toward us!" Liz squealed, clutching her husband's arm.

Kennedy drew closer, made direct eye contact with Decker, and extended his hand. Decker shook it and remembered thinking how firm the senator's hand was after shaking thousands of hands that day. Then the events in his life since graduation from high school turned like the glass panels of a revolving door: failure to reach law school, the farm's punishing debt, Elizabeth's illness and death, his ceaseless, backbreaking farm labor and bitter loathing of the outside world. Suddenly, the President was in front of him riding through the plaza in a limousine heading straight into an ambush in downtown Dallas.

Decker soothed his horses one last time. The storm had begun to weaken and an ebbing wheeze of wind had finally turned to light showers. When the animals quieted, Decker closed and latched the barn door, walked toward the house, and, while sloshing in his boots through the coffee-colored ponds of water, stopped in his tracks and gazed up at black clouds forming like bags of catastrophe in the November sky. An apocalyptic calm had descended over the plains of Iowa.

Once inside the house, Decker tried the phone again. Nothing. As the gruesome events described in *The Book of Time* whirled around him, he remembered the chief rule of thumb for determining truth in witness testimony: record statements as soon as possible after the fact before time and doubt cloud memory. Decker took pencil and paper and sat at the kitchen table scribbling every detail he could remember reading. He listed names, places, and timeframes as fast as he could recall them. After filling nearly an entire page, he asked himself a question that had been at the back of his mind since he first began reading the assassination accounts: What if the characters in the book were real people in Dallas?

Decker was in his truck heading toward north Des Moines

with his written notes stuffed into his raincoat pocket. By the time he reached the city's outskirts, county power had been restored. But he would not call Katherine; Decker wanted to test not only the truth of the *The Book of Time*, he also wanted to test his own sanity. He parked the pick-up, hurried into a drugstore, and collected $3 in change. Closing the door on a pay phone, he sat down and removed his notes. Then he dialed the operator and asked her to connect him to Parkland Hospital in Dallas, Texas.

"Sixty-five cents, please." Decker's trembling fingers inserted the coins.

"Mam, I need some information," he said reading from his handwriting. "I'm trying to locate two doctors. Does a Dr. Perry practice medicine there at Parkland?"

"...Yes. Dr. Malcolm Perry is most definitely a general surgical resident here."

Taking a breath, Decker then asked: "Also—would you know if a Dr. Clark might be on the hospital staff?"

"That is correct. Dr. Kemp Clark is chief of neurosurgery."

"Could you please tell me," Decker continued, swallowing hard, his voice cracking a bit, "if someone was brought into the emergency room after, say, a gunshot wound, would those two doctors likely be the ones attending the victim?"

"They very well could be. Both are attached to trauma. May I ask why you're inquiring about a gunshot wound? Do you know of someone who's been injured?"

Decker hung up.

According to his notes, Doctors Perry and Clark had attended the dying President. Perry was the first to work on Kennedy and had opened a hole in his throat in a desperate attempt to save his life. Clark pronounced the President dead to Mrs. Kennedy. Decker stared at another name and place in what he had written. With cold, nervous fingers, he dialed the operator again.

"Operator, please connect me, station to station, with Dallas, Texas. I want a book depository building whose full name I can't recall. Can you search for it?"

"I have…The Texas School Book Depository on Elm Street?"

"Yes. That's it."

"Would you please deposit 65 cents?"

Decker's fingers could barely feed the coins into the narrow slits.

He listened to his own breathing as two rings followed, then a woman's voice answered: "Texas School Book Depository. How may I help you?"

"Mam, I'm trying to reach an employee working there in the building. His name is Oswald."

"One moment. Y—yes. Lee Oswald works on the upper floors, but I have no way to put you through up there. I can, however, take a mess—"

The phone went straight to the hook.

Decker stood outside of the drugstore shivering in disbelief. In the thread of sunlight that broke through clumps of black clouds, he wiped the sweat from his forehead and neck and crept back down the street toward his truck. He had established that Perry and Clark were doctors at Parkland Hospital just as he had verified that a man named Oswald worked on the upper floor in the plaza's book building. Those people are not fictional characters, he now knew. And if the book was right about them, what else was it right about? As he sped back to his farm, Decker's acid stomach felt as if it were ready to split open.

One hour later John Decker stood at his living room window gazing pensively through the rain-washed panes. What he saw was more of an historical portrait of a broken down farm after a storm rather than his own farm. The entire landscape seemed to have been photographed in the reddish-brown tint of Civil War sepia tones: a sullen, Midwest calm between downpours framing a sagging barn, broken fences, and haggard tree limbs and branches. He compared the run-down wasteland of what he saw to himself. After years of pointless drudgery on this farm, why have I suddenly experienced the most inconceivable event of my life in my own wheat field? Peering out into the distance where he found *The Book of Time,*

14

Decker remembered his favorite quotation from Supreme Court Justice Oliver Wendell Holmes: "To reach the port of heaven, we must sail sometimes with the wind and sometimes against it, but we must sail, and not drift, nor lie at anchor."

Sinking to the chair next to the picture window again, he thought hard about his life 'lying at anchor.' I have languished on this farm since childhood—holed up in it more accurately—saw my law school dreams dissolve, married Elizabeth doomed to break her back helping me conquer the bank's load, and when the debt was nearly paid, watched her die a slow, miserable death. For 33 years I've stumbled through existence in the middle of nowhere. The fact is, I never accomplished a single career dream. I'm nothing more than a hayseed farmboy. I'm the sum total of nothing.

Decker got up and stared dolefully at the last embers in the fire. Was Justice Holmes right? If we sail with the wind, will we eventually arrive at a peaceful port?

Ten minutes later Decker made the most improbable decision of his life. He was on the phone speaking to an attendant at Des Moines International Airport.

"Mam, I want to make a reservation on the next available flight to Dallas, Texas."

II

The runway fell away when Decker's plane, flight 411, became airborne at 6:25 p.m. destined for Dallas. He had bought a Chicago Tribune at an airport kiosk before boarding and found the President's itinerary for November 22: Kennedy would land at Love Field in Dallas and was to motorcade through the downtown area followed by a business speech. He clearly remembered *The Book of Time* describing the President's assassination occurring at 12:30 p.m. But as Decker leafed through the newspaper, he kept reflecting on the transformation in his thinking. Yesterday at this time I would have considered what I'm doing now to be deranged.

15

Do I actually believe the accuracy of the events described in a strange book that disappeared from the front seat of my car? Was Mac right? Am I trying to rectify the misery of my life through some hairbrained fantasy?

The flight was scheduled to arrive at Dallas' Love Field at 8:41 p.m. He'd call Katherine from the airport then sit down with his sister later, describe what he had experienced, and show her his notes. Together they would try to verify more names and facts and attempt to prove the book's truth. Decker estimated that if Katherine became convinced the predicted events were accurate, they'd have over 12 hours to plan a course of action to prevent the President's limousine from passing through Deleay Plaza in Dallas.

A ping sounded in the plane's cabin. A little white light went on above his head. The captain's voice spilled out over the intercom:

"This is Captain Swindle. Unfortunately, Ladies and Gentleman, we're having some difficulties with our landing gear and we're going to have to make an unscheduled stop in Wichita. I'd like to request you fasten your seat belts and place all carry-on luggage securely in the racks above you. You'll find our stewardesses to be very helpful. I'll keep you duly informed."

Wichita?!

Decker fastened his seat belt anxiously. The stewardesses were already moving quickly through the aisles assisting passengers with their carry-on luggage. Decker's mind reeled: if the President parades through the downtown area a little after 12 noon tomorrow, I'd have to be at Katherine's well before that. Will I make it to Dallas with enough time to spare?

When the stewardess reached him, Decker asked, "Mam, how long of a delay do you think we'll have in Wichita?"

"If we're lucky and catch another flight immediately, it might just be an hour or two on the ground," she answered.

The plane was losing altitude. Decker glanced out the window and saw the twinkling lights dotting the plains in the Midwest dusk. What if I'm stranded in Wichita? What if I can't get a connecting flight in time?

Minutes later the stewardesses were in jump seats buckling in tightly. It appeared to Decker as if they were strapping themselves into straightjackets.

Trouble with the landing gear?

The plane sank precipitously. Decker's stomach felt as if it dropped out of his body. Groans went up from people around him, nervous heads turned and bobbed. Then a grim foreboding shot like a wave through the passengers as the aircraft veered to the left and sawed off its flight pattern. In the seat behind him, he listened to a woman whispering the Catholic rosary.

The horrifying image of a plane crash opened up before him. What if the book had nothing to do with the assassination of the President? What if getting me on this plane to die was the real purpose of it all? Decker's fists clenched around the edges of the armrests. He closed his eyes and tried to convince himself he would land safely in Wichita and would get an immediate second flight to Dallas and lose no significant time at all.

The plane veered off sharply again. Worried voices mumbled through the interior. For one horrifying moment, Decker thought the fuselage was going to turn upside down. Several passengers gasped. Something crashed to the floor in the plane's rear kitchenette. Up ahead, a little girl was whimpering. One stewardess strapped to her seat had her eyes closed and was mumbling to herself. A prayer? Does she know something I don't?

Telephone circuits going out in the county—convenient. The truck's flat tire—convenient. The book disappearing from the front seat of the truck—convenient. Was it all to put me on this flight? Am I about to go down with the passengers and crew on this plane?

The airliner slowed in mid-air, then shifted speeds. From somewhere in the middle of the cabin a man guffawed in gruesome contrast to the grim interior.

A second ping went off.

"Captain Swindle again. As I mentioned, we're having a slight problem with a portion of our landing gear. Hitting the runway in Wichita could be a little less than smooth. Be very sure your seat belts are fastened and all luggage is secure. We'll be landing in a few minutes."

A little less than smooth?!

The Wichita runway lights were shooting up in the distance. What if the pilot was lying? What if the landing gear had been damaged far worse than the pilot described? A belly landing?

The airliner swayed like a garden swing in the flush of a summer breeze. Decker sensed the pilot was struggling to keep the fuselage level. The plane tilted to the left, then steadied. Suddenly, it dropped altitude again, then tossed about wildly. The Wichita runway was coming up fast.

Finding that book had nothing to do with any assassination. It was all about destiny: placing me on board a flight headed for oblivion.

Contact.

The plane's walls shook like plywood. The agonizing screech of metal combined with an ugly reverberation from under the aircraft shot through the fuselage's sides and floors. A thick puff of smoke rushed passed the plane's windows.

Gasps and screams filled the interior. The plane was on the ground, careening with a terrifying and unbearable metal on metal sound. A tire or some piece of equipment exploded out from the rear and released a high-pitched whistle. The airliner tilted, then skidded on the runway like an arctic sled on a sheet of ice. Decker's heart sank into his bowels.

Elizabeth, you were the most decent thing that ever happened in my life...

The landscape beyond the cabin window fluttered. Decker unbuckled his safety belt spasmodically, the last thing he thought he would ever do. It was panic-stricken behavior, neuromuscular reaction without thought shooting out of the horror of wanting to free himself from the stifling seat belt that tied him to disaster.

It came at him from the side. A blow he didn't see coming. Decker's head felt as if it had been knocked off the stick of his neck.

The book exploded out of the dirt and shot up like a golden comet...Elizabeth—dancing through the stars...Mac lit a cigarette and tossed it to the truck's gasoline tank, then howled at the explosion...the roof coming off the barn and a hundred horses stampeding away in terror...Kennedy hit in a crossfire...Blood and tissue everywhere...

Decker lay flat on his back on a hospital gurney staring straight up at a ceiling that seemed to be rising away from him. His head ached and his neck felt as if it had been twisted by a professional wrestler. A young nurse held a clipboard, turned toward him, and smiled.

"So, Mr. Decker, a pretty rough landing, eh? You didn't keep your seat belt on, did you?" The woman's voice sounded as if it were coming from a scratchy Victrola.

"What...happened?" he asked groggily.

"Apparently, from what's on the report, you got hit by a flying suitcase, Sir."

"Wha—what time is it?"

The woman looked at her watch. "It's 8:32, Mr. Decker."

"My God..." Decker said, struggling to get up.

"Sir, please lie down," the nurse said placing her gentle hand on his shoulder. "Dr. Crenshaw would like to examine you. You were knocked unconscious. It's possible you could have a serious concussion."

Decker's head pulsed with an awful throbbing. He collapsed back to the pillow and stared up in misery. His shoes and pants were folded neatly on a chair against the wall, but when he looked at them they seemed to be miles away. Decker slid his right leg over the side of the gurney and tried to sit up again.

"Please let Dr. Crenshaw see you, Mr. Decker," the nurse insisted. "There's only one patient ahead of you."

19

Decker complied. His head sank to the pillow. He closed his eyes in misery.

"I'll ask Dr. Crenshaw how long he thinks it will be."

"Just get the doctor, will you, Nurse? I have a lot to do and a flight I absolutely must catch."

It was a very small examination space. A thin, white curtain draped from the ceiling down to the end of the gurney. Someone on the other side was shuffling about in an adjoining examination area.

Decker lay flat and turned his head from side to side to test his neck. The fog was clearing and the last moments of his flight slowly clicked back into place. Beyond the curtain, heavy footsteps crossed over the floor.

"Mrs. McClelland, I'm agent Wade and this is agent Sanders. We're with the FBI."

"Thank God you're finally here," the woman said sounding profoundly relieved.

"Mrs. McClelland, we'd like you to tell us about this document you found."

"As I stated on the phone, I found this book titled *The Book of Time*—the most frightening thing I've ever read. It described the assassination of President Kennedy tomorrow in Dallas: how he'll be shot and killed, how Vice-President Johnson will become the next President. It told everything in shocking detail: the doctors who will be frantically trying to save Kennedy's life and a man arrested for the assassination who works in a nearby building. It was incredibly precise—*horribly* precise..." The woman's voice trailed off emotionally.

On the other side of the curtain, John Decker turned pale and felt for a moment as if he were about to vomit. Grasping the edges of the gurney, he listened to the woman's voice in dream-like suspension.

"Mrs. McClelland, we'd very much like to see this book."

"I don't know what happened to it. As I drove across town to the FBI office to show it to you, I had an accident which is why

I'm here. The tow truck came and when I got back to the car, the book was gone! It described the events surrounding President Kennedy's assassination tomorrow in Dallas. But I'm not crazy. I saw it and I read it!"

"Well, do you know who wrote this document?"

"No, I don't. It had no author, didn't say where it was published. You don't know how bad I wish I could hand it to you now. You've got to warn law enforcement in Dallas! Please take action right away before the President is killed!"

Decker was paralyzed. Absorbing every word the woman uttered, two conflicting reactions exploded within him: joy that he had proof of his own sanity; astonishment that he had crossed paths with another person who also found *The Book of Time* and was now detailing the same events he had read.

"Please try to recall as best you can, Mrs. McClelland: did this document seem like a plan or set of instructions that someone might follow for action against the President?"

"With the details of the doctors' racing to save his life; Mrs. Kennedy's misery; world leaders attending the funeral on Monday? I don't think so. The account was written—as if it had already happened...as if it were *history in a history book...*"

"Could you tell us just how this book described the President being killed?"

"He will be shot while riding in his limousine through Dallas in a parade tomorrow afternoon. There will be shooters with rifles waiting in different locations in front and behind him—along the street and in high buildings. Not only will the President be shot, but so will the governor of Texas who's with him! Please, *warn your superiors that the President is in grave danger and that precautions need to be taken in Dallas!*"

"Now exactly where did you found this book, Mrs. McClelland?"

"It was on a shelf in my library. I'm a librarian for the public school system here in Wichita. I was taking inventory of our books and there it was."

"Was it in the fiction section?" Sanders asked.

McClelland didn't laugh. "Is that supposed to be funny, Sir?"

"And it was just there among the other books—on the shelf?" Wade interrupted. "No one gave it to you? It wasn't mailed to you? No one left it behind in the library?"

"It was on the shelf with other books," she repeated impatiently. "No one gave it to me and it certainly wasn't mailed. When I found it, I checked it against our system. It was never entered into the library inventory; it had no identification in it whatsoever indicating it had never been in the Wichita Public School system or any other system at all. And it had this pleasant glow about it."

"It was glowing?" asked Sanders.

"Yes. A very pleasant, golden glow. But I couldn't find where the light was coming from. No batteries. No plugs or cords."

Wade and Sanders exchanged glances. "Mrs. McClelland, we assure you that we take any potential threat to the President very seriously."

"According to the book, the President will not be protected as he should be. You have to do something."

"Did this document say in what specific way that protection will be compromised?"

"It said Secret Servicemen will be called off from guarding the limousine. The police will not be in places they normally would be for a Presidential parade. The Secret Service will never check the high windows and buildings along the parade route. President Kennedy will simply be left wide open and shot from three sides."

"This book you found said all that?" Sanders asked surprised.

"Yes."

Wade removed a note pad. "I assume," Mrs. McClelland, "you reside here in Wichita?"

"Yes."

"And you had an accident not far from here a while ago—and brought here with a possible whiplash or neck injury?"

"You've obviously spoken with the doctor. Yes, all that's true."

"Have you taken any medication since you had this accident?"

"Yes, the doctor gave me some pain pills. I took two for my neck."

"Mrs. McClelland, I'm going to give you my card that has my phone number. I want you to call me if you find this book or remember just where it came from or if anyone contacts you about it or has any information pertaining to it."

"There *was* a book," McClelland insisted. "I took it from the library shelf. I read it. It was real. As real as both of you standing here in front of me now."

"Books are your trade, your profession, right?"

"You think I'm having a delusion after my accident, don't you?"

"I did not say that, Mrs. McClelland. It's just that we don't have anything concrete here."

"When did your husband pass away, Mrs. McClelland?" the other agent asked.

"Just less than a year ago. You *do* think I'm delusional, don't you?"

Decker could practically see the agony in the woman's face through the curtain. He had processed the interview and tried to guess the odds of two people finding the same book in different states, then thrown together in a hospital emergency room.

"Are you or are you not going to take action?" McClelland pressed.

"Well, Mam," Wade stated, "we are most definitely going to file a report."

"My God," McClelland said. "You're not going to do a damn thing, are you?"

"Mrs. McClelland, we do not have a shred of physical evidence proving this book's existence—which you claim later disappeared. Nor can you connect anyone to it we might be able to question. But you have my word a report will be written and sent to our superiors. All we can do at this point is to turn in our report and suggest you call us if additional details turn up."

"Let me ask both of you a question: Tell me how I knew that the doctor who will work on Kennedy will be a Dr. Perry? A woman judge will swear in the Vice President on the plane going back to Washington: her name will be Hughes. Kennedy's autopsy will be at a naval hospital in Maryland tomorrow night. I never heard of these names and places before today. How did I know they existed? Please explain all of that to me."

"We can't," Wade admitted. "And we're certainly not going to try."

"Again, Mrs. McClelland, I guarantee we will submit a thorough report. We do appreciate you contacting us. If you ever think of anything more, you have my number."

Decker could hardly breathe as footsteps tapped back across the room and trailed off out into the hall. Only a curtain separated him from someone who had also found *The Book of Time* and experienced what he had experienced. Sliding over the hospital gurney delicately, he gathered his clothes and dressed. He thought he heard the woman whimpering as he buttoned his shirt, slipped into his khaki pants, and zipped up his windbreaker. Decker knew he had to confront this person before she left the examination area. He steadied himself, took a deep breath, then reached for the white curtain and threw it to the side.

McClelland was completely unlike what he had imagined her to be. She was a strikingly pretty woman in her early thirties with kind, expressive blue eyes and stylish dress, shoes, and scarf. She wore a navy blue cashmere sweater and matching gabardine slacks that hugged her attractive figure. Standing at a mirror and running a brush through her black, cottony hair, she turned to Decker startled and quickly dabbed her red eyes with a handkerchief. "I beg your pardon, Sir, but—"

"Please excuse me. My name is John Decker."

"I'm afraid I have to get out of here," she blurted, shoving her hairbrush into her purse and snapping it shut. As she began to walk passed him, Decker took her arm.

"*The Book of Time*: strange paper; no page numbers; very fine black print; and a golden glow you can't pin down. The assassination described precisely naming time frames, law

24

enforcement officials, and doctors. A man named Oswald will be arrested at a theatre; the President's funeral will be on Monday at Arlington cemetery in Washington…"

McClelland froze and peered at Decker as if she were staring into the face of President Kennedy himself.

"I found that book, too, Mrs. McClelland. I read it and it disappeared from the front seat of my truck in a rainstorm in Des Moines early this morning just like it disappeared from your car."

"My God," she breathed. *"Des Moines*? How did you—"

"I've been listening on the other side of that curtain for the last 15 minutes. You're lucky you weren't arrested or thrown into a psycho ward, Mrs McClelland."

"Jeannie."

"Jeannie, you just proved that you can dismiss one screwball, but not two. I was on a flight from Des Moines to Dallas when the plane made an emergency landing in Wichita. I also suffered a head injury."

"You were flying to *Dallas*?"

"My sister lives in Dallas. She works in the plaza where the book says the President will be shot in his limousine. I made the decision to go to Dallas and try to sort this whole thing out with her. Jeannie, I nearly had a stroke on the other side of that curtain listening to your account of what you found in your library. Since I discovered the book, I thought I was having some kind of breakdown. But there's no doubt in my mind now that something incredibly real is taking place in both our lives."

"Is it possible," McClelland asked, "that more people than just the two of us found the same book?"

"Yeah, that thought occurred to me. Who knows?"

"Those FBI agents saw me as a mental case," McClelland said bitterly. "You heard them. They're going to 'file a report.' They're probably laughing it up right now at the screwball Wichita librarian who said she found a book off a school library shelf predicting the President's assassination."

"The problem is, Jeannie, the interview you gave those agents is now a matter of record. They know who you are. And they know *where* you're employed."

"But I told the truth."

"Of course you did, but if any harm comes to the President tomorrow you'll be under a magnifying glass. Those men and who knows what other government people will come after you like hound dogs wanting to know how you knew what you knew."

McClelland threw on her peach colored overcoat, buttoned it, and said, "John, could we please get out of this miserable hospital?"

They took a cab to Wichita's Mid-Continent Airport where Decker learned that his connecting flight to Dallas had departed 20 minutes ago. "Another brick wall," Decker stated in frustration. "I've got to get the next flight to Dallas and land well before noon tomorrow. Must land. The flight *has* to land in Dallas before noon."

"John, suppose I went with you to Dallas and confirmed everything you tell authorities? You said it: there might be one crazy person, but not two. I'm saying I'm willing to describe finding the book and every account in it. Wouldn't that be 10 times more convincing than having the whole thing fall on your shoulders alone?"

"You'd actually be willing to do that, Jeannie?" Decker asked in amazement.

"Yes," McClelland said. "And I'd detail everything to the letter."

"Jeannie, that'd be powerful *corroboration*. You sure you want to go through with that?"

"I do."

The couple purchased tickets for a plane departing Wichita at 10:05 p.m. Then they found the airport lounge and over coffee Decker described how he stumbled across *The Book of Time* while steering his tractor and how his good friend Mac thought he was delusional. "I proved Perry and Clark, the doctors at Parkland, to be real people," Decker stated, showing McClelland his handwritten notes.

"And I also proved something, John. The book described Vice-President Johnson being sworn in on the Presidential plane by a woman judge named Hughes. I remembered that name and made a long distance call to the Dallas courts and asked if there was such a judge named Hughes. They said Sarah Hughes was a federal Texas judge in that area. My heart exploded in my ears when I heard that. Then I checked a map. Elm St., the street where the book says the President will be shot, goes right underneath the warehouse building. That was when I got my aide to cover for me at school, took the book to show the FBI, and had the accident. Just before my car was towed off, I realized the book was gone. So many coincidences, John."

"Too many to ignore," Decker agreed. "I also called the building in the plaza and verified that the man the book said will be accused of killing the President really does work there. According to the book, that man will be shot and killed when the police transfer him to another jail on Sunday."

"Exactly," McClelland stated. "By some local nightclub owner, I think." She sipped coffee, then added: "The accounts in the book—so incredibly precise. They described the President's assassination as if—"

"As if they were history?"

"Yes, as if it were history told in straight, objective factual detail; it was like a textbook account written by a source that had complete knowledge of the assassination to the very minute. You know what 'omniscient' means, John? It means 'knows everything.' That's the adjective I'd use to describe whoever wrote *The Book of Time*. What makes it even scarier is the way the book disappeared."

Decker glanced at his watch. "Jeannie," he asked delicately, "did I overhear you say you recently lost your husband?"

"A little over a year ago."

"I lost my wife 2 years ago."

The chilling announcement spilled out of the airport's public address:

27

"Flight 1122 for Dallas scheduled to depart at 10:05 pm has been cancelled. Repeating: Flight 1122 for Dallas..."

McClelland covered her mouth with her hand and her frightened eyes glared at Decker. The couple rushed over to the arrival-departures schedule on the wall and scanned it.

"Jeannie, the next flight to Dallas isn't until 8:50 a.m. tomorrow morning. That cuts it way too short. Impossibly short. There's no way we'd be able to make it to Dallas and have enough time to get to my sister's—by plane. Listen, I've driven from Des Moines to Dallas many times and made it in 5-6 hours. If we rented a car tonight, we could be in Dallas with good time to spare. It's 9:42 right now. We have to find a car within the hour, Jeannie."

Decker rushed to the airline ticket counter outside the lounge where a clerk had just hung up the desk phone.

"Mam, please help us. We want to rent a car immediately."

"Sir, I'm afraid all the airport vendors closed at 9."

"Do you know of some rental agency in the area still open? It's an emergency."

"I wish I could help you, but I don't know of any agencies open at this hour."

The couple hurried outside to the airport rotunda. Staring frozen at the lights in the Wichita skyline, Decker caught sight of a sign on a wall across the drive path: *Go Greyhound!* "Jeannie, we're gonna' have to take a chartered bus."

They took a cab to the Greyhound bus station three blocks away and rushed inside the depot. Decker collared the desk clerk. "Sir, we want two seats on the very next bus direct to Dallas." The man glanced at his schedule of departures. "There's a bus to Dallas leaving here at 7:30 a.m. tomorrow morning," the man stated. "It's a comfortable eight hour trip with four rest stops."

"Not good enough!" Decker shouted, his impatient voice echoing through the building. "*We have to be on a bus to Dallas before midnight!*"

"I'm sorry," The clerk said. "There just isn't one."

Decker and McClelland slumped to a wooden bench in the

corner of the depot. "A 7:30 bus in the morning won't do it, Jeannie. That cuts things too close. It wouldn't give us a reasonable time cushion to work with at all."

"John," McClelland began gently, "I admire your tenacity, believe me, but is this the fork in the road where we have to admit that the obstacles blocking us are saying, 'You can't change what is meant to be'?"

Her doubt did not phase Decker at all. Instead, something very tender swelled up within him when she asked it; something he hadn't felt toward anyone in years. He looked into McClelland's eyes and marveled at what he realized. For the woman who sat next to him on the bus depot bench at that moment was someone filled with true compassion. This Wichita librarian had known him for just a few hours, yet she was willing to endure the risks ahead with him. Decker wondered where he'd be at this moment without Jeannie McClelland.

"Jeannie," he answered softly, "I honestly don't believe this is any such fork in the road at all. Add things up: my plane diverts to Wichita and I'm placed in a room next to a woman on the other side of a hospital curtain who describes the same events I read in the same book that also disappeared for her without any logical explanation. Care to guess the odds on that? Fifty million to one? A hundred million to one? Some obstacles may be thorns right now, but they aren't thorns big enough to prevent me from believing something profound is happening to both of us. I can't believe I'm saying this, but it's as if that book was sent to us through a doorway to time."

McClelland smiled ruefully and ran a hand through her soft, ebon hair. "The irony of us crossing paths is undeniably powerful, John, but is it enough to get us to Dallas in time? I'm sorry," she added, "but the stress of this indescribable, mystifying day has drained me." McClelland shook her head wearily. "I'd give every cent I own to have the key to what is happening."

"Maybe we will have that key some day, Jeannie. But it's very probable we won't know any more than we know now."

29

"Forgive me, John, when I say I hope you're wrong."

"Who could blame you for hoping that?" Decker smiled. "We're standing against huge waves that keep coming in and pounding at us. We have to do our damndest to keep standing, Jeannie."

After a thoughtful silence, McClelland asked him: "Do you have a religious faith, John?"

"I did—once. My mother was very religious. As a kid, she made me memorize many Biblical passages until she passed. Whatever thread of faith I had left dissolved when my wife Elizabeth was taken from me. The fact is I lost all..." Decker's voice broke off emotionally.

"John, my guess is that you probably fought against life's hammer blows like everyone else when they lose a spouse. For what it's worth, my faith evaporated when my husband died."

"And now?"

"John, what I believe now is that God is an unfathomable mystery to our pedestrian minds that grope 24 hours a day trying to shove a square peg in a round hole. And when the square peg doesn't fit, we think God has turned his back on us so we turn our backs on Him."

Decker slammed his fist down on the bench's wooden armrest. *"We can't stay frozen in Wichita, Kansas, Jeannie! We can't and we won't!"*

McClelland was about to say something when two men in business suits entered the bus depot, stared directly at the couple, then moved toward them.

Decker suspected who they might be. He turned his back to the men and quickly whispered to McClelland: "Tell them you were mistaken at the hospital and took too much medication. Tell them you're going to Dallas with me and that we just met."

Impressive identification flashed before them. "I'm agent Blaine and this is agent Greer. We're with the Secret Service. We were contacted by agent Wade who apparently spoke to you earlier,

Mrs. McClelland. We'd like to talk to you. Our office is just a few minutes away. Will you please accompany us there?"

"What's this all about?" McClelland asked trying to appear confused. "You know my name? Are you here to ask me about the accident I had?"

Blaine didn't answer her, but said to Decker: "And you are…?"

"My name is John Decker. Mind if I ask what this is about?"

"Ms. McClelland, we're seeking some information concerning some statements you made about the President."

McClelland tried to appear confused and befuddled. "Oh, well, I did say some things at the hospital—after a minor head injury. But I think I'm OK now."

"Sir, I'm travelling with Mrs. McClelland. I'd like to accompany her if you don't mind."

The agents drove them to a small, unassuming building that stood on a corner of a vacant lot several blocks from the depot.

Blaine unlocked the back door. "Mrs. McClelland, would you please accompany me to a room down the hall? Mr. Decker, would you go with Agent Greer?"

Except for a plain wooden table with a telephone, three chairs, and a writing tablet, the room Decker entered was sterile. A third very tall unidentified man in a dark suit entered and stood against the wall in the corner with his arms folded. He said nothing and his eyes never left Decker.

"Mr. Decker," Greer stated, "May I inquire as to what exactly is your business in Wichita?"

"I was travelling to Dallas for Thanksgiving to visit my sister. My flight was diverted and I had an emergency landing here."

"And your relationship with Mrs. McClelland?"

"As a mater of fact, we met today."

The agent raised an eyebrow. "The two of you just met?"

"That's right. Had a very bad landing and my head took a pretty good knock. Mrs. McClelland had a car accident. We met at the hospital, talked, and found we were both flying to Dallas."

"You're saying you just met and you're traveling together to Dallas?"

"Yes. Is that unusual? By all means, verify it with the hospital if you like."

"Mr. Decker, Mrs. McClelland has claimed she found a rather unusual document. Do you know anything about that?"

Decker felt the wild urge to corroborate McClelland's story and spill everything out right there in the room. The agents would, of course, detain him, interrogate him endlessly, and if anything did happen to the President, it would be the beginning of a nightmare. Decker envisioned being forced to sell his farm and move to another state after reporters hounded him to death about his knowledge of the President being shot. Telling the truth to the Secret Service now would probably mean the end of life as he knew it.

"What document is that? As I say, Mrs. McClelland was going to Dallas and so was I. We just sought a little companionship. She's a very attractive lady," he smiled.

"Did Mrs. McClelland describe anything at all to you about any unusual experiences she had with regard to this document?"

"I can tell you she didn't appear to me to be in the best frame of mind. She also said she was pretty shaken up by her accident here in Wichita. I hate saying it, but she also mentioned she may have mixed up her medications and became a little confused."

A yellow light on the telephone went on. Greer picked up the receiver. "...I see...All right," he said. The agent put the receiver down and studied Decker curiously. "The fact is, Mr. Decker, that Mrs. McClelland made some rather startling statements concerning the President of the United States. Interestingly, some of the details of her story check out; then again, it may be coincidental."

"*The President*?!" Decker repeated, feigning shock. "What is this? As I stated, my plane made an emergency landing here in Wichita. Again, Jeannie and I met at the hospital. She was travelling to Dallas just as I was."

"So, in effect, you're saying you know nothing of any document or book that Mrs. McClelland may be referring to?"

"*What document are you talking about?*" Decker asked, his voice rising. "Sir, the God's truth is I never laid eyes on Mrs McClelland before this day."

"You're absolutely sure?"

"Why wouldn't I be sure?"

"So you did not know Mrs. McClelland before meeting at the hospital earlier?"

"No."

The man standing in the corner glanced at Greer, nodded, and exited the room.

"Mr. Decker, we're going to chalk this entire matter up to Mrs. McClelland's emotional state, the trauma of her auto accident, and a negative reaction to her medication. We see no reason to detain either of you. Mrs. McClelland is through now. Do you need a lift back to the airport to make your flight?"

"No," Decker said, trying to camouflage his profound relief. "Our flight to Dallas was cancelled. That's why we were at the bus station."

Decker waited nervously until Jeannie, pale and agitated, finally emerged from the room down the hall. As they exited the building McClelland whispered, "I told them I was mistaken; that I had overdosed. They think I'm a basket case."

"The FBI turned it over to the Secret Service, then they traced us to the Greyhound station. For all we know, they might still be monitoring us. But none of that changes anything for me, Jeannie."

"What do we do now, John?"

"We keep trying," Decker emphasized. "But if you want to go back—"

"No. I want to see this through. That book appeared to me too, you know."

A truck stop lay at the very end of the street. They hurried toward it, entered, and sat at the counter. After ordering ham and eggs, Decker's eyes noted the clock hanging over the café's kitchen grill.

"It's 11:10," he stated. "No flights to Dallas till after 9 tomorrow morning. Car rental agencies closed. No buses out of here that could put us in Dallas before 12 noon. Jeannie, what about a friend of yours who could loan us a car? I'd be more than willing to pay for it."

A burly, barrel chested man in a red woolen sweater, overalls, and a fisherman's cap pinned with anglers' jigs and hooks was seated on the stool next to Decker. "Hey, Chief," he said, poking Decker in the ribs, "you lookin' for transport to the big 'D'?" The man's glossy, beady eyes met the hope that suddenly sprang into Decker's face.

"Yes, we are!"

"I'm 'bout to be headin' out to Dallas in my rig, Chief. Yur' welcome to hitch a ride. Goin' straight through Oklahoma City, then on to Dallas. But I kin' only take one passenger ridin' shotgun."

Decker glanced at Jeannie's worrisome, but hopeful face.

"If we left now, when do you estimate we'd be in Dallas?"

"Assumin' roads are clear, oughta' make it, say five, five and a half hours."

Fifteen minutes later Decker and Jeannie stood in the truck stop lot next to the biggest rig they had ever seen. The mammoth side panel spelled out "Fortune Trucking Company" in broken, hazy letters. The driver climbed into the cabin and turned the engine over. The rig thundered like a Saturn rocket as Jeannie quickly scribbled her home telephone number on a piece of note paper.

"How are you gonna' make it home, Jeannie?"

"They have cabs here, remember? John, promise me you'll call when you get to Dallas," she said, shoving the paper into the side pocket of Decker's windbreaker. "Promise me that now."

"On my honor, Jeannie. And here's my sister's number and the number of Mac Kellerman, my neighbor." Decker scribbled everything down for her and added, "Jeannie, if anything happens to me, call them and tell them everything. *Everything*."

"John, hear me: heroics are wonderful in movies, but they don't work the same way in real life. I won't lie, John: I'm scared to death at the thought of the risks you might take in Dallas."

"Jeannie," Decker began, "up until today I was a glob of nothing drifting through space. Then I found the book. Yeah, it terrified me, but it also drove me to do *something*. And that something led me here to the biggest comeuppance of my life. I know you didn't intend to give me a gift, but meeting you in that hospital proved there's something in this universe beyond our measly little lives. For that I need to thank you."

Their eyes met meaningfully, then McClelland threw her arms around Decker and hugged him tightly. Elizabeth's anemic, failing face, lying weakly on a hospital pillow passed before his eyes.

"John, I pray that one day you'll come to think again and again about what what you're saying now."

Decker pulled back and looked at McClelland in disbelief.

"We're blastin' off, Chief!" the truck driver shouted from the cabin window. "Gotta' rock!"

The big rolling tires crept away as the rig lumbered off toward the main highway. An emotion Decker couldn't quite describe swelled within him when he caught a glimpse of McClelland framed in the side mirror. She stood alone in the cold watching the rig move off, clutching her purse, standing helpless and frightened in the middle of the trucker's lot. His mind whirled as he fell back against the seat hoping the events described in *The Book of Time* would never come to pass on November 22, 1963. Gazing up at the clear, white stars, Decker was convinced that whether the events occurred or not, he had made the right decision to go to Dallas. Twenty minutes later the rig's rambling, churning engine purred Decker's exhausted mind to sleep.

III

The dream-like seductiveness of Scheherazade reached Decker's ears from the cabin's dashboard radio. His eyes opened and he became conscious of the rig rolling along smoothly at 75 miles per hour.

The driver lowered the radio's volume. "Have a nice siesta, Chief?"

Decker surveyed the passing landscape. "Where are we now?"

"About 25 miles out of Oklahoma City. Point 'O No Return."

"What time is it?"

"A little after 3 a.m., give or take a few centuries. Hey, Chief, didja' know the President's coming through Dallas? You gonna' see him?"

Decker felt a shiver. "I—he is?"

"How long have you been farmin' in Des Moines?"

"I've been—" He stopped short. "How did you know I owned a farm in Des Moines?"

"Musta' said somethin' 'bout it back at the diner. Guess I was eavsdroppin'."

Decker thought back and was certain he had never mentioned anything to McClelland about his farm at the truck stop. "You sure about that?"

"So many technological and scientific breakthroughs are in store down the line right here where we are now."

"Down the line? What do you mean, 'Down the line'?"

"Your entire life run to peak efficiency by advanced computers. Colonies on Mars drilling for oil. Human life expectancy increased to 120-125 years. DNA revolutions eradicating every major disease you now know."

"What's in hell is DNA?"

"Sorry, Chief. Got carried away. You fixin' to see the President?"

"That's the second time you asked me that question. Why?"

"Thought you mentioned it at the café?"

"No. I said nothing about the President back there at that diner."

The driver shook his head. "John, do you believe it's possible to change history?"

36

The blood drained from Decker's face. "What did you say?"

Something palpable existed in the air between them. The noise of the engine had diminished. The driver's voice had taken on a different aspect and tone.

"Let me try to simplify it, John. I'm referring to a cosmic law that insures time's immutability."

Decker couldn't believe his ears. "What in God's name are you talking about?"

This was not the same man he met at the truck stop. The Missouri twang had vanished; the voice was suddenly melifluous and authoritative. Through the windshield, Decker saw the landscape transforming into something new and futuristic.

"*What's happening here?!*" Decker shouted in alarm, pressing against the dashboard, startled at what was taking place. "I've driven to Dallas on this highway many times and never saw any of this!"

"That's because we've detoured."

Decker came forward in panic. "*Detoured?!*"

The driver took his eyes off the road and looked at Decker, yet the rig never veered one inch from its course on the highway. He studied his passenger for a moment, then said in a gentle voice:

"John, it is impossible to change what is destined to be..."

Decker's bones turned to ice. It was the same feeling that rushed through him when he read *The Book of Time*, when he heard his flight would be diverted to Wichita, when he heard Jeannie's voice describe identical experiences on the other side of the curtain in the emergency room.

"But not to worry, John: you're definitely headed in the right direction."

Decker could take no more of it. The enigmas that had stood before him like a succession of walls finally wore him down to he ground. "*Who are you?!*" he demanded to know. "*I'm not getting out of this truck until you tell me who you are and what is happening to me!*"

"John, I'm a helper. Someone who wants very much to assist you to get out of the cul-de-sac you're stuck in…"

It was as if stage lights came up slowly on a very odd landscape that surrounded the rig. The highway bore no resemblance to the highway where Fords and Chevrolets sped in the lanes between white lines. These cars were fluorescent, cylindrical bullets with narrow, horizontal slits of black windows. The roadway seemed to have layers one on top of the other where the cars, if that's what they were, some a bright orange, some maroon, swept off in various directions. They shot along at a frenzied pace darting in and out of traffic, bolting here and there, flashing at the edges, disappearing off to the side.

"Where are we?"

"Another place and time, John."

In the distance, a majestic sapphire metropolis rose from the horizon. It was a city built of silver, towering buildings clumped together forming one radiating entity. Flecks of white and blue clouds drifted passed vertical peaks and what looked like a huge veil domed the entire spectrum. Then some sort of monstrously huge flying machine not quite a blimp, not quite a rocket ship, cruised over the spectacle majestically. Streams of colored light sprayed down from the machine's hull to various points in the city below. Smaller flashes of light seemed to be bolting up to it from ground level.

"Don't worry, John. It's a momentary detour, not a port-o-call. We've been moving toward this moment since we left the diner. The purpose is to convince you that you cannot alter history. And you do need to be convinced because you're swimming upstream against a powerful ocean current that will drown you if you maintain your present course."

"Where is this place?" Decker asked, pointing dumbfounded at the metropolis in the distance.

"A city that is not Dallas. Know who lives there? The 70th President of the United States. Take a guess at whose picture hangs on his wall? President John F. Kennedy."

"*The 70th what?!*"

"A man who will be 45 Presidents into the future, John."

"Into the *future*?!" Decker retorted.

"John, what will happen today in Dallas will be a terrible thing. But you can no more prevent that tragedy than you could change the orbits of the planets around the sun. All that is to unfold will mark a crucial turning point in world history. But it's a necessary turning point. Keep in mind, John: good derives from bad. That city you're seeing, the fine people and the wonders within it, would not be able to exist without the events soon to take place in Dallas. Think of it this way: you could never have a Renaissance without the collapse of Rome; you could not have streamline starships without brave men perishing in winged aircraft in the early 20th Century. A bad marriage that ends in bitter heartbreak and pain can still produce good children and grandchildren. John, you have to understand that o*ne ripple in a pond leads to succeeding ripples.*"

The astonishing vista Decker saw began to fade. Finally, the pitch of night returned and the truck was back on the highway passing along the recognizable landscape Decker knew well. He simply watched the transformation in detached awe.

"You are a very determined, strong-willed man, John. But if you continue along your current course and make an attempt to interfere with immutable history, that city you just saw and all the good people in it could be harmed. And you might also be harmed. The physics of that phenomenon is far too complex for your 20th Century mind to comprehend."

Light began to come up around the rig. A new day was springing into view.

"My '20th Century mind'? "

"We're stopping here, John. We're in Dallas. It's 12 noon. November 22, 1963AD."

Decker looked at his watch. His jaw dropped. "I'm one half hour from—"

The brakes squealed and the truck slowed, then the rig finally came to rest along the road's shoulder. Decker saw buildings in the distance, but they were matchsticks compared to the grand edifices he saw in the sapphire city.

"This is where you get off, John." The driver waited for his passenger to open the door and climb down from the truck's cabin. "Think about what I've said. But you're on the right path."

Decker refused to move. "I want you to tell me why I found that book on my farm," he demanded. "What's the purpose of this entire nightmare? Why did that book appear in my wheatfield describing the assassination when you say it's going to happen anyway?"

"*Discovery*, John. *Discovery.* Now may I recommend you head down in that direction? That is where you'll find precisely what you need to find." The driver pointed off to the right where the road winded into the city of Dallas.

He wasn't sure if he slammed the cabin door, or if it slammed by itself. But he was standing at the road's shoulder as the rig's engine revved up and exploded in his ears. Decker watched helplessly as the truck rumbled off and left him in a draft of exhaust. Behind him a deserted service station slumped with dismantled gas pumps and cracked plywood boarding up its windows and garage doors. Decker noted it, then began to move south on foot.

He walked about a dozen blocks when he pulled up to a small television repair shop. The doors were open and inside a knot of people were riveted to one black and white television screen in particular. Various expressions of shock and horror were pasted on the faces of those pinned to the news. An elderly woman had her hands up to her mouth and cried, "Oh, no!" The reporter's thick voice drifted out to Decker who paused on the sidewalk and listened to the grim words.

"*...To repeat: we have confirmed a report that President Kennedy has been shot in his motorcade here in the Deleay Plaza area of downtown Dallas. It has also been confirmed that Governor John Connolly, also in the limousine, was struck by gunfire. We now switch you live to Parkland Hospital...*"

An arctic chill swept through every fiber of John Decker. He stepped inside the shop and saw several other screens showing chaos at Parkland Hospital. His watch said 12:52 p.m. *The President is taking his last breaths now. Dr. Clark will approach Mrs. Kennedy in eight minutes and pronounce her husband dead.* Decker turned away and didn't want to see or hear any more of the televised reports. As he crept away from the repair shop, his final realization actualized: every word printed in *The Book of Time* had been absolute truth. But why? *Why did it appear to me and to Jeannie?*

Edging along on foot, he moved into the downtown section of the city wondering what Mac Kellerman must be thinking now. Two police cars raced by with spinning red lights and a howling siren, but Decker didn't look up to see them. Weary legs and the desire for solitude carried him up the steps of a church. What he wanted now was to disappear into an interior disconnected from the ugliness that surrounded the city. Exhausted, Decker sank into a back pew, closed his eyes, and saw Elizabeth, young and beaming, as she placed a Christmas roast down on the dining room table. Mac and Jackie Kellerman were there and Mac was whistling and rubbing his hands together at the sight of the delicious feast. Jackie was lifting her glass and proposing a toast to the Decker's.

Liz, if you can hear me, give me the strength to get through this day...

A scuffling drifted up to him. A priest in cassock and white collar was moving through one of the front pews. He was a very young priest in his mid-twenties who appeared to be wiping his eyes with a handkerchief. Decker rose and headed down the aisle slowly. "You have obviously heard the news," he whispered.

The man looked up with moist, sad eyes. "Yes, I've heard. But I'm sorry, Friend, I will be of no assistance to you today. For me the world just ended."

"I assume the church will be holding some kind of service...."

"Well, there will be no comfort coming from me at any such service, I assure you. How could I possibly tell people to be strong when I am weak? Sorry, Friend, but the presence of God is absent for me right now."

Decker wasn't sure he had understood the man. "You are a priest, aren't you?"

"Am I? How can you tell?"

"You're *not* a priest?"

"Friend, I have no glory for a God who could let such a vile thing happen to the President, our country, to the President's wife and children. A priest, for your information, is a mortal human being, stumbling along like everyone else; perhaps you've confused a priest with a cheerleader. Frankly, I don't believe in the walls of this building right now. If you told me I was standing here at this moment in the city of Dallas, I'd doubt you completely."

Decker tried to grasp the man's dilemma. "I'm sorry; I don't think I understand."

"What's to understand? The simple fact is I'm not a hypocrite."

"And you might be...?"

"You can use Brehm." The man wiped his eyes again. "And to make matters worse, I'm all alone here today. The pastor and assistant pastor are out of town. Who would have believed I'd be burdened with this monstrosity on a nondescript Friday in November?"

"Burdened?" Decker repeated. "Is that how you see it? What's the matter with you anyway? Isn't your job to be a rock of strength in the face of your flock's despair?"

"Oh, is that my job? Listen, Friend, I'd be a hypocrite if I spoke to people at all today about 'trusting in their faith'."

"You'd be a hypocrite not to!" Decker shot back. "Shouldn't religion raise people up and not let them down?"

"Is that about it?" the man said sarcastically. "Well, thanks, Friend, but I'd appreciate it if you could keep your bumper sticker slogans to yourself."

Decker's anger was rising. "Mind if I ask why you ever became a priest in the first place? What did you think the clergy was going to be—pancake breakfasts and Friday night bingo?"

He could sense the man was too uncomfortable to debate the issue further. Instead, he brushed by Decker, stomped up the altar steps, and disappeared into the sacristy. Decker lifted his eyes to the image of Christ hanging on the cross above the the altar. Before Elizabeth's death had ripped his faith apart, he believed in what that image represented. Decker turned. People were beginning to drift in through the church's vestibule. He saw an elderly, sobbing woman assisted to a pew by a man, probably her son. Off to the left, a mother with her arms around two small children, all three appearing lost and grief-stricken, lit votive candles and knelt before the little flickering flames. Like a funeral parlor with bereaved family members, a collective whimpering was beginning to fill the church. How can that priest abandon these people? Decker asked himself. The man lives in the guise of piety, then when people need him most, he turns into a coward and jumps ship.

Resolve pulsing through him, Decker had finally reached the end point. Since he boarded a plane in Des Moines, every effort he had made had been thwarted. Every turn taken led him to a thick wall blocking his path. Lines of reasoning were blurred with enigma; rationality and logic had detoured into paradox. Now a two-faced priest was running away from the very horror he, Decker, had been racing toward. Seeing the disconsolate people entering the church, picturing the millions more behind them, was the final straw. Determined to grasp one meaningful shard of truth, deciding that if the sole, meager contribution to this ghastly day was to put a priest in his rightful place, Decker resolved to go that last, final yard. He was heading up the altar steps toward the sacristy.

Inside the room, the priest unbuttoned his cassock. He looked up at Decker with resentful eyes as if waiting for Decker to speak.

"Father Brehm, with all due respect, I'd like to remind you everyone is devastated today, not just you. May I suggest you get a hold of yourself? People are coming into this church looking for answers and comfort. Do you really intend to leave them hanging from a limb? With all due respect, I think you're obligated to get out on that altar and speak to the hurt out there."

"Answers? Comfort?" the man shot back. "I tell you what, Friend, *you* put on this cassock; *you* go out there and lecture on the topic of keeping one's faith in the face of today's devastation. Explain to those folks how a loving God allows a grotesque thing like this to happen. Please be my guest. And while you're at it, throw in a spoonful of the Gospel of St. Mathew and a pinch of St. Paul's Letters to the Corinthians. Go ahead! You have management's blessing!"

He rolled his cassock up into a wad the size of a football and shot it straight at Decker who caught it on the fly.

"Yes, take it, Friend. You would obviously make a much better priest than I. Oh, I'm very serious: go out there and save the masses from the clutches of despair on this inauspicious black Friday. After all, you seem to have all the proper ingredients for a perfectly beautiful blind faith."

Decker clenched his teeth. "You're going to let those people just sit out there and drown in misery? I can't believe that all you supposedly stand for will let you do that..."

"You don't? Well, watch me!"

The man stormed out of the sacristy in his street clothes and the door slammed behind him. Staring down at the crumpled, black cassock in his hands, Decker felt as if the room had tilted. Shuffling feet and sniveling out in the church filled his ears as he collapsed to a creaking, wooden chair. *The Book of Time,* containing the truth of November 22, had finally swept him up to a nondescript little room in a church in Dallas, Texas. What unfathomable power allowed that book to intersect my existence and carry me here? Through a slit in the sacristy's door, Decker could see the pews filling with scores of parishioners praying at the altar railing in silent grief. He wondered how many millions more were at that moment groping for answers in churches and synagogues all over the country. And how many, their faith shaken to its core, cried out for an answer that wasn't coming?

Suddenly, another scene flashed before Decker. It was one he had imagined a thousand times.

An impressive courtroom. A lawyer donned in a fine, three-piece suit stood before a jury summing up his final argument. His defense was brilliant; his words electric and powerful. The efforts led to a winning verdict for the defense and acquitted a man unjustly charged with a major crime. Adulation reigned down upon John Decker as he descended the courthouse steps and made his way through the admiring crowd amidst flashing cameras and microphones thrust under his mouth. He was the country lawyer who had fashioned justice out of the overwhelming odds stacked against him. But the fantasy dissolved into the sacristy's cracked linoleum floor in the same way it always dissolved when the scene returned to the harsh, threadbare present. This time, Decker vowed, it will be different.

Closing his eyes, he remembered a line his mother required him to memorize in childhood. He had turned it over many times through the years, but after Elizabeth died, he thought he had buried it forever. Now the quotation loomed up and he saw the words as if they glowed in luminous neon.

Sitting in the creaking chair and reflecting upon the most inexplicable day of his life, anger and angst finally dissolved; assurance replaced doubt; confusion gave way to certitude. Less than 24 hours ago, I believed *The Book of Time* was science fiction trash. Though I may never find reasons for the events of this day, I now know that book described the authentic, undeniable assassination of a President.

We shove a square peg in a round hole. And when the square peg doesn't fit, we think God has turned his back on us so we turn our backs on Him. Jeannie, he thought: the one shining pearl on a day I'll remember if I live to be 90.

All at once Decker got to his feet and rifled through the room's cabinets and drawers in search of paper. Finding a pen and the back of a blank church calendar, he wrote as fast as his hand could move the instrument over the page. When he finished, Decker studied his scribbled handwriting.

He zipped his windbreaker to the top of his neck and flattened the collar neatly. He combed his hair, dusted his pants, and washed his face at the little sink in the corner of the room. He considered that he could still throw the calendar in the trash, exit the side door, taxi to Love Field, and board the next flight for Des Moines. No, Decker resolved, I will perform the one decent act I'm capable of accomplishing on this pathetic day. Elizabeth, I dedicate what I'm about to do to you.

It seemed like the most surreal, dreamlike ten seconds of his life when Decker's legs strode across the altar's carpet toward the pulpit. He set his notes down, gazed at the grim assemblage and clenched the wooden sides of the lectern with his powerful hands and wrists. He cleared his throat and, in a thick voice, spoke:

"My name is John Decker. I'm from Des Moines, Iowa. Unfortunately, the parish priests are unavailable. It was suggested I address you…"

Heads turned. Surprised whispers flared through the pews.

"I'm obviously not a priest, just an Iowa farmer who stands before you very much unprepared. You will find no eloquence from me today, but I assure you that what I'm about to say comes straight from the heart…"

Decker paused, looked at his unkempt notes, and cleared his throat again.

"The unthinkable has happened to our President and to our country. And it has happened in this city which makes it all the worse for you because Dallas is your home."

"May I ask everyone in this church to consider you're here because of another assassination? Two thousand years ago a Man was crucified for no other reason than his intrinsic humanity threatened the status quo. Had that atrocity not taken place, you would not be sitting here now.

"Years ago I lost my wife. I drowned in despair for years and I reacted to the tragedy by throwing myself into work till my hands bled and my back and legs ached so badly that I couldn't sleep at night. As my bitterness grew, I saw myself as nothing more than a spec of dust blowing at the mercy of the four winds. But from the day I walked away from my wife's gravestone, one question burned in my soul: why do terrible things happen to good people?

"My late mother used to require me to memorize passages from the Bible. Of the thousands of lines in the scriptures she insisted I learn, there is one quotation that echoes back to me now. It's from John, 9:1 when Jesus had met a man blind from birth. The question arose: Who caused this innocent man's blindness, the man's parents or him? Jesus answered:

"*'Neither hath this man sinned, nor his parents: but that the works of God should be made manifest in him.'*"

"That line—*that the works of God are manifest in us*—now dawns like a sun in my mind. My interpretation of those words is very clear to me at this hour. They tell us that good ultimately derives from bad.

"For those who believe President Kennedy's life was rendered meaningless by today's unthinkable horror—may I suggest that we are incapable of understanding how tragic events shape our future. But I would bet everything I own that tragic events often prove to become immeasurabe goodness—upon our personal lives and even upon our country.

"Please," Decker pleaded, coming forward with a surge of the sincerest passion he could muster, "on this bleak day—a day we will remember 50 years from now—as we grope to understand the cruelty that breaks our hearts, we must never forget that God did not kill President Kennedy—Man did. But it is always God who picks up the pieces and creates glory from the tragedies that make us weep."

Not a sound flickered in the church as Decker ran out of words. Gazing out at those before him, he caught sight of a woman sitting in the front pew. She was the twin of Decker's late wife Elizabeth. Dabbing her wet eyes with a handkerchief, she was transfixed upon Decker and looked upon him with an expression of emotional awe. It slammed Decker hard between the eyes. Overwrought, he hastened off the altar, swept through the sacristy, and hurried down the side church steps.

Nearly colliding with an older priest heading up in the opposite direction, Decker froze on the step and glared at the man standing inches from him.

"Excuse me: you are….?"

"Father Huber. I'm sorry, but I have a service to prepare for."

"Just a moment, Father. I thought the other priests were out of town."

"Not at all. I'm the pastor and I'm definitely here."

"The pastor!? Decker repeated. "Father Brehm said—"

"Who?"

"Father Brehm, the young priest here at this church. He said the other priests were gone and he was alone today."

Huber shook his head. "I know of no Father Brehm."

"Hold it! Are you telling me there is no Father Brehm connected to this church? A young priest. Middle to late twenties. Very slender man?"

"Sir, all three priests are indeed here and Father Brehm is not one of them. I never heard of a Father Brehm."

Decker stood flat-footed and dazed. The priest's confused face studied him for a moment, then the man said: "I don't mean to be rude, but there is a special service this tragic day and I am late already."

The priest continued up the steps and disappeared through the church's side doors.

Decker crossed the parking lot on foot with the vivid, flesh and blood image of a man he had spoken with clearly in front of him. He had been there physically in the church, like the truck driver had been there physically in the rig, like *The Book of Time* had been there physically in his wheat field.

I want you to promise me you'll call when you get to Dallas...

Decker wanted only one thing at that moment: a telephone.

In the windless calm of a Mid-West November dusk, John Decker trimmed branches in his apple orchard and thought seriously about the destiny of his country. Finally, he dropped the pruning clippers to the ground, wiped the sweat from his forehead, and gazed off toward his wheat field. The autumn sunset had painted the patch of land where he had found *The Book of Time* in spectacular pumpkin orange.

Decker began to dream again of the lawyer he might have been, but wasn't. About the family he could have had, but hadn't. About the book he could have missed, but didn't.

Discovery...

Tomorrow Jeannie will arrive from Wichita. She doesn't know it, but she's going to be treated to the finest Thanksgiving dinner of her life.

A Glimpse of Time

The clock on the wall in Connor Clifton's computer workoom stopped running the day he broke his leg and its black hands still pointed straight up to 12. Even after six months, Clifton pinpointed 12 noon as the precise time he fell from the loft in his company's computer warehouse. He wasn't sure why, but he liked the clock now more as a symbol of time rather than as a clock that actually *told* time.

Hard drives, monitors, keyboards, metal boxes, and hundreds of wires and cables filled the worktables and shelves in the second bedroom of his Pasadena home. Taking stock of the hardware that tangled around like an electronic octopus, Clifton wondered if his tombstone would one day have "Computer Nerd" chiseled in stone under his name. Through the window, he studied the two workers constructing his new detached garage. The men lifted gray blocks as if they were bars of gold ore, set them in place, cemented, straightened. Is this how the pyramids were built? On the computer screen in front of him, Professor Stanley Laurentia's email confirmed their meeting at 1 p.m.

He shuffled through the books lined on the shelf above his desk: the "Mahabharatha" from Hindu mythology; the Japanese tale "Urashima Two"; the "Honi Ham'agel" from the Talmud; and H.G. Wells' *The Time Machine*. Entertaining stories, he mused, but not a shred of a concrete insight about the mechanics of time anywhere in these supposedly great works of literature. Then he flipped through three inches of printouts stacked on the computer table next to him: cosmic strings, black holes, and Einstein's theory of time dilation. These, he knew, were the very opposite of the books on the shelf: grandiose concepts, but impracticle. No more literature, he promised himself. I need to talk to live bodies and get real ideas.

Professor Stanley Laurentia's book, *The Illusion of Time*, lay on the computer side table. He leafed through the slim volume again, the one pragmatic charge in all he had read. He reviewed his notes penciled in along the margins and pictured Laurentia: a stereotypical physics nerd with unkempt, bushy hair and horn-rimmed glasses who doodled abstruse formulae on cocktail napkins.

Leaning against his desk to support his six-foot-two frame, Clifton grasped his cane and looked curiously at the clock on the wall. It still says 12, he mused. My injury occurred right at 12 noon. Did the clock stop running the minute I hit the cement? "Good thing you're 31 and not 70, Conner," his doctor told him. "A break this bad could have caused you to walk with a limp forever."

Rip Van Winkle goes to sleep, wakes up 20 years later.

Limping on his cane toward the kitchen, Clifton pictured himself teaching a course on time travel. Even if I did, it would be pie-in-the sky theory stolen from books. Plus, I'd be condemned to correcting empty, screwball essays forever.

He lifted the coffee pot, poured, added cream. The porcelain on the side of the mug quoted Robert Frost: "They give us a cup of time and they don't care if we spill it." Swallowing a sip, he remembered an old joke told by a stand-up comic: "The other day I put a cup of instant coffee in the microwave to see if it would go back through time."

No more books, he promised himself. Meet Laurentia today. Pick his brain. Come away with a breakthrough.

Clifton snapped on the radio news in his bedroom as he always did while shaving and showering. He listened to tales of a stock market plunge, the search for a missing child, and details of an indicted congressman. At the end of the news, the announcer stated it was the anniversary of the assassination of President John F. Kennedy. It came at the end serving as "filler" and a "tag" for the morning report. Clifton always hated the network announcer's dispassionate, scratchy voice. He studied his face in the glass: square jaw, curious, light brown eyes, and goatee trimmed to a perfect tuft on his chin. Then he combed his warm, chestnut hair down around his ears and into his medium-length shag style. November 22, he thought as he raised the razor to his throat.

An hour later he was at the Pasadena library main branch reading through his copy of *The Illusion of Time.* It had never been in the county system; nor had Clifton ever found the book in any of the other five county systems he had checked. He located it in an old out-of-print bookshop near the UCLA campus. The review on the jacket said, *"Avant guarde physics...an obscure nugget for those who hanker to understand time outside conventional thought..."* Clifton decided he would review the professor's theories one last time before meeting him.

Laurentia had eschewed meeting at Cal Tech and had, instead, proposed a Starbuck's a block from the campus. Clifton arrived 15 minutes early, but found the professor already sitting in a quiet corner scouring the LA Times sports page. Laurentia recognized Clifton from his cane, got up immediately, and extended his hand.

"Glad to know ya', Conner," Laurentia smiled lightly. "Let's grab some coffee and donuts and go across the street to the park. I get claustrophobia in here."

The professor was the most handsome, bald-headed man in his fifties Clifton had ever met. A dashing figure, he had movie star good looks and dressed in gray, tweed sport coat, matching vest, and blue silk tie. The black sheen on his patent leather shoes sparkled as if they had just been removed from a plastic tuxedo rental bag. Twin, pencil-thin cigars peeked out of his upper coat pocket in front of his dapper silver handkerchief with the garish monogram 'SL'. He walked a step or two ahead of Clifton, and, as he maintained that gap, moved down the sidewalk speaking over his shoulder eating donuts and slurping coffee.

"You said you'd be on a cane, Conner, but never said what happened to your leg. Have you always been lame?"

"I fell from a loft in a computer warehouse a little over six months ago. Broke the femur."

"Ouch. Yes, you mentioned you were in computers..."

"Engineer for Balance Technologies in LA. On disability obviously."

"Jeez, I think I need a new mouse," Laurentia complained. "Does this walking bother you?"

"No. I'm fine."

"So you read my book, then? How in the world did you find it?"

"As a matter of fact, I stumbled upon it in a used bookstore. You can't find it in any conventional bookstore. It's not on line; not in libraries. It's nowhere."

"It's nowhere on purpose, Conner. I self-published it. The crème de la crème do not consider it scholarly. It was a lecture I gave at Cal Tech that caused the roof to cave in on me."

"Your book wiped me out, Professor. So you don't believe in time at all?"

They crossed the street and reached the grass of a public baseball park with several contiguous diamonds. Laurentia tossed donut crumbs to gathering pigeons in the parking lot as he sipped his coffee and murmured, "Ahhh. Did you know Balzac drank 60 cups of coffee a day, Conner? My hunch is that your injury is giving you far too much leisure to worry about the curious subject of 'time'."

"Yeah, but it's also providing an opportunity for me to re-think what I want to do with my life. I'm considering getting out of computers completely."

"Conner, do you know how many emails I get a week? I actually pay my daughter to deal with them. Schizo's who say they've invented a time machine; fruitcakes who announce they went back and saw Christ hanging on the cross. Pat deletes 99 percent of that crap. Yours she forwarded to me because she knows what I like. Your email was long, but sincere; and it had a nice, honest tone. You didn't waste my time quoting Einstein's physics. You're not a woodpecker telling me you've traveled to the year

3000 and saw the world in a geodesic dome. And you live in Pasadena and I'm on leave from Cal Tech. The perfect storm. So we're here, aren't we?

"I'll tell you this, Conner: you're tackling the Great Sphinx of Giza. As a matter of fact, you're staring straight into the deepest abyss of them all. This walking doesn't bother you?" The professor tossed a few more crumbs to the pigeons and blackbirds that were swarming in around him. Then he swallowed the rest of the donuts and washed it all down with coffee.

"To answer your question: I don't believe that 'time' is anything close to what we have come to believe it is. It's a complete illusion, a mental construct." Laurentia removed a pencil-thin cigar from his coat pocket. A beautiful brass lighter shaped like a cube popped out and a tiny flame appeared. He lit the cigar, inhaled, and released a stream of smoke. The lighter snapped shut and shot back into the professor's coat pocket. "But you must also understand that a mental construct must never be confused with an abstraction."

"But you do reject conventional thinking about time, don't you, Professor?"

"Naturally."

A cyclone fence separated the two men from the baseball outfield. In the distance, a father hit ground balls to his 10 year-old son at shortstop. Laurentia placed the palms of both of his hands on the fence and leaned against the wire at an angle studying the figures on the diamond. He puffed on his cigar and continued to speak over his shoulder to Clifton.

"Civilization interprets 'time' into minutes, days, hours, years, clocks, calendars. All of that is nothing more than symbolism. What is meant by that use of the term 'time' is actually the segmenting of the earth's rotation around the sun which translates into the sweep of a second hand around a dial. We look at an old run-down house and say 'time sure took its toll.' 'Time' did nothing of the sort: weathering, termites, and neglect caused that dry rot, torn window screens, and tilting foundation, not 'time.'"

"Then tell me, Professor, what do you think time is?"

Laurentia withdrew the cigar from his mouth and fixed his gaze on the boy and his father in the distance.

"Time is the picture frame around the picture, but it's not the picture itself."

Clifton remembered reading the analogy in Laurentia's *The Illusion of Time*. "I tried to imagine that parallel when I first read it in your book, Professor."

"You see, if I put a cake in the oven, what really bakes the cake? Time or heat?"

"Wouldn't you say heat radiating the cake combined with a specific period of time cooks it?"

"Yeah, that's what most people would say. But the radiation produced the cake. If it had to be time, then how do you explain microwave ovens cooking food in a fraction of the 'time' it might have taken in the oven or on the stove? Imagine a brand new car that is hermetically sealed in a garage the moment it comes off the assembly line. You keep it there for 25 years, come back, put the key into the ignition, it starts right up. All the other cars that came off the assembly line that same day have been relegated to the junk heap. Why? Because of the obvious abuse, poor care, etc. Time didn't wear those other cars down: the negative conditions they were exposed to did the trick. The car sealed up in the garage is just fine. Why didn't 'time' wear it down?"

"Well," Clifton answered, "Obviously, the car that was sealed up didn't suffer any wear and tear."

"You're proving my point, Conner. But it was still subjected to 'time' wasn't it? Yet it's in mint condition. Why? And what about 'time' taking its toll on that house I just mentioned? What if you built it and also put it in a huge hermetically sealed 2,000 square foot plastic bag? You'd come back in 25 years and there would be no dry rot, no termites; you'd have a perfect foundation. How's your leg, Conner?"

Laurentia was following the arguments in his book to the letter. But now Clifton was in front of the man who wrote the concepts and was listening to the voice explain them. He wanted to push the man farther than he had gone in his writing; he wanted the professor to give him a dramatic insight that would change his own skeptical opinions about Laurentia's theories.

"Rest assured, Conner, that when we say 'time' we do mean *something*. And we certainly do need this notion of 'time' so that days, months, and years maintain an orderly civilization. I have no problem there. I use the word 'time' all the—'time.' It's cemented into the lexicon, but as far as I'm concerned, 'time' is probably the greatest misnomer in the English language. I would guess that you noticed that whenever the word 'time' appears in my book it's in quotation marks."

"Yes, I did notice that, Professor."

Laurentia held his cigar between his first two fingers on his left hand, shifted his weight, and leaned against the fence propped up by his other foot. His eyes never strayed from the father and son practicing in the distance.

"You can't live in this world and not negotiate 'time.' But since there is no 'time'—or what everyone thinks of as 'time'—there is no 'time travel' because there's nothing to travel *through*. Your email asked me to reconsider this notion. To me that's utterly ludicrous; what's to reconsider if nothing's there? You might as well ask me to reconsider the concept of leprechauns."

Clifton was excited to be engaging Laurentia's candid narrative. And he thought he knew where it was leading. "Professor Laurentia, could you give me another example of 'time' not existing?"

Laurentia exhaled. "Conner, I'm trying to steer away from deep stuff here such as the sub-atomic particle level. So let me try to make my answer to that as simple as possible...

"There are two great landscapes in physics: that of Isaac Newton and that of Einstein. Newton viewed 'time' as flowing equably for everyone. Einstein destroyed that notion. Good old Albert proved that there is no space *and* time; there is only a *spacetime continuum*. Newton thought of 'time' as dynamic, events developing with the passage of time, like the rotting of that house I just mentioned. Einstein maintained that events don't develop, they just are."

Clifton shook his head. "Sorry, Professor, but I wrestle with that concept. Guess I'm dense."

"Don't feel bad, Conner. Most physicists don't get it either. Look at it this way. Absolute time—for *everyone*—does not exist. See, Einstein believed space and 'time' are inseparable. And this relationship is expressed in the mathematics of his special theory of relativity. But don't spend a moment fretting over it, Conner. Just accept it because it's been proven."

"Wish I could understand these ideas as clearly as you do."

"Conner, you're forcing me to get into my raison d' etre. If you read my book, you know the keystone in all my thinking, don't you?"

"Light?"

"That's right. You did read my book. I believe light is the essence of all existence. Genesis 1:3, '*And God said, 'Let there be light.*' For me that is the greatest single line in the Bible and perhaps the greatest single line ever written. It satisfies all intellectual levels and arguments—from peasants in ancient deserts to the most advanced astro-physicists today. But we better stop here, Conner, because if we go any further, we fall into an unrelenting void. Frankly, I don't care to do that and I don't think you do either. Just think of space as being inextricably bound up with 'time'."

Clifton looked puzzled and gazed out at the two figures playing baseball in the distance.

"What about time travel, Professor?"

"Your email focused on that more than anything else. Why?"

"I don't know why, Profefssor. The idea has taken hold of me for reasons I can't explain."

"Well, the concept does introduce you to the well-known 'grandfather paradox.' You know, you go back and kill your 15 year-old grandfather making it impossible for you to ever exist. But there is also the Novikov principle saying that if by going back an instance gives rise to a paradox, then the probability of that event is negated. 'An event can never cease to be an event. It can never get out of any time series in which it once is.' John Ellis McTaggert said that and I concur."

"Who was McTaggert?"

"A metaphysician, Trinity College, Cambridge. Around 1910 he wrote the "Unreality of Time" which maintained that 'time' was unreal. You read my book, didn't you? Listen, My Friend, you're getting in way over your head. You're steering yourself straight into the greatest Pandora's Box of them all."

"I won't lie, Professor: I have difficulty believing time doesn't exist; that it is, as you say, 'a mental construct.' What I do believe is that 'time' is an abstraction like gravity or love, which, yes, is hard to define, maybe impossible to define, but *must* exist."

"Oh, but gravity is a force whose behavior is irrefutable. As good old Albert taught us: mass grips spacetime telling it how to curve, and spacetime grips mass, telling it how to move. Yeah, I read your email and noted your problems with my arguments. But there's something else you might consider. Your leg feeling OK?"

"Events certainly do occur. And while I regard 'time travel' as ludicrous, I do recognize the possibility that 'event witnessing' may one day be possible."

"Now I found that idea most intriguing, Professor," Clifton said. "I wanted to explore your theory on that."

"All the 'time travel' writers and philosophers have mistakenly confused 'time travel' with 'time alteration' as though they're the same. You know, somebody builds a time machine and goes back and tries to prevent the assassination of President Kennedy. Two distinctions have never been made in this regard: one: traveling back to an event; two: interfacing with the event itself and altering or changing it. Why do we assume that if we witness an event we have to jump in and change something? What makes us believe we're able to 'step into the action'? They have to be separate modalities. No, travelling through 'time' and changing an event is impossible; but witnessing it or accessing it might just one day come to pass. Of course, the Hindu's believe in the Akashi records—humanity's experience from beginning to end in one cosmic library housed somewhere in the cosmos. Edgar Cayce, for example, claimed to be psychic and would go into a trance supposedly tapping into those records. The bottom line is I do hold open the door that it's possible to discover the means to view past events—but the viewer would be absolutely detached from the action."

"So I could go back and watch the siege at the Alamo in Texas, but not change it."

"Conner, please delete the phrase: *'So I could go back.'* You're not going back to the Alamo and never will. Remember, there's no 'time.' Just events, one upon another, brick upon brick, stones of experience that rise up and stretch upward and outward. But as I've said, I believe it may be possible to access past experience. You could theoretically witness pure history denuded of all historical bias. Think of it as camera film of your 10th birthday: you're able to watch it, but you aren't there and you can't change the number of candles on the cake."

"Completely apart from travel back through time, then?" Conner asked.

Laurentia was irritated. *"There's no time so there's nothing to travel through, for God's sake!"* he shouted. "It would be like saying, 'I'm taking a magic carpet ride through the sky,' but there's no magic carpet to ride on! It doesn't exist. If it helps, insert the phrase 'event witnessing.' Maybe one day we'll see events on a super television screen of some kind that will display the Trojan War or the first colonists settling Jamestown. You see, if I light a match, is a record of that action stored anywhere in the universe? It depends upon discovering some way of re-transmitting the event itself—as if it were recorded on tape. I can hypothesize that coming to pass. But it would mean viewing pure truth. And pure truth is perhaps the most dangerous idea imaginable. Wasn't there a science fiction story where a guy invents a machine that shows historical events as they really happened? He was murdered and the machine was destroyed because the truth invalidated too much of the lies that have come to be known as the factual history we've been taught in school."

Clifton could practically see the wheels spinning in Laurentia's head as the professor kept his eyes pinned on the boy in the distance standing at the plate and swinging at his father's lob pitches. He guessed the professor had exhausted hundreds, possibly thousands of hours arguing against the conventional notions of 'time.'

"But I must be honest, Conner: if we ever do discover any form of 'time travel', I really don't think it will be through the courtesy of physics."

"OK, Professor, now take the little kid you've been watching play baseball out there. Won't he eventually grow up 'over time' to hit that ball like his Dad?"

"Conner, what will make that boy grow up and hit a ball," Laurentia said, pointing to the boy on the infield, "is nutrition, exercise, environmental conditions, and genes. 'Time' won't do anything. And if you don't believe me, take a newborn baby and confine it to a closet for 5 years. Its growth will be stunted, mental faculties disturbed, bones, tissue twisted. And by the way, there have been wicked parents who have actually done that to their children."

"Going back to your example of the Trojan War, Professor: you're telling me time's not the stage for historical events?"

"Conner, are you listening to anything I'm saying? There's no 'stage'! If there's a 'stage,' then it's the earth. Forget 'time.' To repeat: it's all about events, brick upon brick, experience leading to more experience. Take that kid again: let's say he grows up and plays for the Dodgers. What gets him there is years and years of practice, good coaching, perseverance, and innate talent. But 'time' didn't put him in a Dodger uniform and never will. Do you see, Conner? Is it sinking in?"

"But according to Einstein's Time Dilation Effect—"

"Let's get something straight: Einstein was wrong," Laurentia stated flatly, biting down on his cigar and squinting his eyes.

"*What*? Einstein was *wrong*?"

"Einstein was a great mind, one of the greatest minds in history, but he erred."

"Where exactly was he mistaken?"

"We get back to light. Einstein, in essence, said that if one could travel at the speed of light, 'time' would slow down relative to someone who's stationary. But how can something slow down if there is nothing to slow down *about*? And please don't tell me it's been tested and supposedly validated, even very recently. I'm well aware that clocks in relative movement seem to run slower than clocks standing still. Not surprising that physicists take that seeming proof and run with it into the end zone thinking they scored a touchdown."

"But if it was tested and proven—"

"It was tested by using *physical clocks and physical testing methods*—even atomic clocks. OK, fine. Seemingly convincing and irrefutable. But if 'time' is an illusion—a mental construct—then any physical test upon it must contain the ghosts of the illusion's essence. Sort of like a ruler trying to weigh pounds. *A physical something cannot measure a non-physical nothing...*

"The big three in physics for Einstein was space, mass, and 'time.' You can see and or test both space and mass, but 'time' can neither be seen nor felt. It would be like inserting love into scientific formulae and inventing a 'love-o-meter' that tests the degree of love one feels for someone. Whatever registers or is measured is at the mercy of the instruments measuring it. You want a person to register a certain degree of love on the 'love-o-meter,' you will get a certain degree of love. But at least love can be felt emotionally; time can't. Einstein *assumed* spacetime and incorporated it into General Relativity. That is, he inserted a force he thought should *be* time. Sort of like the ancient Greeks assumed atoms and molecules without ever seeing them."

"But atoms and molecules exist, don't they?"

"Ah, but atoms and molecules compose matter and we can see matter. We can't, on the other hand, see 'time'—because 'time' is smoke and mirrors. And if you say that days and years compose 'time' in the way atoms and molecules compose matter, then you prove my point because days and years are based on the Earth's rotation around the sun, nothing at all to do with 'time' at all.

"Conner, you're the computer whiz. If I asked you what 'Cyberspace' was, would you say it's out there like planets and stars are out there? You'd tell me I was dead wrong because you know that Cyberspace is essentially, and to its core, *electromagnetics*. Yet the average person thinks of cyberspace as some kind of physical universe filled with web sites, emails, and search engines—as though it were existing like the planet Neptune exists in the Solar System. But there's something far more meaningful here you keep ignoring. And you had better consider it seriously."

"And what's that, Professor?"

"Light! Because when you interface with the speed of light, you enter a realm so unfathomable it is truly useless for the human mind to try and comprehend it. You might as well speculate whether the tooth fairy rides a bicycle down the street or takes a cab. A complete waste of 'time.' Yet the speed of light is the physicist's calisthenics; the scientist's orgasm. And I abhor all of that. Since Einstein catapulted 'the speed of light' and all that it has entailed for physicists ever since Special and General Relativity, the concept of light has come to be regarded as sort of a grandiose tinker toy. And believe me, light is no tinker toy. If you study Einstein, you find that he didn't just mean 'everything is relative.' He meant that *appearances* are relative. And in Stanley Laurentia's book, Einstein might as well have gone down the rabbit hole and discovered the Cheshire cat.

"You see, Conner, Einstein was a physicist who spoke the only language he knew how to speak and science fell in love with him very early on. And that marriage between Albert and his mistress 'physics' continues blissfully to this day. You can bet I've had fights over this issue with many peers especially about Einstein arriving at $E=MC^2$. You know my office at Caltech was once Einstein's?" Laurentia chuckled. "I've become the raspberry seed in my department's wisdom tooth for years. Believe me, I've paid a heavy price for my beliefs. But so be it. Apparently, that's the punishment for thinking outside the box."

"Professor, you have to admit your ideas are quite a package to unload. Were you always a 'creative thinker'?"

"By 'creative' I assume you mean 'cuckoo'? No, I began as a soft spoken physics professor who kissed all the necessary academic butts for twenty years."

"So what changed you?"

Laurentia's eyes twinkled and he took another long puff on his pencil-thin cigar. "Certain things."

"I'd love to know about those 'things.' Mind sharing?"

"Nothing personal, but yes, I do mind and don't really care to go there. Now don't misunderstand me, Conner: Einstein was a watershed intellect in the history of physics. But when he ventured into the area of light—its speed and nature—he took us down the same garden path that most all physicists have gone down ever since."

"And what path is that, Professor?"

"To tackle light with a straight face as though it's a subject like dating fossils or radiator repair that one is able to break down and concretize. He said light was made up of particles and photons. As far as I'm concerned, Einstein led us into a haunted house and showed us ectoplasm. But what in the name of Christ Almighty is ectoplasm?

"Conner, I've gone too far afield already. Everything Einstein concluded is spilled milk for our purposes here, isn't it? I met you today because you sent me a sincere email, seem like a nice guy, found my book, and live in Pasadena. Your passion, Conner, is an admirable layman's romance with 'time.' And I'm willing to have coffee over that. You probe, but you're not a pain in the ass with some jackass preconception that combined with twenty cents wouldn't get either one of us a local phone call."

"Professor Laurentia, you've got a mind-blowing hat full of ideas."

"And those ideas are the reasons I'm on a short leave to

'reevaluate' my positions. *The Illusion of Time* was too volatile. It ruffled too many feathers and caused me to become a pariah at Cal Tech."

"Didn't know that."

"Given your concerns, Conner, I'm not sure you should even be talking to a physicist at all about 'time.' Physics is probably not the gateway you really need. But you consulted a physicist, so you got a physicist's approach. Had you consulted a mortgage broker, you'd have gotten a mortgage broker's approach. The essence we think of as 'time' is probably *something*, but it's not even remotely close to what it's universally thought to be. Perhaps it will never be truly understood at all; frankly, Conner, this may surprise you, but I hope that is the case. Is Man supposed to unlock every damn mystery in the universe? Maybe some things ought to be left to— the mind of God."

"Professor, you quoted Genesis. Do you believe in God?"

Laurentia exhaled a stream of cigar smoke and stared at the little boy in the distance who chased a pop fly that landed over his head. "I leave the barn door wide open for that one. Being agnostic is the physicist's moose handshake, isn't it? Ever meet a religious physicist? I haven't. One does rightfully wonder why. Physicists theorize upon the most infinitesimal particles of matter and explore the most mind-wrenching depths of space—from the edges of creation to black holes to the Higgs Boson and dark matter. They get their minds blown as they uncover reality that gets stranger and stranger, then they turn around and describe all of it as just random crap floating around in an indifferent cosmos. I'm not entirely sure I can swallow that with my coffee and donuts. Were you aware that the first person to propose The Big Bang theory in 1927 was George Lemaitre, a Belgian priest?"

"You *are* certainly different, aren't you, Professor?"

"That's what they say. Well, c'est la vie"

"Professor, what do you recommend I do with this obsession I have about time that won't seem to let go of me?"

Laurentia pulled out another cigar as he turned around and made direct eye contact with Clifton for the first time.

"Forget physics. You need a different path, Conner. May I suggest one? Would you consider talking to a very intriguing guy? His name is Aristotle Protosaultis. He left medicine and began counseling people with very unique concerns such as yourself. He's got a rather amazing intuitive perception and truly cares about his clients. I respect Ari's unorthodox approach which might be right up your alley. He does have a very private practice and takes only referrals, but I know him well and I'll recommend you, if you like. His office is in Century City."

"I'd appreciate that," Clifton said. "I promised myself today I'd stop reading and start talking to people about this thing I have with 'time.' I need live *feedback*. And if this guy can give me that, I'm all for it."

Laurentia reached inside his coat. "Well, you'll get feedback from Ari, I assure you. Now he'll charge you $100 an hour, but he's worth every dime." The professor removed a white card from his billfold which had the counselor's contact numbers.

"What was the medical field this guy left, Professor?"

"Neurology."

The crack of the bat sent a low line drive that hugged the foul line all the way down to the cyclone fence and skidded 20 feet in front of the two men. "Isn't it amazing, Conner, how often the umpire misses the call as to whether a ball was 'fair' or 'foul'? I've seen a hundred blown calls. And no one does anything about it, the errors are never corrected, yet those mistakes influence the outcome of many games."

The professor tossed his cigar butt away and straightened the knot in his tie.

"Conner, I hope you don't think that just because I suggested Ari, it means I think you're a three-dollar bill. Hey, if your leg feels OK, let's go back to Starbuck's and get some coffee and donuts. Unless you think *I'm* crazy."

They headed back to Starbuck's where the professor wolfed

down two huge cinnamon rolls and drank a large cup of cappuccino. He told Clifton about one of his undergraduate students who claimed he had traveled ahead in time 50 years and met his great grandson. The student turned in a paper with abstruse formulae allegedly proving his time travel assertions. Laurentia said the mathematics was hilarious. "Last I heard that kid was working at a company that made toilet seats."

Clifton got back to his car around 2:30 feeling as if a room full of furniture had been moved around inside his head. Turning over the engine, he thought about all that Laurentia had said about 'time' and light. Then his cell went off. It was Protosaultis. The counselor had already heard from Laurentia and said he had a cancelled appointment and had an opening. He invited Clifton to drive over to his office around 4 o'clock, if possible. Clifton agreed, then sped off toward Century City.

The counselor's office door said: "Aristotle Protosaultis, M.D., Ph.D." It was a warm living room of two leather recliners facing one other over a Persian throw rug. In the middle of the room a mahogany coffee table supported vases of pretty red roses and a row of fresh carnations. The walls had large posters: a tropical rainforest, gorgeous coral reef, and a picture of Christ in white with children running to His outstretched arms in a beam of light. A side window looked out across the street where workers poured cement for a future corner block of offices. The window had no screen, but lace curtains shuffled in a light breeze.

Protosaultis was a very slight man in his 40's no more than 120 pounds with a prominent gap between his two front teeth that widened into a large space whenever he smiled. He wore wiry toothpick bifocals and an oversized sweatshirt that said "Pepperdine." Clifton guessed his curiously intriguing, angular face suggested both Mediterranean and Japanese ancestry. But it was his voice, soft and serenely calming, that sent a gentle chill down Clifton's spine which indicated to him that the man was at perfect peace with himself. Protosaultis had just boiled water and asked, "Care for some green tea, Conner?"

"No, thank you."

Clifton began by describing his current career angst and uncertainty about just what he wanted to do with his life. Then he got onto his divorce two years earlier and detailed his accident at work. His broken clock on the wall in his computer room somehow found its way into his narrative, but the subject of time was his central focus.

"I don't know why this obsession with time has taken hold of me," Clifton stated. "But it got more intense after I broke my leg. I'm like an addict and can't read enough or learn enough about it. Not sure I need a shrink exactly, but Laurentia highly recommended you and so here I am seeking interaction and feedback. Guess I'm groping, Dr. Protosaultis; I can't truly say I know where I'm going with any of this. I'm not sure if I've gone a little off the deep end or not."

The counselor listened attentively, his bifocals pinned to the tip of his nose. The entire time Clifton was speaking, Protosaultis grasped the arms of his recliner firmly and never once veered his eyes from the subject across from him.

"First of all, I'm not a shrink, Conner." The counselor smiled good-naturedly and the gap between his two front teeth opened up like a highway. "I was a neurologist, yes, but I left my practice years ago and now implement my own approach. For example, I don't believe in the classic therapist's 'detachment' of saying little and waiting for the subject to disclose he dreams of strangling his father. I get involved. I suggest, dive in; I move concepts around and have no problem editorializing. And if my client says 'Two plus two equals five,' the hairs at the back of my head don't stand up at all. Please call me 'Ari.'...."

"Conner: do you think you could come up with one single incident or event that might be a clue as to why you're so obsessed with the subject of time?"

"The germ of this has existed since childhood. As a kid, I saw every movie and read every story on time travel there was. It was after my accident months ago that this whole fascination somehow accelerated. Suddenly, I had this driving, overwhelming passion to understand time and know just what it is. But it's not a scary thing—I'd compare it to a dinosaur hunter's excitement knowing important fossils are just under the next rock. I keep lifting rocks, I guess, hoping to unlock whatever it is I'm looking for."

"Conner, we're all lifting rocks. But let me try to hone in with greater clarity: try to break down the general subject of time and pinpoint the specific element or facet of it that interests you most."

"Time travel, to put it right out there. In the last couple of years my thoughts have focused on it more and more. Nuts, maybe. Then I found Professor Laurentia's book, emailed him at Tech, and he agreed to see me today."

"Don't think that's nuts at all," the counselor shrugged. "Stanley is an excellent physicist to talk to having lectured and written on the subject. Conner, I'm going to propose a framework. And the pitch is coming straight down the plate. Ready for it?"

"Yes."

"Conner, how old are you?"

"Thirty-one."

"I want you to assume you *have* gone back in time. I'll use the age of 70. Assume that Conner Clifton, at the age of 70, traveled back 39 years to your present. How do you know that this present is not really your past? Can you prove it?"

The notion hit Clifton squarely between the eyes. He now realized what Laurentia meant when he described Protosaultis as 'unorthodox.'

"So when I'm 70, I travel back to right now, age 31?"

"Yes, from 70 back to 31. What I want to know is, where's the body of memory for those 39 years? They have to be some place. And if they are gathered somewhere, how do you access them?"

"Whoa, let me think about that. What about—hypnosis?"

"That's the answer most reach for, yes. Know how many people have been hypnotized? Millions. If hypnosis truly unlocked past and future memories we'd have documented that by now. And other than late night radio talk show mumbo-jumbo, there's no credible scholarship on the subject whatsoever. Personally, I believe past life regression is pretty much suggestion by the therapist."

"So how does somebody retrieve 39 years of memory?"

The counselor laughed. "You're asking me the key for future prediction? If I had that answer I'd be out at Santa Anita race track cleaning up!"

Clifton liked him. Protosaultis had a soft demeanor and a genuinely pleasing whimsicality. He was already grateful to Laurentia for recommending him and was very comfortable sitting in front of the counselor now and revealing his concerns.

"If you experienced time travel when you're 70, for example, that experience might somehow be contained in your present. Could you possibly find a way to tap into that experience?"

Clifton thought hard. This was far from what he had expected when he walked through the counselor's office door. Ideas began dancing around in his head as he imagined a number of scenarios.

"A mental experiment, Conner: Again, you're 70, and you venture back to 31, your present. That's 39 years of time that has to be accounted for. All that experience must be stored somewhere."

"Well, there's nothing I can pinpoint or put my finger on: no recurring dreams, no psychic visions. But then might not that memory be blocked?"

"Can't rule that out at all."

"But the memory would have to be in the mind, wouldn't it?

"Not necessarily. The medial temporal lobe is the region of the brain which has organs of particular relevance used as the storage center for memory, true. But other types of memory exist, too. Look at the athlete—instantaneous physical adjustment such as a skier going down slope, a boxer reacting to a punch in the ring—it occurs in a flash of a second without thought. That's neuromuscular memory. Muscles do what they're trained to do. There's also emotional memory: you hear a piece of music, taste hot apple pie, and a specific, powerful memory is recalled that might even bring you to tears. What impresses me most is your relentless *passion* to understand the subject of time."

"So what does that tell you, Ari?"

"It tells me your drive to *know* time derives from something real. What I'm asking you to do, if you have traveled back in time, is to 'remember forward'."

Through the window, just to the counselor's left, Clifton saw construction workers wrapping up their day's labors. They had been laying blocks of stone on a new structure across the street. He drew a parallel between the building he saw through the window and the building of his own detached garage at home.

"Wow, 'remembering forward.' How do you do that, Ari?"

"Back to the central question: what happens to memory if and when one moves backward? You're 31 and all you know is what you've accumulated to this point, or so you think. Let's look at this mental experiment from the reverse angle: What if at the age of 17 you shot ahead to 31?"

"But I'd know that now, wouldn't I?"

"Would you? Or your memory may just be contained as the complete memory of a 31 year-old man with a composite of intervening experiences. Quite a conundrum either way, isn't it?"

Clifton laughed. "I have to admit, Ari, I never thought of any of this."

"There are many theories about short and long-term memory processes, but we'll leave that to complex medicine. Your drive to butt heads with this subject of time is obviously the crux of the matter. You know this subject is one huge paradox, yet you challenge it and don't seem to tire of the effort. But I am on the train with you, Conner; I'm seated beside you and I'll accompany you to the last stop if necessary."

"Laurentia mentioned the 'grandfather paradox.' It seems self-canceling now, but will it be in 39 years?"

Protostaultis shrugged. "We'll never know 'till we get there."

"Ari, do you even remotely entertain the idea of time travel?"

The counselor shrugged. "Let me put it this way: I was fascinated with the human mind as early as 13. Eventually, I became a clinical neurologist and practiced medicine for years.

Now does that mean that at the age of 13 I 'remembered forward'? I can't say, Conner, and neither can anyone else. But I will tell you that many people have interest in a particular subject or profession in childhood for which there is no nexus, but ultimately it becomes their life's work. Are they remembering forward?

"The universe is paradox. As for memory, I do believe every experience one has in life is stored in the mind—songs learned, friends known, Christmas gifts given and received. But most of it is buried and forgotten. However, I'm of the opinion that those memories can be revived with the proper trigger.

"Ari, something that might relate to all this: when I was in junior high, I used to walk over to the local public high school on Saturdays and summer days peering into empty classrooms and hallways with a strange sense of something, a sort of nostalgic sensibility. My parents said I'd never go to that school and sent me to a private high school instead. Yet I couldn't dismiss the attachment to the other school. Ironically, I ended up transferring to that very public school my sophomore year."

"Most psychologists would probably call that a self-fulfilling prophecy."

"There's more to it. That school became an intersection in my life. I have close friends to this day from that school; even former teachers who I'm in still in touch with. I'm 100 percent convinced that the desire to get to that public school was more than just acting out a subconscious, self-fulfilling script. Could this be what you mean by 'remembering forward'?"

The counselor looked intrigued. "Interesting," he commented. "Keep going with that."

"That phrase 'remember forward'—first time I ever heard it. But it seems to fit the experience. Then I had the accident at work. Since then, fascination with the subject of time is something I can't seem to let go of."

'Or one that won't let go of *you*. You know, Conner, I'd like to go back—and who wouldn't?—and correct many of my mistakes. I'd start with my two ex-wives and never marry them. But then what I learned from them led to meeting my third wife and three wonderful children by her. Had I gone back and cancelled those first two marriages, I'd have never had the beauty of my third wife and family."

"The 'grandfather paradox,'" Conner stated.

"We often wade through the muck to get to the rose garden, don't we?"

"Are you saying that what I'm going through now is for a purpose? To set the table for something to come?"

"In my book, *everything* we go through is to, as you say, 'set the table' for a later purpose. Years ago, when I was practicing clinically, a couple brought their five-year-old little girl to me. The parents thought their daughter might have a brain tumor. She was speaking gibberish all day long. I listened to this child's rambling and recognized something amazing. I referred her to a professor of classics at USC before I rendered any diagnosis. That professor confirmed the little girl was speaking conversational Latin as it was spoken during the reign of Julius Caesar! How was this possible? Days later the little girl returned to normal and stopped speaking Latin in childhood. Well, guess what? That little girl is now a teacher of high school Latin and remains a teacher of classical Latin to this day. The last I heard she was writing a book on the poetry of Ovid. Had she lived over 2000 years ago? Was she tapping into a past consciousness that could assist her future life?

"There are theories of simultaneity—and Carl Jung did outstanding work here—that try to explain déjà vu, for example. You know, you think of someone you haven't seen in 25 years, then you pull up to the gas pump and there she is.

"The chronology of time as we think we know it may be a far cry from what is 'actual time.' Conner, what interests me is that you no doubt have a very real romance with the notion of time. Can I crack the nut for you? I don't know, but I will tell you one of my ironclad beliefs: people appear in our lives for important reasons. They all leave footprints. Some stay for years; others exit quickly never to be seen again. I'm here for you at this moment because for some reason it's important; but you are also here for me, too. I told you I would editorialize, didn't I?"

"Don't apologize for editorializing, Ari. I think it's refreshing."

"Final segment," the counselor announced, glancing at his watch. "You mentioned that your clock stopped, but that you never fixed it. I'm very curious why that is."

Conner shrugged. "I don't have a good answer to that question, Ari. The clock hangs there in my computer work room with the hands stopped at 12. It's now more like a picture of a clock than a *real* clock. Sort of like a wall painting representing time."

"I see," the counselor observed.

"Ari, you said I had a 'romance' with time. Laurentia also used that phrase to describe what I'm going through. Am I suffering from a 'romance'?"

"I won't be disingenuous, Conner. I spoke briefly with Stanley about your concerns. He knows you think he's an eccentric. But Stanley's been regarded eccentric for much of his career. He went against establishment thinking at Cal Tech. But he likes you. As for using the phrase 'a romance with time,' I wouldn't call it that. How about rendezvous?"

"But you both think I've got a loose screw, right?"

The counselor came forward with furrowed eyebrows and a look of concern. "What in the world makes you say a thing like that? Frankly, after engaging you for this short period of time, I think you're as normal as Laurentia; as normal as I."

"Ari, what is your definition of 'normal'?"

"I define 'normal' as a thirty-three and a third record playing at thirty-three and a third speed."

"Well," Clifton laughed, "I suppose that's something to build on."

Protosaultis removed his glasses and tapped the stems on the chair's armrest. "Conner, I'm going to suggest something that will be very simple to do. All I ask is that you won't ask me why I'm suggesting this. Will you go along?"

"Anything that helps. Agreed."

"Conner—fix the clock."

"Huh?"

"Go home and fix the clock. Set it to the correct time and keep it running properly."

"You're suggesting I just fix the clock?"

"As soon as you get home. Simply fix it."

Clifton tried to guess how fixing the clock in his computer workroom could possibly lead to anything significant.

"Just fix the clock, Conner. That's all. Fix it. Do it as soon as you get home."

Driving back to Pasadena, Clifton re-played every word of the session. What an unusual psychologist Protosaultis is, he mused. Laurentia had obviously sought the counselor out for his own personal reasons. I'd give serious money to have been a fly on the wall in the office when he and Laurentia dug into whatever troubled the physicist. There are plastic surgeons for celebrities; guess Ari's a counselor for idea-driven odd balls like me who have obsessions with time. Two blocks from his home, Clifton stopped at a convenience store and bought a package of batteries for his clock.

He stepped through the front door and went straight into his computer workroom. Slipping two batteries into the back of the clock, Clifton set the time to 7:11 p.m. The clock went into place on the wall and Clifton admired the golden, octagonal timepiece as its gentle, measured clicks reached his ears. But he was at a loss trying to understand what starting the clock had to do with the issues he related to Protosaultis.

Through the window, Clifton caught sight of his detached garage still under construction in the evening shadows. Turning on the yard light, he limped over the lawn on his cane and, with a flashlight, inspected the work that had been done earlier that day. The block wall had risen to a five-foot rectangular structure. He ran the flashlight's ray over the smooth brick surface and was pleased with the progress the workers had made.

As he crossed the yard on his way back to the house, Clifton nearly stumbled over an object protruding upright in the middle of his lawn. A book rose from the grass and emitted a pleasant golden glow. How did I miss this on my way out? He asked himself, reaching down, and picking up the volume.

THE BOOK OF TIME

An eyebrow lifted. *The Book of Time?* What is this? Taking the volume into the house, Clifton wondered why anyone would jam a book into his backyard lawn. Once in the kitchen, he turned back the pristine cover:

The Komono Pandemic
2035—2042AD

In 2035AD a human virus originating on the Indonesian island of Komono spread over continents and grew into a universal pandemic ...

Clifton was stupefied. He looked in vain for the author and publisher. Moreover, copyright, place of publication, and page numbers were also missing. Then he continued reading:

...The Komono Pandemic caused 19,457,992 deaths and was not arrested until the Keideker Serum was developed in Stockholm, Sweden in 2041AD...

Clifton held the book out in front of his eyes and studied the golden halo, then his fingers brushed through pages quickly. Where's this gold light coming from? He wondered in disbelief as he felt the unusual printed text. Then he leafed through more pages until he arrived at a second subtitle:

The Arrest of the Komono Virus
May 1, 2041AD

On May 1, 2041AD, Dr. Isaac Keideker and his scientific team in Stockholm, Sweden announced the serum for the Komono Virus after 100 victims inoculated with the cure were clinically proven to be free of symptoms...

Clifton read it with disbelieving, racing eyes.

On May 5, 2041AD, United States President James Eggerstein confirmed that the cure for the Komono Virus had been discovered by Dr. Isaac Keideker in Stockholm, Sweden. Pesident Eggerstein hailed Dr. Keideker as one of science's "Historic Men of Medicine"...

President James Eggerstein?! 2041AD?

Clifton took the book into his computer room and dropped to his vinyl chair trying to understand why someone would plant such a thing in his yard. This did not drop into the grass accidentally; this was purposefully shoved into the ground by somebody who wanted me to find it. Why? When he tried to dog-ear the page and return to the story of the virus, the paper flipped back into place without a crease. Attempting to tear a corner of the page lightly, he found it could not be torn. Clifton removed a pair of scissors and applied the blades to the book's cover. He gripped the scissors with greater force and tried to cut the page again. The blades snapped and broke. It's like trying to cut through steel, he thought. Clifton's numb fingers thumbed ahead a dozen or so pages. He froze when his astonished eyes found the next amazing subtitle and the paragraph that followed:

NovaSol Provides Serum Breakthrough
January 10, 2041AD

Conner Clifton, president of NovaSol Technologies in Los Angeles, California housing the NovaSol LTS400 computer, developed an advanced data encoding system which separated previously unknown organic genetic material that led to the discovery of the Keideker Serum...

Conner Clifton—president of NovaSol Technologies?!

Astounded, he flashed back to the first page and began reading as fast as his mind could absorb the sentences. Twenty minutes later, Clifton put the volume down and exhaled in disbelief.

The Book of Time? The Clifton computer?!

He imagined the workers building his garage had something to do with it. But how could they? The ludicrous possibility of Laurentia and Protosaultis producing the document also shot through his mind. But that scenario was just as ridiculous. Yet— what were the odds of spending the day talking about time to two different men, then coming home and finding a book titled *The Book of Time* predicting events more than twenty-five years into the future?

Out of breath, Clifton called Protosaultis. The counselor's voicemail went on and, in a shaking voice, he left a message: "Ari, this is Conner. It's urgent. Please call me as soon as you get this. I wouldn't be calling if it weren't urgent."

He stared at the amazing document in his hands. This book is predicting a world pandemic in 2041 naming cities, scientists, metropolitan riots, millions who perish from a virus, and world organizations working day and night to find a cure. And I— Conner Clifton—play a significant role in it. This has to be a gag placed in my yard by someone who knows my obsession with time. Examining the book's physical properties again, he wondered who was capable of producing paper that couldn't be folded, torn or cut. And this glow—it has no source.

The measured ticking of the clock on the wall filled Clifton's computer room. *President James Eggerstein?* Wait!

He swung his chair to the front of his computer and with shaking fingers typed the name into a search engine. The web site of Congressman James Eggerstein of Pittsburgh, Pennsylvania popped up in front of Clifton's incredulous eyes. Eggerstein was a 33 year-old politician who was in his first term. He'd be in his 50's in 2041, Clifton projected.

Clifton set the book down on his computer table, then limped on his cane toward the kitchen. Throwing the yard light on, he crept over the grass again. A neat rectangular slit formed in the middle of the lawn. Seeing Laurentia and Protosaultis today, the ensuing discussion about time: all of it is too coincidental. This is just plain nuts.

"Einstein was wrong..."

"Time is a mental construct..."

"Just fix the clock..."

He hurried back into the house, returned to his workroom, and sat down in front of his computer. When he reached for the book, Clifton's hand froze in mid-air. It wasn't on the table.

Jumping to his feet, rifling over his desk, Clifton searched the floor, then the entire room. He limped back to the kitchen quickly, hoping he had left the book there in a moment of absent-mindedness. Then he retraced all his steps from the kitchen to the yard to the computer room and turned everything upside down. The book was not in the house or in the yard.

The cell phone went off. He limped back into the workroom and swiped it. It was Protosaultis. Panting, Clifton spilled the entire episode out to the counselor. "Ari, I took a pair of scissors and tried to cut the paper in that book and the blades snapped and broke!"

"And you say it was gone when you got back from the yard?"

"Yes. Flat disappeared. I was out there one, two minutes, that's it."

"Hmmm."

"Ari, am I losing my mind?"

"Probably not," Protostaultis said. "But I'd like to see you, Conner."

"Thank you! I can be at your office within the hour."

"No, I want to see you at your home. Do you know the city college on Colorado? Be in front of it by the main marquee in 15 minutes. Don't worry. I'll find you."

Clifton was out of the house in two minutes. He raced across town to Pasadena City College, parked at the curb, and began pacing nervously with his cane on the sidewalk as he watched for Protosaultis. Twenty-five minutes later he was still pacing and wondered if the counselor would meet him at all. He was about to call Protosaultis on his cell, when a black SUV cruised up to the curb. The counselor poked his head out the passenger window. "I'll follow you to your house, Conner."

The moment the two men stepped inside Clifton's front door, Protostaultis said, "Now please show me where you found this unusual book."

Clifton picked up a flashlight and led the counselor across the back yard lawn. "Right there," he pointed.

Protostaultis took the flashlight and poked it straight into the slit on the grass. He knelt down and felt inside the narrow hole. "It's a perfect rectangular slit, isn't it?"

"Yes. The same size as the book."

The counselor gazed over at the garage in progress. "Is that the garage you said you were having built, Conner?"

"That's it."

Protosaultis probed around the yard shining the flashlight on the flowers, then worked his way over to the garage and inspected the freshly cemented stones.

"Now, Conner, would you please show me those broken scissors?"

Clifton lifted the trash can in his computer room and picked out the blades for Protostaultis to see. "I don't blame you for wanting proof, Ari. I'd ask for proof if I were you."

The counselor smiled his wide, gap-toothed smile. "Seems we have a healthy conundrum on our hands, don't we? Mind boiling some water; I brought green tea."

Protosaultis was intrigued by the endless parts, disassembled modems, and hard drives in Clifton's computer workroom. "Quite a collection of paraphernalia here, Conner." Then he perused Clifton's collection of books and papers on time that lined his shelves. Finally, he noted the clock on the wall. "So that's the clock. Nice to see it's running," he observed, walking around the room sipping green tea. "Conner, would you mind going through the whole rigmarole again?"

Clifton described the episode and what he read in the book. "This wasn't a Nostradamus-style bunch of cryptic poems that you could read whatever you wanted into them. This was so specific it was like reading a Civil War history book with battles described in order."

The counselor listened carefully, then sat down in the corner with his tea. "What strikes me most, Conner, is the specificity of it—naming people, dates, places..."

"Ari, there's more: I went online and found a 33 year-old Pennsylvania congressman named James Eggerstein. The book referred to a President James Eggerstein. He'd be 58 years old in 2041."

"Hmmmm. I told you, Conner, I'm on the train with you; I'm along for the ride to wherever the destination leads. May I ask a few routine questions? Take any medication in the last 24 hours?"

"No."

"Any alcohol?"

"None."

"Allergic reaction to any—"

"No."

"Were there any head, neck injuries when you fell and broke your leg?"

"For God's sake, no, Dimitri."

"Indulge me, Conner."

The counselor held two fingers in front of Clifton's face and asked him to follow their lateral path with his eyes without turning his head. "Live alone?"

"Of course. Divorced. The last time I saw that book it was right there," Clifton indicated, pointing to his computer station.

"Now, you say the book named a certain doctor who discovered the cure for this virus?"

"Yes! This Dr. Heideker—or *Keideker*, yes, that's it!"

"You're the computer expert. Get on line and see if any such person pops up."

Fingers stabbed at keys. Within seconds, Clifton's eyes

widened and he said, "Listen to this! Dr. Isaac Keideker connected to—Smerud Medical Research, Uppsala, Sweden...Expert in clinical development blah, blah, blah...wrote a book titled *New Biostatistics for the 21st Century*. What do you make of that, Dimitri?"

Protostaultis swirled his tea bag around in the cup. "And the name of that computer company you're supposed to be president of some day?"

"NovaSol! Should have thought of that!" Clifton shouted, his splayed fingers running over the keys again. After scrolling down a page of paragraphs, he said, "No—nothing pops up for NovaSol."

"Of course not," smiled Protosaultis, "if that company is in the future, it wouldn't exist today, would it? Conner, time to start connecting dots: A document with no author or information about where it came from appears in your backyard describing events some 25 years in the future; it names a President who's now in congress; names a doctor now in Sweden; names you and links you to a future computer company. Then this document with the strange properties you've described disappears without a trace. Is that the gist of it?"

"Yes, except that I found it after a long hard day discussing time with you and Professor Laurentia," Clifton added.

The counselor's left eyebrow shot up significantly. "Hmmmm. As I see it, three possible explanations: One, you hallucinated the experience; two, it's the most sophisticated prank I ever heard of; three, you've had a rendezvous with the preternatural."

Clifton rubbed the stubble of beard on his chin. "I considered the garage workers might have had something to do with it, but that's totally out of whack because they speak very little English. And where did the book go in the two minutes I went back out to the yard?"

"Now let me ask this: you said you were divorced. Could your ex-wife—"

"Not a chance, Ari. She moved to Vancouver two years ago and knows nothing about my interests in time."

The counselor shook his head. "I'll be blunt, Connor: there are cases of dual personality where one identity plants or erases evidence against the other identity. It's two distinct people in one body; the right hand never knows what the left hand is doing. But I don't really believe that is what's happening here."

"That's schizophrenia, right? Am I schizo?"

"No. And I'll tell you why: Conner, did you know I was coming over here? Did you have any idea I was going to rush you back to the house after we met and then ask to see the hole in the grass? Even more, we have the broken scissors."

"Had no idea you were coming over, Ari."

"Of course you didn't. But the cherry on the banana split for me is the clock: you fixed it, didn't you? Let's just say that had you been sabotaged by your other identify; it would not have allowed you to start the clock. You're going to have to trust me on that one and accept the psychology of it at face value. No, I rule out schizophrenia."

"Well, I'm at least relieved to know I'm not two people."

"Tell me again: where did you say the virus began?"

"Komono. Supposedly some island in Indonesia, I think."

"I could be wrong, but I do believe there certainly is an island in Indonesia named Komono. Were you aware of that?"

"I—think I might have heard of the place before, but don't think I've ever clearly identified it as a specific island."

"Check it on the web, Conner."

Clifton typed over the computer keyboard and pulled up a map of Indonesia. "Yeah—here it is. Komono sure is in Indonesia."

"Conner, brace yourself: unless we can come up with someone in your life who knows about your obsession with time, someone who took it upon himself to write this book and somehow manufacture its odd makeup, someone who slipped into your yard and planted it, I would have no choice to say we've come face to face with the inscrutable. A phenomenon unlike any I have ever known."

"*Jesus...*"

"A first even for me, Conner, and I've seen more than my share of three dollar bills in my time. That little girl I told you about—the one who spoke conversational Latin—this transcends even that puzzlement."

"Ari, I'm sure glad I met you. I think the garden variety shrink—excuse me, 'counselor'—would have put me on medication. But I do have to say I'm impressed by how calmly you approach all this. Do you ever get hot and bothered about the unusual?"

"The universe is paradox, Conner. Anti-matter; dark matter; quarks. Billions of galaxies and each with billions of stars. Black holes sucking up chunks of incomprehensible space, the Higgs Boson, and on and on. Existence is one grandiose conundrum in which we humans plod along like ants puzzling over a tiny grain of sand that blocks our path so we say, 'What is this mystifying enigma that confronts me?'"

"This isn't a grain of sand, Ari. This is the most incredible experience of my life! I'm shown a slice of the future in which I'm supposedly involved. This glimpse of time is thrown into my lap right after I see a physicist and a neurologist talking about 'time.' Way too coincidental. What do you suggest I do, Ari?"

"You proceed. You live your life normally—because there's no other option, Conner. The harder you try to find explanations, the more you'll probably end up grabbing air. But I'll tell you one thing I do believe: there's important purpose here."

"So I'm going to carry all this with me indefinitely?"

"You'll carry this particular aspect of it, yes. Did the document describe a future wife? Children? How long you would live?"

"No. Just the reference to what I do in the computer aspect of finding a cure for this virus."

Protostaultis shook his head. "Obviously. Because that's all that was necessary. Why this book appeared to you on the very day you picked to talk to people about time and—don't forget, the day you fixed your clock—may never be known."

Clifton worked on it. "Damn! I keep hearing Laurentia saying 'time is an illusion.' If he's right, then where's this book from?"

The counselor raised a finger. "Ah! But Stanley would say it's *not* from time, it's from a *place*. Stanley believes time is a picture frame around a picture, but not actually the picture it's framing."

"Yes, I'm familiar with that metaphor. Ari, do you believe Laurentia is right?"

"I believe Laurentia is no more right or wrong than anyone who advances a theory about one of the universe's greatest concepts: Time."

Clifton gazed out the window. His yard was dark and he could no longer make out the silhouette of the garage. "Ari, if this book truly describes what is to come, then the future is in stone. And if it's in stone, why did the book appear since the events are fated to happen anyway?"

Ari smiled his wry, gaped-toothed smile. "Speculation here, Conner: What if that book you found has nothing at all to do with the future events it described?"

"What are you talking about? The whole point of it was the world-wide virus."

"Was it? Conner, the first thing you hit upon when you walked into my office today was your career dilemma."

"Am I missing something here, Ari?"

"Think outside the box, Conner. I think the timing of all this may just be the point. You found this book just as you stand at a crossroads laboring over your own destiny. You broke your leg and during this recovery period you began second-guessing your purpose and direction in life. You contemplated leaving the computer field altogether, didn't you?"

"Are you saying that book appeared in my yard because it's trying to get me to stay in computers?"

"Finish this sentence, Conner: *The book came to me because...*"

"...*Because*—this proves the future still needs to be determined...*Because*—certain things need to be put into a specific place to...insure a certain future—to insure that virus will be *cured...*?"

The counselor's eyes twinkled. "I'll only say that once you

admit the logic of the book coming from the future, why can't you admit the rest?"

Clifton let out a long breath. "But to say the book came from a *future conscious intelligence—"*

"Don't be naive, Conner! Of course it came from a conscious intelligence! Books don't write themselves. The toughest thing you may be facing is that you will never get any reasons for what you've experienced today. I strongly suggest you swim with the current, not go against it. If I've learned one thing dealing with the human mind, it's to go with the behavior, the experience, and not make the mistake of fighting straw men. I've encountered the most bizarre forms of schizophrenia—but I go *with it.* Had a complete schizophrenic years ago who thought he was Jesus. I said to him, "You know, dogginnit, you're the fifth Messiah I met this week!"

Clifton threw his head back and laughed.

"I told you I'm riding along on the train with you, but I'm not God, Conner. Be content that signs seem to point to a benign power that has singled you out for some important reason. So by all means fly on the tail wind it's giving you; don't fight it. But I do agree: your obsession with time hitting a peak today then coinciding with the appearance of this book is amazingly coincidental. Go about your business, Conner; live your life as you normally would live it and let that which is destined to unfold, unfold."

Clifton's eyes fell to *The Time Machine* by H.G. Wells standing upright on the shelf across from him. He removed it and regarded the novel's cover which showed a man getting into a strange chair that was about to catapult him forward in time. "Ari, could you give me an anti-anxiety prescription to calm me down?"

"No. No drugs. One of the worst things I think you could do now. I will, however, give you a far better RX: When I leave here, I'd like you to plan a day tomorrow spent away from this house; do what you love most, Conner. Stay away from this workroom, your computer, and don't read about time or even think about the subject. If you do this, I think many of your anxieties will diminish. Meanwhile, my office door is always open."

"And if—another book appears with a whole different future?"

"Then you deal with it like you would deal with—a broken leg."

Clifton slept restlessly that night. He tossed about, felt a sudden stab of pain in his leg similar to the pain he felt when he broke his femur. Then he dreamed he was limping toward a book the size of the Eiffel Tower. The book opened. He entered. The book closed.

Early Saturday morning, Clifton stood on his backyard lawn and stared straight down into the rectangular slit again. Then he threw fishing gear, cheese sandwiches and cold beer into the trunk and headed for the beach. He was taking the counselor's advice and would do what he loved most: spend the day surf fishing. The salt air and clean ocean breezes had always been Clifton's tonic for washing away stress. He wasn't sure he could do it, but he would concentrate hard on erasing yesterday's events from his mind.

Flinging his pole case around his neck, carrying the loaded plastic bucket in one hand while negotiating his cane with the other, Clifton edged over the cool sand. It was a laborious trek, but he finally made it close to the water's edge and planted his gear. Taking in a huge breath of ocean air, he studied the killer breakers, then began to assemble his pole and bait his line.

Two metal sardines dangled from a hook and Clifton cast into the shallow foam watching the surf swallow the lures. As the line was drawn out, he threw the reel's catch and braced the pole at an angle in the sand against his folding chair. Ripping the pull-tab off the top of a can of beer, Clifton kept hearing Protosaultis' voice: *"Go about your business, live your life as you normally would..."*

A few sips later, he removed his shoes and perused both ends of the deserted stretch of beach. He was about to reach for his I-pod when he checked his pole: it had dropped to the sand and was rolling out to sea. He hobbled after the line frantically, splashed into the surf, and dashed at the reel inches from his grasp. But the pole swept out, and, as he lunged for it, slipped and fell into the icy water. Stunned by the sea's wrenching cold, Clifton lost complete sight of the line. He was up to his waist in the current, freezing, shivering, searching over the water and hoping the line would snag, tangle, and bob to the surface. He waded about in all directions when the foot on his broken leg stepped down on the point of a shell or rock. Hopping in agony, he reached for his injured heal when the surf crashed in wickedly and knocked him flat. The frigid shock of the blow stunned him and he choked on seawater and struggled to get to his feet. Coughing salty foam, enduring the hammering pain in his foot, Clifton finally caught his breath. But he was suddenly treading water, still searching for a sign of his pole. There, some twenty yards out, he spotted the white line circling like a loose lariat in a white surface cloud. Behind it, though, another swell was growing.

Since the reel catch had been thrown, he knew that if he could grab the line, he'd be able to drag the pole along the bottom and back to the beach. He dived in and began swimming toward the white, bobbing thread in a race to snatch the line, meet the next wave, and body surf back to shore. All at once his eyes stared straight ahead in disbelief at the approaching swell that had grown into a monster. An instant before it swept over him, he filled his lungs with air.

The monster covered him completely. Clifton was underwater, arms and legs flailing in a crazed spasm fighting the vicious current that held him down and tossed him about like a piece of human driftwood. Twisting under the brunt of it, he managed to push upward frantically and shoot to the surface. Gasping for air, trying to stay afloat as he choked on saltwater again, Clifton realized in horror the current was pulling him out. Though he bobbed in the water like a cork, his body was being drawn into the undertow's clutch yanking him into much deeper water. Suddenly, he caught sight of the shore—it was impossibly distant. I'm at least a 100 yards from the beach! *How can that be? How did I get this far out so fast?* But another swell, bigger, mightier, had built and was poised to collapse on top of him. *Help!* Clifton screamed in panic. *Help!*

It covered him like a tarpaulin. He was underwater again, flailing hysterically, this time panic-stricken he wouldn't come up. In the finger-snap of terror, Clifton's mind exploded with the grisly vision of his own death, his purple body washing ashore, the drowning of Conner Clifton, and a phalanx of authorities blanketing his corpse and transporting it up the beach to an ambulance.

Floating in surreal time and space, the subtle, insidious current passed through him like ghostly ripples. He was suspended in the pocket of a weightless vacuum. Small patches of seaweed or kelp brushed across his face like a drifting ocean cobweb, but instead of warring against the undertow, he went limp and, for a few terrified moments, submitted to the sea's will. It freed him at once from the clutch and he sprang to the surface. He was treading water, heaving for breath in wild spasms. Worse, the frightening sense of tiring arms and legs sagged in his limbs. He couldn't swim because he was unable to position himself with enough strength to kick back and pull his arms over his head. Instead, his body bobbed, his eyes bulged, his voice screamed and cracked: *Heyyyyy!*

But in those terrified moments when Clifton had lost complete control of himself, as he tossed upon the whim of the enemy sea, a thought flashed through his mind: *I absolutely cannot drown—If I'm part of the future!*

Anybody—help!

From the side of a surfboard that came in from behind, a pair of hands reached down from the sky.

"Grab the handle," a voice called out. Clifton clasped a man's hand that slid his hand over to a handle on the side of the board. "Hold on!"

The surfboard caught the crest of the next wave and began to ride it in. Clifton couldn't believe what was happening: he was sailing in sweetly to shore. *A miracle,* he cried to himself.

Prostrate, feeling precious sand under his feet, Clifton hobbled ashore and dropped to his hands and knees. He coughed seawater as his lungs fought to regain the rhythm of breathing. Then he rolled over and lay flat on his back staring up at the tissue-like clouds in ecstasy.

"Thank you," his gravel voice stated in profound gratitude. *"You saved my life...."*

A tall, broad-shouldered man in his mid-thirties with a dirty blonde crew-cut, green wet suit, and swimmer's goggles perched on top of his head knelt down sympathetically on the sand next to him. "What happened out there, Guy?"

"Went after my fishing pole. Got knocked in," Clifton coughed. "Can't believe I was underwater so fast...I can't believe it happened that fast."

"It's not hard to do. A few weeks ago a young couple were both swept out. You OK?"

"I think so, yeah. You a lifeguard?"

The man smiled. "Naw, just surfboarding. Heard your calls for help."

Clifton inspected the red, ugly gash on his foot, then sat up slowly and stared out at the unforgiving sea.

"I'm Fred."

"Conner Clifton," he said, extending his limp hand up to the man gratefully. "Thank you, Fred. What in hell do I say?"

"Not a thing, Guy. It's funny—I came this close to not coming out here at all today."

"Thank God you did," was all Clifton muttered as he sat up and stared down the beach at his white plastic bucket. "That's my spot over there," he pointed. "Fred, I won't have you say 'no' to a beer and sandwich."

"Sounds good to me." The man tucked his surfboard under one arm and the two men headed across the sand toward Clifton's bucket.

"There really is good fishing here, Conner. 'Course, you're gonna' have to get a new pole," he laughed. "And remember to hold on to it."

"Believe me when I say a fishing pole's not my biggest concern at the moment."

"You know, I surf here often and I know pretty much every inch of this beach. My family lives a few miles down the highway."

Clifton hobbled along and dismissed his throbbing heal in the grandness of being alive.

"It's a broken leg; I'm not crippled, in case you're wondering. Another week, I'll try it solo."

"How'd you break it?"

"Had a fall in a computer warehouse."

"Ah," Fred said with interest, "so you're in computers then?"

"Engineer."

"Really? An engineer?"

"Yeah. Why?"

"I'm launching a computer company, my second company, in fact. First one went broke. Terrible marketing. Thank God my Dad's got the capital to give me a second chance. I won't make the same mistakes twice, believe me."

The twinge of a ripple shot down the back of Clifton's neck. They had reached the bucket. Clifton picked up a beer and handed the can to Fred.

"Let me guess: the company will launch in Los Angeles. It will be called NovaSol."

The crash of surf hit the shore and exploded like a hundred cannons. Fred stood transfixed on the sand. "Jesus, you're psychic! I just copyrighted the name yesterday! Didn't even tell my Dad the company will be called NovaSol. How'd you know?"

Clifton thought of letting it all fly. What was the difference anyway? *The Book of Time* was a powerful paradox that could either be shoved down deep into the private confines of one's mind or revealed to the very person who would be inextricably connected to his future.

"Fred, strap your hat on. What would you say if I told you NovoSol will become universally acclaimed? You see, one day there's going to be an international problem that NovoSol will help eradicate. So go ahead and move forward with confidence and accept your Dad's investment; yeah, go full steam with every one of your future plans. Trust me, Fred: everything I've described is in stone and is as certain as the waves that hit the shore on this beach right now."

Fred shook his head dumbfounded. "You're playng with me, Conner."

"Not playing with you in the least. Take what I've said as a gift for saving my life. Hey, I'd like to see that building you just leased. I may just tell you more about the year 2035."

"Then you're also gonna' have to tell me how you know all this stuff, Conner."

Clifton pulled the tab on his can of beer. Fred stood on the sand baffled with a face painted in awe.

"Hey, Fred, wasn't there once a great movie that ended with the line: 'I think this is the beginning of a beautiful friendship'[1]?"

Departure Time

Sanford DeShores ripped the envelope and its contents in half, then in quarters, then in eighths. Every emotion to which he said he'd never succumb—disgust, anger, vengeance—exploded within him. He hurled the paper shreds into the fireplace and watched them curl up into black carbon in the tongues of crackling flames. For a flicker of a moment, DeShores enjoyed unabashed, morbid delight.

The terse note from the literary agent was gone, but the written words that shot bullets kept firing at him. He imagined the woman skim-reading every twentieth page of his novel trying to rid the clutter of his book from her desk, then reaching for a stack of pre-typed rejection slips:

> **Sept. 15**
> **Mr. DeShores,**
> **I just don't feel this material is right for me.**
> **Thank you for submitting your novel.**
> **Ada Pandit / Pandit Literary Agency, N.Y.**

Eternal Autumn, my life's work, 457 pages of sterling prose, crafted over three and a half years, holidays spent wrestling with endless editing and re-writing—trashed in two sentences by Ada "who the hell is she?" Pandit. The accused steps up, lowers his head on the guillotine, the blade is released, the head chopped off. Execution without a trial; conviction while the jury is out having cocktails.

DeShores wanted to be out of the house before Eve got home from work. His wife had lived through too many of her husband's

Eternal Autumns, their crushing rejections, and his ensuing, miserable postpartum depression. For this was the night to get plastered. It might also be the time to buy a one-way plane ticket, board a 747 without a stitch of luggage, and fly to the Mexican island of Xochimilco where he'd spend the rest of his life paddling tourists around on colorful gondolas. Or maybe this was the moment to get the car up to 120 miles per hour, throw open the door, and jump out.

DeShores' angry hands pulled back the doors of his spare bedroom closet. A library of rejected manuscripts stared back at him miserably as he took a long, sad breath. Instead of shirts, pants, and suitcases, there were unpublished novels, short story collections, full-length plays, and collections of essays lined along two long, horizontal shelves. The title of each work was printed on a strip of pretty colored paper and pasted to every spine. There they were—scripts dating back to his sophomore year of college standing in stiff attention and awaiting instructions from their beleaguered king who had gotten lost in traffic.

Bolting down the street like a comet, ignoring the corner stop sign and the red light after it, DeShores considered introducing his closet to the same fate as the Pandit rejection: a squirt of kerosene, a lit match, and the end, once and for all, of Sanfred DeShores' tormented literary soap opera. And wouldn't it be sweet to have Ada Pandit bound and gagged inside that closet before I toss in the match? He could hear her tortured screams going up with the flames as he rounded the next corner on two bald tires.

Some vacation in the Caribbean, I write a detective novel. Others join a country club and play tennis and golf, I plow through a book of essays. Why has the drive to write not diminished one scintilla since high school? Who threw the switch when I was born igniting my creative engines and seeing to it they stayed on automatic pilot through my entire life? And why, oh why hasn't one book, story, or essay ever seen the ink of a publisher's press? My writing life has been spent strapped to a theatre seat watching a stinking musical titled "Hello, Rejection, Hello!" which features the ugly, fat ass legs of a 100 Ada Pandits high-stepping in a chorus line macabre. *GodAlmighty, what a filthy waste...*

DeShores hit the brakes and skidded sideways as a white railroad crossing guard descended inches from his front bumper. He caught his breath, red signal lights flashed, and a zephyr raced by in a streak of flashing windows. How could any self-respecting literary agent reject *Eternal Autumn*, the finest novel of the last 20 years? He pounded the dashboard in anger and cursed Ada Pandit, whoever she was, for not giving him so much as a run-on sentence as to why she was rejecting his life's masterpiece.

The blur of the zephyr windows suddenly turned to a 19 year-old sitting at an old Underwood portable typewriter on the kitchen table who couldn't type fast enough. With endless cups of black coffee serving as vitamins, he imagined the title of his three-act play sparkling in lights on the marquee of the St. James Theatre on Broadway. And under the play's title, the name "Sanford DeShores" would light up as hundreds crammed into the theatre each night craving the electricity of a smash hit. Two years later the college sophomore handed the script to his playwrighting instructor, Clayford Whetstone, with all the pomp and circumstance of Oscar Wilde handing *The Importance of Being Earnest* to his producer. "We'll hope for good news, Sanford," Whetstone said, agreeing to read the play and offer his opinion.

Ten days later, the professor invited DeShores to his office for coffee. Excited and wide-eyed, the kid met Whetstone, but slumped in his chair immediately as his teacher took a surgical scalpel and cut through the play like a Texas butcher. The professor was brutal:

"Plot is irreparably contrived. Characters one-dimensional, flat, and cliched. The dialogue is hopelessly wooden; frankly, in parts, it's so terribly embarrassing I cringed. Nevertheless, it's your first play, Sanford, and though horrible, a start. I suggest you toss it into the wastebasket and begin thinking about play number two."

Whetstone described the play's weaknesses in scene after scene, which, to DeShore's ears, was not unlike knocking a phonograph needle across a brand new record and wincing at the unbearable, scratching horror. The kid left Whetstone's office devastated. That afternoon DeShores passed by the college bookstore where dozens of classics whirled round in a book tree: "The Brothers Karamazov"; "Studs Lonegin"; "The Sun Also Rises". For the first time in his life, DeShores despised Leo Tolstoy personally.

A week later, still throbbing from the Whetstone autopsy, DeShores performed an experiment. He lifted a few passages from a William Faulkner novel, inserted them into an assigned short story, and turned the work of fiction into his creative writing teacher. The assignment was later returned with red correction marks circling Faulkner's sentences with a grade of 'C' attached to the comment: "Dreadful phraseology." That signal experience left DeShores with a life-long hatred of incompetent, Charlie McCarthy academics who, if their lives depended upon it, couldn't write a two paragraph precise of a third grader on his way to the toilet.

Alone on a barstool at The Quiet Riot, DeShores said hello to his first bourbon. My life has been lived on a raft adrift in a sea of rejected manuscripts. It began with Clayford Whetstone and now it comes full circle with Ada Pandit. Twenty-eight years of unrelenting, cold-blooded literary rejection has left me with a closet of starving orphan children. God, he thought, recalling the precious weekend he sweat bullets over *Eternal Autumn's* last chapter in a Lake Tahoe motel, I have probably spent ten thousand hours, probably entire years, wasting away at a keyboard. While Eve was across town feeding nickels into a casino's video poker machine, I kept sinking time and precious hope into a business that had no customers. The question is: How much longer do I keep marching across crooked boulevards whose street signs all point to a dead-end that says "Ada Pandit"? Every agent who ever read my work was Ada Pandit, DeShores cursed as he slurped down a second bourbon. Whetstone was Pandit. Academia was Pandit. *They're all Pandits!*

Then DeShores' most despised nemesis, Joselyn Delacroix, popular paperback romance novelist, author of the best-selling

Farquar's Concupiscence, dropped down in front of his eyes like a smelly Halloween witch. Delacroix's agent was Ada Pandit, he knew. How could it be, he asked himself, that a three dollar bill like Delacroix turns out one piece of human offal after another and manages to get her books freshly stocked front and center in the Safeway checkout racks? I could write War and Peace, but Ada Pandit wouldn't be able to flush it down the commode fast enough; meanwhile, Delacroix coughs up literary crap and the publisher grinds her books out like cheese pizzas. Publishers, editors, and literary agents—all of them—they're Vito Corleone's. The New York publishing world *is* the Cosa Nostra, a nepotistic cabal of Mafia dons, a coven of cronies. Who appointed these poltroons to be the gods that reigned over the publishing universe anyway?

Across the bar, a mirror was decorated with Hawaiian leis and silly Fourth of July top hats. The glass in the middle reflected the forlorn face of a man in his mid 40's, a briskly receding widow's peak, salt and pepper goatee decidedly crooked, sad, watering brown eyes, and singed, cherry cheeks. Under his chin, the top flap of his neck had begun to take on the charm of jowls. Instead of a best-selling author living in Switzerland turning out novels his publisher gets on his knees and begs me to write, I was condemned to the life of a two-bit high school English teacher preaching simple composition to freshman whose Humpty-Dumpty essays are slowly sending me to the crazy house. DeShores often wondered if, at the end of each school year, students sold the papers they had written to new freshman who re-typed them and turned them in all over again. In the cheap saloon's background a country singer belted out "If Our Love Were Oil, I'd Be A Quart Low'."

"Shoot me a double bourbon, willya', Boss?"

DeShores' legs finally ate cracked sidewalk cement. Moving toward his car, he could hear the sands of time dropping down through an hourglass. But these sands weren't grains; these were boulders striking the pavement all around him like mortar shells. Gains supposed to have been achieved by now had dissolved into endless streams of envelopes whose contents were two-sentence,

Pandaesque rejection slips. Meanwhile, more manuscripts thickened his closet shelves and took their places like the *Dead Sea Scrolls*—undiscovered, silent, withering. Look at Eve: she has ascended the ladder in the medical profession while I sat on a bicycle for nearly 30 years peddling in place. And it's the Ada Pandits of the universe who have seen to it that I remain on that bicycle peddling faster and harder every year, but never advancing an inch.

No more of it!

Breathing through his nose, DeShores bolted past another red light as he raced toward Portland International. Go ahead DeShores, a quiet, sensible voice advised underneath all the bourbon, buy that one-way ticket for Pago Pago and live out your last years writing final apologetics on papaya leaves in a bamboo lean-to. Spend your final days bearded and barefoot, the voice said, dipping your crudely crafted twig of a fishing line into the surf and combing the trees for dates.

Sprinkles of rain tapped the windshield as he slumped at the wheel of his car in the long-term parking lot. An airliner lifted off the runway and DeShores gazed at it enviously wondering if there were a writer on that flight destined for New York City. And was that writer about to sign a multi-million dollar book contract—*with Ada stinking Pandit?!*

One plane after another glided up and soared off majestically. The bourbon in his blood had turned on funereal organ music— and with it the image of Sanford DeShores, stepping up morosely to his own casket. He looked down at the corpse, his sleeping, waxen face and two arms crossed over a copy of *Eternal Autumn*. As the stream of Portland International 747's slowly faded out, one of the greatest literary influences of his life faded in. It was the novel *Crap Game,* by Raymond W. Sardonics.

He had stumbled upon the book years before when, by chance, he sifted through a bargain book table at Walgreen's. *Crap Game* lay at the bottom of the pile under a mound of children's animal stories and refrigerator repair manuals. DeShores bought the tattered paperback for 50 cents and, out of boredom, began reading the novel that night in bed under a soft lamp. *Crap Game* quickly unfolded before his eyes as one of the most brilliant works of fiction he had ever encountered.

It was the story of Donald Simple, a New York life insurance salesman, in the midst of a mid-life crisis. Simple was beaten to a psychological pulp by his weak, hypochondriac wife, Olive, and the three evil Simple children. From the moment Simple stepped through the front door of his cramped two-story townhouse after work, he had come to despise his entire domestic life and everyone in it. Most of all, Simple dreaded hearing the endless whining laments Olive's nasal tones rained down upon him. The woman was a human weeping willow incapable of holding a serious, adult opinion. Every day, it seemed, she stayed in bed a little longer complaining of a series of undisclosed ailments doctors could never quite diagnose. She whined and moaned about her reckless sister Octavia, her petulant, nagging mother, Beatrice, and Simple's 12 year-old daughter Morgana who had announced she was through with school. Simple thought he was losing his mind.

One night Simple walked down to the townhouse basement and constructed a crap game table. It was a professional looking, Las Vegas style crap table created to scale with a green felt surface that included "Pass Line," "Don't Pass," "Any Craps," and even "Horn Bets." Whenever Olive presented Simple with a new problem or dilemma, Simple would head down to the basement, pose a question whose answer was either 'yes' or 'no,' and throw the dice. If he made his point, the answer to the question would be 'yes.' If he crapped out, the answer would be 'no.'

The Saturday after Simple created the crap table, Olive stated she was unable to get out of bed at all. Whining under the blankets, she told Simple her sister Octavia wanted to move into the townhouse. "Could she, Donald? Could she?" The weak, muffled question asked under the blankets. Simple went down to the basement and stood before the crap table: "Should I let Octavia move in?" he asked aloud. Then he rolled the dice. His box point

98

was 9. Simple threw again: 6. He threw a third time and rolled a 7: craps. Simple marched back upstairs and informed Olive that Octavia would *not* move in.

Soon after, Olive became semi-hysterical over just what to do about their daughter's chronic school truancy. "Should we put her in a special school, Donald?" Olive creaked from under the covers one afternoon. Simple went straight for the basement. He rolled the dice: 12. Craps. He informed Olive that their daughter would stay where she was and face her problems like an adult.

Simple's marriage rapidly deteriorated to the point where he could no longer stand to be in the same room with Olive, let alone climb into bed with her. At that time Simple had an insured client, Carlisse Montenegro, whose husband had been thrown 200 feet from an amusement park roller coaster. Carlisse was everything Simple ever wanted in a woman. After thinking about making an advance toward her for weeks, Simple finally went downstairs to the crap table and closed his eyes. "Should I ask Carlisse for a dinner date?" He picked up the dice and threw them over the table: 11. Simple made an appointment with Carlisse to discuss her insurance policy at her home. At the end of the appointment, Simple asked Carlisse to dinner. She accepted.

The crap table took complete control of Simple's life. It solved his problems; it cured his anxiety. But the dice did not just make lucky decisions for Simple; it made *correct* decisions. I've created a miraculous instrument to control my destiny, he reasoned. Simple was giddy thinking that his worries were over forever.

Relying on the crap table, Simple's relationship with Carlisse deepened. Eventually, the dice indicated to Simple that he should move swiftly and divorce Olive. It led him to high-powered insurance prospects and the closing of many sales. It recommended buying income properties. Moreover, Simple created a system whereby the "Horn Bets" and "Lines" on the crap table corresponded to certain NASDAQ stocks. He rolled the dice to see which stocks to buy and which to sell. He made hundreds of thousands of dollars. Finally, the crap game told Simple to marry Carlisse, move to

Beverly Hills, purchase a 12- bedroom home, and begin buying failing bankrupt shopping centers.

One afternoon, Simple came home early from the office and found Carlisse in bed with another man. He was crushed. How could this be after the crap game told me to marry this woman? What do I do? He stood before the crap table and asked, "Crap Table, should I *kill* Clarisse?" Simple tossed the dice and closed his eyes. When he opened them, the dice lay quietly and unambiguously on the green cloth: 7.

Later that evening, Simple tossed a portable radio into Carlisse's bubble bath and electrocuted her. The District Attorney ruled the woman's death had been an accident.

In the days that followed, Simple grew lonelier and more miserable than he had ever been in his life. "Should I move back to New York, Crap Table?" Simple threw snake eyes: 2. He remained in Beverly Hills and began frequenting singles bars in search of a new woman.

One Saturday evening, Simple got into his BMW and sped toward a posh cabaret on Rodeo Drive. He had gone only a few miles when the brakes on his Mercedes failed. Simple went over the freeway ramp and plunged to his death.

The final scene of *Crap Game* showed Olive, Simple's ex-wife, tossing the dice in front of Simple's original crap table in the New York townhouse basement:

"Should I kill the man I paid to loosen the brakes on Donald's BMW?"

DeShores believed *Crap Game* was everything a brilliant novel should be. It contained powerful, vivid characters; it was incisive, metaphorical, possessed rich, black humor; the narrative prose was cheesecake; and, above all, *Crap Game* was a page turner so compelling it drove him to read the entire book in one night.

Yet *Crap Game* never won a Pulitzer Prize and never appeared on a best seller list. The author did not win a Book of the Month Club award, and, in fact, no one DeShores ever spoke with had even heard of *Crap Game*. But what depressed DeShores most of all was that the author of *Crap Game*, Raymond W. Sardonics, took his own life a year and a half after the book was published. Sardonics' body was found hanging nude upside down in his bathroom with a post-it stuck to his nose and a one-line sentence: "I simply refuse to be part of a world that dumps my novel onto the 50-cent bargain table at Walgreen's."

This is the whirlpool I twist 'round in, DeShores concluded dolefully. Do I need to build my own crap table and start tossing the dice to get the answers that have eluded me? He turned the key in the ignition of his Toyota and skidded out of Portland International's long-term parking lot. No, boarding a 747 today or tomorrow or the day after tomorrow was the bourbon talking. And just where did I think I'd go anyway—to see Ada Pandit?

DeShore's right foot slammed down on the brakes and the car skidded sideways and nearly crashed through the window of Broomhilda's Donuts. He was breathing through his nose again, sitting at the side of the road watching wheezing windshield wipers slosh back and forth over drizzly beads. An idea was taking root fast and it was sprouting into a beautiful oak tree there in the rain in front of DeShores' red, heartbroken eyes.

Just who in God's name does Ada Pandit think she is? On what throne in which 30 story Manhattan high rise within what streamlined executive office bustling with editors waving mega-million dollar book contracts did this woman dwell? Ada friggin' Pandit. Does the woman actually sit at her desk as Nigerian slaves fan her off with palm fronds?

DeShores' self- pity finally yielded to somber resolve. When do I ultimately come to terms with the masked identities who have reigned over me in two-lined rejection slips for 28 years? Do these abstractions ever take human form in front of my eyes? Do I ever confront them? And if I did come face to face with these arrogant swellheads—precisely what would I say and do?

Twenty-eight years of writing have whittled down to this day, to this hour, DeShores realized in a moment of supreme clarity. Ada Pandit is not simply a literary agent mailing a rejection slip to an amateurish novelist in Hortense, Georgia whose fiction was a bad ham on rye. Ada Pandit hurts good authors writing seriously. She is the publishing world incarnate. She is every dreaded razor-thin envelope with a bad two-sentence rejection circumcision to which I have been subjected. She is why I have a closet full of unread, unpublished manuscripts and not a Book of the Month Club award hanging over my living room fireplace. Ada Pandit is the contract never signed; the royalty check never cashed; the bottle of champagne never uncorked. She is an ulcer, an anxiety disorder; she's ventricular fibrillation and a brain infarction rolled into one bad attack. She's the "toss" in the sleepless night's "toss and turn"; she is the foreman of the jury who actually enjoys standing up high and tall and, with the hubris of a Greek king, proudly proclaims with a smirk, *"Your Honor, we, the jury, find that the defendant's novel, Eternal Autumn, is not fit to be published."* Ada Pandit is Professor Theodore Whetstone. And Theodore Whetstone is Ada Pandit.

The granddaddy of scenarios unfolded before DeShores' widening eyes like an Arthur Murray dance chart: a flight to New York, an appointment at the Pandit Literary Agency. He'd be, say, Maximillion Moncrief, editor and CEO of Misnomic Press, a new publishing house about to launch production in Los Angeles. He would introduce himself and establish a connection with one of the New York's most successful literary agents: Ada Pandit. He'd be dressed like a bank president and smell of Mennen Skin Bracer. He'd carry an impressive briefcase with a little chain locked to his wrist. "Ms. Pandit will see you now, Mr. Moncrief," the beanpole secretary in buckled shoes would say to him holding the door open wide, showing him her loose dentures. He'd stride across the office with his head held high and, once in front of Pandit, he'd throw open his briefcase, remove all 457 pages of *Eternal Autumn,* and crash the two pound manuscript down on her desk with a sonic boom that rattled shelves in Hoboken. Then he'd lean forward on his knuckles six-inches from Pandit's nose. The lines in DeShores' face would shoot out like sparks; his eyes would have torches behind them; his lips would be as red and moist as Bella Lugosi's when he gazed upon a sleeping Wessex virgin.

"Several days ago this novel was returned to me by you, Ms. Pandit, and rejected in two sentences. What's interesting here is that I purposely stuck pages together at various points in the book and those pages are still stuck together. How can this be, Ms. Pandit? You never read my novel, did you? I've come 2,800 miles to find out *why* you never actually read my book. It couldn't be because I'm plain old Sanford DeShores and not Joselyn *stinking* Delacroix, could it, Ms. Pandit?" DeShores would be clenching his teeth; there'd be spittle at the corners of his mouth; his bulging pupils would be like those of a man falling through an elevator shaft directed by Alfred Hitchcock.

Pandit would grope for the handle and, with a lip quivering somewhere between rage and ambushed stupefaction, she'd emit feeble, apologetic gibberish:

"Well, ah, I for one thought you had talent, Mr. DeShores. Your book has a great deal of, ah, merit. But it's a tough market. We just couldn't muster enough enthusiasm for this project, however. What I strongly suggest is that you get back on your horse and, ah, punch out another fine manuscript that we all know will light up the sky!"

DeShores would then unleash every bit of dirt and filth that had accumulated in his psyche since Professor Theodore Whetstone cut through his first play with a buzz saw a quarter century before. Frightened, Ada Pandit would call security whereupon a beefy, six-foot-two house dick would lift DeShores by his lapels and punt him back into the elevator. But what, in the big picture, was there to lose? If dumping 28 years of pent-up anguish over unjustified literary rejections in the face of Ada "Corleone" Pandit gives me an orgiastic catharsis, then lead me, Dear Ringmaster, to the circus midway.

The windshield wipers were on high power flashing back and forth and keeping time with DeShore's heartbeat. All very nice, reflected DeShores, considering the scenario in the cold light of objectivity. And filled so nicely with the words and pictures of sweet justice one sees in movies. But do I have the guts to go through with it? Could I actually board a DC-3, fly to New York, go to the building, the office and desk of Ada Pandit with the same smoldering resolve I'm feeling now? And once there, would I utter the words I've been dreaming of uttering for over two and a half decades? Does Sanfred DeShores have the gold balls to actually march through Stalingrad?

Eve was in the kitchen manufacturing one of her world class roasts. "Sanford, I was thinking we'd have Phil and Marla over tonight for wine and cheese. You OK with that?" she called out, unaware her husband hadn't heard one word she uttered and was at that moment in the spare room standing in front of the open closet doors.

Dating from his first play to the master copy of *Eternal Autumn,* the scripts filled the closet space like lost scrolls from the ancient library of Alexandria. DeShores sank to the edge of the daybed as his eyes roamed over the works that translated into tens of thousands of hours of characters, plots, and keen prose polished to perfection with a jeweler's cloth only to be thrashed by a filthy white envelope and nauseating New York postmark originating from Ada Pandit.

I'm through with writing, DeShores concluded softly sans trumpets. I'm written out. Done. Spent. But that doesn't mean you win, Ada. God, no.

Tears the size of pumpkin seeds dropped from the corners of DeShores' eyes.

I'm raising the flag at the Alamo before I go down, Ada. I'm coming to see you.

II

Getting the appointment at the Pandit Literary Agency had been surprisingly easy. DeShores identified himself as Maxmillion Moncrief, CEO of Ground Zero Books in Los Angeles, California.

"Ms. Pandit can see you on Friday, the 23rd. Would 2 p.m.

be convenient?" a sweet voice chirped. "I hope that coincides advantageously with your schedule while visiting New York, Mr. Moncrief?"

"Very advantageously," he replied. "Most wonderfully, magnificently, insuperably advantageously."

That evening Eve sat quietly and watched her husband pace back and forth in the living room nursing a bourbon and soda. Drops of liquor spilled onto the hardwood floor as DeShores ranted on about 28 years of blood and tears injected into his scripts as he declared he had now reached the pitiful end of his writing life. "But it will be reached with an exclamation point," he added with burning eyes fixed on the coffee tables' plastic swan. "I'm committed. I'm flying to New York. Eve, if you think my resolve's going to fade in the wind, guess again. Pandora's going to get 28 lousy years of what she's got coming."

Eve listened to her husband with controlled sympathy. When DeShores finally talked himself out, she observed:

"You apparently need to do this, Sanford. You know what? Go do it. Let it wash the demons out of your system. Though I've questioned why you do what you do, especially when I see your pain when the rejections come, I check myself because I know you're wired to write just as we are all wired to do something. My question is: Do you know what you'll say to this literary agent when you come face to face with her?"

"Better than you could possibly dream, Eve."

"If I had to bet, I'd say this trip will re-charge your batteries. You'll write again."

The glass of bourbon stopped short an inch from his lips. "The question is: re-charge my batteries for *what*?"

"A leopard doesn't change its spots, Sanford. You're not going to quit writing. Writing is your mistress. She'll be there tomorrow waiting for you faithfully whenever you decide to knock at her door."

"Eve, please, let me handle the two-bit metaphors. I'm the one who's supposed to be the bad writer here."

"You've never been a bad writer, Sanford, and I've told you that for years. You're a wonderful writer. And the best writing you do is when you create solutions for problems that show a deep, sympathetic understanding of human behavior. How many times have I told you that? But you don't hear it, never heard it, and never will. How many times have I admitted to being jealous of your gift? I couldn't write a thing worth reading beyond an administrative spreadsheet. That's my gift to mankind: brittle hospital reports that I see as a big bag of trail mix."

"At least it performs a service. At least people read what you produce."

"Uh-huh. But it's sterile writing. You have the gift to create flesh and blood characters that have passion and problems the reader can relate to and learn from. How I wish you could allow that to be your one, true satisfaction. But you have this relentless drive to be published. So fly to New York or Timbuktu or wherever, tell Pandit off, then stay in a nice hotel suite; see a musical; sleep in; take a carriage ride around Central Park, get drunk. My hope is that a light will go on from all this and you'll discover a new incarnation."

Two days later DeShores requested a substitute for his English classes, packed his bags with his best suit, and placed *Eternal Autumn* into his briefcase. Eve drove him to the airport, hugged him, and wished her husband good luck. DeShores' insides beat with an unwavering purpose as he moved through Portland International, but when he stepped up to the airlines check-in counter, the clerk raised an eyebrow.

"Sir, what was your intended departure date and time?"

"Today, 1 p.m."

"Funny. These tickets say November 22, 1 p.m., all right, but the—I'll be right back."

The ticket was shown to a supervisor. The two men went to the computer and spent ten minutes scanning the screen. Then the supervisor stepped back to DeShores and said, "An obvious typographical error here, sir. The day and time are printed correctly on this ticket, but the year," he laughed, "is 1963. Your flight is for November 22, 1963. Never quite ran into this one before."

"Well, what can we do about it?"

"I don't think there's a problem at all. You paid by credit card and still on Flight 411 for today at 1 p.m., unless, of course, you'd prefer to go back in time and depart on November 22, 1963," the clerk chuckled.

DeShores didn't laugh. The error was rectified and, as he waited for his flight to begin boarding, he bought a New York Times at the magazine rack and sipped coffee at a bagel kiosk. Flipping through the pages, his eye caught a squib saying it was the anniversary of the assassination of President John F. Kennedy. DeShores was struck by the coincidence of the typographical error on his ticket—1963—and its significance to the assassination anniversary this very day. He also read that Kennedy was officially pronounced dead at 1 p.m., his exact departure time. As he took his aisle seat and strapped in, a trace of adrenalin shot through him. Foreshadowing? Is this plane doomed? Is it destined to go down in Buzzard Roost, Montana?

Twenty-five minutes into the flight, DeShores' sights settled back into proper focus. He sipped champagne and watched ragged mists of clouds sifting by his cabin window like torn shreds of taffy. He recalled the black afternoon 28 years ago when Professor Theodore Whetstone sent a fist into his sophomore kidney. He saw countless rainy afternoons thereafter pushing a pen over excited paragraphs that made chapter after chapter breathe. He saw himself in a robe with tonsillitis pounding keys as he created characters from nothing. He saw wintry Christmas holidays writing lines that seemed to pour out of the pencil before he seemed to have conceived them. But he also saw the awful razor-thin envelope that inevitably appeared in his mailbox coming like a dreaded medical diagnosis announcing the mass was malignant.

As the champagne buzzed between his ears, DeShores engaged a wonderful fantasy. He would appear at Pandit's office and would say and do all that he resigned himself to say and do. But after slamming his manuscript down on the agent's desk, Pandit would miraculously reverse herself. "Now, let me take a second look at this novel, Mr. DeShores. Yes. Yes! You know what: on second thought I think I *will* represent you. Hold on for a minute, Sanford, while I contact Milicent Darkbloom, chief editor at Random House. Don't worry, she'll offer you a hefty contract because I have plenty of clout." That dream's a rotten egg, DeShores reasoned, shaking loose from the reverie. I might as well expect Pandit to meet me at the tarmac, genuflect, and hand me the Pulitzer Prize.

His plane landed as smoothly as a teacup upon a Victorian queen's saucer. A little after 3 p.m., DeShores sat comfortably in a cab as it crept through Manhattan toward the Tevere Hotel on West 57th St. Knowing the Pandit Literary Agency was only several blocks away, he asked the cabbie: "Driver, would you please cruise by The Sansom Building?"

The cab snaked along until DeShores beheld the huge, multi-storied edifice with a golden revolving door at ground level. Nothing too fine for Ada, is there? He craned his neck out of the taxi's window and peered skyward at the 22nd floor imagining Ada Pandit holding court up there among the serfs in her literary kingdom. Ethiopians probably dance there now, he mused. Perhaps I should arrive tomorrow on a donkey offering frankincense and myrrh.

Arriving back in his room at The Tevere Hotel, he removed *Eternal Night* from the briefcase and took a hard look at the masterpiece in his hands. Tomorrow at 2 p.m. this time bomb will go off on Ada Pandit's desk and my justice will be delivered the moment I blow away that woman's cockamamy arrogance. What happens to me after that will be immaterial. Let the gods present me with my golden justice.

It was after five when he sauntered into the hotel's Woodpecker Room for the cocktail hour. Sporting a white dress shirt, blue sport coat, and dapper, silver ascot, DeShores imagined himself the new John Updike, toast of New York where adoring fans waived copies of *Eternal Autumn* they desperately needed autographed. Instead, the lounge sagged with a dozen regulars who had wolfed down most of the complimentary cheese cubes from plastic bar trays. In the far corner, a disconsolate business man buried his head in his arms covering three empty shot glasses. A Rubinesque woman, pendulous, torpedo bosoms scarcely contained by her skin-tight polka-dot cocktail dress, stuffed herself with a plate of meatballs on toothpicks and laughed like a hyena. Her companion was an emaciated man in purple suspenders whose toupee reminded DeShores of a battle helmet. From an unseen speaker, Sinatra's *It Was Just One of Those Things* drifted out scratchily, then suddenly began to skip:

> A trip to the moon—
> On gossamer wings
> —on gossamer wings
> —on gossomer wings...

"What can I do ya', Doc?" asked the midget bartender who reminded DeShores of Danny DiVito. The man's little arms wiped the bar's surface with a towel that smelled like over-cooked artichokes..

"Best Merlot ya' got. Say, no piano bar tonight?"

The man didn't laugh. "Fer dat yeh heve ta' go across da' street."

"What's across the street?"

"Da' Steinway Company," he wisecracked.

"Just got in from Portland," DeShores bragged.

The cork shot from the wine bottle with a crisp pop. "'Zat so? Bizness in town?"

"Oh, yes," DeShores replied. "Business that should have been taken care of a long time ago. Tomorrow, in fact, I'll be settling a life-long score."

"Sounds serious. Wish ya' luck, Chief." The bartender vacuumed the $10 bill DeShores had thrown down.

"Keep it," DeShores offered.

New York at last, he sighed, glancing at his watch and projecting that in less than 19 hours he'd be face to face with the great Sphinx of Pandit. He was surprised by how good he felt about his decisions as he carried his Merlot to a tiny cocktail table in the lounge's corner. DeShores sipped his wine with a wonderful air of satisfaction and told himself that Eve had been right: my batteries will be re-charged here in Manhattan. Maybe I'll take a carriage ride through Central Park fog after all and sip cognac and enjoy the stallion's horseshoes clickety-clacking on cobblestones. Suddenly, a club or group entered The Woodpecker Room. Middle-aged and elderly men and women carried books and notepads to a large booth next to DeShores. He read some of the titles they placed on the table: *Why Your Mind Is Not Really Your Mind; Who Thinks the Thoughts You're Thinking? Consciousness: Does it Exist Outside of Us?*

A peppy and spirited man who could have been 90 turned and asked DeShores if the group could borrow the chair at his table.

"Certainly. Say, what organization is this?"

"We're mambers of "The Mad Tea-Pawty Society," fans of John McTaggert, the philosophur."

"Afraid I'm not that familiar with him."

"He wrote *The Unreality of Time*, a critic of Hegel, friend of Bertrand Russell."

"Pretty heavy stuff. You meet here often?"

"Once a month. You're not from New Yawk; from the coast, right?"

"How'd you know?"

"Ratired speech teachur from Baston, Mass for years. Hobby was always nailin' down Americun accents. I'm gonna'guess yah from nawth of San Francisco, but not as fah nawth as Seeahtul."

"Hey, that's pretty good. Portland, as a matter of fact."

"Well, pick up yur drink and drag yaself on ovah for a chawt..."

Within minutes DeShores became the Mad Tea-Party Society's centerpiece. "Just flew into New York," he beamed proudly, straightening his ascot. "On business."

"Which is?"

He hesitated for a moment, then answered, "Well, I'm a writer and I'm meeting with a literary agent tomorrow."

Everyone seemed impressed. "Do you write philosophy?" one woman asked.

"I think just about all writing is philosophy, wouldn't you say?"

"What books have you published?" asked another.

DeShores paled and wanted to crawl under the table, but he deflected the question saying, "Well, don't think you'd be familiar with any which are sort of local, niche technical things; anyway, hoping this, ah, meeting tomorrow will result in something significant."

"But what's your area?"

"Fiction."

Heads nodded all around the table.

"But do you think there's as much truth in fiction as non-fiction?"

DeShores brightened. "Oh, yes; perhaps more so. I've always believed that if you want to learn about an historical period, for example, the Victorian Era, just read a novel by Charles Dickens. Good novels lend more insights into a particular period than sterile history books, in my view."

A woman in the corner had started taking notes.

"Where do you get your ideas?" a man asked.

"I believe that the human mind is a muscle; train it to think a certain way and it'll respond. If you write enough, you develop a talent where imagined characters and stories take on a life of their own."

"My problem was always grammah," complained the elderly man.

"Forget grammar. It should be the least of your concerns. Grammar is science; it's easily corrected. But you've got to have a solid beginning, middle, and an end that keeps the reader turning the page or you won't ever have a story worth reading no matter how impeccable the grammar."

Two others at the cocktail table also began jotting his words down. Suddenly, DeShores felt as if he were back in the classroom, except that this time he was lecturing students who cared; students who were hungry to learn. "One of the oldest paradoxes in fiction," he began to expound, is 'Does plot come from character or does character come from plot?' If I had to bet my mortgage, I'd say that everything comes from character." Suddenly, everyone at the table was scribbling notes. "As a matter of fact," he continued, "Henry James, a major American novelist of realism said, 'What is character but the determination of incident. What is incident but the illustration of character'?"

"Would you please repeat thawt?" the elderly man asked unable to get the entire quotation verbatim. "'*What is character* ....'"

Nearly two hours later, DeShores' lecture to The Mad Tea-Party concluded with light applause from grateful admirers. He had lectured on character, plot, suspense, irony, and dialogue. It was one of the most fulfilling experiences he had ever spent engaging the topic of writing. He ached a bit thinking he'd be returning to high school freshman who looked upon these very same ideas as noise akin to nuts and bolts rattling around inside an empty coffee can.

What a joy they were, he reflected, as he strutted out of The Woodpecker Room feeling more like Tom Wolfe than Sanfred DeShores. Those folks saw me as an important writer; they would have probably paid a fee to hear me proselytize. The trip to New York was worth it just to sit in the Woodpecker Room and hold court with The Mad Tea-Party Society.

But once back in his suite, DeShores removed *Eternal Autumn* from his briefcase and the Jezebel of New York reared up like Madame Blavatsky. She's Torquemada; the supreme metaphor for the New York publishing syndicate conspiring to send fine writers to the dreaded gallows. As he skimmed through his novel, DeShores went further: this isn't a trip to Manhattan, he reasoned; it's a crusade to the Holy Land. Am I not acting on behalf of every Sanford DeShores who was condemned to oblivion by their respective Ada Pandits? Is the bar of literary justice now calling me to the stand?

Thank you, Mad Tea Party, for your faith in me, he thought, as he slid his novel back into the briefcase. Tomorrow at 2p.m, Sanfred DeShores, an army of one, will conquer Gaul.

He slept restlessly, waking, tossing and turning, then finally dreaming he was standing on the top of a book with millions of pages. In the distance, he could see China and the Pyramids. Below him, however, Ada Pandit crawled along the dirt like a cockroach. He tried to snuff her out, but she squirmed free and disappeared into the table of contents.

In the morning, the Pandit magma flowed undiminished. This is surely the day, DeShores declared to himself in the shower; I will not retreat an inch. For breakfast he enjoyed expresso waffles with mocha drizzle at an upscale café a block away, then took a brisk walk through New York side streets before returning to The Tevere Hotel. He dressed ceremoniously in his fine 3-button, pinstriped, charcoal vested suit and spit-polished, Florshiem shoes. But before he left, DeShores peeked once again at his novel and promised to the cover sheet: "You did not live in vain." Then he placed the manuscript into his briefcase and stepped into the hotel elevator with the pride of a defense attorney about to turn the tables in court for his falsely accused client, *Eternal Autumn*.

A yellow cab pulled to the sidewalk of the Sansom Building at exactly 1:45 p.m. DeShores gazed up at the slick, gray walls. Pushing through the revolving, brass doors, the elevator ascended a moment later, but DeShores did not see himself in an elevator at all: he was on an assault craft riding in toward Utah Beach. For this was Operation Neptune on D-Day, wasn't it? Rejected fiction writers everywhere are counting on me, aren't they? I've been at sea for 28 years and now the beach is finally coming up fast. I will hit the ground running with bayonet fixed to my M-1 and destroy Ada Pandit and her moronic stooges.

When the doors parted on the 22nd floor, DeShores stepped off and stood for a supreme moment glaring at the gold letters etched on the glass before his eyes: "Pandit Literary Agency." His watch said 1:55 p.m.

He stepped into a silent, empty interior and walls framed with photographs of the agency's authors. Joslyn Delacroix's idiotic smirk and beehive hairdo lay in the center of the array. A very young woman dabbing her eyes with a handkerchief suddenly appeared around the corner next to the reception desk. "Oh! May I help you?" She was startled to see anyone in the office at all.

"I'm Maximillion Moncrief of Ground Zero Books in Los Angeles," DeShores stated grandly. "Please inform Ms. Pandit I'm here for my 2 p.m. appointment."

The woman paled. "Oh, my God," she said moving quickly to the front desk and flipping through pages in her appointment book. "I'm so, so sorry. Mr. Moncrief, I'm afraid—"

"Yes? Afraid of what?"

"I'm afraid," she repeated, looking up at DeShores with a nose that suddenly turned to rosacea red, "Ada Pandit—*passed away* early this morning..."

Had soft mud, or even soggy sheetrock composed the floor beneath his feet, DeShores would have gladly plunged straight down through 22 levels of urban, downtown Americana. But this was the Sansom Building in Manhattan where concrete and iron constructed mighty edifices preventing even the king of buffoons from falling through 22 floors and desolving into the soup of his own miserable stupefaction.

"I beg your pardon: she—*what*?"

"Yes, oh, yes. All of her appointments today were contacted and cancelled. But we couldn't reach you, Mr. Moncrief. I myself tried to find a number for Ground Zero Books in Los Angeles, but was unable to locate your company."

Swallowing what seemed like an unmentionable ball of muck, DeShores placed his hand upon the desk for physical support. "No, we're...very...new..."

"I again apologize so profoundly," the woman offered turning the appointment book around for him to see. "Yes, here it is:

Maximillion Moncrief, Ground Zero Books in Los Angeles. But no number. I'm so very sorry you had to go through this, Mr. Moncrief," the woman offered with great regret. "Sorrier than I can express."

"You're telling me—*Ada Pandit died this very day?*"

The woman dabbed her eyes and nose again. "Yes. About 9 a.m. at her home in Queens."

"And you're her secretary?

"I'm one of them. Yes. Kathy Kirshner."

"Had—Ms. Pandit been ill for long?" he groped.

"She was in her late 70's, and, yes, was ill, but no one really knew just how sick she was."

"I obviously never met her. Was just trying to form a mental picture..."

"She was such a wonderful woman, Mr. Moncrief. No agent anywhere was more respected than Ada Pandit. Always going the extra yard for her clients who loved her in return. No one in the entire publishing industry ever had a bad word to say about her. In my opinion, if Ada Pandit wasn't a saint, then saints don't exist..."

"A *saint*?" DeShores repeated dry-mouthed.

"As far as I'm concerned, she was. I came to New York two years ago and had nothing, knew no one, not a dime in the bank. Ada hired me and advanced me $1000 to help me get started. Later, she refused to let me pay her back. I remember we had an editor here at that time who had a paralyzed son in need of one of those motorized wheelchairs that cost a fortune. Ada just took care of it quietly and decently." The woman's eyes flashed red again and the handkerchief dabbed the cherries under her eyes. "None of us here believe Ada's really gone. So kind, so sweet, especially given her recent amputation..."

"Her *recent amputation?*" DeShores asked in a voice just above a whisper.

"Ada had her left leg amputated about five years ago. Diabetes. Never a complaint. Not one. And once she was well enough after her surgery, she returned here to the agency and just picked up where she left off not missing another day of work."

"I'm...sorry."

"Mr. Jardine will be taking over the agency. Do you want me to have him call you?"

"No, no. That won't be necessary."

"I'm so sorry we couldn't contact you. Our agency is completely stunned..."

"Under—standable. Would you—express my sympathies to Ms. Pandit's family?"

"Mr. Moncrief, I hope you didn't make the trip to New York just for this one appointment."

"Oh, no. I was here to meet with editors anyway," he lied. "I wasn't inconvenienced at all. Please express my condolences to Ms. Pandit's next of kin."

One minute later the elevator doors parted. DeShores head groaned with a rotten throbbing as he considered that he was plunging through Dante's Ninth Circle of Hell. Weak-kneed, he shuffled out of the lobby's revolving door and signaled a cab with a sunken, waving posture. DeShores wasn't sure which of the emotions that pulsed through him he was now supposed to be feeling most: guilt, pity, or naked humiliation.

"Driver, take me to the closest saloon you know of," he ordered, unbuttoning his collar and tossing his tie across the seat. "And get me there yesterday."

Eve's words sang to him like a twisted, church hymnal: *"Maybe a light will go on from all this and you'll discover a new incarnation..."*

Ada Pandit was dead.

DeShores wobbled into a saloon filled with a party of young advertising executives. A hired clown passed out colorful suckers to company employees who were laughing and whooping it up over some big account that had been closed. Alone in a corner booth, he stared into the depths of a bourbon trying to connect dots that did not want to be connected. It's done. It's over. The climax erased in a flicker. The play ended 15 seconds after the house lights dimmed and the curtain went up on Act I.

Of course, no one at the agency contacted me because I didn't want them to have my number. For had they been able to call and cancel, that would have meant not coming to New York. And not coming to New York would have meant not striding into the Pandit Literary Agency like Caesar crossing the Rubicon to punch Pandit between the eyes with a devastating right cross. But, no, any chance to score my addled justice was unplugged. Instead, I became Jerry Lewis staggering to stage center in a sold out Metropolitan Opera House wearing only boxer shorts who slipped on a banana peel and fell straight on his corpulant keister.

Ada Pandit died the very day I arrived in New York...

Every one of his literary sensibilities was crowned with the crooked irony of the toast he gave up at that moment. "To Ada Pandit," DeShores declared with glossy eyes, raising the bourbon high in the woman's honor. "To the literary agent with whom I played Kick-the-Can for a week, but who saw to it in death 'twas I whose can ultimately got kicked."

DeShores slurped down a second bourbon and winced at the heartburn. Don't call Eve, his inner voice warned. Oh, God, no. That would multiply my idiocy tenfold at the moment I need it least. Slamming the empty shot glass down on the table, he stood up weakly, but not before catching his face in the bar mirror. There in the glass peered Maximillion Moncrief, a Barnum and Baily clown with bulbous nose and hilarious elephant ears. Hello, Everyone: I'm the CEO at Ground Zero Books in Los Angeles, he whispered to himself acidly as he moved over the Manhattan sidewalk buzzing from the liquor's sting. Anybody here wanna' get published?

"Central Park, Driver," he barked, sinking into a second cab's back seat. "Anywhere, any place or part of Central Park. Any patch of grass, thicket of shrubs, lagoon, pond, or nook with a psychotherapist in a kiosk."

A 12 year-old boy wearing a baseball cap backwards

skateboarded by and nearly knocked DeShores on his rear end as he crept along a lonely dirt trail under arching trees and crooked hedges. Suddenly, his briefcase, *Eternal Autumn* within it, felt as if it were loaded with bricks. DeShores stopped and collapsed on a park bench, set the briefcase down, leaned back, and closed his moistened eyes.

...In my opinion, if Ada Pandit wasn't a saint, then saints don't exist...

What's wrong with me? How did I ever descend into this self-righteous, adolescent dime melodrama titled "The Poor Rejected Writer"? What a damn fool dunce Sanfred DeShores turned out to be. God help me if I ever poke at another typewriter key again...

Off to his left, he spied a rusty drinking fountain. He stepped over, pressed the button with his thumb, and tasted air. Go home, DeShores, face the music. Admit to Eve you're an obtuse, empty suit and, while at it, apologize to her for every post-rejection convalescence you ever put that decent woman through. And don't forget to—"

His eyes fell upon a short, circular retaining wall curving around the back of the fountain. Protruding from the cement, a book glowed in a little halo of a pleasant golden light. He stepped behind the fountain, peered at the volume oddly, and slid the book out. As a few drops of cement crackled to the ground, he noted the perfectly rectangular empty slit left in the wall. A delicate, soft hue emitted from the volume in his hands as he studied the cover's title.

THE BOOK OF TIME

The *Book of Time*, DeShores chuckled cynically as he inspected the very unusual print. The perfect denouement to my Commedia dell'arte. Yet a strangely, beautifully printed book, he said to himself. What's a thing like this doing stuck into a cement wall behind a rusty drinking fountain in Central Park? He tried to pinpoint the source of the golden halo as he turned back the cover. Then DeShores tottered as if he'd been knocked back on his heels:

Sanford DeShores Wins Pulitzer Prize
November 22, 2031AD

American novelist Sanford DeShores was awarded a Pulitzer Prize for literature in New York City on November 22, 2031AD at 1 pm UT. President Jon Bauder acknowledged the author's contribution to humanity for a lifetime of work glorifying individual growth potential and human interaction...

Struggling to cope with what his brain told him were the words on the page, DeShores sank to the park bench again and read what was printed.

...World Global Literary reported that the books of Sanfred DeShores have sold more than 57.4 million editions in physical and cyber form...

He raced ahead, read and re-read portions of the impossible accounts of Pulitzer Prize winning author Sanfred DeShores. He jumped up and shot over to the hole in the retaining wall, peered into it, and examined the cement edges. He went back to the bench and picked up the book again. Flipping wildly through page after page, he found excerpts from his own works, some he knew well because he had written them, some unknown to him containing future titles and dates. He came to a two-page Pulitzer Prize acceptance speech in which he referred to *Eternal Autumn.* They're my words, DeShores realized joyously, his shaking hands holding the book as if it was a lost Biblical manuscript proving once and for all the existence of Christ. Then he flashed back to his two bourbons at the saloon. Did the bartender drug the booze?

Hyperventilating, he jammed *The Book of Time* into his briefcase and raced back over the Central Park dirt path. When he reached the street, he waved frantically for another cab. Who could have known I'd be walking down that particular Central Park lane in New York City at the specific moment? *Who wrote that book then placed it in that hole in that wall for me to find?!*

"Driver—the Tevere Hotel! Now!"

He stared senselessly at the briefcase sitting on his lap. He told himself that it was indeed a briefcase; that he was actually riding in a New York taxicab; that he was very much conscious and existing in real life in North America on on the surface of planet Earth. As the cab shot off into traffic, DeShores swallowed to see if he was able to swallow at all; then he pinched himself to see if he felt it. Slowly, he opened the leather briefcase. *The Book of Time* lay on top of *Eternal Autumn* in a pleasant spray of golden light. He flashed through the pages one more time seeking the author and publisher. Finding neither, he brushed his fingers against the black print and thought that of the thousands of books he had held in his hands, he had never beheld a volume like the one he was holding now. DeShores read the incredible headline again:

Sanford DeShores Wins Pulitzer Prize
November 22, 2031AD

Get back to the hotel, call Eve, start with page one, and quote these very words to her over the phone! Then ask her to affirm that I just read these words to her, then have her affirm I've been her husband for 22 years, then have her affirm I'm Sanfred DeShores from Portland, Oregon, then have her ask me questions about my past to affirm I haven't lost my goddam mind!

Rushing into his suite, he placed the briefcase flat on the bed. Then he lifted the top as if he were lifting the lid of the lost Ark of the Covenant. Instead of *The Book of Time*, however, DeShores stared at the cover page of *Eternal Autumn*, the only manuscript there. In crazed disbelief, he yanked his novel out, looked inside the satchel's pocket liners, and searched the floor of the room and under the bed. He retraced his steps madly—the hall, the elevator, the lobby—and out to the sidewalk in front of the hotel where the cab had let him off at the curb. He raced back up to his suite and stood in front of the briefcase feeling as if he were sinking helplessly into the horror of an African quicksand.

I've had a coronary thrombosis...I need emergency medical attention...

What is happening to me? DeShores asked himself, taking dazed, backward steps, staring at the briefcase in as if it were Houdini's empty straightjacket. Two bourbons don't create delusions like this. I held that book, touched the paper, read the words. It had to have fallen out in the cab. Is it lying on the floor of the back seat of that cursed taxi now as it sifts up to a corn dog kiosk in Coney Island?

That book went into my briefcase and it stayed in my briefcase and my briefcase stayed on my lap. And I closed and snapped the top shut and it never left my hands...

Had he been stranded on a planet of ice circling in Andromeda, DeShores could not have felt more alone in the universe than he did at that moment in the middle of downtown Manhattan. The Tevere Hotel was suddenly the House of Usher. New York City was Transylvania. The people moving along Manhattan sidewalks were zombies staggering through Night of the Living Dead.

Yet another cab. And another anxiety-ridden safari through the city. DeShores slumped in the back seat heaving as if he'd just run the Boston Marathon. His eyes were closed when he said: "Driver—Bellevue Hospital—*I'm having a stroke...*"

Forty minutes later DeShores paced in his underwear in the examination room of Dr. Fritz Oppedahl, M.D. The doctor was a diminutive elf of a man with wiry glasses and lenses the size of coffee can lids. A mop of brown hair scrambled on top of his head as though he had just awakened after a hangover. A pair of glossy marbles peered at DeShores with detached, psychoanalytical interest. Then a nasal voice asked, "How can I help you, Mr. DeShorts?"

"Before you throw the net over me and send me to the funny farm, Dr., please hear my story."

Oppedahl listened with genuine interest. Then, as the tale dragged on, he took the wooden chair against the wall, turned it backwards, and sat down with his arms on the neck gazing up at DeShores like an enthralled child listening to his grandfather's bedtime storytelling.

"That's quite a yarn, Mr. DeShorts. I can imagine your consternation. May I examine you?"

Oppedahl scribbled notes in a medical file folder as he took DeShores' vitals.

"I held that thing in these very hands, Doctor!" DeShores held his hands straight out for Oppedahl to observe. The doctor examined them. Brown, glossy marbles squinted up at DeShores.

"Very anomalous, I'd say. I simply don't know quite what to make of your story, Mr. DeShorts."

"But you don't believe me, do you, Doctor? Am I or am I not having a stroke?"

"Other than your extreme anxiety, I find nothing physiologically impolitic. Don't think a stroke is the culprit here."

"I've lost touch with reality. What about a nervous breakdown? What do you think, Doctor? *Am I having a nervous breakdown*?!"

Oppedahl shook his head in bewilderment and removed a tablet from his lab coat pocket. "I'm giving you a mild prescription for valium. But when you get back to Portland, think seriously about talking with a professional counselor about this episode you had today in Central Park, Mr. DeShorts."

DeShores paced back and forth in frustration. "If the book wasn't real," he asked, shivering in his underwear, "why did I fly back to the Tevere Hotel after I found it in the park? What made me do that, Dr.?"

"Simply take one of these tablets as per need every 4-6 hours," Oppedahl suggested, zipping off the prescription from his tablet.

Oppedahl, make a statement, for Cri-sake, you asinine jackass!

"Are you or are you not going to give me a medical opinion, Doctor?"

The physician didn't flinch. "The key factor is: what do you plan to do about this unorthodox experience you think you've had, Mr. DeShorts?"

"*Do about it*?! What *can* I possibly do about it?"

Oppedahl chuckled. "You know, Mr. DeShorts, I do a bit of writing myself. In fact, I'm wrapping up a medical suspense thriller right now. It centers around a buxom blonde intern who gets involved with a proctologist that—"

"And—your point, please, doctor, your *point*?"

"Was coming to that. The devil's in the details, Mr. DeShorts. The solution is always in the details. If it were Sam Spade, he'd say you need to examine the minutest detail of the case to discover the linchpin."

"But what does that actually *mean in this case, Doctor*?" DeShores demanded to know, shivering flat-footed in his purple boxers. "Please—exactly what are you *getting at*?"

The tip of Oppedahl's forefinger bounced off his upper lip. "You said you found that book in a hole in a cement wall, correct? Would that hole still be there?"

"Yes!" DeShores exclaimed. Overcome with joy, he nearly kissed Oppedahl on the lips. "Yes, of course it would have to be! It most certainly would, Dr.!"

Why didn't I rent a car? DeShores asked himself collapsing in another cab's back seat as he directed the driver to Central Park. Several fruitless searches, stops, and U-turns ensued before DeShores finally identified the sidewalk that led to the path that winded to the drinking fountain. "There!" he shouted. "That's it! Pull up there, Driver!"

He practically jumped out of the cab before it slid to the curb, then raced along the shrub-lined path. Fifty yards ahead, he pulled up with his hands on his knees gasping for air, but the drinking fountain was in sight straight ahead of him and behind it the cement wall loomed like Valhalla. Out of breath, DeShores crept toward the fountain. A wondrous euphoria overtook him as he examined the empty, rectangular slit and the particles of cement lying on the ground below. Sinking to the bench next to the fountain, he closed his eyes in ecstasy. Yes, cement, he repeated in joyous awe. Wonderful chunks of cracked, magnificent, sublime cement...

The Book of Time was real. I am not having a mental breakdown. Through some inexplicable miracle of the universe, destiny has informed me that I will one day be awarded justice for my life-long literary hell.

A whimsical DeShores practically tap-danced through security at JFK, then boarded a red-eye flight for home and took an aisle seat that felt like a stash of silken pillows. He did not feel he was in the same skin of the Sanfred DeShores who left Portland. As the plane soared into the clouds above the New York skyline, the events of the week fell one against the other like dominoes: the Pandit rejection, his adolescent, reckless reaction; recalling *Crap Game,* flying to New York; the Woodpecker Room, Pandit's death—*The Book Of Time.* Who wrote that book, where did it come from, and where did it go? But in the big picture, does it matter? Fate, destiny, God or all three have gifted me due process. Questioning why the school bus that whizzed by two inches from the bumper of one's idling Ford didn't kill the driver is useless, isn't it?

Then the incident at Portland International flared up. Why was November 22, 1963 printed on that ticket? Why was the departure time 1 p.m.? Since the moment the Pandit rejection burned in my fireplace, I've been led around on a leash by wondrous irony. And DeShores knew irony well; Professor Theodore Whetstone had embossed it upon his literary sensibilities like a sterling silver signpost. And Whetstone's voice came back to him and was in his ears as clearly as if the professor were sitting in the seat ahead of him and suddenly stood up, turned, leaned forward on the headrest, and opined: "Irony has purpose in literature, Sanfred, because it has great significance in life."

New York airspace had fallen far behind and the in-flight movie had begun. But DeShores clicked on the cabin light, took out a pen, and began listing the key elements of his odyssey: Yesterday was November 22, the anniversary of the Kennedy assassination. My ticket misprinted the year and inserted 1963, the very year of the assassination itself. Then I arrived at *JFK* Airport. Kennedy's death; Pandit's death. JFK died at 1 PM; my flight departure time was 1 p.m.

November 22?!

He jumped up in his seat so abruptly that it jostled the sleeping Armenian couple sitting ahead of him. *The Book of Time* said I would win the Pulitzer Prize on November 22, 2031! Grandly bewildered, DeShores came face to face with his salvaged destiny. It is the proof. The notary's stamp. Whoever He or She may be who sits at the control stick piloting Sanfred DeShores' pilgrimage through some unfathomable doorway to time—I bow to you so grandly.

...You're a wonderful writer. And the best writing you do is when you create solutions for problems that show a deep, sympathetic understanding of human behavior...

DeShores had to restrain himself from exploding from his seat and running down the aisle in the middle of the movie and hollering like an escaped mental patient: *"Hey, Everybody! I, Sanfred DeShores, will one day win the Pulitzer Prize for literature!"* He laughed out loud when he realized the movie being shown was Back to the Future.

Sprawling in the reverie induced by a glass of wine, DeShores gazed down upon the boxed townships spilling across the Mid-West. Twinkling lights passed slowly under the plane's snail-like forward pace. Somewhere down there, he thought, a young Sanfred DeShores is getting pistol whipped by his own Professor Clayford Whetstone. But—what if Whetstone had actually liked my play when I was in college, raved about it, told me I was the next Arthur Miller? Suppose he had sent the play to his New York connections and they, in turn, loved it and produced it? Critics would have smashed that thing to bits because it really was terrible. And given my 20 year-old glass ego, the drive to get back on the horse and punch out the next script might have been crushed. Was the pain Whetstone inflicted upon a naive college sophomore less a heartless act of cruelty than a cardinal act of mercy? Did Whetstone's grim critique in the privacy of an office feedback session actually save me from my own literary implosion? Yes, Whetstone gave me my redemption by teaching me that at best I had written a rough draft. A lesson that in the long run made me soar to greater heights. And at the peak of those heights I wrote *Eternal Autumn.*

The light dimmed from Whetstone and gradually highlighted Raymond Sardonics, author of *Crap Game.* But DeShores now bathed in a new perspective. Sardonics is no hero of mine, he reasoned; not any more, he isn't. That man crafted his own black comedy in which he cast himself as existential hero. He took the easy way out. Raymond Sardonics was an abysmal clown, a weak, self-loathing coward; he was a man who caved, a gutless flop who bailed and ended up slithering on his stomach toward his own oblivion.

A charm of lights strung across the landscape below. Yes, DeShores wondered, how many writers under those lights now are perspiring over the keys of their word processors laboring to turn out a novel? How many of them are fashioning characters from air and plots from scratch—and all of it destined to be annihilated by the dreaded white envelope containing the scythe of a rejection slip? May they all persevere through their personal Ada Pandit's and keep moving forward and realize their innate talent.

DeShores set his bags down in his living room a little after 8 a.m., closed the front door quietly, and headed straight to the spare room. The closet doors pulled back, his eyes widened. There they were—the manuscripts, neatly filed, indexed. But now it was different. For opening those closet doors was akin to Ali Baba entering the whimsical cave at Baghdad. He could see that what now filled those shelves was the product of a rare gift; one that could chisel plays, essays, and novels from cold blocks of stone at will over the course of 28 relentlessly creative years. Despite any agent, publisher, or critic whose rejection slip indicated otherwise, DeShores saw his thousands of pages as pegs climbing a ladder to a New York odyssey where a reconstructed writer, not a beleaguered Ada Pandit, emerged as the shining central character.

"Sanford? You're back," Eve said sandy-voiced, appearing

in the room's doorway tying the sash of her robe. "How did things go?"

"How did things go?" He lifted the master copy of *Eternal Autumn* from the top shelf and looked at the cover page that symbolized far more than he could describe to his wife. "Eve, if my right arm was amputated without anesthetic it would hurt less than admitting right now that the contents of this closet amount to one, immense rough draft. *Every* manuscript's a rough draft—no matter how 'finished' the writer thinks it is. Pandit's rejection was a rough draft. Whetstone was a rough draft. Our marriage is a rough draft. Everything that lives and breathes in life—is an on-going rough draft in time."

"What's going on, Sanfred?" Eve asked with concern. "Obviously, something important happened in New York."

Eternal Autumn was in his hands and DeShores looked down at it as if it were a newborn infant held by its father for the first time.

"A great deal happened. Gabriel's trumpet sounded, Eve. My *real* departure time is now. Who can say—if I work hard enough and polish these rough drafts with enough sweat and tears, I might one day win a Pulitzer Prize."

Precious Time

"Dick, suppose I went back in time," Morley suggested, "and blew up the log cabin where 10 year-old Abe Lincoln was eating breakfast. There'd be no President Lincoln, the union would not have survived the Civil War, the South would have seceded, and, more than likely, it would have been the end of America as we know it today."

Morley's sardonic laughter shook the house. "Even if Man reaches the year 3000, he'll never be able to travel either ahead or back through time. And as for 'psychic powers'—that concept is even more hilarious than the idea of time travel."

"Why, Quint? Why couldn't psychic prediction be possible?" Newsom asked.

"Dick, predicting the future would mean the future already exists. And if that were true, then it negates human free will. Are you ready to trash that?"

"OK, but our present is the future to those who lived before, right? To them *we* are their future. President Reagan is President Roosevelt's future, am I not correct?"

"When Roosevelt was alive, that was his present. As soon as the present moment's over, it's flushed down the drain of time. Gone. Don't you see the paradox in all this, Dick? And the paradox should give you pause. It's there for a reason."

Quint Morley was an enormous hulk of a man who stood six foot-five with legs and arms like redwood logs. His trademark green suspenders and bright red bow tie gave him the appearance of a figure one would see at the entrance to a boardwalk funhouse. His full head of white, spongy hair, bushy white eyebrows, and prominent rectangular jaw, lent to an intimidating persona—which he manipulated at all times. But Morely was as imposing psychologically as physically, his voice roaring in a deep foghorn blast that could weaken marble walls. Far more than a bulldog, however, he was an articulate, intellectual with a Ph.D in history who thoroughly researched the subjects he detested most until he became an expert in their loopholes. And he did it for one purpose: to reduce his enemies' asinine superstitions to pulp.

"No one in the history of the planet has ever been able to specifically predict major events, Dick—other than those who have correctly perceived trends based on statistical probability and such. But psychic prognostication is mumbo-jumbo; it's not part of the rational universe."

Dick Newsom crossed his legs in the easy chair across from Morely. He was a good-hearted, amiable man in his early 40's with a Sears-catalogue, Brooks-Brothers physique. Usually dressed natily in slacks, white shirt, and casual sport coat, Newsom was a very likeable man with premature grey hair parted on one side slickly, inquisitive blue eyes, and a genuine personality that tried to find the best in people. Always a respectful listener, Newsom considered all points of view thoughtfully before offering an opinion on any matter. His best friend Morely said it often: "Dick, I like the way you don't insert words into a discussion until you feel your ideas are germane. You don't ramble; you look before you leap. And you're an even better sounding board."

"Quint, have we truly explored every aspect of the human mind? Why couldn't someone possess an aptitude that taps into a dimension, an extra-perceptive sense of some sort, or links up to a force we know nothing about and actually sees what will happen?"

"Because as I just stated," Morley argued emphatically, "that would mean that future events exist as a physical event before they've occurred. The assumption is by all standards utterly cockamamie. Every attempt by so-called psychics to predict the future is nothing more than idiotic, imbecilic generality. And generality is the psychic's bread and butter. If you don't believe me, go to a psychic who reads tarot cards, tea leaves, or palms and ask them who will win the World Series this year. They can't do it. Suddenly, their 'psychic powers' collapse like a cardboard outhouse. They're reduced to moronic statements like, 'You'll be receiving important news from the East very soon.' A generality they probably stole from that morning's newspaper astrology. But they take your money, don't they? Ever wondered why a psychic charges a fee? If they're psychic, why aren't they applying their psychic powers to the stock market and making millions?" Morely laughed sardonically, but Newsom had heard it all before.

"Just try to pin one of these jack 'o lanterns down some time and ask: 'I have a playing card in my wallet. Tell me the suit and card's number.' Or: 'Give me the five digits of the house address I grew up in as a child, and please put all five digits in order.'"

Newsom held out his wineglass as Morley poured him more vintage Cabernet.

"What *would* convince you, Quint? What would make you say psychic power did exist?"

"It would have to be something very, very specific and unambiguous—a future event using dates, names, places that are irrefutable. Something like, 'The winner of the Illinois Power Ball two weeks from today will be Mrs. Eleanor Easterhog, 42 year-old cleaning lady, 435 Park Ave., Seaweed, Illinois.' But you'll never see it, Dick. And you'll never see it because 'psychics' are all higgledy-piggleddys."

"Undoubtedly, some psychics are charlatans, Quint. But eliminating the riff-raff, what about Nostrodamus and Edgar Cayce? From what I've read, they were pretty impressive."

The lines in Morley's face tightened. "Neither Nostradamus nor Cayce correctly predicted anything, Dick. For example, they both said 1999 would be Armageddon. Nostradamus wrote these cryptic poems that were, in effect, Rorschach tests in verse—and people have been reading whatever they want to read into them for centuries. He said 1999 would be the 'zero' year and the US would split apart. Remember Y2K when civilization was going to be thrown into chaos as computer time clocks rolled back to the year 1900? People were actually buying food rations, storing water, and hooking up to windmills. Dick, we went from 1999 to the year 2000 without a whimper."

"The mind may be the most amazing thing in the universe," Newsom argued. "But I'm just not totally convinced that it's incapable of connecting up to extra-sensory perception."

"Now animals are supposed to get very antsy just before an earthquake," Morely shrugged, "but even if that's true, it's attributable to sensing atmospheric conditions. That I can accept."

"I'm not talking about animals and atmospheric conditions, Quint. I'm talking about accurate prediction of future events in specific detail."

Morley held his arms out wide. "Well, where are these prophets, Dick? Tell me. Where were the psychics warning us of the Loma Prieta earthquake that hit the San Francisco Bay Area in 1989? Where were these same people in 1980 contacting the Secret Service or FBI that somebody would shoot President Reagan? Why didn't anyone come forward to scream that the Space Shuttle would blow up in 1986? But man, oh man, they sure come out of the woodwork *after* it happens, don't they?"

Newsom sipped Morely's vintage Cabernet. "I'll say this: I'm going to be front row center Friday night when you debate Sylvia Thorne on the Tracy Show."

Morley looked as if he had just swallowed castor oil. "One of the most revolting scam artists on the planet, Dick! I've researched this woman. She knows no shame and charges $500 for a half hour telephone consultation! And the saps who buy her act just can't whip their credit cards out fast enough to line her pockets. They ask her questions like: "Is my late husband Harry happy in heaven?" Thorne eats these jackasses for breakfast. 'Yes, honey," she answers, "your husband Harry is very happy and he is praying for you in Heaven.' Then the victim bawls on the phone and says, 'Oh, God Bless you, Sylvia, you're a saint.' I'm telling you, Dick, somebody's got to stop these people. But I've got a big surprise for Ms. Thorne Friday night that will send that woman back to Palookaville."

"What are you gonna' do, Quint?"

"You'll have to tune in to find out. But I guarantee you I've done my homework and I'm gonna' throw this shyster one big curve ball that'll make the network ratings fly off the charts. You see, Dick, I don't mind a guy standing on the street corner shouting, 'The end is near!' What I do mind are the piranhas who charge serious dollars and prey off the pain and heartache of bereaved, hurting people, especially the elderly. Legally, you can't touch them, of course, so it's up to those of us who stand for accountability to take the reins and expose them for the rip-off artists they are."

Morley continued to pace around the room like a grizzly bear that had caught the scent of a dead carcass. "The Loch Ness monster, UFO bases in Anarctica, remote viewing— I've squared off with every nut supporting these hippogriffs—and never, *never* do they offer one scintilla of credible, irrefutable evidence. It's always a cloudy blip shooting over the mountain or a plesiosaur sticking its head out of the water in a lake in Scotland that nobody could properly photograph. And, as you know, Dick, every single time I debate these three dollar bills I score a knock out."

The lecture went on for another 45 minutes centering on academic scholarship as the intelligentsia's true religion. Finally, Morely brought the wineglass to his lips, swallowed the rest of the Cabernet in three successive gulps, and wiped his mouth with his sleeve. He threw off his green bow tie, dropped his suspenders to his waist, and finally added: "More than anything, the fertilizer of psychic powers and extra-terrestrial's flitting around in our skies is a testament to the ignorance of the American intelligence and the depths to which we've deteriorated. Statistically, Americans aged 20 to 34 spend less than seven minutes reading per day. That's a scary trend. And scholarship? It went down the toilet years ago when television sitcoms and video games replaced Shakespeare and Tolstoy with Batman. Today public schools honor classes like wood shop and cooking as much as time-tested literary classics. American minds traded critical thinking skills for a cream of wheat mentality a long time ago.

"And an after life? Dick, we're carbon-based entities craving food, sex, and a Mercedes, then we die. Nobody here but we homo-sapiens, plants, animals, and a whole lot of H20 crammed onto a ball of rock circling a star. No alien spacecraft creating apocalyptic messages in crop circles; no fourth dimension in the Bermuda Triangle sucking up aircraft; no Area 51 with dead aliens on ice; no New Jersey Devil; no Louisiana swamp monster. Nothing of the kind. Zilch. Zero. Just a bunch of folks caught in bumper to bumper traffic praying for the week next summer when they can pass through the turnstiles at Disneyland and crowd into line for Space Mountain."

"That's a pretty cut and dry, gray world you live in, Quint. No room for anything beyond the meat and potatoes on your dinner plate?"

"As I keep saying, Dick: Where's the incontestable, dramatic film footage of a flying saucer parked in Yosemite? It's nowhere. And it will never *be* anywhere. But let's get back to the original point about psychic powers.

"Everything I've said applies to the 'psychic' because these folks are an empty sack of barn yard refuse running a carnival three-card Monte. The only predictions I believe in are actuarial insurance tables guaranteeing 18-25 year-old males will get into more auto wrecks than octogenarians."

"Well, Quint, this debate you're doing Friday night with Sylvia Thorne should really light up the sky. Phil Tracy has sure been promoting the deuce out of it."

"Thorne despises me, you know. She'd put a bullet between my eyes if she thought she could get away with it. She sees me like they all do: the guy who pulls back the curtain in Oz showing a con artist at a control panel speaking into a microphone. But if I'm the raspberry seed in their wisdom teeth, I'm thrilled to be it," Morely proclaimed. "Frankly, I wouldn't be surprised if Thorne cancelled for Friday night. But if she did, I'd go it alone and disclose precisely just how she's been hosing innocent people for years."

"You think Tracy will lean on you more than he leans on her just to give her the edge?"

"Phil Tracy's no different than any other television talk show host who stuffs his integrity into an Arbitron rating. If Phil Tracy could get 100,000 more viewers to tune in tonight by doing a show on aliens from Proxima Centauri now living in Palm Beach and disguised as Jews, he'd do it. He's a gutless wonder who got where he is by kissing the butts of flimflam Jakes of every brand and degree. But he's not stupid: he knows Joe Sixpack has made him what he is. The problem for those of us who value academic scholarship is that Joe Sixpack and his soccer Mom wife have the combined IQ of a toadstool. But Tracy doesn't care. Ever see his home? Eight bedrooms, tennis courts, and an Olympic size swimming pool with Roman arches."

Morley poured the rest of the Cabernet into Newsom's glass. "Dial in Friday night, Dick. I think you'll find it quite educational. By the time I'm through with Sylvia Thorne, she'll be running for the exit with her coat over her head."

"When's your flight?"

"Tomorrow morning."

"I'll be watching, Quint," Newsom toasted. "But something tells me it's Thorne who'll be needing all the help she can get."

Once again, Newsom's head filled with his friend's pedantic opinions as he left Morely's two-story brownstone. Quint hasn't changed one degree since college, he mused. Newsom drove off recalling his introduction to Quint Morely on the practice football field their freshman year at the University of Cincinnati. Newsom carried the ball around left end and Morely exploded from his nose guard position and leveled Newsom driving him two feet into the ground. The 19 year-old suffered a broken collarbone, concussion, and left the field in an ambulance. But Morely visited Newsom every day, lumbering down the hospital hall after football practice with ice cream and magazines. They played cards, discussed history, and talked about life after college. Finally, the nurses would arrive and ask the imposing visitor to leave whereupon Morely would demand to see the chief of staff who he engaged in a lively debate concerning the stupidity of hospital visiting hours.

Newsom came to believe that if a gene governed cynicism, Quint Morely possessed the prototype. He cringed during a history seminar one afternoon his senior year as he watched Morely launch into an ugly argument with a professor who stated that the existence of the historical Jesus was problematic. Morely stood up and scorched the man for his shameful scholarship. After a shouting match ensued, Morely called the professor an "insufferable baboon" driving him from the lecture hall and prompting the appearance of campus security. From that day on, Newsom realized how deeply Morely despised personal conviction not supported by incontrovertible proof.

A year after graduation, Morely married his high school girlfriend Sharon Lee. The couple did well until the birth of their son, Stephen, Newsom's godson. Morely tried, but the relationship between father and son deteriorated. The Morely's divorced five years later, Sharon took Stephen to New York City, and Morely never saw his son again. A day after Sharon and Stephen left Cincinnati, Morely made it clear to Newsom that Stephen's name was never to pass from Newsom's lips again. But Newsom believed Morely's estrangement from his son crushed him and the heartache probably lay at the core of the man's cynicism.

Stephen Morely, however, saw his Uncle Richard as an adopted father. He wrote to his uncle often and Newsom, in turn, never missed sending Stephen a Christmas present or birthday money. Newsom used endless opportunities to persuade Stephen to reconnect with his father, but young Morely wanted no part of it. Meanwhile, Quint Morely ascended the ladder of popular culture publishing one book after another pulverizing extra- terrestrial UFO's, astrology, reincarnation, and especially psychic charlatans. Newsom knew that if Morely could get away with it, he would load up a bus filled with psychics and send it over the cliff at Mt. Whitney.

Yet Morely was forbidden from visiting the Newsom home. Vera, Newsom's wife, once told her husband: "He's an obnoxious bully when you get right down to it. He's a human axe that cuts vulnerable people up. His instincts are to destroy, not create. Frankly, I think he's a lonely, miserable oaf and probably a lush who'll end up in a drunken stupor that will send him over the cliff. Never invite him over here, Dick. Never."

On his way home, Newsom found himself at the local library combing shelves for books on the psychic realm. One volume in particular caught his eye: *26,280 Hours: The Prediction of the Assassination of President John F. Kennedy* by Ruth Ann Decker. Newsom skimmed the jacket, was hooked when he read the first few pages, then checked out the volume.

From the beginning, he was absorbed by the account of the author's mother, Jeannie McClelland, who had been a county librarian in Wichita, Kansas in 1963, and her father, John Decker, an Iowa farmer. One day before the assassination of the President, Decker's parents found a very strange book titled *The Book of Time*. The volume allegedly predicted not only the assassination of the President in very specific detail, but events of the early 1970's. Ruth Decker described her mother's tale of how she met her husband, John, in a Wichita hospital the same day they both found the book, how the book disappeared, and the efforts of her father to travel to Dallas and prevent the assassination. The story detailed John Decker's odd experience in a diesel truck that took him to Texas; and his inexplicable experience in a Catholic Church confronting a priest whose existence could never be proven. Decker returned to his Iowa farm, married Jeannie McClelland six months later, then died in a tractor accident three years to the day of the President's assassination, November 22, 1966, thus the title 26,280 *Hours*, the number of hours in three years.

But shortly before marrying Mclelland, Decker undertook to

document, to the best of his memory, all that he remembered *The Book of Time* had forecast. Moreover, he had two attorneys sign an affidavit confirming what he had written with the instructions that the envelope containing the affidavit not be opened before 1980. Decker's writings were placed in a mailer and sent to the attorney's law firm where it remained sealed in their possession with a postmark date of October 21, 1964. On her 20th birthday, May 1, 1984, Ruth Decker opened the envelope in the presence of the two original attorneys. The men then signed new affidavits stating the seal on the envelope had never been broken.

The contents of the envelope totaled 17 pages written in John Decker's hand. It described the assassination of President John F. Kennedy, the Viet Nam War, President Lyndon B. Johnson's decision not to seek reelection in 1968, the election of Richard M. Nixon, his resignation in 1974, and the American withdrawal from Saigon, Viet Nam in 1975.

Newsom was electrified. He read the Decker book from cover to cover in one night. Why haven't I ever heard of this story? As he crawled into bed and turned off the nightstand lamp around 2 a.m., Newsom wondered just how Quint Morely would explain the affidavits filed by the two attorneys in 1980 proving the accuracy of John Decker's future history written in 1964. He imagined Quint strutting around his living room with a glass of Cabernet jauntily dismissing the entire story as hogwash:

"Listen, Dick, isn't it obvious? The lawyers were bought off by the Decker woman so she could write a best seller. The whole thing's brilliant marketing pure and simple."

II

"Tonight! Psychic Sylvia Thorne verses skeptic Quentin Morely! They will debate the psychic realm. You, the viewer, will decide!"

Phil Tracy, his gleaming white teeth, wavy salt and pepper hair combed straight back, appeared on the screen flanked on either side by his two guests.

"I'm Phil Tracy and welcome to the Phil Tracy Show. But there's more! Later in this program a psychic experiment that will pit Sylvia against Quint in a test of psychic powers you will not want to miss!"

Wearing his trademark red bow tie and green suspenders over a checkered, chartreuse shirt, Morely's confident demeanor contrasted sharply with Thorne's. The psychic sat rigid and dour, her frazzled gray hair, plain, white sweater, and unflattering crow's feet casting her grandmotherly against the larger than life cartoon of Morely who looked as if he were ready to drill for oil. A silver cross hung from Thorne's neck and, from time to time during the show, she fingered it nervously with her right hand, especially when she was on screen.

"Sylvia, first to you," Tracy began. "Critics claim you and other psychics engage in empty generalities, but never specifics. Your reaction to that?"

"Well, it's simply not true, Phil. I correctly foretold the crash of United Airlines Flight 200 in 1999; I foretold that Y2K would never be a problem; and I forecast the Bush-Gore election last year would be historically close and would lead to a high court crisis."

"Back to Flight 200, Sylvia: Did you actually warn authorities in advance of the crash?"

"Oh, I tried and tried to get through to the FAA. But no one would listen. One nice man did try to follow up, but let's be frank: public officials fear ridicule from higher-ups if they were to write reports based on a psychic forecast. I've spoken to many public officials who have privately told me they will never file a report based on a forecast. Regrettable, but what can I do about it?"

"Sylvia, where do you claim your powers come from?"

"My ability to forecast events comes from God, our Savior. Sylvia Thorne is simply a conduit for His will. He decides what will be taken seriously. He is in control of all human events just as He is in control of those He selects to be His messengers."

"'Beware of false prophets,'" Morely hooted from the other side of the table, "'who come to you in sheep's clothing, but underneath are ravenous wolves!'²"

Thorne did not look at Morely, but kept her eyes downcast. "I think, Mr. Morely, you're the last person in the world who ought to be quoting the Bible—especially since you're an atheist. As I was saying, Phil: He sends His messages through me, but it is to glorify His word, never to glorify the person of Sylvia Thorne. If He chooses to bestow powers upon me, those powers come directly from Him and pass through me as they would pass through a conduit."

"Good enough, Sylvia," Tracy smiled. "Now to you, Quint: why are you such a pain in the rear for people like Sylvia who claim to be psychic?"

Morely came forward leaning his massive chest against the table. His white eyebrows furrowed; the corners of his mouth tightened. "Because, Phil, these blowholes engage in generalities we could all make. As for Ms. Thorne's purported warning to the FAA prior to the crash of Flight 200—Crapola! I investigated that, spoke to people at the FAA, and they said Sylvia Thorne never called them. But there's a larger issue here, Phil. If Sylvia Thorne is psychic, why doesn't she spend at least three-quarters of her time helping police find missing children? Or why doesn't she offer her services to medical researchers desperately seeking the cure for diseases like MS and Alzheimer's? Psychics like Thorne never do that, Phil, because they can't."

Tracy turned to Thorne. "Sylvia, have you ever assisted law enforcement agencies in their attempt to locate missing persons?"

"Yes, Phil, I most certainly have. Many, many times. In the Kathleen Garfield disappearance I told police she was not going to be found in Rockford Park where they were, at that time, tracking with search dogs."

"That's where she *wasn't*, Sylvia!" Morely shouted angrily. "Why didn't you tell them where she *was*? Tell us now, Sylvia! Tell us: Where is Kathleen Garfield right now? Help the police, Sylvia;

help Garfield's grieving family. *Sylvia Thorne, I challenge you in front of millions of viewers: Tell us all where Kathleen Garfield is at this moment?!*"

Thorne looked flustered, but kept her eyes lowered and grasped the cross around her neck with the fingers of her right hand. "Phil, what is most important of all to understand is that I am able to foretell events only when God our Lord wills me to foretell them. I proceed at His pace, showing patience to His due course as He sees fit—to accept His time scale, to use me as His conduit. Sometimes I have all or most of the information; in other cases, only bits and pieces. But as mysterious as His way is, I trust in Him that there will always be a Divine reason for either complete or incomplete knowledge at a particular time."

"What a convenient trap door!" Morely shouted again from his side of the table. "What a crock of pure cow dung!"

"Now, now, Quint, let's be civil," Tracy admonished lightly. "So let me now turn to you again, Quint: what proof do you have that Sylvia Thorne is *not* psychic?"

"This isn't rocket science, Phil," Morely replied looking directly at Thorne. "Ms. Thorne, do you charge $500 an hour for private telephone consultations?"

Thorne shifted uncomfortably. "That is patently untrue," she said with a quivering lip and eyes fixed on the table in front of her. "No one knows the pro bono work I do: I've never charged any law enforcement agency I've assisted when advising in a case involving a missing person. And, Mr. Morely, with all due respect, you know nothing about the money I privately donate to charitable causes."

Morely looked baffled and held his arms out wide. "Why do you need to give money to charity, Sylvia? Why don't you just tell your favorite charity what the winning horses will be tomorrow at River Downs racetrack so they can play them and make millions?"

"Our Lord's realm does not extend to a crass race track or games of chance, Mr. Morely..."

"Hold that thought right there, Syliva," Tracy interrupted.

"Folks, we've got a real donnybrook on our hands tonight as expected. We'll take a break for some messages and when we return a very special psychic demonstration right here on the Phil Tracy Show!"

Newsom and his wife Vera saw it all from their living room couch. "There will always be a Quint Morely," Newsom observed shaking his head.

"I didn't like him when I first met him," stated Vera, "and I like him less now. He's a self-righteous oaf and an arrogant blowhard. For the life of me, Dick, I don't know why you associate with Quint Morely. How do you tolerate this man's gigantic ego?"

"I'll never say Quint is pretty, Vera, but I'll tell you this: if I was in a foxhole in combat, I'd want Quint Morely next to me. If you think about it, Quint's number one problem is his brutal honesty. He candy-coats nothing. You know where you stand every minute. How many people can you say that about?"

"Honesty's one thing, Dick, but having tact and respect for another human being's point of view is another. Is it possible for this man to engage an opponent in a debate without stooping to insult them and referring to their beliefs as 'cow dung'?"

"What's worse, Vera: Quint telling you to your face that you're a hypocrite for scamming people or some ass-kissing friend telling you how wonderful you are when they really can't stand you? Also, keep in mind, Vera, I'm Godfather to Quint's son. I take that role seriously."

The handsome face of Phil Tracy appeared on the television screen again.

"Now I'd like to inform our viewers that we're about to conduct an exciting experiment in which both Sylvia Thorne and Quint Morely have agreed to participate. Here's the deal:

"Our program director, Steve Bloom, asked Quint Morley to come up with one question and its answer that has to do with a name from Quint's childhood. Earlier Quint did just that, wrote both the question and answer on a piece of paper, and placed it in this sealed envelope." Tracy held up the envelope for the camera to see. "No one opened this envelope after Quint Morely placed the question and answer into it. So only Quint knows the contents. Now we'll ask Sylvia Thorne the question Quint wrote. If Sylvia responds, we'll open the envelope and read the answer. Fair enough, everyone?"

"All right, Sylvia, let's put it to the test. Meditate, concentrate, or whatever it is you'd like to do. Quint, would you now tell us what the question is inside this envelope I'm holding?"

"Who was my eighth grade teacher?" Morely bellowed loud and clear.

"All right. Sylvia Thorne, tell us: *"Who was Quint Morely's eighth-grade teacher?"*

Morely said nothing, folded his hands on the table, and looked smug. Thorne brought her fingers to her forehead and closed her eyes. Her lips moved in a silent whisper, her right hand came up to the cross on her throat and felt its edges.

"Again, the question, Sylvia: *"Who was Quint Morely's eighth grade teacher?"*

"...What I'm getting," Thorne groped softly, "is...*Green*... No, I'll refine that to *Greenwhich*, or something very, very close to *Greenwhich*...A woman whose name was...*Mrs. Greenwhich*... Yes. My answer is *Mrs. Greenwhich*..."

"All right," Tracy said, "we shall now see. Folks, I'm going to open the envelope..."

Morley was grinning like a circus clown. Thorne looked comfortable, but appeared to be concentrating hard.

Tracy slit the top of the envelope with a letter opener, then removed a small piece of notepaper. "Folks, here is what Quint Morely wrote: "My eighth grade teacher was—*Mrs. Phyllis Greenwhich*...Sylvia, this is nothing short of remarkable!"

"Well, Quint," Tracy said turning to Morely, "I think you're now forced to admit that Sylvia Thorne has demonstrated a rather impressive use of psychic power."

"She proved nothing," Quint stated, brushing it aside. "What Ms. Thorne did here tonight is no different than what she has always done; and that is to engage in a complete ruse. Her performance is one-hundred percent bogus."

"*Bogus*?" Tracy repeated in disbelief. "Quint, did she not name your elementary school teacher correctly?"

"I certainly did give the question and the answer to your program director earlier and he certainly did put it into the envelope and sealed it. "However," Morely continued, removing a document from the folder on the table in front of him, "this is an official transcript from James Monroe Middle School in Youngstown, Ohio. It depicts my elementary school records sent to me just two days ago. Could we please get a good shot of this?" The camera focused on the document and zoomed in slowly. "As everyone can plainly see, my eighth grade teacher was *Harriet Glimmer*, not anyone named *Greenwhich*. I never knew anyone named *Greenwhich* in my life. It's a name I made up and wrote down for your program director."

Tracy was stunned. Thorne looked as if she had been stripped from the waist up.

"Just a minute," Thorne broke in out of breath, her cheeks puffing, "I was asked to reveal the contents of the envelope and I did just that!"

"Afraid there's a bit more than meets the eye here, Phil," Morely continued. "Unfortunately, your program director, Steve Bloom, has, in my opinion, committed a serious breach of professional broadcast ethics. At some point after I wrote the answer, Mr. Bloom showed it to Sylvia Thorne. In my opinion, I think Mr. Bloom should be fired for a shameless attempt to boost your show's ratings! Don't you think he should be fired, Phil?"

Tracy looked as if he'd been whacked in the face. "Ah, well," he groped looking around for support, "listen Folks, I assure you I had nothing to do with—Steve, did you know about any of this?"

"And it's all true, isn't it, Sylvia?" Morley asked, glaring at Thorne as if she were Mata Hari.

Inaudible words were uttered off camera as Tracy struggled

for control. "Folks, we'll be right back after this break while our staff sorts this out..."

"My God!" Newsom observed, jumping off the couch in his living room. "This is a first even for Quint!"

"Did we just see the Phil Tracy Show or are we watching the Quint Morley Hour?" asked Vera. "This guy, your friend in the foxhole, is one piece of work. Whether Thorne's psychic or not, I still say Morely's a blowhard."

"Even after he shows Thorne to be a fraud? Vera, this woman has preyed off bereaved people like the mother of Kathleen Garfield—you still say he's a 'blowhard'?"

"Yes, Dick. I do. The man's a meat grinder. He goes to war with anybody who disagrees with him. He gives me the creeps."

"Vera, no question he's unsavory; I won't argue that. But isn't Quint performing a service? How many naive people have been taken in by this woman? How many who might have paid her good money will now think twice about it? I say, 'kudos to Quint!'"

Phil Tracy's somewhat composed, but somber face reappeared on the screen.

"Folks, let me give you this fast breaking story: *Sylvia Thorne just stormed out of the studio!*" Tracy's laughter lay somewhere between incredulity and shame. "That's right: Sylvia Thorne is gone with the wind, flew the coop, made tracks! Quint, what's your reaction to what's taken place here?"

Morely's immense form came forward against the roundtable, his bushy eyebrows nearly joined in one long line across his forehead. "Sylvia Thorne's behavior speaks for itself, Phil. But I didn't come here tonight to show Sylvia Thorne for the fraud she is and merely lift the lid off her crooked racket. I came here to dramatize the dirty rot in all psychic jingoism. Psychics are scam artists, con men who use God, the Bible, and most of all predictable generalities in people's lives that, along with two bits, couldn't buy a local phone call. But I'm a reasonable man; I keep an open mind. Therefore, I am going to issue the following challenge to all psychics everywhere right here and now on the Phil Tracy Show..."

The camera zoomed in on Morely. His huge face and head filled the screen.

"If you people out there are truly psychic, gain public credibility by assisting the police; help them find missing children; work with scientists desperate for a cure for diseases like MS and Alzheimer's. Or, if you prefer, call your local church and tell them what the winning Power Ball numbers will be tomorrow so they can make millions and pay their debts. But for God's sake, stop preying upon the elderly and grief stricken parents, widows, and widowers to whom you give nothing but cruel and useless false hope! Stop using God as the 'force' behind your empty powers. I challenge astrologers, Tarot card readers, palmists, spiritualists, and psychics everywhere to step up to the plate and prove me wrong. But just one asterisk: if you do step forward, you'd better have specifics for all your prophecies. Or better yet, why don't you freeloaders go out and just get a real job?"

It was painfully obvious Tracy wanted the segment to end. "Well, quite a finale here tonight, Folks! I'm sure we haven't heard the last of this and I assure you we'll be tracking further developments...Next up: Orville Peckham will tell us what it's like to be taken aboard a UFO and given a medical examination by aliens maintaining a base under Mongolia."

Newsom punched the air with his fist. "What a bombshell! Talk about the hen flying straight into the fox's den! Quint wasn't kidding when he said he'd send Thorne back to Palookaville. You'll have to admit he did exactly that, Vera."

Newsome's wife wasn't convinced. She sat with her arms folded. "I still think Quint Morley is the king of gasbags," she observed.

II

Newsom sat at his desk in his office at Trademark Life Insurance shortly before noon on Monday morning. He smiled over the touching birthday card from his godson and read the lines detailing Stephen's excitement over a new career as a paralegal in New York City. When his land line rang, he knew it had to be Morely.

"What do you think of Sylvia Thorne now, Dick? Ha!"

Newsom held the phone six inches from his head to prevent damage to his eardrum.

"Quint, let me just say—"

"Didn't I tell you I'd have that Cyclops running for the exit?" he bellowed. "Whoever dreamed that dame could run so fast! I don't think anybody's sure if Thorne opened the door on her way out or went straight through it!"

"She looked awful, Quint. I'll bet she's having a few drinks in Palookaville right now."

"Did you read where they fired the program director?"

"No kidding?"

"I met with management after the show. You should have seen Tracy at that conclave, Dick. He was livid. And Bloom sat there like the guy who just swallowed Porky Pig. Ha! Dick, I'm buried in requests for guest appearances on talk shows from here to Cucamonga! Dick—I'm scalding hot!"

Newsom stared at the colorful birthday card in his hands. The irony of Quint's words going off in his ears at the same moment he held an affectionate remembrance from Stephen, his godson, wasn't lost on him.

"Oh, hey, Dick—Happy Birthday! Have I ever forgotten September 10? Have I?"

"No, you haven't," Newsom laughed lightly. "I've always appreciated you remembering, Quint."

"Dinner on me at Alfred's. Sky's the limit. But not tonight, though; Gonna' do the Ted Marks show."

"Well, I'll try to listen, but I'm working here till about four, then I'm driving up to Sandusky to meet Vera who's swinging over from her sister's in Cleveland. We'll play some golf and lounge around a few days."

"Sounds like a plan. Dick, wasn't she pitiful? Didn't Thorne come off as Broomhilda?"

"Tell me, Quint, how in the world did you know the program director had shown Thorne the answer?"

"*Ha! Ha!* It's an old trick. I sure did write the question and answer down, put it into a plain white envelope, licked it, sealed it, and handed it to the program director. But what that imbecile Bloom didn't see was that I also put a little dot in the bottom right corner of the envelope. When Tracy held that envelope up before the live cameras, the envelope was sans the dot. That told me the envelope had been opened, the answer shown to Thorne, and my slip of paper inserted into a second duplicate envelope. But I have to confess: I didn't know it was Bloom who showed the answer to Thorne; it could have been anybody. But really, what's the difference?"

"Always one step ahead of everybody, right, Quint?"

"I have to be when I face these frauds, Dick. Count on that dinner soon, though. Gotta' run. Supposed to get a call from the producer of the Marks Show to confirm. I'll be in touch. Happy Birthday, Buddy, and try to listen to the show tonight if you get a chance."

Newsom stared again at Stephen's birthday card. He never believed for a minute that Quint Morely was truly the bulldozer he wanted everyone to think he was. Behind the sound and the fury, Newsom knew, Quint suffered great pain at his estrangement from his son. But he also knew that living with Quint was like living with a seething volcano. He re-read his godson's touching letter describing his new career at the law firm of Lansworth and Grebb in Manhattan:

"Uncle Dick, the opportunity's incredible and I do value it more than anybody knows. I'm not going to blow this, Uncle Dick. Plus, the view from the World Trade Center is spectacular. I think Mr. Landsworth is impressed. He asked me to go to lunch next week. BTW: I just bought a new Armani suit!"

Quint Morely may be the most celebrated cynic in America, he may send an army of Sylvia Thorne's to Palookaville, he may sell

10 million books, but he'll never know peace in his heart until he establishes a relationship with his son. Newsom resolved that when he got back from Sandusky, he would try again to bring Quint and Stephen together.

Newsom left Cincinnati a little after 4:30 p.m. With golf clubs in the trunk, a zippered travel bag and that morning's Cincinnati Post lying on the seat next to him, he glided lazily along Interstate 75 north to Sandusky. Neither his birthday nor the prospect of a few days R&R dimmed Morely's voice in his ears. What a contrast, he thought, between Morely's scathing bluster and Stephen's warm sincerity. It's almost as if Stephen is not Quint's son at all: he looks like Quint, has Quint's affectations, but lacks any innate desire whatsoever to grind his antagonists into a pulp.

A few miles from North Baltimore, Newsom swung off the highway for lunch. A little ice cream freezer stood adjacent to a pond of ducks and geese that drifted serenely over its surface like colorful, wooden decoys. He brought a sandwich and a cup of coffee back to his car, then listened to his cell phone alarm go off in his shirt pocket. Newsom grimaced. He had left the phone's charger in the top left desk drawer in his office.

Out of the corner of his eye, a pleasant, yet strange golden halo resonated. A book, one he never placed in the car at all, sat in plain view on the passenger seat next to him.

THE BOOK OF TIME

Baffled, Newsom lifted the book off the seat. He turned to the first page and read the black, embossed headline and the grim passages that followed:

Terrorist Attacks On America
September 11, 2001AD

At 8:46 a.m. on September 11, 2001AD the first of four commandeered commercial airliners struck the north tower,

93rd—99th floors, of the World Trade Center in New York City executing an Islamic Terrorist Attack upon the United States of America...

At 9:02 a.m. a second commandeered airliner struck the south tower, 77th—85th floors, of the World Trade Center in New York City...

How did this thing get into my car? Flashing through the first dozen pages, Newsom re-traced his movements since leaving Cincinnati: tossing his golf clubs into the trunk, throwing the overnight bag and newspaper on the front passenger seat, and locking the side door. I drove straight out on 75 and didn't stop until I pulled into the freezer. I would have seen anyone slipping this book inside the car when I bought a sandwich. And I saw nobody.

At 9:37 a.m. the third commandeered airliner struck the first floor, west wall of the headquarters of the United States Department of Defense complex in Arlington, Virginia, United States of America...

At 10:06 a.m. a fourth commandeered airliner crashed in an unpopulated area 80.6 miles southeast of Pittsburgh, Pennsylvania, United States of America...

These events take place on September 11. That's tomorrow, Newsom knew. He flipped back to the front of the book, but couldn't find the name of a writer or publisher. The absence of page numbers also struck him as very odd. After failing to find the source of the golden halo, he read more passages:

...At 9:59 a.m. the south tower of the World Trade Center collapsed...

...At 10:28 the north tower of the World Trade Center collapsed...

...The terrorist attacks were directed by Saudi Arabian Osama Bin Laden, leader of the political revolutionary organization Al-Qa'ida, an Islamic radical sect whose objective was global war against its western enemies...

...Casualties totaled 2,977 deaths including 2,606 deaths in the

World Trade Center and surrounding areas, 265 on four airliners, and 125 at the Defense Department headquarters in Arlington, Virginia once known as the Pentagon...

Struck? Crashed? Casualties totaled? The whole thing's written as if these events have actually taken place.

The Book of Time? Newsom's fingers ran over the cover's pristine, black letters. The print was smooth, yet firm to the touch; the inner pages were composed in the same way—small, black print raised on very unusual gold paper. Dumbfounded, he read the unpronounceable names of 19 Islamic terrorists involved in the hijacking of four American planes. Great detail framed the accounts of one American defense mishap after another as the hijacked planes got through the cracks in American security and reached their targets. He read how the President, the Vice-President, and cabinet members were rushed into secret command centers in Washington, D.C. Separate pages listed the names of nearly three-thousand victims who perished in the catastrophe. At a loss, he shot ahead to the book's final, chilling lines:

George W. Bush, 43rd President of the United States of America, responded to the attacks of September 11, 2001AD by launching a Global War on Terror composed of a multi-national force led by the United States of America, the United Kingdom, Australia, Spain and Poland, all conducting military operations in the countries of Iraq and Afghanistan commencing on March 20, 2003AD.

A sense of dread pulsed through Newsom. He examined the book's paper carefully. Folding the first page in half vertically, he watched it flip back without a crease. He tried bending the paper a second time. That, too, shot back into place. Newsom quickly unzipped his overnight bag and, taking a pair of scissors, tried cutting lengthwise across the top of the cover. The metal blades snapped and broke. Newsom was stunned. *Whoever put this on the front seat of my—*

Stephen!

The car door flew open. The birthday card his godson sent

him referred to the "spectacular view from his floor" in the World Trade Center! The gruesome image of Stephen working in one of the trade center towers as a plane crashed into it made Newsom nauseous. But that, he thought, assumes the attacks described here correctly predict the catastrophe, he reminded himself. And that just isn't possible. Some warped novelist dreamed up this terrorist attack story in New York to create a sick work of fiction. But then—what kind of book has a glow with no apparent source? Or paper that can't be cut?

He rushed around to the trunk of his car and removed the crow bar under the spare tire. Placing the book on the cement, he rammed the slanted point of the bar straight into the cover. He thrust the bar into the book a second and third time. Stunned, Newsom stepped back and glared at *The Book of Time* lying undisturbed on the cement in a halo of gold.

Scrambling to grab his cell phone on the dashboard, Newsom froze. Hell! It needs re-charging, he remembered. Newsom jumped to the wheel, circled around the freezer, and sped off on 75 north again. The only rational explanation for this is that someone placed this book on the passenger seat before I ever left Cincinnati. But why didn't I notice it on the seat when I first got into the car?

A red light flashed in his rear view mirror. Good! I want a cop!

Newsom pulled to the shoulder and tried to calm himself. Heavy footsteps crackled along gravel behind him. The officer leaned into the window. "May I see your license? Did you know you were doing close to 90?"

"Officer, give me a ticket, I really don't care," Newsom said breathlessly, "I have a dire emergency on my hands and need to get to a convenience store. Do you know the nearerst one?"

"Please wait here a moment."

The reflection of an Ohio sunset glared off the rear window as the officer walked back to his patrol car. The dashboard clock said 5:42 p.m. Newsom picked up *The Book of Time* and again read the lines describing the account of the first plane striking the World Trade Center at 8:46 a.m. That's Eastern Time, he knew, less than 24 hours. He pictured a metropolitan holocaust occurring tomorrow in New York City. The discussion with Morely about psychic power came back to him. He imagined the nasty adjectives Quint would use to describe *The Book of Time.* Utterly cockamamie! Morely would howl.

The officer leaned in to Newsom's window and handed him his license. "Mr. Newsom, proceed straight ahead on 75 north exactly 2.8 miles. Take the right turnoff at exactly that point. Another 243 feet and you'll come to a service station and mini-mart. They carry cell phone re-chargers there."

"That's very precise, officer. Thank you…"

A bizarre moment passed in which the two men locked eyes. Newsom knew the officer had detected his agitation.

"It would be a lot safer for you if you obey the speed limit."

"I will. Having a very stressful day is no excuse, I guess."

The officer nodded sympathetically. That was when Newsom noticed the man did not carry a firearm, but a plain belt sans bullets. Nor did he have a baton, handcuffs, or even a badge.

"Well," the officer stated, "The convenience store is just up ahead, Dick."

"How—how did you know my name?"

"It's on your license. Think of me as a helper."

"Oh sure. Sure. A helper. Thank you."

The odd stare in the man's dark, glossy eyes went straight through to Newsom's bones.

"And Happy Birthday."

"How did you—"

"Your birth date's on your license." The officer tipped his cap. Footsteps crackled along the gravel again as the man turned and walked back to his car.

Frozen at the wheel, Newsom watched the officer's vehicle drift passed. He blinked: the county or city seal or emblem on the passenger door was a scrambled mass of letters that was little more than a watery blotch. He rubbed his eyes: the patrol car's license plate was blank.

Pulling back onto Interstate 75, Newsom drove no more than a quarter of a mile when the realization exploded: *I didn't tell that man my cell phone needed re-charging!* His eyes scoured the highway ahead in all lanes. The patrol car was nowhere in sight. Newsom then glanced down at the passenger seat and a second horror seized him. *The Book of Time* was gone.

The car fish-tailed wildly to the shoulder again, tires spit gravel, brakes screamed. In the dust cloud swallowing his car, Newsom rifled through his overnight bag and tore the pages of the Cincinnati Post apart. He jumped out and raced around to the passenger side, threw the door open, searched frantically over the front and back seats, then shook the floor mats. Perspiring against the side of the car, Newsom wondered if he were having a stroke. He felt himself for numbness, then recited the alphabet backwards to test his speech and mental faculties. Would my mind be this lucid if I suffered a hemorrhage?

No one placed that book on the passenger seat next to me, yet it appeared there. I read about the terrorist attacks occurring tomorrow, September 11, in New York City in plain English. Then the book was gone. And a policeman without a badge or gun somehow knew my cell phone needed re-charging. *Another 243 feet and you'll come to a convenience store*? I have to be losing my mind.

The service station mini-mart was precisely where the officer said it would be. Newsom roared in and raced passed the clerk at the island gas pump who was helping an elderly woman fill her tank. He found a phone charger inside the mart, tore the plastic package apart furiously, and, with shaking hands, connected the charger to his cell and plugged it into a wall socket. Then he tried to calm himself by placing a cup of tea into a microwave. As he watched the liquid circle on the plastic dish, Newsom was hit by a cannon ball: the Decker book!

Ruth Decker, who wrote *26,280 Hours*, claimed her parents found a book in 1963 predicting John F. Kennedy's assassination— that book was also titled *The Book of Time*! It, too, disappeared soon after it was discovered. The author stated that her father, John Decker, had encountered strange people when he traveled to Dallas to warn of the President's killing. And I just met a strange man who knew my cell needed re-charging, though I never said a word about the battery being dead. When Newsom's phone gained full power, he snatched it, threw money down on the counter, and bolted for his car.

He ran through every detail he could remember about John Decker's 1963 odyssey. The man left Iowa and met his future wife in a hospital when his flight diverted to Kansas. According to his daughter, Ruth Decker, she would have never been born had Decker not boarded a plane to Dallas. Morely's words about psychic prediction echoed back: *Predicting the future would mean it already exists. If that's true, then it negates free will.* Was Quint dead wrong about free will? And was that not the only thing he was wrong about? No man is infallible, Newsom reflected. Not even Quint. Maybe my problem has been that I viewed Quint Morely as an intellectual demigod.

The Ohio landscape was invisible. Newsom's fingers gripped the steering wheel tightly. Sweat trickled down the sides of his face. He added the elements up in sane, chronological order: Morely's harangue on psychic prediction. Finding the Ruth Dekcer book recounting how *The Book of Time* appeared to her parents. Discovering the book himself which described a terrorist attack in amazingly precise detail. Meeting a very strange policeman with no gun, badge, or license plate numbers who read his mind. Finally, the book disappearing on the passenger seat.

Newsom wiped the sides of his face with a handkerchief. He couldn't deny it: his experiences paralleled those of John Decker. Even if finding a book describing a national tragedy in less than 24 hours were the only similarity between Decker and me—that would be enough. But there's that strange policeman who said—*he was a helper*!

Another lightning bolt struck Newsom. His car swerved as if it hit an oil slick. It skidded to the side of the road, jerked to a stop, died. A helper? *A helper for what?* To help me get to a convenience store to re-charge my cell so I could call Bev and then call Morely so I could call Sharon and ultimately call Stephen? Sensing a growing disconnection from reality, Newsom remembered how Ruth Decker wrote that the book appeared to her father, John Decker, for what he ultimately believed was a purpose. *Did that book also appear to me for a purpose?*

Where is the logic and reason in a book that tells of future events? Suddenly, the words of the finest teacher Newsom ever had, Professor Wilson, a geometry instructor at the University of Cincinnati, rushed back to him. One afternoon Wilson had been discussing the forumula for finding the hypotenuse of a right triangle. Newsom didn't remember how the professor got on to it, but he began to compare the hypotenuse, the longest leg of the triangle, to Einstein's space-time. The teacher then began digressing about time itself. He said something to the effect that time had a fluid quality like that of a running creek: sometimes it streams by fast; sometimes it's stagnant; sometimes it swirls around in little eddies. Was time an eddy? Wilson asked his mesmerized students. Are we all in one grand eddy with present, past, and future swirling about us?

Newsom's fist pounded the steering wheel in frustration. At worst, what could happen if I accepted what *The Book of Time* says will take place tomorrow? I'd be warning my godson to stay out of Manhattan for no reason. If it comes to that, I'll gladly live with the ridicule of being the boy who cried wolf. A small price to pay for a cleansed conscience.

In one pulsating moment of surreal deduction, Newsom convinced himself that the most fatal decision of his life could be denying the events described in *The Book of Time* and failing to warn Stephen. However irrational it may seem, I have to accept the book's truth that disaster will occur tomorrow in New York. The alternative is unthinkable.

Driving to Sandusky was now out of the question. Sweating in panic-stricken time, Newsom turned around and headed south back to Cincinnati. For this kind of time was detached from the time in which he existed two hours ago; that was common time adorned with carefree, thoughtless movement. This kind of time was alien time. This was palpitating, conscious time where precious minutes tick by like huge cinder blocks hammering down one after another in front of your obsessive purpose. The clock was the enemy in this kind of time. The clock cut into your psyche while it fought hard to destroy you and draw closer with every breath always reminding you that passing minutes were now little timebombs.

Interstate 75 seemed to stretch into infinity. Newsom realized that reaching his godson was now the most important thing in the world. He veered off into a rest stop, killed the engine, and got out to breathe fresh air. When he felt a bit more composed, he called Bev at her sister's in Cleveland.

"Bev—my old friend Walt Freeman passed away," he lied.

"Oh, God. Dick, I'm so sorry. What happened?"

"Boating accident. I think it'd be good if I was there for Carolyn. I've already spoken to her. I'm turning south right now and heading back to Cincinnati."

It was now passed seven in New York and even if he did reach Stephen's law firm, an after-hours office voicemail was sure to go off. He needed to call his godson directly which meant reaching Sharon first. And access to Sharon meant going through Morely. His stomach turned inside-out just thinking about calling the man now. A confrontational tone would have to be used. Newsom took another long, deep breath, then speed-dialed Morely.

"Quint, listen carefully: I need to get in touch with Sharon in New York. Could you give me all the contact numbers you have for her?"

"What in hell for?"

"Quint, just give me Sharon's numbers. And—I want you to be at my office in two hours."

"Excuse me. *Be at your office*?!" Morely repeated in disbelief. "Dick, I told you: I'm Doing the Ted Marks radio show tonight. And it's a big one. I'm dueling that Collin Fenster clown who claims he's established communication with his dead mother. I can't cancel my appearance now, Dick."

"You can and you will, Quint. Cancel the show!" Newsom demanded. "And give me the numbers you have for Sharon!"

"*Cancel?* Dick, there's something in your voice I don't like. Are you in Sandusky?"

"No, I was on my way there, but I turned and I'm heading back to Cincinnati."

"What in hell for? Dick, are you in trouble?"

"Sharon's numbers, please, Quint…"

Morely gave Newsom Sharon's cell number. "Dick, I need more than a Humpty-Dumpty riddle here. What in hell's going on?"

"Trust me for just a few more hours, will you? When I see you back at my office, I'll explain everything."

"*Trust you?* This sounds ominous. I don't like this, Dick."

Newsom had had enough of Morley's blather. "Quint, for once in your life, shut your goddamn trap and listen! Think you're capable of one simple act of compassionate understanding?"

"Jesus, Dick, you never talked to me like this—ever. But you're telling me plenty. You *are* in trouble."

"Yes, I'm in trouble. It's urgent. Be at my office in two hours, Quint," Newsom demanded, trying to end it. "Just be there."

Newsom clicked off, then punched in Sharon's number and listened to her voicemail. "Sharon, this is Dick Newsom in Cincinnati. It's urgent. Please call me when you get this message. My cell number is…."

Still piecing together just what he'd say to his godson, Newsom knew that his warning could never include a shred of ambiguity; he had to make it crystal clear to Stephen that he was to be nowhere near Manhattan tomorrow. When his cell went off, he prayed it was Sharon, but it was Morely again.

"Dick, I don't know what the hell's going on with you, but I've got a show to do tonight and it's a powerhouse. Furthermore, I don't like you putting the screws to me, Pal! I've crammed good research into this program and I plan on sending this guy Fenster into orbit.

To cancel now would look like I'm caving to this blockhead. But if I did cancel, it had better be for one damn good, urgent reason."

"Quint," Newsome said in a cold, harsh tone he had never used to Morely, "*you bet your ass it's for one damned urgent reason. My office, two hours. I won't say it twice.*" The cell phone snapped shut. Newsom pulled an anti-acid table from the overnight bag on the front seat. As soon as he swallowed it, his cell went off again.

"Hello, Dick! How the hell are you?"

"Hello, Sharon," Newsom laughed weakly. "I'm trying to reach Stephen. I have no numbers for him. He sent me a card and I'd like to catch up with my godson. Hey, how are you?" he asked blankly, grabbing paper and pen from the glove box.

"Life is good. We haven't talked since I moved to Albany, have we?"

"No. So you're in Albany then, not Manhattan?"

"Yes. I moved to Albany right after Christmas."

"Sharon, do you have any idea if Stephen would be at work right now?"

"Oh, no. He goes to his buddy's in Queens every Monday night to watch the football game."

"Sharon, about what time does Steve usually get into work in the morning?"

"I imagine around eight or nine. Anyway, here's his cell..."

Newsom's shaking hand scribbled the number on the front page of the Cincinnati Post. "Sharon, I'm sorry, but I've got a call coming in from Bev and her sister is ill. Lemme' call you again soon when we can talk. Listen: if you talk to Stephen before I do, would you tell him to call me right away? It's very, very important I speak with him, Sharon. Really. Promise to reach you later..."

The dashboard clock said 6:42. Newsom thought hard about his next call. Pressing the buttons for Stephen's cell carefully, he closed his eyes, his godson's voicemail went off, and he spoke the words distinctly:

"Stephen, this is your Uncle Dick. I want you to call me the moment you get this. *Please.* It's serious. It's urgent." Newsom left his number, closed his cell, and prayed.

He was back on 75 again streaming south. Newsom's disconnection from reality was palpable. The highway's broken white lines flashed under him like other-worldly bullets. Morely's diatribe returned: *Psychic prognostication is mumbo-jumbo…It's not part of the rational universe.* But what in God's name was the rational universe? What could possibly be rational about describing events before they occur? Days slip by hour after hour like legs stepping over sidewalk cement one after another or breaths taking in air as we move through space never questioning the clouds above our heads or the blades of grass under our feet. We just do. We just act. We just live. Then, without a hint, something unworldly strikes us like a powerful spotlight in a pitch black corridor. The heart pumps fast. The legs go numb. The brain cries for reasons. We reach for sanity's handle, but logic is sand and we grab air. Standing naked, one is left with the realization that *something* momentous exists in a realm beyond our senses. Something imperceptible. Something that passes through a doorway to time.

The last leg of highway back to Cincinnati filled with unthinkable words and reasons Newsom never dreamed he'd ever utter. He now knew what he'd say to Stephen, but what about the calls after that he would make to authorities? Contact with the FBI would undoubtedly beg the ultimate question: "Sir, just how do you know this terrorism will take place tomorrow?" "Well, you see, I found a book predicting terrorist attacks in New York and Washington—just before the book disappeared from the front seat of my car." The absurdity of it was laughable. Newsom wished he still had *The Book of Time* in his hands so he could repeat precisely how the plane hijackers broke through security. Incontrovertible facts rule the investigative world, not ludicrous books predicting the future. Authorities will see me as a screwball no matter what I say. If Quint is the friend I hope he is, he has to help me through this. But convincing Quint Morely of what I read in *The Book of*

Time might prove to be tougher than convincing the FBI. Newsom grew weary just thinking about facing Morely.

When Newsom arrived at the Emory Building, Morely was there pacing like a caged lion. He looked angry and grim as the two men walked up to Newsom's office on the third floor.

"Quint," Newsom began as he sat down behind his desk, "what I'm about to tell you is going to challenge every skeptical fiber in your being."

Newsom took a long breath and recounted the inexplicable experience of finding *The Book of Time* predicting the attacks on the World Trade Center, the thousands destined to die, and the "War on Terror" and invasions of Iraq and Afghanistan in 2003. Morely listened to every word, but looked as if he had just swallowed rotten eggs. When Newsom described the book disappearing from the front seat of his car, Morely's face and neck turned red.

"And this is your idea of a 'damn good reason' Dick? I don't know what prescribed medication have fried your synopses or just what slammed into your head and gave you a hematoma, but I am absolutely stunned you had the balls to demand I be here—*to listen to this crap!*"

"Quint, it happened!" Newsom pleaded. "As incredible as it sounds, it happened!"

Morely got up with eyes that searched the ceiling for patience, then he spoke to Newsom as if it was all he could do to keep from throwing his friend through the office window.

"It's rot! Pure bullshit, Dick! Who paid you off—Sylvia Thorne?"

"*I said it happened!*"

"Oh, did it now?" Morely shot back. "Did you fly up 75 on fairy wings? Maybe you saw Isis or Heimdall or the Oracle at Delphi. Did you see them, Dick?

"You know, Dick, I can't help but recall that discussion at my place a week ago. I may not have shown it, but I was disturbed by your defense of the 'psychic sphere' which, at the time, I chalked up to the spirit of debate. But this mound of compost you're dumping on me now—and getting me to flush my radio gig tonight down the toilet—this is beyond the pale, Dick."

"Quint, I don't blame you for doubting what I've told you. And I'm aware it runs contrary to everything you believe, but on my mother's grave, I have told you everything I read in that book to the best of my recollection."

"You cost me tonight, Dick. You denied me a key appearance just to come here and hear this cow plucky. I would have sold a lot of books off that show, but what's far worse is that I'll now be seen as weak and caving to that horse's rear Fenstra. And that is more unpalatable to me than losing money."

"Is that what you're worried about, Quint? Appearing 'weak'? Do you realize the ramifications if I'm right? I don't pretend to have a rational explanation for what I experienced out there on 75, but I found that book in my car. I read it. It was as clear as my words right now about what will happen to the World Trade Center buildings. And, yes, the book was gone without a trace. I'll say it one last time, Quint: *That book appeared on the passenger seat of my car and described a terrorist attack tomorrow that will take almost 3,000 lives!*"

Morely shook his head as if he were profoundly disgusted with his old friend. "And I guess I need to repeat to you: the future is just that—events that haven't happened! Describing what will occur tomorrow or the day after tomorrow is an impossibility of nature. To accept that a book, without an author or publisher, of all things, could prophesy events in the kind of detail you've related is to get in bed with all the Sylvia Thornes of this world. And that sickens me beyond words."

"For one second, would you consider what it would mean, Quint, if that book described what will happen tomorrow?"

"Dick, if I were to accept even one percent of what you've shoveled here, I would, in effect, be rejecting every principle and cannon I ever stood for: 25 years of writing and research against the clown-frauds of this world. And that is just not going to happen,

Pal. If I didn't know better I'd swear this was some kind of test to prove Quint Morely is the 'King of Imbeciles.' Well, guess I flunked the test, Dick, because I officially pronounce your book and its prophecies one-hundred percent pig shit!"

"All right, let's suppose it is," Newsom said losing patience. "Let's assume I had a brain infarction out there on 75; let's say I hallucinated the whole thing. Why can't you wait till tomorrow morning before you say I've gone off the deep end? Will you at least do that, Quint?"

"There *is* no possibility you're right!" Morely countered angrily. "The whole thing's moronic! To assume any of this happened is to toss reason and scholarship into the sewer and accept a universe that spins on psychic prophecy. No, Dick, you hung me out to dry tonight. You denied me a key radio appearance and cut off my balls. And I resent it. It's a test, isn't it? Problem is, the test sucks stinking air and precious time that I could have spent knocking one more Sylvia Thorne clay pigeon out of the sky."

Newsom had reached the release point. After listening to Morely's long-winded annihilations of the world's plasticity, he erupted with what had lain dormant for years.

"That's what it's really about, isn't it, Quint? The superhero who has to gun down his clay pigeons so he can stand up and say: 'I'm St. George, dragon slayer, look at me?' Quint Morely, the protector for all us poor, dumb, unenlightened folks standing up against the world's con artists. Ah, but it's not about flashlighting the Sylvia Thorne's, is it? Because it was never really about spotlighting sham. Quint Morely's mission in life is *control*. And control is the name of the game for you, isn't it? And control means power. But what tears me apart, Quint, is the fact that your son Stephen works in the tower that book says will collapse tomorrow.Yet you'd rather remain faithful to your cynicism about an irrational universe than accept any possibility your son might die in a terrorist attack."

Newsom struck the primordial nerve. Morely's eyes narrowed in hard on his friend with a look of grave intensity.

"You just crossed a very big line there, Dick," Morely shot back acidly. "And as far as I'm concerned, you can't cross back over it. We've been friends a long time, but you can't unscramble eggs. Afraid this tears it between you and me, Dick."

"What a shame I can wait less than 24 hours to find out if I'm nuts, but you can't."

"I'll tell you what: I won't wait another 15 seconds to declare that Quint Morely wants nothing more to do with unhinged Dick Newsom."

"Then so be it," Newsom stated.

Morely turned his immense back on his old friend and stormed out of the office.

Completely spent, Newsom realized that even he had underestimated Morely's iron intransigence. He regretted asking Morely to meet him at his office. *Why didn't I just get Sharon's number and then call Stephen? I should have known Quint would never accept my incredible story. Quint Morely is the Rock of Gibraltar times 10 and even his son's mortality doesn't put a nick in the limestone.* Newsom slumped at his desk with his head in his hands. *Where did the The Book of Time come from and how did it get on the front seat of my car?*

Newsom's cell went off. He froze and glared at the phone lying face up on his desk as if it were a hand grenade.

"Hi, Uncle Dick! It's Stephen! My Mom said you were trying to reach me. Hey, we haven't talked in way too long."

"Stephen, where are you right now?"

"I'm at a friend's in Queens for the Giants game tonight."

"Steve, listen very carefully—more carefully than you've ever listened to anyone in your life.

"OK," he said, the excitement draining from his voice.

"Your law office is in the World Trade Center, right?"

"Yes. The north tower."

Newsom's mouth went dry.

"Steve, just hear me: *Do not, repeat do not go into work tomorrow at the World Trade Center...*"

"Huh? What's that, Uncle Dick?" he laughed.

"I want you to stay as far away from the World Trade Center as you can possibly get. Stay out of Manhattan altogether..."

"Hey, what's this all about, Uncle Dick?"

Newsom paused. He wanted his words to sink in, then he said, "Steve, there's going to be a very dangerous security problem in that building tomorrow morning."

"*Jesus! Are you kidding me?* How do you know this, Uncle Dick?"

"I wish to God I were kidding, Stephen. I am telling you—and again don't ask me how I know this—s*tay out of Manhattan entirely and miles from the World Trade Center....*"

"I don't believe I'm hearing this, Uncle Dick. This is totally bizarre."

"You bet it is. Let me repeat: *stay out of Manhattan. Don't go near it anytime tomorrow.*"

"Mind telling me how you—"

"I can't tell you! You have to accept what I'm saying! I can't tell you anymore than what I've said. Trust is the number one issue here. If you ever trusted me or had any respect for me whatsoever, trust me now. Is that clear, Stephen?"

"Uncle Dick, do you have secret ties to the government?"

His Godson had given him an unexpected opening. "Y-Yes," he lied, "I do. But that's as much as I'm able to say."

"Wow! This is unreal. I never heard you use this tone of voice before."

"Can you trust me, Stephen? Will you do what I am asking?"

"Yeah. I can. Guess I'll stay here tonight in Queens, I suppose."

Newsome exhaled. "Good. There can be no misunderstanding here. *Stay away from Manhattan tomorrow morning.* And I'm also going to ask something else of you: say nothing about this to your mother in Albany until after tomorrow. I want your word."

"All right. OK. Uncle Dick, is there going to be some kind of SWAT team action against organized crime or something like that?"

"You're on the right track, Stephen. Now don't ask me any more questions. Just stay clear of Manhattan, say nothing to your mother, and you'll have nothing to worry about."

"Agreed. I absolutely will. God, Uncle Dick, never knew you had ties to the government. You sure don't seem like the undercover type."

"Stephen, do you have any friends who also work at the World Trade Center?"

"Not really. As I told you in the birthday card, I'm new and don't know anyone yet. This is pretty scary. I guess I have to say—thank you for calling me and warning me. I hope you haven't jeopardized your position. You've blown my mind, Uncle Dick..."

"I understand completely. Stay with your friend in Queens. *Just stay there.*"

"All right. I will."

"Stephen. I have to get off now, but I want your word in stone you won't go near Manhattan. You'll be fine. I'll talk to you after tomorrow and by then things will be clear. Just do as I say, Stephen. I'll talk to you soon."

Newsom closed his watery, weary eyes and snapped his cell phone shut. A massive headache pounded the sides of his head, but he knew he now had to make calls from an untraceable phone. How, he asked himself, do I convince the FBI I'm not a psycho? And if the World Trade Center buildings in New York are disasters waiting to happen, can the catastrophe be prevented no matter how many authorities I contact? Didn't I just change a part of history by warning Stephen? Or was that in itself destined to be? He removed two aspirin tablets from his desk drawer, popped the pills into his mouth, and swallowed them with water.

The elevator doors parted and Newsom hurried out through the building's lobby where he nearly collided with a janitor mopping the tile floor. Suddenly, the room tilted crookedly: it was the police officer who had stopped him on Interstate 75. But the man was now dressed in a brown maintenance uniform. A name was sewn just above the shirt pocket, but it looked like it was encrypted. The two men locked eyes in the same strange way they did when the officer pulled him over.

"You're—the officer who stopped me," Newsom breathed.

The man leaned his mop against the wall. "Yes I am, Dick."

Newsom now knew. For a mighty truth was manifest in that simple admission. Whatever irrational events imbued the last several hours—they were at that moment finally and officially stamped real by this man appearing to him for a second time in the lobby of The Emory Building.

"Think of me as a helper. Dick, you need to know that if you went ahead and warned public officials, you would create devastating havoc to yourself and to your family."

Newsom sagged. "It's all going down in Manhattan tomorrow, isn't it?"

"Yes, it is, Dick. *One ripple in a pond leads to succeeding ripples.* You can't turn those ripples back to their origins and change or alter them. Physical laws exist for very specific and important reasons.

Newsom whispered, "Tell me: what is the meaning of that book appearing to me?"

"It's about *discovery*, Dick. What you've done with what you've had to work with is admirable."

"So—I'm shown a horrible, tragic picture of the future—but I can't do anything to stop it."

"No."

"Just tell me: Where did *The Book of Time* come from?"

Newsom watched the man gather his mop and bucket with a slow precision. "I'm sorry, but you're incapable of comprehending the answer to that. What you need to do now is to look ahead—to a future that will stand on the legs of what you've experienced today. *Discovery.*"

The man smiled, then walked straight out of the Emory building.

Newsom wanted to ask endless questions, but was caught helpless in the vice of the moment's paradox, unable to move, standing transfixed, he could only bask in the comfort and supreme satisfaction that came from warning Steven, his godson, in time.

Paralyzed, Newsom saw the man dissolve into the September dusk.

Arriving back at the house after 10, Newsom's exhausted frame collapsed on the living room couch. Poor Quint, he thought. Stubborn, bull-headed Quint. If events in New York prevail tomorrow, the king of cynics will take the plunge of a lifetime.

His heavy lids closed. Behind them the day's events rained down like a hundred volcanic fragments. Moments before dropping off to sleep, Newsom remembered that today was his birthday.

His eyes popped open at the scuffle of Bev coming through the front door. He didn't think he had the energy to describe the impossibile to her. But he tried.

The appalling network footage had flashed across the television screen for too many hours. Bev watched the live news reports from New York with anguished, red eyes. Newsom sat next to his wife transfixed in silent contemplation thinking about nearly 3,000 fatalities.

"Dick, that book—whatever it was, wherever it came from— led you to save Stephen's life." Bev broke down completely. "A miracle," she repeated through a burst of tears. "A mir—"

"I'm numb, Bev. Totally numb. Sorry I had to lie to you about Walt. Guess I didn't take much time to reason things through like I should have out there on 75. The pressure of time crushed me."

Bev dabbed her eyes with a tissue. "In my eyes, you're a hero, Dick."

"I'm no hero," Newsom stated. "I just did."

"Tell me, how in God's name will this country ever cope with this evil day?"

"The same way we coped with Pearl Harbor, the darkest days of World War II, and the Kennedy assassination," he answered.

"And all the other events in our history we thought would tear America apart."

Bev was still wipping her eyes when she crept into the dining room and quietly set down dishes for lunch. Unable to watch any more news reports, Newsom turned off the television. He had just taken a step toward the dining room when the front bell chimed.

It was Morely. Though the big man filled the entire doorway, he appeared shrunken and dazed.

"Dick, may I please come in?" he asked softly, his ashen face forming a haggard expression Newsom had never seen on the man's face before.

Bev stood frozen at the dining room table. Morely stepped inside the house. Newsom closed the door behind him.

A long silence passed, then Morley said:

"Do either of you know how hard it is to go from the Grand Inquisitor to the village idiot in less than 24 hours?"

"Quint, please, there's absolutely no need to—"

"Oh, yes, there is a great need to, Dick. And I hope you *both* listen," Morely added with an acknowledgement to Bev watching from the dining room. "It's taken me hours to drum up the guts to walk up your front steps and ring that bell."

Morely swallowed hard. "My father beat the living tar out of me from the time I was a child. Then one night when I was about 14, he came at me with a leather switch. But by then I was bigger than he was. I took him on with a piece of steel pipe and nearly killed him in front of my hysterical mother who never recovered from that experience. Do you know what he did for a living? He was a counselor for down-and-outers at a Protestant church. It led me to despise hypocrisy in all forms, brands, and degrees. Psychics, astrologers, and jingo artists of every stripe turned into Sylvia Thorne. Battle wounds leave very red scars, Dick. My psychological evolution after that isn't rocket science, is it? I'm sure you can both connect the dots."

"Dick, Sharon called me earlier today hysterical and bawling her eyes out. She told me you called Stephen in New York and convinced him to stay out of Manhattan. As for what you described happened to you on 75, I'm at a complete loss and won't even try to offer a syllable of an explanation. What I do know is that I owe you light years of apology. I'm ashamed of everything I said and ashamed for walking out on you last night.

"Dick, the bottom line here is that you proved that time is more incomprehensibly mysterious than I ever dreamed. Ten thousand Quint Morely's will never be able to debunk that truth.

"For the record, Dick, I always knew you were communicating with Stephen. Sharon told me years ago. Did I mind? Why should I? If Stephen had to have a surrogate father, I'm glad it was you. The plain truth is you're the man I never was."

Newsom waved him off. "Please don't say that, Quint."

"What happened to America today is an abomination. We still don't know how many thousands died, but thanks to Dick Newsom, one of them was not my son."

Morely's remorseful eyes filled up, then he added in a thick, throaty voice, "So here I am reduced to an imbecilic jackass with my hat in my hand; the prodigal son returned to say he wasted too much hot air abroad chasing gnomes when he should have stayed home caring for precious time. Guess there's nothing more to do than slay the fattened calf, right, Dick?"

"Quint," Bev interrupted walking into the room, "I won't lie; I disliked you for years because I thought you were a wrecking ball pulverizing good people. But I can only imagine what it took to walk up to our front door and make these admissions, though, to be honest, I still don't believe my ears. Quint, I think I speak for Dick when I say we're not only stunned you're here; we're in awe of your humility."

"There's no question Bev speaks for me, Quint," Newsom smiled.

"Thank you. Also, you need to know I spoke with my son just two hours ago for the first time in too many years. He's inconsolable. When Stephen gets a hold of himself, he's going to call you, Dick. Guess you've turned me into a believer, old Friend: positive transformation is born out of tragedy."

"Quint," Bev asked, "would you join us at our table? Will you sit down and pray with us for those who didn't make it today? And, God forbid, if there is going to be a war, for those who may not make it in the years to come?"

Morely wiped his eyes with the back of his hand. "I'd be honored to sit at your table if you'll have me, Bev."

The three of them stepped into the dining room quietly. Bev set a plate and silverware down in front of Morely. Newsom brought out a fine Merlot, filled Morely's wineglass, then raised his own glass in the air to toast the best friend he ever had. "Welcome home, Quint."

Bev lit three memorial candles around the table.

"Thank you, Dick. It's good to be home."

Collection Time

Hauling from your attic or basement absolutely free.
No packing or crating. Must have items in boxes.
Specializing in retired folks. 916-923-1140.

Haydin read the ad in that morning's Sacramento Bee several times and wondered if it could be worded more effectively. A dozen phone calls in four days and a dozen trips to the dumps had left him without one collectible item.

The 1960 Plymouth Savoy sailed to the curb of 189 Dexter Drive in Sacramento on four bald tires, a dented right fender, and small U-Haul trailer tagging behind like an orphan caboose. The run-down Victorian looked like a house that was ready to slide off its foundation, but Haydin loved it the moment he saw it. Pushing back the broken garden gate, he stepped along the cracked, weed-strewn stones that lead to the porch and noted dry rot everywhere on the building's facade. The screen door hung on one hinge and nearly fell off when he opened it to knock. This place is a pot of gold, Haydin said to himself.

"So the ad was legit?" the old man inquired. "A little too good to be true. Gotta' be a catch here." He was in his 80's, a bean pole sagging in industrial work clothes. His smile revealed an absence of upper teeth. A Dr. Grabow pipe stuck out from his mouth. Threads of white smoke puffed continuously from the pipe's bowl.

"It's 100 percent free, Sir. The catch is I don't pack, crate, or stack junk. Your items must be boxed or I won't haul anything."

"Well, everything's ready just like the ad stated in the paper. I'm Clem. Come on in. Let's get started."

The house's interior looked as if it had been trapped in a 1940's time warp. Dusty stuffed chairs filled the living room where newspapers were taped over the windows as curtains. A wooden dining room table on pencil-thin legs supported a phonograph with old 73 records stacked on its turntable. In the room's two corners, faded lamps looked as if they had been on President McKinley's coffee table. Yet the more Haydin saw, the more excited he became.

"The outside door's broken, so you'll have to come and go up the basement stairs through the kitchen."

The old man led Haydin to a long piece of string hanging from the ceiling over the basement door. Then he tugged on it and opened the door as the descending wooden stairs lit up below. Haydin followed the old man down the creaking planks.

"Sir, those old 73 records on that phonograph—would you be interested in selling them?"

The man stopped and turned around to Haydin and seemed mildly irritated. "If I did that, how would I be able to listen to Xavier Cougat?"

Haydin toured the basement quickly and surveyed the project before him. To anyone else, the sea of cardboard boxes and wooden crates stacked one on top of the other was a trash headache. To Haydin it was one, vast treasure chest. Waffle irons, silverware, garden tools, and books filled the boxes from wall to wall. In the basement's corner, an old Norge refrigerator stood alone covered with cobwebs.

"Wow, a Norge," Hayden observed. "I love old Norge's."

"You can have that icebox, too, if you want it. It doesn't refrigerate, though."

Haydin opened the door. The interior was crammed with a wooden console of sorting drawers, spiders, and dead moths. He pulled out one of the drawers and found scores of nails, screws, and nuts.

"You're gonna' have an aching back carrying these boxes up and down the stairs, Son."

"Not at all, Sir. I'm in better shape than Charles Atlas."

The old man laughed so hard he began coughing and wheezing and had to sit down on one of the boxes to regain his composure.

Haydin was a short, compactly-built, robust 17 year-old. He suffered from severe acne that his mother monitored with routine appointments to the dermatologist. A red, fiery crew cut flared across the top of his head; his face and jaw were full, his brown eyes permanently alert. Always in trademark white T-shirt, jeans, desert boots, and a thick set of keys that dangled from his belt, Hayden had a furniture mover's arms, shoulders, and thick, stocky ankles. Though he hated school, Haydin was innately intelligent and had no patience for studies that he thought would be of no benefit in later life; instead, he applied his efforts to a business or math course he knew would be useable in the 'real' world. But his greatest talent lay in his intuitive entrepreneurial business sense empowered by the belief that the future would one day be kind to things old. For Haydin's dreams were founded on the joy of finding pearls in the oysters of trash. *Today's trash, tomorrow's treasures* was the slogan he had decided upon for his future business card.

"I just have this little agreement, Sir." Hayden removed a paper he had folded in his back pocket. "This simply says you permit me to dump this clutter and will not hold me responsible if I happen to take anything of value contained here. In other words, when it's gone, it's gone, Sir."

"There's nothin' of value here, Son, or I wouldn't be lettin' you haul it outta' here." The old man took a pen from Haydin and placed the paper on his knee.

"And, Sir, if you could please write the date next to your signature."

The old man signed the agreement stating aloud as he wrote: "Clem Hutchison. And the date is June four, Nineteen-hundred-and-sixty eight."

Haydin took the paper, folded it, and shoved it into his back pocket.

"Mind if I ask what you get out of this free hauling, Son?

He was always prepared for the question. "A good friend of

mine gives me the tin, copper, iron melt-down value of the junk. Usually, I don't make much, but pennies add up, Sir."

"Well, here's a buck and a quarter for your dedication, son. I'll leave the front door open for ya'."

Clem left a strong trail of Bond Street tobacco in the unventilated basement air as he crept back up the stairs. Putting on his cheap garden work gloves, Haydin knew that 99 percent of the contents of the cardboard boxes before him were destined for the Sacramento trash heaps. Weeding out the other one percent, discovering the diamonds in the rough, that was the heart and soul of his efforts. That one percent, Haydin knew, could be converted to cash.

After loading a dozen boxes into the trailer, Haydin returned to the basement and flipped through a carton of worn out dictionaries, travel guides, and auto repair manuals. When it came to books, Haydin's rule was to leaf through the pages carefully. He knew people used books as hiding places for currency, often forgetting about the money or dying before they ever spent it. In his very first haul, Haydin discovered a ten-dollar bill stuck between the pages of a George Washington biography.

He skimmed through a few volumes, then lifted out an ancient Webster's Dictionary with a ragged, torn cover. Just before tossing it into the box, Haydin noticed an old baseball card pressed against the inside back cover. "Wagner, Pittsburgh" it read. The card was smaller and slimmer than common cards in wax packs sold in stores. Needs to be checked out, he told himself, slipping the card into his shirt pocket.

Loaded to the brim with boxes and cartons, the trailer was covered with a tarpaulin over its top and secured with ropes. As Haydin pulled away from Dexter Drive in the Plymouth, he totaled the day's fare that would not be dumped: two brass lamps, a set of china cups and saucers, a Daisy bee-bee gun in serviceable condition, an old Eliot Ness rotary telephone, and the Wagner baseball card.

Haydin's good friend Carlton, the Sacramento dumps'

manager, roamed the gravel roadway alongside the Plymouth as it rolled up to the dumps' entrance gate. The manager wore his usual flannel shirt, red hunting cap, soiled jeans, and military infantry boots. A Chesterfield cigarette hung from his chapped lips permanently and he smiled at Haydin through broken teeth. "Anything foul here, Haydin?" Carlton lifted the tarpaulin on the trailer and inspected the contents. Satisfied, he threw the cover back over the top.

"Everything's clean, Carlton. No leaking oil drums; no poisons; nothing flammable."

"OK, let's say 50 cents. Had quite a bit of excitement out here last night," Carlton stated. "A hysterical woman came in just before closin' and said her husband accidentally dumped her mother's weddin' rings and emerald necklaces. Worth thousands, she said, cryin' all over the whole lot. 'Parently, the gal hid the jewels in TV dinner trays inside the garage's busted washing machine. The husband, who knew nothin' 'bout it, paid a hauler to clean out the garage. 'Naturly, he tosses dem' treys into his truck, den dumps 'em here. The woman gets home, finds out, and has a nervus' breakdown. We spent mos' two hours after closin' sorting through piles o' rubbish. It was a miracle, but we did find that julry. Then that lady started bawlin' again and tips me twenty bucks."

"Exactly why I always have my customers sign a contract," Haydin stated. "It's scary to think of the valuables people throw out with their garbage."

"This actually ain't a dumps, ya' know. It's just the dirty end a' the rainbow," Carlton laughed. "Just appears ta' be a heap o' rubbish. I told you 'bout the bank teller who sifted off a little over $25,000 in cash over time, kept it in wooden barrels in his backyard tool shed. He put old engine parts on top 'o the dough to make it look like trash. Then his son guts the whole yard, tosses out 'dem barrels, dumps 'em here. The investigators caught the guy and he admitted what he'd been doin', but it was too late. 'Dose barrels were covered for weeks 'fur it was known. That twenty-five grand in cash is still residin' out here someplace," Carlton added, waving his arm from left to right.

Haydin looked at the near horizon. Just beyond the foreground where trucks, cars, and trailers were unloading rubbish, hills of lush, green grass encircled the Sacramento dumps.

"That grass you see, Haydin, is coverin' fill. Underneath lays buried treasure. Rules don't allow us to dig there or I'd be bringin' in a bulldozer plowin' it up yesterday. The rules regardin' what you dump are gonna' get strictur, Haydin. Pretty soon you'll be payin' $2 or $3 to come in here plus you'll hav' ta' gift wrap your garbage and tie it with a pretty little pink ribbon jus' to git thru the main gate."

"Anything for me today, Carlton?"

"Nope. Pretty slim pickin's last few days. But I know what ya' want. If I see any toys, comic books, sports cards, oddball collectabulls, I'll put 'em aside fur ya'. Oh, and hey," he added, reaching inside his flannel shirt pocket, "this might prove intrestin'. My wife's mother in Elk Grove needs her attic cleaned out. She's 'sposedly got some nice old radios. Here's her number. Meantime, I'll keep mah eyes peeled. If anybody can strike gold in this crap, it's Haydin Kravitz." Carlton's cackle could be heard from one end of the dumps to the other.

Haydin shoved the paper into his t-shirt pocket. "Appreciate it, Carlton."

The Plymouth and its caboose crackled over the uneven, dirt-clod roadway. When Haydin found a space, he backed the trailer in and, as he began tossing the boxes and crates into the trash heap, added up his expenses for the Sacramento collector's convention. He had just paid the $15 deposit for the display table, but that left him with a $20 balance, money he still needed to buy a new pair of pants and a dress shirt, spare cash to make change, and $5 to print business cards. He estimated the collectibles he had now might gross him about $60. But it wasn't enough; he needed more inventory.

Haydin stepped inside the front door of his home a little after

6 p.m. Mr. and Mrs. Kravitz sat grimly watching television and waiting for their son in the living room. Haydin knew what was about to be unloaded on him.

"Haydin, get in here," Mr. Kravitz ordered. "We got a call from your counselor at school today. You're grades equal a goddam low D average. Near an F. She also said you've been absent a lot lately. Is this true?"

"Don't worry, Dad. I'll bring my grades up. I'll pass."

"Haydin," Mrs. Kravitz said, "Mrs. Bumgartner said you were in danger of not graduating. Are you aware of the seriousness of that?"

"I said I'll pass, Mom. I'll be fine."

Mrs. Kravitz looked very concerned. "You simply can't flirt with not graduating, Haydin. Your high school diploma is everything. Nobody says you have to go to Harvard, but you must graduate and get your certificate."

Mr. Kravitz was more adamantine. "All this bologna collecting trash, hauling back and forth to the city dumps—it's the reason you're in this fix. Well, that's now ancient history. Beginning tonight, you'll hit the books like you was at Stanford. You will bring your grades up to at least a C. In the meantime, I'm clamping off on all these hauling expeditions. Is that crystal clear?"

Haydin couldn't believe his father demanded it. "I have three set appointments with customers this week, Dad. I've even got an ad running in the Bee."

"Then cancel the goddam thing!" Mr. Kravitz shouted. "Now I want to see you in your room."

"And," added Mrs. Kravitz, "don't forget you have an appointment right after school tomorrow with Dr. Dahl at 3:30 p.m. I can tell your acne's worse."

Mr. Kravitz threw back the door of Haydin's room and shook his head in complete disgust. "Look at this goddam place, Haydin. You can't even move in here. It looks like the Sacramento dumps. You're almost 18, graduating from high school, and you still collect comic books and children's toys? Your grades are a disgrace.

Forget attending a decent state college; you wrecked that chance a long time ago. What are you going to do with your life—spend it collecting rusty garden tools and Lone Ranger dolls?"

"Dad, what I've been thinking is that after I graduate, and I will, you might see your way to loan me a couple hundred bucks to open a collectible's store."

"What?! *Are you nuts?!* You're telling me you'd actually consider trash as a business? Haydin, I can't believe my own son spends good hours hauling garbage and taking it to the dumps. It makes me wonder if you're mentally ill. Get it out of your head: your life with trash is over, Boy!"

"I dump the trash, Dad. The rest may have value that can be turned into cash."

"*A baseball card has value*?! You're living in fantasyland, Haydin; all these comic books have warped your mind. And it scares your mother, too. If you think people are going to pay good, hard-earned money to buy a Superman comic book, then you're out of your goddam mind. And even if I was rich enough to loan you a hundred or a hundred-fifty to put into such a lunatic scheme, I wouldn't do it. It would teach you nothing but foolishness, plus it would mean you'd have to pay back money you'd never have because you'd never do any goddam business. You need to hunker down and find a good trade like I found when I started selling waffle irons. And you'd better find one goddam fast, Boy, because this ain't the Hilton Hotel you're livin' in. I've reached the release point. My friends ask me what my son plans on doing after high school and I evade the question because I'd have to say, 'Haydin plans on a career at the dumps picking through garbage looking for old Howdy Doody puppets.'"

"That's not fair, Dad."

"That's what you're doing, isn't it? Looking through rubbish to find toys and games—*and doing it free, for God's sake!*"

"I do it free to get more clients and more clients means more basements and attics that could possibly have valuables. Plus, my customers usually give me a tip that covers gas."

"Haydin, your obsession with junk isn't normal. I sometimes wonder if I should go back and investigate mental illness in the family history. The fact is, fascination with crap has taken over your life which is not a goddam healthy thing to have. The trash in this room belongs in the garbage can."

"Yesterday's trash, tomorrow's treasures, Dad."

"Don't get cute with me! Look at these pictures scotch-taped to your walls: monsters, and vampires. Over there, you've got Lucky Lager beer bottles and Davy Crockett air rifles, goddammit. And those stacks of baseball cards—they're for kids. Haydin, are you 17 or 10?"

"Dad, I don't use tacks on the posters because it puts holes in them and decreases the value. Secondly, it's my opinion that someday those baseball cards may one day get $1, maybe $2 a piece."

"I also notice you're starting to store more trash in the basement because you've obviously run out of room here. God, where's this leading?"

"I was hoping that in a year or two I'll have a store where I can make a living off collectibles. When I start making a profit, I'll hire a couple employees to go to the attics and basements and dumps while I mind the store and supervise the whole operation. Then dough will really roll in. If you help me, Dad, I'll promise you 10 percent on your investment."

Mr. Kravitz looked as if what he had just heard made him nauseous. "That has to be the most idiotic, cockamamie plan I ever heard, goddammit. Well, I'm hacking this pipe dream off at the neck. I'm nixing it now and for good."

"Why, Dad?"

"This is why!" Mr. Kravitz walked over to a shelf lined with colorful, metal Revolutionary War soldiers. "Eighteen-year-olds don't play with goddam army men, Haydin!"

"I don't play with them, Dad, I *collect* them. Old is good, Dad. And I happen to believe that a lot of this stuff is going to increase in value in a few years."

"Godammit, why can't you go to proms and play baseball or football and graduate with a nice average?"

"I'm not the prom type, Dad. I don't have dates because of my acne. Girls don't like me. I'm not good looking plus sports will get me nowhere 'cause I'm not athletic."

"This is it, Haydin. You're forbidden from collecting one more scrap of trash—until you make at least a C average in your courses. I told your counselor I'd be monitoring every step you take, so get it through your noggin' I'll know your grades and every period you cut school. Am I clear? Not one more hauling expedition to the city dumps 'till those grades come up to at least a goddam C!"

The bedroom door slammed hard behind Mr. Kravitz. The windows and shelves rattled causing some of his metal soldiers to fall to the floor.

Haydin looked around at his room dolefully. Movie posters covered every inch of the bedroom's wallpaper: "The Giant Squid," Time Menace," "Conquest of the Spider People," and "Dracula's Wives." Besides neatly stacked three-foot columns of comic books and teen magazines, there were shelves holding sports cards, Lionel trains, and record albums. One corner filled with Roy Rogers and Hopalong Cassidy lunch buckets. Rockets, airplanes, and plastic characters such as Woody Woodpecker, Mighty Mouse, and Donald Duck puppets hung from the ceiling on strings. Collectibles filled so much space that Haydin had to inch carefully through his room just to get to his bed and the desk next to it.

From somewhere beyond, the voice of Mr. Kravitz suddenly boomed through the hollows of the Kravitz house: *"Get to your homework, Haydin! And graduate, goddammit!"*

Haydin's eyes roamed over to his desk. The novel *Moby Dick*, the last book required in his English class, lay on its side serving as a launch pad for a foot-high plastic Saturn rocket. From the little he read of the sea story, the novel gave Haydin the chills. Why are kids forced to read so much junky fiction that has a whole chapter on a minister's sermon? Fiction doesn't connect to real life.

Who could possibly be interested in a story about a miserable sea captain who sets out to harpoon a whale just because it ate his leg?

The next afternoon, Haydin's English teacher, Mr. Lysurges, asked Haydin to stay after class.

"Right now you've got an F, Haydin," Lysurges stated flatly. "And if you don't start turning in your homework and improving your test scores, you'll fail and not graduate. Tomorrow is the final essay I've been talking about for weeks. My suggestion is to apply your efforts and write the best 200 words you ever wrote. Meanwhile, I hope you're planning on reading *Moby Dick* from cover to cover so you can pass the final exam on it with at least a C."

Lysurges rambled on about paragraph structure and phraseology, but Haydin didn't hear a word of it. His mind was fixed on making it to Corky's-U-Haul-It tomorrow after school, renting the trailer, and discovering just what Carlton's mother-in-law stored in her attic.

A sullen Haydin Kravitz sat in his English class the next day with two blank sheets of lined paper in front of him. Mr. Lysurges worked his way down the aisle passing out the test essay question. "Students, you have one full period to complete the essay. You may use only dictionaries and a number two pencil. You'll be graded on spelling, grammar, and organizational structure. There's absolutely no talking."

Haydin took the paper from Lysurges and read the question: *"Explain the most important thing in the world to you and describe its significance in your life."*

He did not have to think about the topic at all. Haydin simply took his pen and wrote the title at the top of the page: "Garbage, Trash, and Junk." Forty-seven minutes later, he finished the essay and began to proofread his writing:

Garbuge, Trash, And Junk
By Haydin Kravitz

My firmly held conviktion is that almost evrything you'll will ever need to know about homo sapeans is contained in their garbuge cans. Garbuge tells you what a person eats, the money he owes, whether he's a Cathlic or a communist, whether he plays Pinnocle or Old Maid, whether he hates his dog or beats up his mother-in-law. Show me a man's garbuge can and I'll show you a man's favorite deserts, bounced checks, and dirty sexuall fantasees.

Garbuge is the scummy Enciclopeedia Britaneeka of our lives because the secrets of a person's life are always squeezed in between torn nylon stockings and empty cans of Fresca. It doesn't take a NASA outer space scientist to know that a garbuge can loaded with Pepto Bismol bottles indicates the homeowner has a bit too much intestinul gas. Either does a person have to have a creedentul in sykology to know that a garbuge can filled with dead rats indicates the house needs a little comet cleansur. Last week I heard that big corperashuns now use "garbuge spies" to dig into the dumpsters of other big companies to find out what secret invenjuns they will be coming up with next. To me that's real smart and I would have no trouble filling out an aplikation to be a secret garbuge undercover agent any day.

Show me a garbuge can with magazines of naked women and I'll show you either a man without a girlfriend or a guy with a wife that looks like Joe Lewis. Show me a garbuge can loaded with cigarette cartons and I'll show you a man who coughs flem at 6 a.m. Show me a garbuge can with a lot of peanut brittle boxes and I'll show you a man with many denshurs. Ferthermoore, a garbuge can brimming with empty exullent wine bottles like Franzia leads you to conklude that whoever owns that garbuge would never be caught dead at a two-bit Italyun restaurant drinking karbonated Vino.

Garbuge cans, boxes of trash and junk have told me more about the owner of the house than if that person had taken a personality test at Napa State Hospital and sent me the answwur sheets. Because in between rotten lettuce and canselled cheks hides Xhibit A for a future murder, rape, and bank robbury. Lift up whiskey and gin bottles and you'll see broken promises to Alcoholiks Enonimous. Find torn-out Sears catalogue piktures of little girls in underwear, and you're saying hello to a weirdo who's probably lurking in the bushes underneath your front window as you now read this excullent paragraf.

To conclude, the significance of garbuge, trash, and junk in a person's life is one-hundred pursent factualistic. I know this because I collect trash as a business and trash is garbuge's illajetamate child. Personally, I've seen garbuge and paper documents proving the owner of the house hated his own mother. I've seen boxes of craked records by Xavur Coogat. What did that tell me? It told me that the ocupant hated Elvis Prezlee. In other words, all of the clues of human behavyur, the meat and patatoes of life, you might say, is simply waiting for you in a person's garbuge can. But you better get over to their can quick because that garbuge is headed for the Sacramento Dumps where once it arrives only Carlton, the dumps' manager, will have the pleasure of properly analysing it for its valu.

In conklusion, garbuge tells us more about a person's life than all the doctor's reports, psykologist's hypnotics, and school distric tests rolled up into one and tied with a pretty junior prom corsaje. A person's past, present, and even future resides 100pursent in garbuge. Garbuge is the punkuation mark in the essay of human remains.

And so I grandly conclude finully, beyond the shadow of a doubt as they say on Perry Mason, that all this is the significunce of garbuge. Long live garbuge!

The End
Haydin Kravitz, Senyor

Five minutes after the dismissal bell, Haydin flew out of the school parking lot bolting straight for Corkey's-U-Haul-It. He ignored his appointment with Dr. Dahl because another visit to the dermatologist was completely meaningless. What's Dahl going to do, give me another prescription for a cream and lecture me about "sebashus glands" and avoiding French fries while Mom sits there in her overcoat crying?

When Haydin pulled into the gravel lot, Corkey looked surprised to see him.

"Haydin, your father called this morning. He asked me not to rent you any trailers."

"*What*?! Since when do you take orders from him? This is a free, capitalist country. Corkey, don't you want to make a profit?"

"He says you're truant from school and if I were to rent you a trailer I'd be part of whatever the problem is and he'd name me in a police report. I don't want problems, Haydin."

"I'm not truant!" Kravitz shouted. "I just came from school!"

"Sorry, Haydin. I can't let you have a trailer until your Dad clears it."

"Fine. It's really sad you turned out to be a communist, Corkey. From now on I'm taking my business over to Mac at 100-Percent-You-Rents."

Haydin stormed out and headed straight for 100 Percent hating his father for calling Corkey. You just declared war, Dad, he shouted aloud gripping the steering wheel tightly as he swung the Plymouth into the rental yard. And you're gonna' lose every battle when I start rakin' in big dough.

As soon as Haydin walked into the office, a woman behind the desk at the trailer rental removed a message pad. "Is your name Haydin Kravitz?" she asked. "A Mr. Leon Kravitz called here and said the police are looking for you."

"Nobody's looking for me!" Haydin shouted. "Just rent me a trailer, will you please do that, Mam?"

"Not if the police are looking for you. We don't cotton to that sort of thing here...."

Twenty minutes later Haydin pulled into Always Rents. The two brothers who ran the yard said his father had called there, too. Haydin exploded again and the Plymouth's tires burned rubber bolting out of the lot. Haydin began to wonder if his father had called every trailer rental company in the state of California.

Flipping through the yellow pages inside a phone booth, he found Ace of Spades Rents. "This is Haydin Kravitz in Sacramento.

I need a small trailer. Got one?" He was relieved when he found that Mr. Kravitz had not called Ace of Spades.

Less than an hour later, Haydin, with a trailer tagging behind, pulled into the driveway of Carlton's mother-in-law in Elk Grove. She was an enormous black woman, well over 350 pounds, and moved like a wheezing mastodon in a housecoat. "Come on in, Mr. Kravitz," she said. A long, grey ash, longer than the cigarette itself, curled down off the tip of the Lucky Strike dangling from her mouth.

The woman signed the hauling agreement and tipped Haydin $2.50. Then she led Haydin to the pantry where she let down a ladder from the ceiling. After slipping on his garden gloves, Haydin climbed the steps and pushed aside cobwebs to see about thirty boxes and cartons filling a dusty, sloped-roofed attic. Carlton had been right about his mother-in-law: several old radios were packed tightly into a huge banana box. Haydin guessed them to be at least twenty-years old. But he knew he'd never make it to the dumps before closing; and loading the trailer would have to be kept out of his father's sight. He'd park it at his grandfather's, then after school the next day, he'd dump the trash and later return the trailer to Always Rents. Though exhausted, Haydin was very satisfied when he left Elk Grove.

Mr. Brossard was in his backyard painting the arms of wooden garden chairs when Haydin walked into his grandfather's kitchen and helped himself to a plate of Texas chili warming on the stove. Brossard had seen Haydin back the trailer in and, after putting down his paint brush, headed into the house, slammed the screen door, and confronted his grandson.

"Haydin, the loaded trailer in the driveway indicates to me you had another hauling excursion today."

"Correct, Gramps."

"Boy, you are one head-strong young man, I'll say that. Fact is, your father called here looking for you. He wants you home immediately. He's very hard-nosed about you not hauling anymore.

Apparently, somebody at a trailer rental place called your father and told him you tried renting a trailer over there."

"Also correct."

Brossard shook his head. "All this does is stir the cauldron, Haydin. Ya' know, you and your father may be on the outs, but your mother is going through emotional torment during this hell. I'm worried she could have a nervous breakdown."

"Gramps, a major collector's convention is coming to Sacramento. I've already paid a $15 deposit to reserve display space, but if I get more inventory, I can make some decent dough. My goal is to make enough money to pay the rent on a store and start a business that will end all this crapola."

"What you need to learn is that there are a lot of ways to skin the same cat. You can get pretty much what you want in this world, Haydin, but ya' won't get it by tellin' your father and mother to go to hell."

"Gramps, I never once told my father and mother to go to hell."

"You've done it without words, Grandson, by disobeying their wishes. Your Dad said your Mom was waiting for you at the doctor's, but you never showed. That's tellin' somebody to go to hell without using words."

"Who do you blame, Gramps? Who dropped the first A-Bomb and started this war? Who calls the trailer lots and tells them not to rent to me? Who?"

Mr. Brossard was exhausted. "This is really getting' to me, Haydin, and I don't need it. I'm reachin' the end-point here."

"Gramps, I'm gonna' clear this crappola up pronto. But I have to be at that convention and that means hauling and going to the dumps today and tomorrow. But would you come on out to the trailer right now and give me your opinion of the couple items I just collected?"

When Haydin lifted the tarpaulin over the trailer and showed his grandfather the old radios, Brossard's stern mood turned to sunshine. "My God, look at this," he breathed, reaching inside and carefully lifting up one of the sets.

"Haydin, this is an old Atwater-Kent cathedral style radio. We had one in our living room when I was a kid. This honey is from the early 1930's, I can say for sure. My Dad bought one of these and we thought it was one of the world's wonders." Brossard dusted off the mahogany cabinet with his handkerchief, turned the tuning dial, and admired every inch of the set. "Then over here ya' got a Zenith and an old Philco, too. These are all Cathedrals from the 1930's. They're scruffy, but we might be able to improve on their condition."

"Think they have any real value, Gramps?"

"These sets will surely catch the eye of anyone who appreciates old radios. Tell ya' what, Haydin: let's make a deal right here and now: you go back home tonight and mend fences, and I'll do what I can to restore the finish on these radios to make them look nice for your convention."

Haydin smiled for the first time in days. "Gramps, it's a deal. Can we hook these babies up and see if they play?"

Mr. And Mrs. Kravitz were watching Ozzie and Harriet when Kravitz walked into the living room. Mrs. Kravitz was startled to see her son. Mr. Kravitz scowled, but did not take his eyes off the television screen.

"Why'd you call all those rental lots, Dad? My name's mud at those places now."

"I'll tell you exactly why. You're under age and you can't do anything without my consent. Plus you're truant, godammit."

"I'm not truant! I took a big essay test today in English, in fact. I'd bet anything I got a B. Dad, you crossed a big line when you screwed me up with Corkey at the trailer lot. Up until now he's been my number one lifeline."

"Maybe it's about time you swallowed that medicine."

"You purposely failed to show at Dr. Dahl's," Mrs. Kravitz put in wearily. "And I can tell your acne is definitely worse. You need to go to your appointments."

"I'm sorry I had to do that, Mom. I didn't mean to leave you high and dry, but first things need to come first. And anyway, what can Dr. Dahl do for me he hasn't already done?"

Mr. Kravitz was beside himself. "The worst of it is you went on a hauling expedition after I specifically told you not to, godammit!"

"And to add to all this," said Mrs. Kravitz, "your counselor called again and said you're getting a notice of failure in English."

Haydin shrugged. "Those are just dumb, paper warnings they use to cover their rears. I said all along I'd pass. Is anybody listening here? What is this crapola?"

"You're hangin' over the edge by your fingernails, Boy. Obviously, none of this scares you enough to change your behavior."

"No, it doesn't, Dad, because I said I'd pass. You obviously don't believe me."

Mr. Kravitz roared with sardonic laughter. "*Believe you*?! With your track record? You've lied, deceived, disobeyed, and left your mother sitting like a damn jackass in the doctor's waiting room for her son who stood her up. Now we're supposed to believe you?"

"Ya' know, Dad, I'm just plain sick of all your bullshit."

"You won't speak to me like that in my house!"

"Fuck it!" Haydin shot back as he flew up the stairs to his room.

Mr. Kravitz jumped up aghast. "*What's that*?! What did you say, Mister?"

The moment Haydin rounded the corner to his room, he felt as if the roof of the house had caved in on his head. The wallpaper was back, the magazines, toys, baseball cards, plastic characters, games, everything had been cleaned out. Only his bed and desk remained on an immaculately vacuumed carpet next to an open window that let in fresh air. His jaw dropped as he stood in the doorway paralyzed with disbelief.

"I had it all dumped, Haydin," his father said standing behind him. "And I'm glad I did it. Furthermore, hand me the keys to your car. You're confined to this house."

Mrs. Kravitz stood behind her husband wiping her eyes. "Oh, Haydin, why didn't you obey your father?"

"You dumped my collection?" he breathed in complete amazement. "You ruined me."

"Yes. I did dump it. And you'll never know where I dumped it either. Now give me those car keys."

Haydin whirled around in a fit of near insanity and took his father by the collar. *"You dumped my collection!!"*

Mrs. Kravitz screamed.

Father and son were nose to nose. Kravitz's eyes bulged in shock and rage as he tried to break free from Haydin's powerful grasp. But Haydin shoved him up against the wall. Crying and whining, Mrs. Kravitz tried to pull Haydin away from her husband, but she had little strength and could do nothing except fall back weakly. Canned laughter from Ozzie and Harriet drifted up the stairs underneath Mrs. Kravitz' sobs.

All at once Mr. Kravitz' feet went out from under him and he was flat on the floor. Haydin slipped and landed on top of his father.

"You dumped my collection, Dad?! Why—why did you do that?!!"

"You no good son of a bitch! Get out of this house now!"

"No, Haydin! Please, no! Let your father go!—Please, Haydin!"

Father and son were locked frozen peering into each other's raging eyes. Mrs. Kravitz was sobbing and tried pulling her son's shoulders back in vain. Finally, Haydin stood up over his father, his furious red face glaring down at him with clenched fists at his sides. Then he turned, bolted down the stairs, and raced out of the house with his father's curses alive in his ears:

"Get out! You're no son of mine! Don't ever come back to this house, goddammit!"

II

Brossard was in the kitchen polishing the Cathedral radios when Haydin burst into the house. "Your mother just called me crying like a baby. Do I understand that you pushed your father down on the floor?"

"That's crapola, Gramps! He slipped and I accidentally fell on top. Did Mom also tell you Dad cleaned out my entire collection? Everything I had is gone, Gramps! My own father dumped years and years of collectibles like he was throwing out the garbage. Did Mom tell you any of that, Gramps? *Did she*?!*"

Brossard looked troubled, but could see his grandson had been pushed to the edge. "I'm not sayin' that was the best way to handle matters, Haydin, but you're also outa' control, Grandson. You've got to get back *into* control. Your life can't go on like this."

"He destroyed my collection, Gramps!" Haydin kept repeating as he stalked about the kitchen in misery. "My own father cut my legs off and called me a 'no good son of a bitch'...."

"Oh, Haydin," Brossard said, tossing his polishing cloths aside wearily. "What in the name of Christ are we gonna' do here?"

"I know I'm not going back to that house, Gramps. I'll sleep on the sidewalk or on a park bench before I go back there."

"Haydin, your collection can be replaced—but your relationship with your parents can't."

"I'm wiped out for the convention, Gramps. I don't have enough inventory to even have a decent display table now."

"You and your father need a cooling off period. I'm gonna' call your mother tonight. For the time bein', you sleep here in the dayroom. But it's on the condition you go to school every single day and do your homework. This must be your number one goal, Grandson. Your collection, this upcoming convention, all that comes way after your education. Agreed?"

"All right. Yes, agreed, Gramps."

"I want to be clear, Haydin: the first time you break the agreement, you're out of my house. No second chances, if, ands, or buts. Because if you do go back on the agreement, then yur' makin' a fool of me and I won't have any part of that."

"I won't make a fool out of you, Gramps..."

"For what it's worth, Haydin, I never graduated from high

school. And that made all the difference in my life. My working years was spent diggin' ditches for the gas company. Believe me, you don't want to go down that road, Grandson."

"I will never dig ditches, Gramps. I'm going to be a highly respected collector."

"Don't like beatin' a dead horse, Haydin, but you can't scrap an education. You may not see it now, but failure to get that graduation certificate subtracts from your lifetime bargaining power. It effects your income, your future relationships, and, most of all, your mind. You've got to value that school you go to; value your teachers who don't make much money teaching you proper English. Does any of this mesh inside that hard head of yours?"

"Yeah. I suppose so," Haydin said, wiping his eyes.

"You're at a crossroads, Grandson. There's a lot at stake right now. The steps you take today will stay with you forever."

Brossard let a few moments pass hoping his words would sink in.

"All right, then," Brossard continued. "Now two of these radios still work. I'm not sure what's wrong with the other one."

Kravitz hadn't even noticed the old Cathedral sets. "Gramps, you're a genius! These radios look great! I'm sure I can get top dollar for 'em!"

"Just required a little tender lovin' care and some good resin polish."

Later, Brossard made a chicken stew for his grandson and placed a tray of sliced white bread down in front of him. Sitting at the other end of the kitchen table with a plate of pork 'n beans, Brossard decided it was time to tell his grandson a story.

"Haydin, I'm goin' to tell you an account that actually happened to my brother Albert in the hopes it will have a great effect on you. Now listen to this story, every word of it, and never forget it...

"Years ago my brother Albert, your great uncle who you never knew, owned a second-hand store up in Placerville. He dealt in everything and anything: washing machines, stoves, piping, nuts and bolts, and a little office equipment. One day a guy walks in,

191

very well dressed and spoken. He's starts lookin' around Al's shop and tells him that he's in search of a gray, three-drawer, metal file cabinet made in the 1940's. Well, Albert had one or two metal cabinets, but they weren't the ones. Then this very well-to-do lookin' man told my brother Al why he wanted to locate the metal file cabinet...

"He said that when he was 16 or so, he and his father had a terrible falling out. The argument was over his stayin' in school—because this man, then 16, wanted to go into the Navy. But his father wanted him to finish high school first. The son had a hard mind of his own, though, joined the Navy anyway, and ended up disowning his parents. He never laid eyes on either his mother or father again. Yet for years the father laid money away for his son intended to be given to him when he graduated from high school. Over time, the father hid the cash in his metal file cabinet. It stood at about $500 which was a fortune in those times, believe me.

"Years later, the father passes, then, shortly later, his wife, the man's mother. One day the son receives a letter. It says': "Mail to my son, Franklin Boss, United States Navy." You see, after Boss' mother passed away, the bank foreclosed on the house. The agent for the bank held an estate sale getting' rid of everything includin' a grey, metal file cabinet. He came across a letter and sent it to the United States Navy which forwarded it on to Boss' current address. Boss received the letter from his father which described the file cabinet, the money it contained, and, if you ask me, a great deal more about the entire broken father-son relationship. Long story short, the son got in touch with the real estate agent who told the son that much of the office equipment had been sold to a second-hand dealer durin' the house's estate sale. For years that son combed every second hand store in the area searchin' for that metal file cabinet. Haydin, that son turned out to be Franklin Boss, founder of First National Trust of California."

"Did he ever find the file cabinet, Gramps?"

"Well, this is gonna' tell ya' plenty about my brother Al's integrity, but after he heard the whole story, Al told Boss he had bought a file cabinet at an estate sale years before which did fit the description of the one Boss was lookin' for. But it was a cabinet Al had used for years in his back office—behind his desk. He said it was a 1940's style metal filing cabinet with three drawers. 'But it ain't got no money in it and never did,' Albert told Boss. Boss asked if he could look at the file cabinet and examine it. The two men emptied the cabinet's contents, turned it over, and sure enough, there was a small tin container screwed into the bottom with five $100 bills inside. My brother Al told me that Boss broke down and cried right there on the spot."

"Well, at least he got the money, Gramps."

"Haydin, the point of the story isn't the money. It's the dedication Franklin Boss had to finding his father's cabinet. And if you ask me, it was dedication stemming from something the father had written in the letter to the son when he was in the service. It's also my opinion that Boss suffered endless heartache and misery over disowning his parents after joining the Navy. But as time went on, it became harder and harder to go back and patch things up with his father. Franklin Boss didn't need or want the $500. He was acting out of respect for his father's wishes as a way of saying, 'I'm sorry, Dad.' Albert, God love him, gave Franklin Boss the cabinet. And guess what? Boss turned around and handed Al the $500 for his honesty. One of the last times I ever saw my brother Al, he took me to the home office of First National Trust of California. Right there in the lobby was the metal filing cabinet with a rope around it and a sign that said, 'Home Is Happiness.' As far as I know, it resides there to this day."

"Grandson, no matter what injustices you think your parents have committed, think very hard before you disown them. Years are like walls. And as years pass, those walls get higher and thicker. You may never climb those walls if you don't climb them now when they're small…"

Haydin had lost his appetite and pushed back the bowl in front of him. Brossard picked it up and took it to the sink.

"Here's the deal, Haydin: unload what you want to keep here

at the house, disconnect the trailer, and go straight to school tomorrow. Then come home and dump the trash. When you're done there, I want you straight back here to complete your schoolwork. Tomorrow I'm gonna' go over to see your parents before this whole thing blows up into World War III."

"It won't do any good, Gramps. Dad's skull is made of cement."

"Grandson, I've been dealin' with cement skulls all my life. Now when's this convention you keep talkin' about?"

"Two weeks from Friday. It runs the whole weekend. But now my collectibles are gone. What am I gonna' sell?"

"You have the radios. What else?"

"The radios, an old baseball card, an Eliot Ness telephone, a set of china dishes, some garden tools, couple other things. Worst of it is, the ad in the paper still has my home phone on it. If anyone calls over there, Mom or Dad will answer and you can kiss those customers good-bye."

"Tomorrow I'll call the paper and change the number to the house here."

"Thank you, Gramps. I really appreciate everything you're doing."

"Those are just words, Haydin. I want you to *show* me your thanks by going to school and putting 1000 percent effort into passing your courses and graduating. Agreed?"

"Agreed."

"Now go do your homework. Meanwhile, I'll see if I can get that other radio in working condition."

An hour later Brossard peeked through a crack in the doorway of the day room and saw his grandson sitting at the small desk. He smiled when he saw Haydin reading *Moby Dick* by Herman Mellville.

The next afternoon during lunch, Haydin sat with Mrs. Bumgartner, his counselor, and Mr. Lysurges, in Bumgartner's office. Lysurges had shown the counselor Kravitz' essay on garbage.

"I'll say this," Lysurges commented, "it's different."

"It certainly is," Bumgartner agreed. "Now, Mr. Lysurges, did Haydin write the minimum no of words and did he stay on the topic?"

"Somewhat."

"And you gave him a 'C-.'" Bumgartner said handing Haydin the essay.

"*A C-* !" Haydin exclaimed, coming forward on his chair and taking the paper in disbelief. "Are you kidding, Mr. Lysurges? This essay deserves at least a B. I went into all kinds of examples here."

"Now, Mr. Lysurges," the counselor interrupted, "Since he got a C-, will that allow him to pass?"

"Haydin's right square on the line," Lysurges said. "He could go either way at this point."

"And what would push him over that line toward passing?"

"His performance in the next couple of weeks. His attendance. Motivation. Oral response in class. Homework—and Haydin's homework record is very poor, Mrs. Bumgartner."

"Haydin, I'd like to hear your thoughts on this."

He cleared his throat. "My answer is that I don't get why there's a C- grade on this paper. I think it's obvious you don't like me, Mr. Lysurges."

"Not true," Lysurges stated. "The grade is for inferior organization. You had a lot of examples, yes, but they were lacking cohesion, structure; a sort of junk heap of ideas. The spelling and grammar are atrocious. However, you did get a C- which I thought was generous."

"*Generous*?! Oh, man," Haydin complained, "I'm gonna'appeal this decision to the state Board of Education."

The counselor stepped in. "Now if Haydin did do extra credit, Mr. Lysurges, would it then push him into a positive area?"

"Normally, I don't give extra credit, Mrs. Bumgartner. If a student doesn't do the regular class work, extra credit becomes extraneous. What's the point of doing extra credit if you're not doing the regular work? Haydin needs to forget about extra credit and concentrate on the assigned classwork."

"Man, oh, man," Haydin complained again, "this is communist. I think the governor needs to know about the illegal grading system at this school."

"Mr. Lysurges, I'd like to thank you for coming in. Haydin, will you please stay a few more minutes?"

After Lysurges left the counselor's office, Bumgartner said, "Haydin, I was on the telephone with your father. He's made me aware of the difficulties you're having at home."

"Yeah. I moved in with my grandfather."

"Yes, he alluded to that. And I'm sorry to hear of it, Haydin. But your father said he laid down rules you didn't follow."

"What rules didn't I follow? He asked me to get out of the house and I certainly did follow that rule. But did he also tell you that he dumped all my collectibles that took me years to build up? Did he tell you that those collectibles were valuable? He just dumped everything like it was the trash left over after a drunkin' New Year's Eve party. Did he tell you any of that, Mrs. B?"

"No, he did not, Haydin. It sounds like you and your father have reached an impasse—at least for now. And your grandfather—how do you get along with him?"

"Perfect. He's the greatest guy there is and the smartest man in the world. Look, Mrs. B, all I care about is graduating. I don't give crapola about grade point average cause I'm not going to Cal or Stanford. Getting the damn certificate on June 17 is the name of the game here. Now you just read that essay I wrote—maybe it's not an A+, but it's a strong B at least. Any reasonable man or woman would agree to that without a bribe to say so."

"I never second guess teachers' criteria, Haydin."

"Lysurges has criteria? Sure fools me, Mrs. B. As I see it, he marks down grades in his grade book at home as fast as he can so he can start drinking cocktails with his loose girlfriends."

"I think that remark is uncalled for, Haydin."

"Well, I think it is true and I think the school board should investigate Mr. Lysurges' lesson plans—if he has any."

"Haydin, I spoke to all your other teachers today. You're

passing in Wood Shop, Physical Education, Social Studies, and Art, though barely. The sore spot is English. Mr Lysurges said the class is reading *Moby Dick*. Are you making progress on that book?"

"I'm up to page 29."

"Haydin, I've been your counselor for three years and you have never clearly expressed your plans after high school. What are they exactly?"

"To have my own collectibles business; to deal in rare items people can't get anywhere else. I want to become an established collector where even the experts seek me out for advice. I'm not talking about a pawn shop or a second-hand store, Mrs. B; I'm talking about a first rate national enterprise.

'You see, Mrs. B, the day is coming when stuff you now see lying around the house in your closets and drawers, stuff you now look at as trash, will be valuable. Comic books, baseball cards, movie posters, even record albums will all be worth 10, 20 times their face value today. But just having this stuff won't be enough: you'll have to have it in very good condition or what is known as 'mint.' Finding just one decent collectible, though, means you have to go through a lot of trash in people's attics and basements. Most all of it is crapola I take to the dumps, sure, but there's diamonds in garbage if you keep looking real good."

"That's a very precise vision, Haydin. I would hazard a guess that it's also very hard work hauling junk around."

"It is. I've hit my head a coupla' times and saw stars, fell down basement stairs, and swallowed some cob webs, but ya' have to take the bad to get to the good, Mrs. B."

"Wouldn't you say the first step to achieve your goals is to graduate from high school?"

"Maybe it is. And I am trying, Mrs. B, believe me."

"And wouldn't you say your father also sees the importance of that first step?"

"Look, Mrs. B, I see where you're going. But there's a million ways to skin a cat. You don't dump a person's most valued possessions without telling him and then say, 'I'm glad I did it.'"

"Haydin, I am going to talk to Mr. Lysurges about offering you extra credit to get you into passing territory. But if he offers it, you must do it and do it well."

"Are we about done here, Mrs. B? I've got to get to get over to the Sacramento dumps and see Carlton before he closes the gate."

Haydin raced back to Brossard's, hitched the trailer to the Plymouth, and headed straight for the dumps. Carlton was wading knee-deep in a mound of trash as Haydin found a spot and backed in the trailer. The manager was cherry picking items out of the rubbish and throwing them into the tote bag over his shoulder. Gradually, he worked his way over to Haydin.

"Heard ya' did a good job at my mother-in-law's, Haydin. Come away with anything good?"

"Some old Cathedral radios. My Gramps is fixing them up to look real sharp."

"'Spose you're pretty set for the convention, eh?"

Haydin looked sick. "Don't ask. My father dumped my entire collection, then kicked me out."

"*What*?! You kiddin' me?"

"Carlton. What I need is inventory—and I need it fast."

"Glad you said that," Carlton smiled. When yur' done, come on back to the office. Got some intrestin' stuff I've been holdin' fur' ya'."

Twenty-five minutes later, Carlton opened his desk drawer in the manager's office and removed two cigar boxes. "Bottle tops, Haydin. Some guy dumped all these bottle tops. Good thing I happened to open these boxes soon as I saw 'em in a pile."

Haydin picked through them. "Thank you, Carlton. Bottle tops are nice, but they're not exactly in great demand right now."

"That ain't all. How 'bout sheet music?" Carlton pulled up some 50-70 pages of sheet music tied with twine. "And how 'bout this sack o' baseball cards, too. Must be hundreds o' cards in here. Take 'em all. That's 'bout it, except for two bags of human teeth I found yesterday, but I converted the gold crowns into twenty bucks cash and bought my old lady some pilla' cases."

"Thank you, Carlton," Haydin said, looking through the cards. "I'm gonna' have to get these valued."

"Why don't ya' take a spin over to see George Ishikawa in Auburn, a pawn dealer who knows his soup to nuts. And he's clean an' honest, a man who won't take ya' fur' a ride. He'll be glad to tell ya' what ya' have in actchual dollars. Then when ya' go to the convention, ya' got a good idea of what to ask fur'. Hell, Ish might even want to make ya' an offer for some stuff right there."

When Haydin got back to his grandfather's, he stared in amazement at three shiny mahogany radios lined up on a card table in the living room. The radios' wooden finish glistened as if they had just been stocked on a retail showroom's shelf.

"Gramps, they look like they just came out of the factory! They're in mint condition!"

"All of 'em work, too. That third one just needed a new plug."

"Carlton, the manager at the dumps, gave me some cool stuff today. I'm planin' on going up to Auburn to see a guy who values stuff like this."

Brossard handed his grandson a slip of paper. "A fella' who called this morning. Said his father died and he needs the basement hauled. Claims his boxes will be ready for pick up day after tomorrow."

"I'll call him right now."

"No, you won't," Brossard corrected sternly. "You'll call him after you do your homework. Which brings up the sore spot again. I saw your parents this morning. Haydin, your Dad's a tough nut to crack, but I can tell that deep down he's sorry for what he did. Your Mom cried the whole time I was there and I don't like seein' my daughter cry, Grandson. They both want you back home."

Haydin stared hard at the radios on the card table, but said nothing.

"Ya' gotta' go back and deal with your parents. Wanna' end up like Franklin Boss?"

"Gramps, you couldn't drag me back to that house now if you chained me to a Mac truck and threw it in first gear. Kick me out in the street if you want, but I won't go back there and see that empty room and those ugly bare shelves that make me vomit."

"Haydin, the longer you're here, the more it affects even my relationship with your parents."

"I'm tryin' to accomplish something important, Gramps. This convention is more than just a weekend spree. I need to establish contacts, get phone numbers and meet people. I even plan on printing some business cards. I have to make an impression while I'm there."

"And I say your horse is still way before your cart. You need to pass your courses and graduate first. You've got the rest of your life for collection time, don't you think?"

"Gramps, let me move in with you just until I can get an apartment, I'd pay you rent."

"And if I did that, your parents would hold me responsible and never forget it. I've already crossed the line as far as your father is concerned."

Haydin removed the English essay from his back pocket and showed it to Brossard. "I'm trying, Gramps, really I am. Look at this essay; I got a C-, though it should be a B. At least it's not an F."

"Will that grade allow you to pass?"

"Mr. Lysurges says I'm on the fence."

"How 'bout your other classes?"

"Passing in every other class. It's Lysurges who's the crapola in the ointment."

Brossard shook his head and let out a long sigh. "I don't know, I don't know, Haydin. Don't get this English teacher on your bad side. Whatever this man does; whatever this man says, bite your lip. Crawl for this guy from here to there if you have to, but if you make this man your enemy, you'll be a dead in the water and headin' for summer school."

"Gramps, let's get one thing straight right now: I will never go to summer school," Haydin swore shaking his head emphatically. *"Never, never, never...."*

III

Brossard sent Haydin down to the store for some milk and cheese so he could call his daughter. Mrs. Kravitz said her husband was disgusted with Haydin for throwing him to the ground. Brossard said Haydin told him Mr. Kravitz had slipped; Mrs. Kravitz said she wasn't sure what happened, but the war between father and son was giving her sleepless nights. Brossard convinced his daughter that a short time apart was best for everyone. He guaranteed he would oversee Haydin's homework and make certain he never missed a day of school. It was agreed that Haydin would stay with his grandfather until after the convention.

The next day Lysurges and Haydin met during the lunch period.

"Haydin, I do see modest improvement in your work and in your attitude. Your father came down to see me during my prep period this morning. I appreciate his concern."

Haydin was incredulous. *"My father came down to see you?!"*

'Yes. And a very nice gentleman he is."

"And a very nice gentleman he is?"

"We discussed your domestic situation at home and I'm not unsympathetic. I'm sure it has all had a negative effect upon your academic performance. But you've got to stay on track, read all, not part, of *Moby Dick*, answer the study questions, and take the final exam."

"Which I am doing, Mr. Lysurges, believe me, I'm trying. But it's a thick book and it's not easy to understand the point of it."

"Well, perhaps you might identify with Captain Ahab. He was blinded by revenge and it caused his extirpation."

Upon hearing the asinine word 'extirpation,' Haydin followed his grandfather's advice and just bit his lip.

That afternoon Haydin met a man named Grant at his deceased

father's house in Fair Oaks. The modest home was empty except for cardboard boxes filled with rubbish that Grant had moved into the living room and hallway.

"I loaded everything in the front of the house to save time and effort. Dad was a doctor. A lot of medical instruments and medical paraphernalia are here. Just haul it and dump it."

"Thank you for making this easier, Sir. It saves me steps, Mr. Grant."

"I'm leaving, but here's the house key. Lock up when you're done and slip the key under the flower pot on the porch." Grant opened his wallet and slipped Haydin a crisp $10 bill. "Nobody works for nothing."

Grant signed Haydin's agreement, then Haydin began picking through the boxes. He found medical books, clothes, kitchen utensils, blankets, and run of the mill household items. But there were hypodermic needles, stethoscopes, and four very old microscopes. They all looked similar, yet strangely primitive and alien to the microscopes Haydin had seen in high school biology. These need to go to Auburn, he decided.

Sifting through the remaining boxes, Haydin pulled off the newspaper from the top of another box and the contents dazzled him: Nine very old saxophones, some gold, others silver, lay stacked in a crate. Some were formed like a clarinet, others had the familiar "J" shape. All were in excellent condition. Jeez, I might get at least $20-$50 here, Haydin guessed.

Saturday morning the Plymouth Savoy drifted into Auburn where Haydin had a 9 a.m. appointment with George Ishikawa at Ishi's Coin and Gold. Every one of his collectibles were with him and though he had no idea of their value, he was prepared to engage the "sales flinch" to get top dollar.

If Haydin learned one thing from his father, it was the sales flinch. The Sales Flinch was a painful facial reaction to an offer that said in clear body language the price was ridiculously high. "Leon, this paint is 75 cents a can," the clerk at the paint store once said to Mr. Kravitz. Haydin's father looked as if he'd been stabbed through the heart with a spear. "Oh, Gawd, Lou," Mr. Kravitz moaned, "I need six cans of this paint and the total cost will break me. Ya' know, my wife had to see a doctor and needs all this expensive medication. Can ya' make it 50 cents a can, Lou?" According to Mr. Kravitz, the Sales Flinch was required behavior in any transaction whenever price was negotiable in the business world.

George Ishikawa was a diminutive, extremely shrewd Japanese pawn broker with a narrow, pock-marked face. He sported a Jack Webb crew cut with widow's peak and thick, horn-rimmed glasses fastened to a large jeweler's loop. He dealt in coins, gold and silver items, sports memorabilia, and guns. Ishikawa bought and pawned thousands of watches, jewelry, silverware, and rare magazines; shotguns, pistols, and even 1920's machine guns stood on their stocks against the front wall. Regarded as one of the best antique appraisers in the area, Ishikawa was an honest buyer and seller known for his integrity.

Haydin lined the long glass counter with his radios, saxophones, microscopes, sheet music, stamps, bottle tops, and baseball cards. Ish's eyes grew wide when he saw Haydin set down the Wagner baseball card. He immediately reached for a thick catalogue on the shelf behind him and began thumbing through it.

"This is Honus Wagner's card. He played around the early 1900's. It's very rare and known as T-206. The 'T' stands for 'tobacco' because companies used to put these cards into cigarette packs." Ish inspected the card under his jeweler's loop, then looked up and said, "It's in very good shape. I'll give you $75 in cash for it right now."

Haydin was stupefied, but executed the sales flinch to perfection. He looked as if Ishikawa had just kicked him in the groin. "Ya' know, Ish, I knew that was a very rare card. See, I've just got all these big expenses for the convention hitting me." Haydin waited, but the shop owner did not make a higher offer.

"What about these microscopes, Ish?"

"What you have here are old monocular style scopes that look like they're from the early 1900's. They would be highly desirable to someone who collects these old instruments."

"And the dollar value?"

"Keep in mind that value is whatever a buyer is willing to pay and a seller is willing to take. The catalogue may say $10, but if the item hits the buyer between the eyes, you can throw the book out. I'd have a hard time selling them; microscope collectors are rare. But I'll guess, maybe, $15 apiece if the party was interested...

"Same thing with these radios. They're 1930's Cathedral sets." Ish plugged one in. The light went on around the dial and the radio began to warm up. "Looks like they've been recently refinished; they're in excellent condition, though. I do like them. How about $15 for each one?"

Haydin executed the sales flinch again and appeared to be greatly disappointed by the offer. "Ish, I put so much work into these cabinets. I spent $5.50 just refinishing every one of them with expensive polishes."

Ish was already thumbing through his musical instruments catalogue. "And then you have these saxophones here," he went on. "These appear to be phones from the 1920's. I believe this is a Buescher sax; this other one here is about late 1920's, a Wonder soprano sax. I'll offer you $45 for all three."

Haydin's excitement over Ish's offers boiled inside him, but he kept his sales flinch firmly in place. "To be honest, Ish, I'm thrown for a loop. Just thought I really had so much more dollar value here, dogginnnit. What about these bottle tops, Ish?"

"Worthless."

"And this sheet music, Ish? I haven't even untied the twine. Go ahead and see what you think."

Ishikawa cut the twine. "This old sheet music might get you 10 or 25 cents per sheet if the buyer wants them." The dealer began to sift through the pages. "This music is from the 1930's and 1940's, very nice if a music lover—wait a minute, this one, look at this..."

Ish picked up one of the sheets.

"Unless it's forged, this is George Gershwin's autograph,

Haydin." The dealer examined the signature closely through his jeweler's loop. "Unfortunately, I don't authenticate autographs, but if this is actually Gershwin's signature, well, you might have something here. See, singers and song writers used to appear at music stores and sign sheet music to promote their music."

"I've heard the name 'Gershwin.'..."

"One of America's greatest song writers, Haydin."

"Gee, you sure know your stuff, Ish."

"And here's another one. Holy Cow, *God Bless America* autographed by Irving Berlin. If these signatures are real, Haydin, you've got some prized autographs."

"Was this guy Berlin big?"

"Still is the biggest. If you authenticate these signatures, I'd be willing to offer, say, $20 apiece for them."

Haydin rounded out the profit in his head and grew dizzy. Now he knew exactly what he had. If Ish refused to go higher, Haydin was confident he could get more at the convention. "I don't know, Ish," Haydin said as though disappointed, waiting for the shop owner to up his offer. "I'm on the fence." Haydin waited, but Ishikawa said nothing. "Guess I'll keep these and watch them grow more valuable with time."

"If I were you, I'd see an autograph expert. Where do you get your inventory, Haydin?"

"To be honest, Ish, I spend a lot of time at the dumps."

The pawn dealer laughed. "Makes sense. Most people have no idea what they're throwing away. Or their relatives die and their children dump everything and can't get the house on the market fast enough. To them, a basement means nothing but trash and they end up tossing out items like this Honus Wagner baseball card."

Haydin gave Ish $2 for his appraisal efforts, then headed into downtown Sacramento to pick up his new business cards. He was thrilled just to look at them and couldn't wait to show them to his grandfather.

Haydin Kravitz
Professional Collector At Your Disposal
"All Your Trash Hauled in a Jiffy"
916-923-1140

The morning of the convention, Haydin loaded the Plymouth Savoy with his carefully packed collectibles, then sped toward the Sacramento auditorium complex dressed in shirt, tie, and slacks. His head swirled with excitement as he took his designated parking space at the back of the auditorium in the far right corner lot. Hand trucks moved about everywhere as collectors unloaded their inventory from their cars and pick-ups. Haydin also wheeled in his merchandise proud that he was now a bona fide, professional collector.

Over 200 tables filled the auditorium with impressive showcases of gold and silver coins, guns, sports equipment, and antiques. Haydin's display table was the smallest one in the auditorium's showroom, nearly lost in a thicket of tables toward the rear. None of his items were priced; his strategy was to force the customer to make an offer, then bargain, and, if necessary, use the sales flinch. The display table filled with the 1930's radios, old microscopes, sheet music, saxophones, dinner china and polished silverware, the Eliot Ness telephone, and the Honus Wagner baseball card. Haydin was very proud of his shiny new business cards which he fanned out across the table.

When the doors opened at 10 a.m., a modest stream of collectors filed in. But after an hour, hundreds were roaming the aisles. Finally, a tall, slender man stepped up to Haydin's table and seemed intrigued with the microscopes.

"I love antique scopes. I'm a radiologist and collect them for my office. What do you want for the whole batch?"

"Well, Sir, why don't you just make me an offer?"

The man inspected each one. "They're nice. How about $60 for the lot?"

Haydin almost fainted as the man reached for his wallet. Every muscle in his face strained to execute the sales flinch. Haydin looked as if he were in great pain.

"All right. I'll give you $72.50 for them," the man said. "That's as high as I can go."

"I think we have a deal here, Sir."

Two men in their 20's with unkempt hair, beards, and psychedelic shirts appeared and inspected the saxophones. "Do these play OK?" asked one man as he blew hard into the smallest sax. The other man had already pulled out a money clip thick with greenbacks. "How's about $35 for all three of these phones?"

Haydin performed the sales flinch to perfection.

"I can see $40," the man offered. "No more."

Haydin stared down at the instruments as if they were old friends he found painful to part with. He shook his head as if he were completely uncertain.

"Fifty bucks for these three. Take it or leave it."

Haydin accepted the offer.

By early afternoon, the microscopes, saxophones, dish sets, some of the sheet music, and about 25 baseball cards had all been sold. Haydin had grossed $212.

Suddenly, the face of George Ishikawa stood before him.

"Hi, Haydin. I won't lie: I really liked these old Cathedral radios. How about fifty bucks for all three?"

Remembering the pawn dealer had originally offered him $45 for the instruments, Haydin executed the sales flinch. "Ish, you know, I spent several hours refinishing these—"

"Sixty bucks. You say 'no,' I walk away and I don't come back. But please, Haydin, no more sales flinches."

Haydin was embarrassed, but had to laugh. "You gotta' deal, Ish."

When the convention closed at 5:30 p.m., Haydin had $287 in cash.

Nearly unable to contain himself, Haydin stood in the middle of the auditorium, closed his eyes, breathed in the stale, auditorium air, and had not one doubt that this would be his life. He carried what he had left in a cardboard box to his car in the far corner of the convention's lot thinking of nothing but two-hundred-and-eighty-seven dollars cash. I'll give Gramps half of it for rent and for all he did for me. *This proves my future is in collectibles!*

As he turned the key in the door of his Plymouth Savoy, the two men who had bought the three saxophones stepped out from behind a Cadillac parked next to the car. One of the men brandished a long copper pipe and rushed over to Haydin. "You drove up the price on those saxes," he said nastily. "You took me to the cleaners. You owe me, Pal."

Haydin set the box down. "Are you kiddin'? Nobody forced you to—"

Before he could utter another sound, the man swung and cracked the pipe across the side of Haydin's head. Stunned, Haydin staggered back against the Plymouth, then dropped to all fours. The second man picked up the box of collectibles; the man with the pipe stood over Haydin and wanted to make sure his victim would not get to his feet. Haydin's aching eyes stared at red beads of blood that dropped onto the pavement.

"OK—I'll give you your... money...back..."

A second blow whacked Haydin at the back of his head and more blood trickled down to the pavement. He lay on his side in dazed agony, then tried to get to his feet, but his legs felt like twigs and collapsed under him. Haydin fell to the cement again. Writhing on his stomach, Haydin sensed the jiggling horror of strange hands rushing through his pants pockets as human words were spoken underwater. Then another blow whacked him on his spine. Haydin thought his back had been split in half.

...You dumped my collection, Dad! Millions of baseball cards pouring down from the clouds upon a field cluttered with old radios...You're no son of mine!...The whale—a planet-sized beast coming straight at him as he tossed a harpoon at it weakly, missed, and waited for the monster to blow him apart... Gramps—help me!

When Hayden opened his eyes, two firemen were gently assisting him to a sitting position. One of the men had taken a cloth and wiped the blood from the side of Haydin's face. His eyes focused straight ahead at the Sacramento dumps filled with rats the size of dogs and dead people strewn about through the rubbish heaps. Carlton was sifting through trash and picking human teeth out and tossing them into his tote bag. Suddenly, his spine, sending throbs through every inch of him, felt as if it had swelled to the size of a tree trunk.

A police officer suddenly squatted down and said, "Son, can you respond to me?"

"...Uh-huh..." Haydin answered weakly, feeling as if his head had gone through a washing machine's spin cycle.

"What day is it?"

"The—convention...day."

The words "Sacramento Police" were printed on the side of a black and white door that seemed to exist at the far end of a telescopic lens. Haydin stared at the words trying to make sense of them. Inside the car, an officer sat at the wheel and listened to a woman's walky-talky voice squawking out gibberish. A small knot of on-lookers had crowded around mumbling words as they peered down at the boy sitting on the cement. Slowly, sensible images began to merge. Then as if awakening to a terrifying realization, Haydin reached for his wallet in panic.

"This is your wallet, Son," an officer stated. "We called your parents off the ID. They're on their way."

Haydin opened his wallet. The cash was gone. His head sank and it took all he had not to break down in front of all the people that had gathered around him. "My money's gone!"

"You got robbed and beaten up, Son," the officer said. "They tagged you pretty clean. Be glad those guys didn't have knives. These snakes case these shows, then wait for dealers to leave at closing time knowing they carry cash. It's usually drug money. Did you get a good look at whoever robbed you?"

"I'd recognize them in the dark..."

Mr. and Mrs. Kravitz pulled up and jumped out of the station

209

wagon. Mrs. Kravitz was crying. Mr. Kravitz had an odd, confused expression as he looked down at his son sitting on the pavement.

"Honey, are you all right?" Mrs. Kravitz asked, putting her arm around her son's shoulder and hugging him tightly.

"Mom, I need to give the cops a good description of those assholes."

"Might be a good idea to sit a bit longer, young man," stated the officer. "Do you folks want to call for an ambulance?"

"No," Haydin refused. "I don't need no ambulance."

After filing a report, Haydin's parents drove him to Sacramento Medical Center where Brossard was waiting. An emergency room doctor examined him, then said he wanted to send him to radiology for x-rays. An hour later Haydin emerged in the corridor with a white bandage over the side of his head. Mrs. Kravitz winced when she saw her son's face, a blotch of worsened, red acne. Mr. Kravitz said, "You need to go home and lay down, Haydin."

"Those cockroaches stole my money," Haydin kept repeating. "They need to pay."

"The money doesn't matter," his mother said. "The doctor says you have a concussion. We'll take you home and—"

"I'm staying with Gramps," Haydin stated flatly.

A thick silence filled the air in the corridor as Haydin's parents and Mr. Brossard watched Haydin walk down the hall toward the exit.

The four of them left the center and walked toward the station wagon in the parking lot. When they reached the car, Mr. Kravitz stepped forward. He made no physical contact with his son, but he cleared his throat and uttered the words in a whispered voice: "I'm sorry I threw out your collection, Haydin. I regret doing that…"

"Dad, I want to get one thing straight: I never pushed you down on the floor in the hallway."

"Right. Yes," Mr. Kravitz agreed, staring down at the ground.

"I want to make something else clear to everybody," Haydin declared, addressing his parents and his grandfather. "What happened today don't affect me one bit. I'm gonna' start collecting again from scratch. They can beat me up physically, they might even kill me, but they will never destroy my dreams."

"Collections can always be replaced," Brossard smiled gently. "But remember those other things we talked about? They can't."

That night Brossard prepared a special hot tuna casserole and set it down in front of his grandson.

"Those apes cleaned me out, Gramps. If I ever see 'em again, I'll kill 'em."

"Weren't you cleaned out once before, Haydin? Didn't you deal with it and come back and make over $250?"

"All I know is I'm gonna' borrow Carlton's .38 Smith and Wesson. I'll be waitin' for 'em at the next convention. And when I see 'em, they're sayin' hello to lead straight between the eyes."

Brossard looked as if he had just swallowed vinegar. "Haydin, that's the worst, dumbest thing you could possibly do. And I promise you that if you do that, you're outa' this house for good. Now listen to me, Grandson: you've got a cast iron disposition and you have to learn there's a world of difference between self-confidence and ignorant revenge. You may destroy your enemy doing that, but you also destroy yourself, too. Let the universe take care of those bums because it will, I assure you."

"I hope they choke on the $287."

"Grandson, I think you missed a significant thing that happened tonight: it was your Dad saying he was sorry. For him that was like Germany admitting it started World War II. You know, some kinds of feelings don't come easy for some folks so they cover it all up in a hard, leathery outer shell. But your father said he did wrong and I hope you heard it; it may have ben the one important good that came out of this lousy day. You may find this unbelievable, Haydin, but I sense that dumping your collectibles is now harder on your Dad than it is on you."

Brossard wanted to say more, but knew he had to change the subject. He slid a piece of paper across the kitchen table toward his grandson. "This real estate agent called today and said he needs a detached garage in Isleton cleaned out. Says there's plenty of old stuff in there. If the doctor gives you the OK, then this might just be the opportunity to start building your collection back up."

Three days after the convention, Haydin finished *Moby Dick*, answered all of the study questions and turned them in to his English teacher. Later that afternoon, he was in Mrs. Bumgartner's office meeting again with Lysurges.

"You're going to pass, Haydin, but not by much. According to Mrs. Bumgartner, you'll graduate. All you have left is to take the final on *Moby Dick*."

"Well, that's pretty good news, Mr. Lysurges. But I still don't get why that Ahab guy had to die in the end. I think he should have killed that damn whale and gone back to Nantucket and sold the oil."

All Mr. Lysurges could do was throw his head back and laugh out loud.

"His lust for revenge overcame his reason, Haydin. It destroyed him."

Mrs. Bumgartner stared at the bandage on the side of Haydin's head. "We all heard what happened to you at the convention, Haydin," she stated sympathetically. "And we're all very sorry."

"I'm starting all over again from the ground up, Mrs. B. You'll be reading about me some day."

The counselor smiled. "You know something, Haydin, I believe I will one day. I have to say: you're the first student I've had in 16 years of counseling whose dream was to collect junk."

"I won't lie, Mrs. B and say my senior year was fun, because it sure had its hills and valleys. The biggest amazement was when my Dad came down to see you, Mr. Lysurges. I never thought I'd live to see the day my father would ever set foot on any campus I ever went to."

"You mean your grandfather, don't you Haydin?"

"No, my Dad. You said it was my Dad who came down that day."

"Did I? I'm sorry, Haydin. I meant your grandfather. It was

your *grandfather* who came down that day and told me how hard you were working and how dedicated you were to passing English. Yes, it was Mr. Brossard."

Haydin drove away from school with moist eyes thinking just what his grandfather meant to him. He wished his own father had the same understanding and common worldly sense his grandfather possessed. Gramps is the wisest man I know, yet he never graduated from high school. Why was Dad born to be such a thick-headed box of rocks? For the first time in his life, Haydin wondered how his father's father must have treated his son to make him act like a communist.

Six days later, the Plymouth Savoy, its trailer tugging behind, pulled up to a dilapidated little cottage in Isleton. The house was a two-bedroom flattop shoebox with a detached garage at the end of an unincorporated road. The dwelling looked like it had been through an artillery bombardment, but Haydin kept telling himself that pearls existed inside little oysters. A man wearing a thick black toupee, loud checkered sport coat, yellow, western string tie, and checkered slacks was adjusting a for sale sign on the tiny scratch of lawn.

"The house is being sold," he smiled. "What I need dumped are all those boxes in the garage. Thanks a million. The key is hidden in the tiny slit just under the garage's window ledge." The agent winked, did not even offer Haydin gas money, then walked off and headed down the broken sidewalk.

The detached garage resembled a creaking mass of soggy cardboard. Not a strip of original paint was left anywhere on its exterior. Haydin lifted the crooked door and stared at crates and boxes of kitchen utensils, gardening tools, rotted electrical wiring, and what looked like used, oily automobile parts. Yes, pearls exist inside little oysters, Haydin said to himself as he slipped on his gloves and thought how great it was to be back in the collection business.

Twenty-five minutes later, he had hauled all but one of the crates into the trailer. A very large cardboard box sat under a disconnected sink and packed tightly with filthy bathroom towels and bedding. As always, Haydin poked through the contents with a stick to be sure it was all rubbish. As he sifted through the dirty woolens, he noted a pleasant golden glow coming from the bottom of the box. A flashlight must be on down here, he thought. After pulling back the last blanket, he discovered a fine, polished book lying face up. The soft glow from the volume was like that which came from a small table lamp.

THE BOOK OF TIME

It looks brand new. Probably a children's toy, Haydin thought, lifting the book from the box. Where's it get the power to produce this light? The instant he turned back the cover, the cement floor beneath his feet tilted:

Haydin Kravitz Museum of Popular Culture
March 21, 2028AD

The $250 million, 17 acre Haydin D. Kravitz Museum of Popular American Culture opened March 21, 2028AD in Sacramento, California, USA, housing 11,456,987 collectible pieces ...

Huh? What is this crapola?!

...Seventy-Seven year-old Haydin D. Kravitz who designed the museum with architect William Penn Rose, welcomed 12,029 visitors and dignitaries to the grand opening of the complex recognized as the world's greatest showcase for the history of 20th Century popular culture...

Haydin raced the book back out into the sunlight. Panting and out of breath, his eyes couldn't read fast enough.

...The centerpiece of the museum is the Leonard Brossard Memorial Plaza leading to 25 separate museum galleries containing exhibitions in sports, comics, coins, stamps, domestic household artifacts, motion picture materials, and music memorabilia...

...Dedicated to the memory of his grandfather, Kravitz

unveiled the museum's front portal shrine on opening day and stated: "To my grandfather, Leonard Brossard, my guiding light of inspiration. Without his loving efforts toward the completion of my education, this museum would not have been possible."

The words were insane to Haydin. He flipped ahead several pages and found a paragraph that he had to read twice to believe:

...Taking nearly three years to complete, the museum won the International Solarium Award for outstanding modern Architecture which cited its "Novel interconnection of exhibitions, restaurants, arcade centers, and theatres which interface a masterpiece latticework of adjacent arboretums, footbridges, salt and fresh water pools, and the museum's private transit system shuttling visitors through the exhibits."

Hurrying back inside the garage, he ripped through the box's towels and bedding analyzing the sides and bottom of the cardboard box. What was this book doing in this box under the sink? Then he read forward:

...In a ceremony celebrating the opening of the museum, California Governor Stephanie Hillmyer acknowledged Haydin Kravitz as "Not just the greatest collector and impresario of popular American culture in American history, but an immeasurable force for achievement in education."

Oddly, his garden gloves, grimy as always from his hauling labors, had not left a smudge on any of the pages he had touched. Pressing his soiled palm down on the book's cover, he found it remained spotless. He repeated the action, this time smearing his hand all over the cover's surface. Not a grain of dirt or grime was transferred. He picked up a screwdriver and gently twisted its point into the book's cover. But not a mark was made. Hurrying out to the trailer, he pulled a small ax from his box of garden tools. He set the book down on the cement floor of the garage with its spine facing up. Then he hacked the ax down squarely on the binding. The tool exploded out of his hands and smacked against the garage wall. Haydin's fingers stung, but not one scratch appeared anywhere on *The Book of Time.*

"If I didn't know better, I'd swear you hated good books, Haydin..."

The man who had adjusted the front yard's for sale sign was leaning against the half-opened garage door. He was smiling.

"I—just found this book here," Haydin said startled. He eyes fell to the volume lying on the cement floor near his feet. Haydin was speechless.

"I'm afraid the book cannot be damaged in any way, Haydin."

"What do you mean, Sir?"

"It's impossible to transfer so much as a pencil dot on it."

"Huh? What do you mean?"

"Instead of trying to damage it, why not read it?"

He picked up the book and held it out for the agent to see. "What is this? Do you know where this came from? Did you pack this into that cardboard box under the sink?"

The agent laughed. "No, I did not, Haydin."

"Mind if I ask just what real estate business are you with, Sir?"

"Well," he laughed, "I'm not really a real estate agent at all."

"You're *not?*"

"No. Consider me a 'helper.'"

"A helper? For what?"

"A helper to get you through your unusual experience here today. Haydin, that book is saying something very important to you."

A disturbing rush, a sense of other-worldliness crept through the shadows of the old, detached, wooden garage. "Sir, this book's talking about *me*. How's that possible? What's happening here is scary, Sir. And to be honest, you're a little scary, too."

"Haydin, there is absolutely nothing to be afraid of."

"There isn't? *This book's predicting my future!* Now I sure hope what I just read here *is* my future, but I'm not sure I want to turn another page because I'm worried it might tell me when I'm gonna' die."

"Save your worries, Haydin. You have many years ahead of you, much of it based on what is taking place right now in this old garage. Don't look upon today as a day to fear; look upon it as a day of great *discovery*."

Haydin shook his head. "I still don't get it," he stated. "Where did this book come from, Sir? Did you write it?"

"No. Haydin, I heartily recommend you not waste one more bit of energy testing the book's physical nature. I absolutely promise that one day you will have a much better understanding of what happened here than you do right now."

The man smiled pleasantly, turned, and stepped to the side of the house out of view. Haydin stood dazed and confused for a few moments, then ran out to the tiny scratch of lawn and looked in all directions. He stood flat-footed and speechless when he saw no trace of the man anywhere. Haydin crept back into the garage and picked up *The Book of Time* from the cement floor. He opened it again and re-read one paragraph in particular.

...Not just the greatest collector and impresario of popular American culture in American history, but an immeasurable force for achievement in education."

It's about me, he thought breathlessly. I don't get all these words, but it's all about me when I'm in my 70's. And that man. Who was he?

A strange sense came over him as he shoved the book under his arm and slammed the garage door closed. He put the key back in the window slit, raced to the trailer, and placed the book inside one of the boxes. Then he slung the tarpaulin over the top and tied the ropes around the canvas firmly and carefully. The Plymouth Savoy exploded away from the Isleton cottage as if the car had roared off into the start of the Indianapolis 500.

Brossard was spraying his front yard roses with a garden hose when Haydin rocketed to the curb, the trailer fish-tailing behind. *"Gramps! Gramps, you gotta' see this!"* Haydin cried as he jumped out of the car almost before it screeched to a stop in the driveway. "You're not gonna' believe it!"

Brossard listened to his grandson's story. "All right. Let's see this book you found..."

Haydin untied the ropes and threw the tarpaulin back over the top of the trailer. He tore through every box and crate frantically trying to find the book that was not there. As Brossard watched his grandson flinging the rubbish from side to side, he realized Haydin had probably suffered more than a concussion the day he was attacked at the convention.

"Gramps, it was here! Honest! I had it in my hands, read it, then put it carefully into the crate and tied the tarp on tight! I'm telling you the truth!"

Brossard was worried, but listened patiently to his grandson's heated narration a second and third time.

"You don't believe me, do you, Gramps?"

Brossard did not want to ignite Haydin's frazzled fuse. "Could it have fallen out of the trailer?" he asked lightly.

"No! I tied the tarpaulin over the top of the trailer tighter than a ten dollar mouse trap." Haydin sat down on the grass, his weary head falling into his hands. "Maybe, maybe it did fall out of the trailer…I don't know…"

Brossard studied his grandson sympathetically. He was moments away from picking up the phone and calling his daughter and recommending she take Haydin back to the doctor to be re-examined."

"*Wait a minute!*" Haydin jumped up excitedly. "Hold on! If that guy I saw today wasn't the real estate guy, then where was the actual one? And how did I know the key was in the slit on the ledge of the garage window? That's not something you'd guess, Gramps."

"Haydin," Brossard asked gently, "was it possible that man you saw *was* the real estate agent?"

"No, he wasn't, Gramps! And he said he wasn't." Haydin removed the phone number on the slip of paper his grandfather had given him. "Whose telephone number is this, Gramps? *Whose*? I say we call that number right now and find out. And I'm gonna' let you make that call, Gramps. Go ahead. Do it. If the man who answers says he is the real agent and saw me today in Isleton, then send me to the Napa State Hospital crazy house."

Brossard reluctantly agreed. "All right," he said, hoping the call would force Haydin to realize the truth. "I'll make the call and we'll see what's what."

Haydin followed his grandfather into the kitchen. Brossard took the slip of paper, exhaled, and dialed the number.

"Hello, my name is Adrian Brossard, the grandfather of the boy who hauled for you today. I—Yes?...Oh, yes, I see...*Is that right?...*" Haydin watched his grandfather's face contort into disbelief. "The fact is—the trash has *already* been cleared. How'd we know where the key was? Well, er, the garage door was left open, I think my grandson told me...No, no, you're very welcome."

Brossard set the phone down on the cradle slowly and stared blankly through the kitchen window. "The agent said he had car trouble today and couldn't make it to the house. Said he called here to cancel couple times, but nobody answered the phone. Guess I was out in the yard and didn't hear the phone ring."

"See, Gramps! It's true! The book was real and that man I saw was real!"

Brossard looked as if his deceased brother Albert had just pulled up to the curb in his 1947 Buick.

"I saw the future, Gramps!" Haydin shouted. "I don't know how, but I saw it! That book was right: Someday, I'm going to be the greatest collector in the world!"

Haydin skipped and danced and sang around his grandfather's kitchen. He was happier than any 17-year-old boy Brossard had ever seen.

The old man simply sank dumbfounded to one of the kitchen's wooden chairs. "Excuse me, Grandson, but I think I need a stiff shot of Johnny Walker..."

On graduation day Mr. and Mrs. Kravitz and Mr. Brossard watched Haydin stride across the school's gymnasium stage to accept his high school diploma. But Haydin's mind wasn't on the certificate in his hands; it was on *The Book of Time* found at the little cottage in Isleton and the strange man he met there.

After the exercises, the graduates and their families crowded into the main school parking lot. Mrs. Kravitz hugged and kissed her son proudly. Brossard shook his grandson's hand and said, "You did it, Haydin, but now it's on to real life." Mrs. Bumgartner appeared and wished Haydin good luck, followed by Mr. Lysurges who congratulated his ex-student and presented him with a shiny new edition of *Moby Dick*. Finally, Mr. Kravitz stepped forward with some difficulty.

"Congratulations, Haydin. As you can see, everyone is proud of you. And so am I." The words twisted out of his father's mouth raggedly and with obvious difficulty. Then, staring down at the ground self-consciously, Mr. Kravitz added, "Haydin, there's a little empty building over on South Fourth. It has a $25 monthly lease. Your mother, Gramps, and I would like to pay the first year's rent on it as our graduation present to you—if you still want to set up a collectibles shop..."

Haydin couldn't believe his ears. The long, emotional silence was palpable in the air around all of them. Finally, Haydin extended his hand to his father and, with glossy eyes, said, "Thanks, Dad, Mom, and Gramps. You guys won't be sorry. I will one day be a success and pay all of you back ten times worth."

They had all taken about 20 steps toward the Kravitz' station wagon when Haydin stopped as if he had just realized something important. He reached inside the pocket of his white shirt and pulled out the Honus Wagner baseball card.

"Hey! It's T-206!" he exclaimed joyously. "Holy Cow, I forgot I still had it!"

Mr. Brossard chuckled. "Think you might get a few bucks for it, Haydin?"

"Gramps, if you think I'm sellin' it, you're crazy! I'm gonna hold on to this card and watch the value skyrocket. God," Haydin said shaking his head, "who knows what this will be worth in, say—30 years?"

Gambler's Time

The dealer stood waiting impatiently. "Sir?"

Sitting at the blackjack table's left end, Buster had not yet turned over his hole card. He had already 'seen' it: the seven of clubs. But he stole a glance at the card underneath anyway to assuage suspicious eyes. The queen of diamonds lay face up giving him 17. "Stand," he cracked to the dealer.

The dealer flipped over his hole king for 14. An automatic hit snapped down on the table: a Jack. The dealer had 24. He broke.

"You're rich, son!" the woman behind Buster shouted.

The dealer stacked $1,800 in chips on the green felt cloth at Buster's station for his fourth consecutive winning hand. The pit boss stood behind the dealer and studied the table's left end player with keen, intense eyes.

Buster's face paled. As a small fortune piled in front of him, he thought he was floating in outer space.

The dealer collected the spent cards and tucked them under the deck neatly.

Buster's cold hands pushed all of his winning chips into the betting circle letting the $1,800 ride. The woman behind him whistled. The man seated next to him murmured, "You're definitely in a zone, Guy. Hope the angels stay with you."

It was the biggest bet of Buster's gambling life. His mouth was cotton dry. He wasn't sure he could swallow. What if the trick vanishes from under my feet? What if I lose it all?

Hole cards flashed around the table. But Buster did not have to turn his over: he 'saw' a red nine face down. The second cards snapped at their stations face up. Buster shivered when he saw his top card: a black two which gave him 11. He peeked underneath and made sure the pit boss saw him check it. Then he shot a glance at the dealer's hand and 'saw' his hole seven. With his king showing, the dealer had a hard 17 and would have to stand.

Wins and busts recorded at the other stations, then it was Buster's play at the left end slot. The next card to be dealt would be the queen of spades. Buster had already 'seen' it.

Divorce clean and simple. Put the house up for sale, get what we can, after we pay off the loan, we split what's left and go our separate ways...

With the unnerving resolve of a man creeping along a 30 story skyscraper's narrow window ledge, Buster turned over his hole nine. "Double down," he breathed.

He cloned his bet. A total of $3,600 in chips stood on the green, felt table for both of his hands. The dealer sent Buster the one card he was allowed: a black lady. Buster had 21.

When he turned the queen over, the pit boss gaped at the card. The woman behind Buster cried, "Good Lord!"

He had 'seen' the black queen just as he had 'seen' all the other cards face down. The numbers and suits were as vivid as if they had lain face up on the table. Buster was not sure he would be able to keep himself from imploding as the dealer stacked $3,600 in pretty blue and pink casino chips at his station. *What is happening to me?*

The pit boss signaled for a new dealer. The old dealer collected the spent cards and thumped the table twice with his fist. Buster tipped him $20.

Seconds later, a heavy-set, older woman with a grim Aunt Gertrude snarl stepped in as the replacement dealer and tapped a new deck of cards. She broke the cellophane wrapper quickly and began shuffling like a Barnum and Bailey magician.

The casino floor tilted under Buster's feet as he dumped over $8,000 in winning chips into a plastic coin bucket. Practically feeling the pit boss' breath blowing down his neck, he left the table quickly. "Can't believe he's quitting," someone remarked over his shoulder.

You can see the boys whenever you want on the condition that you give me 24 hours notice so I can arrange to be somewhere else...

Standing at the cashier cage, he asked for $1000 in cash and a check for the balance of his winnings. The cashier prepared his paperwork, but Buster didn't believe he was there in the casino at all. Rather, he saw himself in his room at the Gables Motel, sitting on the edge of his bed, reaching for his underwear. *I dreamed the two hours I spent here,* he told himself. *I'm still in my room. I'm still dressing. I never left the motel.*

The cashier placed a casino money order on the counter, then began counting out ten one-hundred dollar bills. The last hundred snapped down crisply, but when it did, four blue sevens suddenly came into focus in the middle of Ben Franklin's face. Buster blinked. He blinked twice. Four blue sevens was the iconic symbol for the casino's premier slot machine payoff: $250,000. The building's doors might just as well have blown open at that moment sending in a slashing cyclone that tore the gambling arcade to a million bits. *Four blue sevens...This...isn't...real...*

Buster crept away from the cashier's cage on rubber knees. The green exit sign lay in the distance straight ahead, but that was not what he saw: to his left, a row of signature dollar slots flashed a line of four Lake Tahoe 7's atop their silver crowns. The machine at the far end of the row caught his eye.

The gamblers in the aisles dissolved; the cranking of slots and clink of change on metal faded. There was no snapping of cards anywhere, no rolling of dice, no casino elevator music or clickety-click of spinning roulette wheels. Buster floated in a noiseless vacuum, the anomaly freezing him with panic; yet the lust to reach for the stars burned within him like a furnace.

I don't want to lay eyes on you again—ever. I want no communication with you at any time. I get sick just knowing you're a mile from me, Buster...

The casino's cacophony came up slowly in his ears. Along the carpet, gamblers stood before slots watching the thump-thump-thump of cherries, lemons, and bells lining up unevenly in the disappointment of another lost pull. Buster exhaled, then crept toward the lonely, unattended machine at the end of the aisle. With the delicate care of a safecracker turning a combination lock in the dark, Buster removed a silver dollar from his pocket, lifted his arm slowly, fed the piece into the coin slot, and brought down the handle. His heart raced, his throat thickened. The machine's wheels turned their spinning blur. An instant later the window's images clicked into other-worldly precision before Buster's wondrous eyes.

Blue seven. Blue seven. Blue seven. Blue seven.

The air went out of his lungs.

Ohhhhh MyGod!...

John Phillip Sousa's "Stars and Stripes Forever" exploded from the box. Red and white lights flashed. A crowd filled in fast, the aisle jammed with smiling faces that were genuinely happy for Buster. Applause broke out. Hands touched and patted his back as if other gamblers couldn't wait to catch Buster's contageous good fortune.

Attendants arrived. One man began copying numbers and writing them down on a clipboard. There were three men in suits who stepped in, one of them turned a key into the side of the machine. He heard the garble of speech and the crush of those packing in tightly to behold four blue amazing seven's lined up in the slot's horizontal window.

The rest was a blur. The shaking of hands, a brisk walk down a long carpeted hall, a security guard in front and behind, driver's license, signatures on paperwork, and, 45 minutes later, the casino manager handing Buster a check for $250,000.

"When you're ready to leave the casino, Mr. Cody, we can provide security to accompany you to your car, if you would like..."

Buster's heart pounded so violently when he sprang from the parking lot that he thought the hammering would break through his ribs and kill him. He pictured how his life would be transformed. He saw himself paying off Judith for the hell he put her through.

He envisioned enrolling his sons in private school and paying off his mother's mortgage. Yet all of it dwarfed under the terror of the visions—what if I keep having them? What if I begin seeing things not related to gambling?

Panic turned the steering wheel; fear pushed down on the accelerator. Taking wild, meaningless lefts and rights around Stateline, he glanced into his rear-view mirror repeatedly checking for cars that might be tailing him. He had once read of a huge million dollar casino winner who left a club and was later found near railroad tracks beaten, robbed, and left half-dead. Breathing through his nose, he swung here and there, one turn, then another, watching for suspicious cars. When he was sure it was safe, Buster pulled back onto Highway 50 and bolted away from Stateline. It was then, as he stared into on-coming traffic, that a new panic seized him: *What if I saw my car going over Echo Summit?*

His shaking hands could barely deposit the casino check at a Wells Fargo ATM. Fumbling over the paperwork as his car idled at the window, Buster prayed with all his strength that the trick was a once-in-a-lifetime, 50-million-to-one, inexplicable freak of nature that would soon dissolve. He simply wanted the entire experience to be gone.

Buster closed the curtains in his room tightly, double-latched the door, and jammed the neck of a chair underneath the handle. Then he threw off his clothes and jumped into the shower letting the hot water massage the back of his neck and spine. He breathed the steam; he scrubbed thoroughly with soap as if the trick were dirt and grime that could be washed away. *I just lived the dream of every gambler in the world,* he thought, *but seeing through things scares the shit out of me.*

A marriage is built on trust, Buster. And you destroyed the little trust we had left...

Firing the bath towel into the corner, Buster peered at the dazed face staring back at him in the mirror. *I'm over $250,000 richer, but the money did nothing to change my round, nondescript face. I have a friggin' laborer's face, the face of a man consigned to* a lifetime of graveyard and factory swing shifts. Had my face been a piece of plywood, it would fit nicely on the wall of a building going up with all the other unremarkable pieces of plywood. I was never pretty. If somebody had to shape together a face out of clay in 15 minutes, that would be my lousy face. My head is a honeydew melon with eyebrows. The truth of it is that Judith always despised my face. She despised it as much as she despised my compulsive gambling. Will $250,000 buy me a new face?

Stepping back from the glass dejectedly, he noted how his light brown, 38-year-old head of hair had thinned fast in the last year. He ran his hands over the top of his head and detected that now he could see patches of his scalp *through* his combed hair. He had never had much of a physique and stood, in his stocking feet, five-feet, five-inches tall. I'm not fat, not thin, just a sack of average, male skin and bones. Buster seldom thought about his left leg being shorter than his right leg; the special shoe he had worn since childhood was effective and allowed him to come to live with the handicap just as one came to live with a missing finger. Buster Cody is the definition of nondescript, he reasoned. As he examined the clump of gray hairs on his chest twisting like ugly little threads, Buster also theorized, and not for the first time, that his entire adult life spent chasing the pot of gold in Tahoe and in Reno was his way of trying to even the score against the fate that punished him by making him an inferior mound of human compost.

Slumping in his underwear on the edge of the sagging mattress, Buster added up thousands and thousands of dollars blown on blackjack, slots, and dice in countless shoe-string trips to Stateline and Reno. And what was my return on investment? Before today, it was one-tenth of one percent of what I put down on red. But that was *before* today. Today settled the score, didn't it? I'm a quarter of a million dollars richer, yet I'm petrified to step out the front door because I might 'see' what's behind the walls in the next unit as I pass by.

You told me you'd quit, Buster. You said you'd get help, but you're the same old Buster Cody stuck in denial, betting grocery money at a blackjack table, controlled by a pipedream that some big payoff is just around the corner...

The manager was playing solitaire at his desk in the motel's main office. Buster handed him his room key and told him he wouldn't be staying another night after all. "Trust everything was satisfactory, Buster. Were the blackjack tables good to you this trip?"

This vagabond fly-trap is where I've spent a hundred nights. The motel manager knows my name and knows my game. How bad is that?

Before walking away, Buster caught the deck of cards on the manager's desk. He had been playing blackjack. He 'saw' the top card: the two of diamonds lay face down. He rushed out of the office. He vomited into the bushes behind the Gables Motel.

The 1978 Toyota slid into Vista Point between Stateline and Meyers. Buster wanted the magnificent panorama of the lake's soft, blue waters and distant snowy peaks to work on his acid stomach and growing fears. The Tahoe Queen, the lake's Mississippi river boat, drifted from left to right like a drugstore postcard of a white and gold riverboat on sapphire glass with the words "Wish You Were Here." Envying the passengers he could see on the Queen's deck, Buster wondered what it must be like to relax in pure vacation serenity and know simple peace of mind in a world without gambling.

He sat on one of the viewing benches near the water's edge as his eyes continued to follow the riverboat inching its way across his field of vision like a beautiful piece of driftwood. *I could probably buy that friggin' boat right now and set up a tourist business here at the lake. But what good would it do? I'd never enjoy a minute of it because I would always be down at the casino.*

The house is in escrow and closes on the 20ᵗʰ. After that, we're through, Buster...

A tall, lean man in his forties with a Roman nose and harsh face sat down at the opposite end of the viewing bench. His wintry overcoat was buttoned to the neck. A silly tam-o'-shanter with a red, woolen bulb sat on top of his head and tilted to one side. He was fiddling with a stack of large, vertical cards, checking off items with a pencil, then arranging the cards in a certain order. Buster knew exactly what he doing: the man was a sports handicapper shuffling parley cards. Buster felt a twinge of pity for the man. How many thousands has this guy flushed down the drain in sports books betting his kids' Christmas money on a statistical certainty that, in the end, was vacuumed by the casino?

"Any luck this week-end?" Buster asked just to make conversation.

The man laughed. "All my teams lost."

"I'm sorry."

"Don't be. The worst thing that can happen to a gambler is to win. By losing and by continuing to lose, you get a few inches closer to mental health. Winning feeds the compulsion," the man added. "It's like an addict shooting up with more heroin. Losing, and I mean losing the mortgage or your entire paycheck or your wife's inheritance, puts you on pace to ruin. And a gambler with a compulsion needs ruin because it ultimately breaks him. A winning streak is the worst thing in the world that can happen to a gambler; and a windfall jackpot is the road to damnation."

The words exploded in Buster's midst as if the man had tossed a lit stick of dynamite in his lap. The ironic relevance of the man's reference to Buster's last two and a half hours made him wonder if the man had been in the casino and witnessed all that he had won.

"What's your game, Pal?"

"Blackjack. Slots. Occasional dice," Buster answered, regretting he had started the conversation at all.

"How'd you do this weekend?"

"How'd I do this weekend?" Buster repeated, weighing the immensity of the question. "I won."

"My sincerest condolences," the man smiled sarcastically.

Buster threw his gaze over to The Tahoe Queen. The riverboat was heading down to dock at Stateline.

"Pal, hate to say it, but that's the worst thing that could have happened to you."

The man's tactless demeanor was agonizing. "Mind if I ask why you gamble if you have all this friggin' wisdom?"

"I play within the confines of what I can handle; what I can afford to lose. And when I've reached that point, I have the discipline to walk away. Do you have that same discipline, Pal?"

The Tahoe Queen released a few cream puffs of steam, then its quaint whistle shot into the air and echoed through the lake's basin.

"Hey, listen, you have no idea what I can and cannot do."

"Calm down, Pal. My point is that even if you're thousands in the black, you'll blow through it soon enough. Then, before you know it, you're up here again fallin' into a brand new hole that's deeper than any of the holes you fell through before."

A second stick of dynamite went off in Buster's midst. "'Scuse me?"

"Before you punch me between the eyes, I'm Ed."

"Buster."

"Listen Buster, gambling has two roads: one is recreation, enjoyment, blowing a few bucks, then moving on to a restaurant, the beach, or taking in a show. The other road is the driving compulsion that you not only have to win, you have to win big time—it's the monkey on your back that makes you cling to that dice table by your fingernails. That second road poisons your entire life and destroys relationships."

Buster winced. He took a breath and fought off the thought that the man had the perfect philosophical wisdom regarding gambling's destructive power.

"Which world are you in, Pal? Able to win a little, then pay your motel bill or auto insurance? Or do you keep falling through the hole and blowing every dime you've got?"

"Ed, I don't know a thing about you," Buster began cautiously, "and I don't know what your history is, but I'd like to tell you something that might just test your theories to the limit. Would you be willing to listen to what happened to me today?"

229

The experience of 'seeing' cards poured out of Buster. He told Ed how it began as soon as he sat down at the blackjack table that morning. Then he described 'seeing' the four blue sevens on the hundred dollar bill and striking the casino's premier $250,000 jackpot. The man fixed his eyes on the distant Tahoe peaks and seemed to listen with genuine interest.

"That's quite a tale," Ed observed, resting back, his arms stretched out over the viewing bench. "But now I'm gonna' whack the ball back to you with a surprise. Your story isn't all that unusual."

"It isn't!? What do you mean?"

"I've heard of this happening to others. And not just to gamblers. In all walks of life."

Buster breathed a mild sigh of relief. "To be honest, I've been terrified since I left the casino."

"Don't be. Your 'trick' as you call it, is a bolt from the blue. It never lasts."

Buster was incredulous and came to the edge of his seat "*It doesn't*?! How are you so sure of that, Ed?

"I know it from first-hand experience."

"Ed, my wife despises me; my kids don't know who I am; until today I've been drowning in debt. But now, even after winning what I won, I shake like a leaf at the thought of 'seeing' another card face down. A dream come true for some, maybe, but not me. On the one hand I'm greedy and want as much as I can get; on the other hand this—psychic power or whatever the hell it is—is a friggin' nightmare. I'm shaking, Ed. Right now, I'm literally shaking just thinking about seeing another card face down."

"As far as I'm concerned," Ed began, "the term 'psychic' is a misnomer. It's a false label for experiences that have no basis in reality. Two weeks ago I was thinking of an old buddy I hadn't seen in over 30 years. I went into a grocery store and there he was standing in front of me at the check-out stand. Did I have a 'psychic' encounter? Not as far as I'm concerned."

"Then what is it, Ed? What's your explanation for what I'm going through?"

"Let me put it this way: we all want neat little stepping stones of experiences to lay a nice logical path in front of us. Problem is, some experiences have missing or crooked stones leading nowhere. What I'm saying, Buster, is you're no different than anybody else: you expect predictable, tidy bows on your packages of experience to be scotch-taped nicely with bright birthday paper folded neatly at the corners. But as I see it, life's a bloody box with torn edges and inside there's a toy with broken parts that has no fix. Why do birds, immediately after hatching, begin to attack another egg in the nest with a mutated chick inside that hasn't even cracked the shell yet? Scientists call it 'instinct.' What the hell is 'instinct'? No one's ever defined it. People came up with 'instinct' for the same reason they came up with psychic—it's a linguistic mattress tag dealing with the serendipity of 'seeing' cards face down."

Buster was overwhelmed by the man's perception. "Ed, you're quite a philosopher. What the hell do you do for a living anyway?"

"I'm a shop machinist."

"Friggin' intellectual stuff for a machinist, I'd say."

"Buster, I have a Master's Degree in Sociology from Cal, Berkeley. I do what I do for the dough because teaching Sociology and ten cents won't get you bus fare."

The Tahoe Queen finally docked in the clump of villages near the casinos. Tiny white steam clouds released from its smoke stack and a few whistle toots shot up. Neither man said anything for a few moments.

"Where you from, Buster?"

"I live in Oakland."

"Super. May I make a suggestion? Visit the CEP—Center for Extra-Sensory Perception at Cal. They deal with these kinds of experiences. Let 'em test you. It's the best outfit around for this sort of thing. Don't worry: they're not touchy-feely, New Age screwballs. They have a very clear-minded approach to the paranormal. They're expensive, but, hey, you're rich now, right?" Ed laughed.

Ed glanced at his watch as if he'd just remembered something and stood up. "Have to be going, Pal. Nice meeting you. Hope I offered some helpful feedback. Seriously, Buster, consider heading over to the CEP and getting help."

Buster wanted Ed to stay and explore his experiences in greater depth, but he extended his hand and said, "Thanks for listening, Ed. I may just pay a visit to that center in Berkeley. God, I hope you're right about all this being a bolt out of the blue."

"If I were you, Buster, I'd enjoy your—powers—while they last."

Buster watched Ed cruise off in his car. Then he turned back to the lake and stared pensively into the clean blue waters as if his entire gambling history were surfacing from its depths. All those years and only one trip up here when I left in the black, he thought. Yet I lived a losing script over and over. Why does a man commit economic suicide by putting his hard-earned dollars down on the horse proven, *destined,* to come in last? But today that horse won the race and balanced the books. Buster sank to the bench again and went back over Ed's words. An anger began to course through his blood as he added up all the rotten casinos in his past and the hurt they gave him—in money and in heartache. He saw scores of trips leaving Reno in misery with just enough money to get home. He thought of the elaborate lies he had concocted to Judith that masked his gambling trips; he re-played the times he missed his son's baseball games and back to school nights because he couldn't deny himself the blackjack tables through a fast trip to Stateline. If the trick is still there, should I go back down to the slots and tables and use the gift I have to break the friggin' house—in appreciation for all the casino's in Reno and Tahoe that broke *my* house?

Twenty-five minutes later, the doors at Caesar's split apart and the red carpet was under Buster's feet. The fresh peach scent was in the air; the clank of slot machine levers and spinning wheels rang in his ears. He was heading straight for the left end seat at a

$25 minimum blackjack table. Five one-hundred dollar bills went down on the green felt table and the dealer placed three stacks of chips in front of Buster's station. He slid it all into the betting circle.

A hole card flew at him, he steadied himself, then glanced at it: he 'saw' the three of clubs. The trick is alive and well, he thought with supremely mixed emotions as he looked at the dealer's hole card and 'saw' her nine. A Jack flashed at his station for 13. He peeked at his hole card to deflect suspicion, then noted the dealer's up card was a six which gave her 15. She'd have to take a hit. Two other players finished their hands, then it was Buster's play. He studied the deck and 'saw' the eight of Diamonds would be next.

"Stand," Buster stated, forcing the dealer to swallow the eight.

The dealer snapped down the card and broke. She paid Buster $500 in pretty chips.

Buster purposely lost the next three consecutive hands with modest bets of $25, $30, and $35. It was the set-up for the fourth hand when he pushed $1,500 into the betting circle. Immediately, the pit boss turned his eyes to Buster's station.

His hole card, a queen. The dealer's hole card, a nine. Buster's card on top was another queen for 20. The dealer showed a seven. She'd be taking a hit on 16.

After the other players ran their hands, Buster took a hard look at the deck and shuddered: a fat ace of spades sat face down and would be next. "Split," Buster said, separating the queens, creating two hands, and placing another $1,500 on the second hand. The ace came his way and he turned over his hole card to show his blackjack on the first side. He pointed to his second hand indicating he wanted a hit. The dealer flashed him a nine for 19. "Stand," he stated.

The dealer turned over her hole nine, then hit with a red 7. She broke with 23.

Buster won $2,250 for his blackjack hand, and $1,500 on the second hand for a total of $3,750.

The pit boss flinched when he saw Buster split the queens.

Splitting face cards wasn't smart and went against the odds; but Buster always seemed to beat the odds. The pattern was obvious: he was a player who lost tiny, insignificant bets sandwiched between huge bets that always won.

The pattern repeated on the next two hands. Buster lost on plays with $20 and $30 bets, but on the third hand, he shoved $3,750 into the betting circle at his station.

Make it good, Buster, he warned himself. This will be your last friggin' hand at Caesar's before they kick you out for counting cards.

He was dealt a hole ten and a five giving him 15. The dealer's hole card was a king with a nine showing for 19. After the others played out their hands, Buster looked at the deck and 'saw' the three of spades face down. "Hit," he indicated. Buster had 18, but it wasn't good enough. He looked at the deck again and 'saw' a blushing red ace of diamonds.

"Please hit me."

Butster had 19. If he stood on the hand, he would simply push with the dealer.

His eyes narrowed in hard on the deck. His chest thumped with the beat of his heart. He 'saw' the most beautiful thing he could have wished for.

"Hit," he whispered.

The dealer flipped over the two of clubs. Buster had 21.

But he had completely forgotten to glance at his hole card and had played out the entire hand without once peeking at the 10 underneath. The pit boss noted it and had also noted Buster's repeated glances at the deck in the dealer's hands. Either the deck was marked and the dealer was in on it, or Buster was counting cards. The boss rejected the later because at no time did Buster study any of the other hands around the table. As the dealer stacked Buster's chips, the boss memorized the face of the man at the left end seat; moreover, his picture had been taken by the 'eye in the sky.' The pit boss quickly relieved the dealer, but it was too late:

Buster was already heading for the cashier's cage with two buckets containing over $7,800 in winning chips.

...You ruined Christmas for me and the boys, Buster. I want you out tomorrow morning...

A crap table stood between Buster and the casino's exit doors. A huge woman well over six-feet tall blew on the dice in her hand. "C'mon home, Baby!" she shouted. The dice spilled over the green felt table: nine. But it wasn't a nine; it changed to a seven, then it turned back to a nine. Buster knew what the trick was saying to him.

He stepped in and put $1,000 down on "Any Seven." The woman blew on the dice and called out, "C'mon big nine—*do it now!*" Then she fired the dice against the table's far wall.

Seven. The woman crapped out. But Buster won. His odds had been 5-1. He collected $5,000 more in winning chips.

Buster left Lake Tahoe with over $275,000 and a stomach that felt as if it had been pulled apart from two separate directions. At one point, while speeding over Echo Summit, he thought he was being followed. He slammed on his brakes near a rest stop, attempted a quick U-turn to lose the car, skidded on gravel, and nearly plunged over the cliff. Panting in terror, staring straight over the precipice and into his own annihilation, Buster had no doubt in his mind whatsoever that it was his winnings that nearly killed him.

Detouring in Sacramento, he pulled into a drugstore and bought a deck of Bicycle playing cards. Through the two hour drive back to the Bay Area, he set the deck down on the seat next to him and, as he drove, tried reading the top card. It was when he reached Vacaville that he noted a fuzziness had crept in around the edges of the cards he 'saw.' Let the trick be fading, he prayed. Let it go away for good. I've won enough. The ledger's clean and I've learned what I needed to learn. I don't want one more penny.

When he got back to Oakland a little after 9, Buster cruised a familiar side street off Broadway. In front of the empty house he and Judith had once owned, a 'for sale' sign stuck into the unkempt lawn with a 'pending' notice perched on top. The Christmas tree that sat in the front window 12 years ago came back to him nostalgically. It was his first Christmas with Judith, a happy time in his life, two years before Jeffrey was born. He also remembered the day after that same Christmas when he lied to his wife that he had to see Mrs. Cody and her lawyer about straightening out points in his mother's will. After breakfast, Buster bolted straight for Reno.

I called Ted. He tried to cover for you, but I got him to admit you two never went to any ballgame. You drove up to Tahoe alone, didn't you, Buster?

When Buster got back to his apartment, he played one game of harried solitaire after another. The fuzziness around the edges of the cards had grown stronger, but he could still 'see' the numbers and suits face down. Finally, he thumbed through the phone book and found the listing for the Center for Extra-Sensory Perception near the Cal, Berkeley campus. He noted the hours and promised himself he'd skip work and show up when the doors opened the next morning. Buster felt like a man parachuting out of a plane at 5,000 feet and staring down into a completely alien world.

I found a receipt from the Gables Motel in your coat pocket, Buster. The date was...

Buster closed his eyes. God, let there be somebody at this friggin' center who can help me...

II

Dr. Gretchen Cardeau, Ph.D., was Buster's examiner. She was a tall, slender woman whose hair was pulled back and tied in a scalp-tight bun. After an hour of paperwork and a lengthy in-depth interview, Buster began hours of hands-on testing.

He was shown pages with a dozen empty squares and told to write the name of the object that belonged in each square.

He sat in front of a wall of one-way glass wearing earphones and listened to a voice on the other side reciting nursery rhymes.

Buster was then shown a dozen photographs and was asked to select the picture of the person who had been reciting the poems.

A miniature house with five identical doors was placed in front of him. Buster was asked to identify the door with a red ball behind it. The test was repeated several times.

He stood before a long, horizontal shelf of photo albums and was asked to select the album containing the picture of Abraham Lincoln.

The next to last test took the longest. Buster was asked to lay on a couch with a blindfold. He was read a long work of prose with key words deleted. When Cardeau came to a deleted word, she paused. Buster had to suggest the word he thought had been removed.

"It's nearly 4 p.m., Mr. Cody," Cardeau stated. "There's just one final test I'd like to try."

The examiner placed a deck of playing cards face down on the table in front of Buster. "Without touching the cards, Mr. Cody, tell me what the top card is."

Buster's heart skipped a beat. He stared very hard at the deck, but 'saw' nothing. Cardeau shuffled the cards and repeated the test several times. Buster could not 'see' anything other than the red and blue zigzag design on the top card. The trick was gone.

"Tomorrow morning I'll present my findings to the rest of the staff. We will review your tests and arrive at a consensus. Come in around noon, Mr. Cody, and we'll go over the results."

That afternoon, Buster worked very hard to clear his mind of all that had happened in Lake Tahoe. He drove around Oakland, then ate at the finest restaurant in Jack London Square. He took a couple of drugstore tranquilizers—which did absolutely nothing to diminish his anxiety—and went to an evening show where he forced himself to concentrate on the movie.

The next day, Buster sat in front of Dr. Cardeau. The psychologist rifled through a folder of clipped paperwork and notes. She looked up, folded her hands, and said:

"Mr. Cody, we can't find one shred of convincing evidence

to prove you have any extra-sensory abilities whatsoever. You checked out as being dead center in the 68 percent range of the general population that, beyond random statistical chance, cannot accurately forecast anything outside the predictive norm."

"So you don't think I'm psychic then?"

"Well, we prefer the term 'extra-sensory,' but no, there's no indication of that."

"Dr., what do you think happened to me in Lake Tahoe?"

Cardeau exhaled. "There are case studies in the literature, similar to what you have described, though not necessarily connected to gambling. In almost all of those instances, the sensory perceptions were powerful, but brief. My conclusion, and my colleagues concur, is that your experience was a purely temporary and inexplicable phenomenon. Precisely what it was and why it happened, no one knows."

"Actually, Dr. Cardeau, this is the very best news. I want this ability, or power, to go away forever. It's a nightmare."

"Of course, if something were to crop up again, we'd be happy to see you." The psychologist handed Buster her personal business card.

Buster breathed a huge sigh, closed his eyes, and slid back in his chair profoundly relieved.

"Now, Mr. Cody, keeping in mind my background as a psychologist, may I ask you: Do you feel you have a gambling problem you'd like to do something about?"

Behind Cardeau, a small, oval window looked out into a modest garden plaza of landscaped yellow roses and geraniums. Buster stared hard at the flowers.

"Dr. Cardeau, I've never amounted to much of anything in life. My birth certificate should say 'nondescript person' on it. Had low grades in school; never accomplished a thing. I was born with one foot shorter than the other so I was never good at sports. Not one remarkable personality trait; no unusual skills at all. No awards, achievements, or plaques. The only certificate I ever had was in traffic court. You know those boring, dull, cheap paintings of cows grazing next to a barn that hang in people's dining rooms? That's me. I'm that painting. For 20 years I've worked at a bottling plant packing crates of soda. That's me again: an empty, nondescript soda pop bottle. I'm the white napkin you wipe your mouth with; in a row of plain bingo folding chairs, I'm one of them; in an orchestra of accordions, I'm the guy in the back row hitting wrong notes. Even the test results you just gave me says it all: I fall into the 'norm'.

"There has been one and only one thing I have excelled at in my life: cards, dice, slots, and the nags. I can't tell you the times I headed into a casino not hoping to win $100 or $500, but desperate to win thousands—all so I can turn around and say, 'Look at me, Buster Cody: I know gambling and I won big time and Joe Success, millionaire CEO of Monster, Inc., can't do that!' Dr., I'm pretty sure that what drove me to gamble is the everlasting hope of capturing what I think was stolen from me when I was born—uniqueness.

"And now—I win the sweepstakes with all its bells and whistles. And what do I learn? That wealth is a haunted house. I haven't had one moment of peace or satisfaction since I deposited $270,000 in my checking account. All that money hasn't fixed a thing in my life. I'm still Buster Cody with the same plain old lousy face and the same cardboard existence. My wife is divorcing me, my kids hate their father. What's happening to me, Dr. Cardeau?" Buster came forward with tears in his eyes. "What's this all about?" his voice cracked. "I just won a fortune and I'm falling...falling completely apart..."

An hour later Buster watched the bustle of university students moving in all directions on the corner of Oxford and Telegraph Ave. in Berkeley. Look at all these future Dr. Cardeau's, he thought. No, I will never be a college graduate or have a degree, but I can pay my debts off, he resolved; and I can wipe the gambling clean from my life forever.

An Oakland Tribune paper box stood a few feet away. The banner headline read: "A's Take Giants 5-0 In Game 1."

Buster sailed west over the Bay Bridge to his mother's in Daily City. Mrs. Cody was in Phoenix with her ailing brother and Buster had promised to install a telephone answering machine while she was gone. After buying Radio Shack's best device, he picked up beer and a pizza and headed to the house to relax and watch Game 2 of the World Series between the Oakland A's and San Francisco Giants. He patted himself on the back for going through with the testing at the CEP, but the fear of 'seeing' cards came and went. What if the trick comes back? The image of jumping out of a plane at 5,000 feet returned—but he was still in the air and hadn't landed yet. Buster was waiting to see if he'd plunge on solid ground or drop straight into the spike of a tree.

While hooking up his mother's answering machine, he tried to focus on what he would do with a quarter of a million dollars. He decided he'd make good on what he bled from Judith's inheritance; he'd put the boys in private school; he'd pay off credit cards; he'd let Judith keep the equity from the sale of the house. And after I do all that, he resigned, I will go back to the CEP and ask Dr. Cardeau to help me get rid of my gambling compulsion.

The game was in the third inning when he turned on the television, put his stocking feet up on the coffee table, and bit into a warm slice of pepperoni pizza. Judith and the boys were still weaving in and out between balls and strikes and Buster wondered if a new life with Judith were possible. The question is: Do I truly want to go back with that woman? Do we have one essential thing in common?

The grandfather clock ticked pleasantly in the corner of the living room. Buster switched off the game in the eighth inning when the A's seemed to have clinched it. Then he collected the empty cardboard pizza boxes and beer cans, went out the back door, and stepped to the side of the house to dump the garbage. He lifted the trash can's lid and was about to toss in the refuse when his arm froze in mid-air. A golden glow shone pleasantly from a book lying face up at the bottom of the can. He peered at it oddly, then reached down and lifted it out.

THE BOOK OF TIME

The trash fell into the can and Buster closed the lid. Puzzled, he brought the book into the living room where he began reading:

Loma Prieta Earthquake
Northern California, USA
October 17, 1989AD

A 7.1 wave magnitude earthquake whose epicenter was the Forest of Nisene Marks State Park in Santa Cruz County, northern California, USA, struck at 37.04 North, 121.87 West near the San Andreas fault at 5:04:45 pm local time...

The dislocation resulted in 63 deaths, 3,757 injuries, and destroyed physical structures, highways, transportation, housing, and utility lines throughout the state's northern region...

Buster's eyes fixed on the date: October 17, 1989. Can't be. A misprint, he said to himself. That's the day after tomorrow.

The ensuing pages filled with accounts of the earthquake's damage and destruction in San Francisco, Santa Cruz, Hollister, Palo Alto, and Oakland. He skimmed over detailed reports of fires, landslides, and collapsed buildings. Must be a geologist's report estimating potential earthquake effects, Buster guessed. What is Mom doing with this friggin' document? And the date of this quake—October 17, 1989—two days from now? And the precise time—exactly 5:04 p.m.? What kind of dumb geology is this?

Buster flipped through pages and noticed the absence of numbers. His eyes bulged when he came to the list of victims who died in the disaster followed by the names of thousands injured and precisely what those injuries were. Chills raced down his spine. This thing is actually naming people who will die day after tomorrow.

He marveled at the book's strange physical makeup. It was tough as nails, yet somehow supple. He traced his hands over the unusual black print. Flipping back to the first few pages, he looked for the author or the name of the government agency that produced the book, but found nothing. Then he flipped the book over and examined its spine trying to find the source of the gold halo. This is impossible, Buster told himself. The phone pressed to his ear. Buster dialed Phoenix.

241

"Uncle Dave, can I please talk to Mom?"

His eyes were fixed on *The Book of Time* lying face up on the coffee table, its soft golden glow springing around it like a pretty halo. "Hey, Mom, I'm at the house and I—"

"Did you install that recorder?"

"I did. And that's why I was calling. But, hey, listen, Mom, I want to ask you: did you happen to throw anything into the outside garbage can before you left?"

"That can should be clean as a whistle, Bus. Veronica wiped the house spotless a day before I left."

"So—you left nothing in there, then?"

"I said *no*. There shouldn't be anything in there. You oughta' be able to eat out of that can it's so clean. Why do you ask?"

"Oh, I just had a pizza and dumped—"

"And that's why you're calling me? Listen, Bus, I want that kitchen spotless when I get back."

After hanging up, Buster took *The Book of Time*, sat down, and began to read more accounts. He was hungry for the sentence, reference, or the attribution that revealed the source of the strange thing he had found in his mother's trash can.

...A 23 by 15 millimeter portion of the upper deck of the San Francisco-Oakland Bay Bridge, eastern cantilever, collapsed to the lower deck at 5:04:54 local time killing Mr...

He turned a few pages, then he caught a second baffling headline:

Major League Baseball
World Series Cancelled
October 17, 1989AD

The dislocation occurred prior to the third game of the 1989 Major League Baseball World Series at Candlestick Park, San Francisco, California, between the San Francisco Giants and the Oakland Athletics...

The Oakland Athletics won the first two games 5-0 and 5-1 at the Oakland-Alameda County Coliseum in Oakland, California on October 14 and 15, 1989AD...

Because of the death and destruction in the northern California region, Commissioner of Major League Baseball Fay Vincent ordered a 10 day postponement of the third game of the Series which was played on October 27, 1989...

Huh?!

Buster's jaw dropped as he studied the box scores of all four World Series games, two of which hadn't been played. According to the book, the A's would sweep the Giants in four games; moreover, batting averages, pitching statistics, attendance figures, and gross ticket sales for the entire four games were printed before his disbelieving eyes.

He looked at the blank television screen across the room. How could this book, a book I found minutes ago, accurately report the score of Game 2 when I turned that very game off in the eighth inning? And how could it report the friggin' results of the next two games—when they haven't been played yet?

He switched the set on quickly and watched transfixed as the highlight replays of Game 2 moved across the screen. The Oakland Athletics won it 5-1 precisely as *The Book of Time* reported.

Flying through more pages, Buster paled when he read the next bold heading:

The Collapse of the Cyrpress Freeway
Oakland, California, USA
October 17, 1989AD

A 2.0 kilometer portion of the upper level deck of the two-level Cypress Street viaduct on Interstate 880 in the city of Oakland, California collapsed at 5:04 p.m. killing 42 people...

He read the sentence three times to be sure he had read it correctly.

Jesus!

The collapse of the Cypress? Judith leaves the bank in Oakland

and picks up the boys at the after-school program, then drives home over the Cypress around 5 p.m.

The Book of Time slipped from his hands. In the corner of the room, the grandfather clock ticked off like gunfire.

He ran out to the trash can and threw off the lid. He picked through the cardboard boxes and beer cans he had just dumped, then poked the bottom of the can with a stick not certain just what he was looking for. How could anyone write a book like that then toss it into my mother's garbage can?

A thought reeled back to him in horror: he had skim-read the list of people killed in the earthquake. *My God, were Judith and the boys on that list*?!

Buster raced back into the house and knocked over the living room end table. The lamp crashed to the floor as he dived in vain for *The Book of Time*.

But it was gone.

Panic-stricken, he searched the living room and every other room in the house. He threw back closet doors, opened cupboards, and yanked out bedroom drawers. He ran to the front yard searching for someone he thought must have taken the book from the room and was now hurrying down the street with it. Then he raced into the small yard behind the house, rattled the locked bedroom windows, and combed the garage for some sign of a break-in. Buster stood on the cold cement of his mother's garage and wondered if the pizza had been food- poisoned to affect his mind.

Crazed images whirled through Buster's head as he sped across the Bay Bridge back to Oakland. An insane logic had taken hold: if a book could predict the final scores of games that hadn't been played, was it also capable of accurately predicting an earthquake that hadn't occurred which it said will kill people? He imagined Judith and his two sons driving over the Cypress at 5 p.m. on Tuesday and heading straight into the unthinkable. A ripple of fear shot through him when he passed the bridge's toll plaza and identified the dreaded Cypress freeway in the distance.

Buster's fists tightened around the vinyl steering wheel. It was Sunday night, but he needed to see Dr. Cardeau. Heading up Telegraph Ave., he grabbed the first pay phone he could find and called the CEP. He left a desperate message demanding an appointment first thing Monday morning with the psychologist. His voice shook as he explained it was urgent, an *emergency*, in fact.

Dashing back to his car, Buster nearly collided with an aged black man negotiating the sidewalk on a crooked, wooden cane. The man could not have weighed more than 125 pounds, wore an Oakland A's baseball cap, and licked what was left of a vanilla ice cream cone.

"Got the time, Boss?"

Glancing at his watch as he flew passed the man, Buster said: "It's—7:25."

A hand was inches from the car's door handle when Buster heard the incredible words over his shoulder:

"Boss, what do you think about that book you found?"

Buster wheeled around. "What's that? What did you say?"

The man deposited the rest of his ice cream cone into a sidewalk trash can. His meek, smiling face, brown eyes and pearl white teeth reflected distinctly under the glint of the street light. He had the physical appearance of a man in his 70's, yet his sharply youthful movements were like those of a young athlete who needed no cane at all.

"Do you still doubt *The Book of Time* is a work of fiction?"

The next question rolled off Buster's tongue shakily as if it were the most natural thing in the world to ask. "Sir, tell me: is there going to be an earthquake on Tuesday?"

The man looked grim. "I'm afraid there is."

"Is there some way to prevent it?"

"No, Buster. There isn't. History is immutable."

"Imm—u—*table*? Who are you?"

"I'm your helper."

"My *helper*?"

Buster felt as if he were stuck in place, suspended in a chamber of weightlessness completely detached from the real sidewalk he stood upon, the real Telegraph Ave., the real space of Oakland, California. He was about to ask a second question when the man raised an emphatic finger toward him and added:

"Now may I tell you something important, Buster? You're anything but nondescript. Follow your intuition as you have been doing to this point and you'll discern how truly unique you are."

"Was—winning all that money connected to finding the book?"

The man smiled.

"Give me an explanation! All this craziness that's happening to me—Explain it!"

"Discovery, Buster. *Discovery...*"

"I'm sorry," Buster said near tears, shaking his head from side to side. "I can't cope with this friggin' insanity any more."

"You most assuredly *will* cope, Buster. Trust yourself and follow your instincts." The man tipped his cap and sauntered off.

"What about my wife and —!"

The man ignored him and hastened at a pace that seemed unusually swift for someone his age. Buster stood spellbound as he watched the figure turn the corner around the side of a building. "Hey! Wait a minute, Mr.! Talk to me!"

Buster ran toward the corner, but the heel of the special shoe on his short foot caught on a crevice in the sidewalk, buckled, and broke off. *Dammit!* Buster tried to shove the heel back into place. When it failed to re-attach, he limped to the corner frantically and, staring down the cross street, blinked in disbelief. It was impossible, but the man was already two blocks away, a lone figure turning right again on his wooden cane, vanishing after passing under the white light of a street lamp.

Buster was in his car speeding around the corner, combing the cross street, searching every inch of the city block for the man—bus stops, alleys, diners. He peered into storefront windows, cruised adjacent blocks, and shot through a parking garage. But he couldn't find the man wearing the A's cap.

Rushing into a pharmacy, he bought a package of tranquilizers, then found a water fountain and gulped two tablets. He closed his eyes and took measured breaths.

MyGod...

History is immu—table...

Back at his apartment, Buster thumbed through a dictionary and found the word 'immutable': "Not capable or susceptible to change." The man was saying that you can't change history, Buster reasoned, but then why did he also say 'follow your instincts'? On the one hand, events can't be changed; on the other, I'm supposed to follow my intuition. If I was crazy, Cardeau would have known it. And she would have said so, wouldn't she?

The telephone was in his hands. He thought of calling Judith and spilling everything out to her. Then he caught himself and wondered if he could reason with the woman at all. Either she'll hang up on me when she hears my voice, or she'll hang up when she hears my story. The phone went down. Buster swallowed another tranquilizer, applied a warm cloth to his forehead, and lay back on the couch. Those box scores in *The Book of Time,* he kept thinking. Those friggin' World Series scores for games that have never been played. The quake and the Cypress flared up: Judith, Jeffrey, and Billy were sailing up the freeway's on-ramp at 5:04 p.m. on Tuesday. Seconds later the car was crushed in a cloud of smoke and debris. He closed his eyes in misery. It's not going to happen, Buster swore to himself. I will never let it happen.

With paper and pencil in hand, he sat at his kitchen table and plotted the steps he'd take beginning in the morning and continuing until 5 p.m., the day after tomorrow. When he finished writing, he applied the warm cloth to his forehead again. What about the $275,000 that now sits in my checking account? Then he re-lived the terror of nearly going over the cliff at Echo Summit. Buster's leaden, tired eyes closed. He finally dropped off to sleep a little after 11.

On Monday morning Buster drove to Amalgamated Bottling in Emeryville and walked into his manager's office. "Max," he announced, "thanks for everything, but I'm through. I quit. Nice working with you."

Before Max could say anything, Buster was out the door.

As he left the factory for the last time, Jose cruised passed him along 66th Street in the lunch wagon and waved. Jose didn't know it, but he would never see his best customer again.

He called the real estate agent to make sure the house was on track to close escrow on the 20th.

From West Oakland, he retrieved his telephone messages. Cardeau agreed to see him at 2:30 that afternoon. He called the Extrta Sensory center at Cal and confirmed his appointment.

He dialed his mother in Phoenix who stated she wouldn't be back for another week.

Then he took a deep breath and called Judith at the bank. She hung up as soon as she heard his voice.

That afternoon Buster sat in front of the psychologist and described as clearly as he was able the appearance of *The Book of Time* in his mother's trash can, its disappearance in the living room, and the very strange man on Telegraph Ave. The psychologist listened patiently and processed his every word.

"Dr. Cardeau, do you think I'm losing my mind?"

"First, Mr. Cody, let me ask you: are you still able to 'see' cards?"

"No. I've played a hundred games of solitaire and don't 'see' a thing now. I can't do it anymore. The trick's definitely gone. For that I'm thankful."

"Now as to this book predicting the earthquake tomorrow," she sighed, shaking her head, "I must say I draw a blank there. And this strange man you encountered—"

"I know, I know," Buster agreed, "Too hard for a professional such as you to believe it. I'm in a strange, supernatural zone, Dr. Cardeau. Here," he said, placing a receipt down in front of the psychologist, "I brought my bank statement which would prove

I have over $270,000 in my account, which might prove the trick happened in Tahoe, but, no, I can't prove I found that book in my mother's garbage can and can't prove I met that man on the street. Maybe it's all Karma or punishment or whatever you want to call it for giving the back of my hand to my wife and kids for years. And yet, Dr. Cardeau, something that man said has stayed with me: he said the whole thing's about *discovery.*

"Mr. Cody, what do you think was meant by that word *'discovery'*?"

"I have no idea, Dr. Cardeau. Absolutely none. But right now my focus is tomorrow, October 17th. My wife picks up my sons every afternoon around 4:45, then drives home over the Cypress. I'm terrified, Dr. Cardeau, and my insides are twisted into a sickening knot just thinking about what I read in that book, but I guarantee you that as sure as I'm sitting in this chair in front of you, my wife and sons will never get close to that friggin' freeway tomorrow. See, Dr. Cardeau, I'm one-hundred percent convinced there *is* going to be a very bad earthquake at 5 o'clock—and the Cypress freeway will go down and people will be killed just as the book said. And worse, there's nothing anybody can do about it because it's immutable history."

The psychologist had been scribbling notes and suddenly looked up. Then she shifted a bit uncomfortably at what she had heard as her keen eyes narrowed in on the troubled man on the other side of her desk. Cardeau could not recall ever having a client quite like Buster Cody.

"Whether you're right or wrong, Mr. Cody, we'll certainly know the truth of the entire matter in less than 24 hours, won't we? But what's important right now is that you believe in this disaster and might place yourself in some needless danger."

"All I can tell you is that I will do whatever it takes to prevent my wife and two boys from ever getting near the Cypress."

"I understand, Mr. Cody. I do understand that."

"By the way, Dr. Cardeau," Buster asked, "I don't suppose you'd be driving the Cypress yourself tomorrow around 5 p.m.?"

Cardeau exhaled. "After what you have told me—probably not."

Buster cruised along Judith's duplex all afternoon and into the evening. Her bottom right unit remained dark and, after deciding to confront her, he finally walked to the door and rang the bell several times. No one answered. Returning to his apartment around 10:30, Buster played a dozen more games of solitaire to convince himself the trick was gone. Then he watched a television talk show until 1 a.m. which featured a woman who predicted that an asteroid would strike the earth in late 1990. Buster's heavy eyes finally closed and he fell asleep on the couch and dreamed of a strange baseball game in which neither team scored any runs, hits, or errors.

On the morning of the 17ᵗʰ, Buster called the elementary school in Oakland to confirm Judith had dropped off his sons.

He went to a jewelry store, bought the finest Rolex watch the store carried, and set the dial to the precise local time.

He drove up to Auto Row in Richmond, traded in his Toyota for a new Mercedes, and paid the difference in cash.

Around noon, he cruised the bank to be sure Judith's car was tucked into its stall in the employee parking lot.

As he pulled away from the bank, a powerful doubt began to sweep over him. He went back and forth on the idea that *The Book of Time* had been a hallucination. The sense was so acute, he pulled off the freeway to a side road, shut off the engine, and tried to pick the theory apart. Sitting at the wheel, Buster examined every line he remembered reading. He wanted a loophole, a crack in the logic of the earthquake's account proving the entire book was flawed. He remembered reading an article in "Reader's Digest" describing mass hallucination. It stated that the phenominon needed a widespread social fear like UFO's or satanic possession to spread through the public consciousness. But finding a book predicting a 7.1 earthquake with a precisely stated epicenter and newspaper-like accounts of death and the names of casualties was different. And what about the man on Telegraph Ave.? Was he also mass hallucination?

Slamming the dashboard in frustration, Buster narrowed

everything down to Game 2 of the World Series. The key is there, he reasoned, because it printed the correct score of that second game and included accurate statistics. And if that book sat in Mom's trash can for longer than a day, it would mean that it correctly predicted the scores of the first two games as well. Which proves it knows the outcome of all four games. And that would mean the book is correctly predicting the quake. The dashboard clock said 2:34. In less than 3 hours, I will know if I need to be locked up in Napa.

The key turned in the ignition. A foot pressed down on the accelerator. Buster sped off into traffic and headed back toward downtown Oakland trying to understand what the man on Telegraph Avenue meant by *discovery*.

III

Buster looked hard at Judith's black Ford parked quietly in the employee lot behind the bank on Broadway. Standing in front of the car, he glanced around to make sure he hadn't been seen, then released the hood's latch. He propped the hood, proceeded to rip off the distributor cap, pulled out the spark plug wires, disconnected the fan belt, and shoved the strap into his pocket. Then he closed the hood quietly and quickly walked down the sidewalk toward his Mercedes.

Sailing up Broadway a little after 3 p.m., Buster stiffened with dread as he turned on the radio and listened to the first strains of the World Series preview show for Game 3.

"And so—San Francisco faces off against Oakland which has a two game advantage. Today, the Giants will try to come back at Candlestick Park hoping to notch their first win of the 1989 World Series at home..."

He pictured 42 innocent lives, now at work, sitting at school, at home, or already on the road, destined to go down in the crush of the Cypress freeway collapse. But my wife and my sons won't be among them, he promised himself. I'll go down before they will...

It was 4:14 p.m. when Buster marched down the hallway of his sons' elementary school on Ninth St. and entered the main office.

"I'm Mr. Cody," he said to the vice-principal. "My two sons are in the after-school program here. I'm picking the boys up a little early today."

"All right, Mr. Cody. Would you please sign the release card? And if you could also provide me with the parental code."

"The code?"

"Yes, the code, Mr. Cody."

"The—ace of spades," he answered softly, forgetting all about the verbal code that had to be given to release his sons.

The ace of spades...

"Mrs. Cody and I are separated. She had some car trouble and will call later. I'd like to leave a note for her and would appreciate you reading it to her over the phone."

Tried calling you twice. Took the boys to a show.
Let's talk later tonight. –Buster

"Your sons are in the schoolyard, Mr. Cody. I'll call them."

Ten minutes later, the boys appeared in the office doorway with surprised expressions. Jeffrey, 9, Billy, 7, looked at their father as if he were part father, part sphinx.

"What are you doing here, Dad?" Jeffrey asked crinkling his nose.

"Oh, I thought I'd take you guys to a movie. How 'bout a show? We haven't been to one in a long time, have we?" He glanced at his watch.

Buster and his two sons headed down the long corridor. The boys had trouble keeping pace with their father's rushed, quickening steps.

"Hey, Dad, how come we're walking so fast?"

He hurried his sons out the school's main doors and down the front brick steps. When he reached the bottom, he froze in his tracks. Judith had turned the corner and the pair came face to face.

"Why am I looking at you, Buster?" Judith asked with cold, accusing eyes. "What are you doing with the boys?"

"I thought I'd take the boys—I left you a note."

"And you ignore our agreement and don't give me notice?"

"I called you at the bank. You hung up, Judith. I tried to let you know."

"You're not taking the boys anywhere, Buster. You know the agreement."

"How'd you get here, Judith?"

He bit his lip as soon as he asked the question.

Her eyes set in on him with deadly contempt and she said it slowly: "*You* vandalized my car, didn't you, Buster?"

"Whadoya' mean?"

"God, Buster," Judith nearly broke down crying, "Why do you do these kinds of idiotic, irresponsible things? Why are you such a bastard of a loser, Buster?"

The broken record played its sour melody in his ears once again. The tip of his wife's finger was in inch from his nose as she tore into his long list of sins and character flaws.

Jeffrey and Billy, his two sons, had to stand there and see their mother and father split apart. His heart ached even more when he considered that he was the reason. But he had to keep his focus: he knew the four of them were minutes from an event they would probably remember for the rest of their lives.

"I need to talk to you," he said. "Something has happened."

"Oh, Buster," she scolded, waving him off as she had waved him off so many times before. "Something's always happening in your sad, pitiful life."

"Listen to me!" he shouted into her face. "I just told you something has happened! A—tragedy. Can you understand that? Can we please spare the boys any more of this friggin' crap and talk to each other like human beings?"

The boys went into the front seat of Judith's borrowed car. Buster closed the door and he and Judith moved off to the side. He glanced at his watch again: it was 4:45. "So how'd you get here?"

She was seething with her arms folded and wasn't about to stand there and subject herself to his cross-examination.

"For God's sake, Judith, can you answer one civil question?!"

Fire was in Judith's eyes. "I got off early, couldn't start my car, then I called a garage. A mechanic came over and told me someone vandalized my motor. Had I known it was you, Buster, I'd have had you arrested. I called my sister. She loaned me her Chevy so I could pick up the boys. Thank you so very much, Buster," she added acidly. "You're going to pay for this—every damn penny of it..."

"Yes, I will pay for it," he agreed. "In fact, I'll buy you a new BMW, Judith..."

"Don't mock me, Buster," she spat back at him, her voice cracking.

Stalling for time was key. His wife could bring a sledgehammer down on his head, but if he distracted her, kept her talking, she and the boys would never leave the school parking lot and would never make it to the Cypress freeway.

"Judith, I've been a liar, a bum, and caused you and the boys nothing but friggin' misery. But in the last couple of days there have been—*events* that have changed my life. Yes, I vandalized your car," he admitted, removing the fan belt from his pocket to prove it. "I did it to keep you from driving the Cypress freeway because there's going to be an earthquake that will hit it and cause it to collapse. A big one, Judith. People will die. It's only minutes from happening right now."

Judith shook her head in disgust at her husband's ability to out-do even his own feckless incompetence. "Did a bookie in Reno give you odds on it, Buster? You're a big shit, you know that? You're the all-time, grade-A jackass. I prayed for you; I offered things up for you; I found you a good counselor which you lied and said you were seeing. But you never saw him, not even once, did you? Most of all, Buster, you hurt the boys who really have no idea who their father is. Where oh where does your self-destructive behavior come from?"

"Keep talking," he said. "I really deserve to hear this."

"Don't patronize me!" Judith screamed.

It was going to have to happen here, not at the empty construction site where Buster had planned to drive his sons to endure the quake. But he was glad Judith had appeared unexpectedly; for they would all be together now and Buster would have no doubt about where anyone would be when it hit. As Judith's excoriation of him raged on, as the next few minutes dropped off, Buster's perception of his past sins—compressed into moments of grand remorse—moments in which he saw his endless lies, the naked destructiveness of his compulsive gambling—could now be exchanged for one life-saving act of contrition.

Judith continued to chastise him, but Buster's eyes roamed over the school building: it was an ancient, two-story brick structure that looked like it should have caved in years ago. Now he and his wife, the boys in the car, stood in its shadows. Behind the school, at the end of the parking lot, he noted the flat plain of a grass soccer field.

"Judith, we're moving over to that soccer field. Now!"

Buster threw the car door open and yanked his sons out. "Guys, I want you to get over to that soccer field. Now! Go!"

"Why, Dad?"

"*Move!*"

"What are you doing, Buster? Have you totally lost your mind?!"

"We need to get away from this building!"

Judith took Jeffrey's arm and tried to pull him away from his father. Buster took his wife's wrist and twisted it until she cringed and let her son go. "*Buster!*"

She whacked her husband across the face with the back of her hand. The boys cried, then she slapped him again. The vice-principal, who had been watching the confrontation from the school steps, ran back inside the building to call the police.

Unable to move Judith far enough away from the school building, Buster finally took his wife's head in both his hands. His face had contorted into madness; his eyes bulged with fury and panic. Through clenched teeth Buster screamed:

"Woman—do you understand English? There's going to be an earthquake and people are going to die!"

They were the words of a man who had gone off the edge. Judith slapped him again and a little cut opened on the side of his face. Then she tried to break away. The boys came to their mother's defense, hating Buster, punching and scratching at him as they tried to get their mother free from their father's cruel hands.

Finally, Buster picked his wife up by the waist and carried her across the lot as the terrified boys tried to pry their mother loose. When they reached the edge of the soccer field, Buster and Judith collapsed to the skin of the worn, yellow grass. He released his wife and gulped air on all fours. The boys clung to their mother moaning and crying. Judith wept as she hugged her sons tightly. Buster had no doubt his sons would probably kill him if they could.

On his hands and knees, Buster finally caught his wind as the face of his watch peered up at him. It was 5:04 p.m.

I did everything possible, he resigned, listening to his own anguished breathing in his ears, still thinking *The Book of Time* could be a hallucination; that the man on the sidewalk had been a hallucination; that all the misery he had accumulated since Stateline, Nevada was one, grand hallucination.

Judith clasped her arms around her sons. All three of them were huddling and crying a few feet away from Buster. He looked at his watch for the last time.

The ground began to roll. It was a mild shaking at first, then seconds later it seemed as if the entire city block wobbled on casters.

Telephone poles swayed. Street lights swayed. The school building swayed. Chunks of brick fell from the school's second story and crashed to the tops of cars in parking slots directly below where Buster and Judith had argued moments before.

Judith and the boys were paralyzed. Judith screamed, "My God!"

Buster thought he saw the sidewalk in front of the school rippling up and down.

The vice-principal and another woman were caught on the school's brick steps, their faces drawn and white. Hunching back into the doorway arch, the second woman screamed. The principal braced herself with her arms in the frame of the door.

Somewhere not far off glass shattered into the sound of a thousand panes crashing to cement.

It lasted for 21 seconds of horror, yet it seemed to Buster as if it went on forever.

An unnatural stillness, a noiseless vacuum followed. Buster, Judith, and the boys were frozen. They waited, listened, breathed.

Somewhere in the distance sirens wailed. Shouts rang out down the street. Horns honked, car brakes squealed. Buster wasn't sure, but he thought he heard the ugly metal of cars smashing into one another.

Judith looked at Buster as if he had transformed into something supernatural.

Turning over on his back, Buster opened his eyes and stared straight up at the cloud-flecked sky. His thoughts were on the 42 who were not as lucky as the four of them were at that moment on the yellow grass of a soccer field in mid-town Oakland.

Winding around the last curving stretch of mountainous roadway, Buster descended into the Lake Tahoe Basin. In the distance, the vault of the lake spread its cobalt blue waters across the spectacular glistening landscape. Conifers, ponderosa, and sugar pines thickened into a universe forest; along the highway random patches of snow clumped like cotton wads; the scent of pine duff floated through the open car window like wonderful perfume. Buster breathed all of it in with exhilaration. This time, however, the vista's grandeur wasn't a signpost for beckoning blackjack tables and dollar slots. This time Buster drank in the splendor of Lake Tahoe's natural magnificence.

The manager at the Gables smiled broadly. "Buster, your usual room? Hey, didja' know the blackjack tables started sizzlin' when they heard you was comin'?." he laughed out loud.

Buster went to his room, shaved, took a hot shower, then put on a clean, white shirt. Back at the wheel of his car he paused a moment before turning the key. How many times have I backed out of this same slot at the Gables then shot like an excited comet for the casinos? Cruising Highway 50, the structures flashed passed like familiar movie set facades: motels, ski chalets, pancake shacks, and t-shirt shops opening early May doors to Mr. and Mrs. Suntan. His heart beat a little faster when he spotted the first casino marquee on the Nevada side.

If you place a shot glass and a bottle of scotch down in front of an alcoholic—he'll resist if he's clean. Is Buster Cody truly clean?

Caesar's glass doors slid away and Buster stepped onto the red carpet. The fresh, peach scent reached him first, then the slots' bells and cranks clanged in his ears. Walking the same aisle he walked a hundred times, he passed a crap table where a player had just donated his one-inch stack of chips to the dog bin. The pit bosses patrolled like wardens; the girls at the change cages snapped down greenbacks to gamblers already deep in the red; the roulette wheels clicked in time as the little elusive ball skipped over the green and red plastic squares.

A blackjack table was in front of him and players sat at their stations like stiff-necked dummies. A heavy-set man with a huge, sagging stomach had just thrown his losing cards down disgustedly, then walked off uttering filthy curses for the entire casino to hear.

Buster claimed a seat in the middle of the table and slipped a $5 bill on the betting circle. The dealer replaced it with a chip and shuffled the deck. A moment later a card flew at Buster face down. He waited, held his breath. Finally, he stared at the card and 'saw' nothing. And when he glanced at the dealer's hole card, he also 'saw' nothing. Buster closed his eyes. "Thank God Almighty," he whispered, exhaling from the bottom of his lungs.

The four of diamonds shot over to him face up. He peeked underneath: a king. He had 14. The dealer showed a ten of spades. "Hit me," Buster said.

A queen flew at him for 24. He broke. He felt wonderful.

Then Buster did what he had never been capable of doing in his entire gambling life: he rose from his seat at the blackjack table and walked away heading straight for the casino exit after losing his first and only hand.

The arcade's mystique, the slots' spinning lemons and cherries, the dice tumbling over pass lines—lent nothing to him. Lady Fortune, who promised rainbows then made you dig for the mortgage, wouldn't be getting another dime from Buster Cody. The casino was a dreary, flat-lined universe, a tepid glass of water in front of a man who wasn't thirsty. All of the playground scenery dissolved behind him. Just before stepping through the sliding glass doors, Buster took a left into the Men's room. I passed, he thought joyously. I'm clean.

He entered a stall. He closed the door. He wept.

Forty-five minutes later, a dozen people stood in front of Buster as he inched in line to board The Tahoe Queen. He took a lone seat on the upper deck, stretched his arms and fixed his eyes upon the Everest-like Sierra peaks dusted with the powdery magic of snow. Crisp alpine air filled his lungs. He closed his eyes. An idea he had considered before returned: What if I had used *The Book of Time* to bet on the outcome of the 1989 World Series? I could have made millions. But then, Buster Cody's no longer a betting man, is he?

Star Time

The black Mercedes rolled along Sunset Boulevard, threaded its way through downtown Los Angeles, and headed straight for the freeway. Not wanting to glimpse so much as a crumb of the passing landscape, Suzanne Deanna slipped on her wrap-around dark glasses and slumped gloomily in the back seat of the limousine.

"Mickey, forget going to Mel's," she told her driver. "Drive me back to Malibu."

Deanna pulled the cell phone out of its case and called her husband. The chirpy tone had gone to a second ring when her eyes locked onto the dreaded billboard she wanted most to avoid:

SEA BREEZE
Starring Christopher Wild and Suzanne Deanna
Just when do you put love on automatic pilot?
OPENING SOON!

"*Ugh!*" she moaned, looking away as though she'd just seen a corpse in the trunk.

"Hello, Suze."

"Jon, I just saw the final cut. It's horrid. On a one to ten, it's a minus seven. The Gestapo on the cutting room floor decimated the picture. Every one of the location shots in Barbados with one exception was stripped down to chewing gum. *Sea Breeze* is road kill. I think I'm physically ill, Jon."

"Let's not jump to any conclusions yet, Suze. That's commonly a reaction to a first raw screening. Final cuts may yet be made."

"I know when I've seen a bomb, Jon. The whole picture is a tour de force of two-bit editing. The worst imaginable. Suzanne

Deanna stars once again for Vantage Pictures as a brainless, semi-nude twit."

"In which scene?"

"How about right after the opening credits dissolve? And I so, so wanted this picture to work," her voice cracked. "I *needed* it to work, Jon. I feel betrayed. And so damn lousy."

"Are you headed home now?"

"I just left the studio."

"Good. Shoot back here and we'll regroup..."

"Jon, how are you feeling?"

"Good. Better. Just get here, Suze..."

Tossing the cell phone to the seat and closing her eyes, Deanna tried not to hyperventilate. I'm being flushed down the tubes into film oblivion, she mused. I've been cut to pieces in a public place by editing that belongs in a slaughterhouse. I'm so ashamed, the actress thought as she brushed away tears.

Suzanne Deanna was a raven-haired, 28 year-old actress with flashing violet eyes, chiseled cheekbones, Victoria Secrets runway figure, and head turning peaches and cream complexion that, combined with her sensuous, full lips and devastating smile, began stopping traffic when she was 16. It was Seville, though, who perceived far more than a devastating face and body in the actress. From his first glimpse of her, the director saw the gems of intelligence and depth beneath the surface. "Suzanne, you've got the sensuality of an Ava Gardner or Grace Kelly," he often told her, "but more importantly, with time and the dues you'd have to pay, you could one day realize the stature of an Ingrid Bergman."

Vantage Pictures, however, saw Deanna as a brainless siren. In three years she had appeared in *Hollywood Castaway*, *In Search of Camille*, and *Casting Couch*. The studio then rushed her into the well publicized *The Dread*, a superficially intelligent science fiction horror that promised much, but ended up frightening no one except studio executives who had to swallow millions in losses. When she read the script of *Sea Breeze*, Deanna saw the picture as a career breakthrough. But the studio pared it down to Suzanne Deanna draped in a bed sheet; Suzanne Deanna in towel stepping out of the shower; close-ups of Suzanne Deanna in threadbare, French bikini on the hot Barbados sands. The movie's best dramatic scenes were excised; and the screenplay's wit and humor misshapen into terribly pruned, unintentionally laughable dialogue. Vantage Pictures saddled me to a blind horse, whacked it, and sent me over the cliff, she thought in nauseous misery. Riding in the back seat of the limousine, she glared at the snake-like freeway gridlock and tried to comfort herself with the one jewel in her Hollywood experience: marrying three-time Academy Award winning director Jonathon Seville.

Vantage Pictures had invited Seville to the studio hoping he'd direct at least one picture there. The director accidentally caught Deanna shooting a scene in *In Search of Camille*. Who is this woman? He asked, dazzled by what he saw, critiquing Deanna in the shadows behind the cameras. Seville sensed unrealized depth in the actress well beyond her physical sensuality. That afternoon the director sent the actress a dinner invitation. She accepted.

The evening with Seville was electrifying. An hour into it, Deanna wondered if she had been awarded a personal clinic in the art of filmmaking. From screen writing to art direction, Seville blazed a trail through the fundamentals and subtleties of making motion pictures. His command of production and his insights into obscure details overwhelmed her. In the midst of it, Seville disclosed his passion to write and direct his magnum opus, *Stars of Gold*.

"The picture is the saga of the Mansfield family," he confided. "*Stars of Gold* follows four generations of film makers—actors, directors, writers—beginning at Essanay Studios in Chicago in 1910 to the high tech wonders of modern Hollywood. Financing will be a huge mountain to scale; and it may just have the biggest budget in film history, but I swear to you, Suzanne, this airship will one day soar into the clouds. Count on it."

Jon Seville relegated every man Deanna had ever known to a pale ghost of wisdom and tenacity. Nondescript, average features, tousled, thinning brown hair, slim build, and worn, tweed sport coat, Seville was all encompassing, supremely confident, sensitive, and intellectually mesmerizing. She sat transfixed as Seville sketched his grandiose plans for his project into the early morning hours. His passionate brown eyes flashed when he said, "My output will require 6-8 hours a day at least. Therefore, I'm taking two years off from directing to write the screenplay—the only way *Stars of Gold* will ever get done." When she arrived back at her apartment just before dawn, Deanna was breathless.

After several dinners with the director and a romantic trip to Catalina Island, Deanna looked into the mirror and resigned that Seville represented the substance missing in her life. This man has taught me as much about myself as he has taught me about film. Three months later, the couple was married in Cancun.

Jon Seville, the light of my life, she mused. Gazing out at Malibu's ocean vault through the Mercedes' tinted windows, Deanna recalled the day months before when she sat secluded at her husband's film lecture at USC. She had taped his presentation and listened to it until she practically had memorized it. Removing the player which she kept in the limousine's back seat compartment, she pressed the play button, closed her eyes, and heard Seville's voice resonating with haunting irony:

"Good casting, terrific screenplay, and even riveting performances are sucked up into the black hole of bad editing. Bad editing in film isn't just cinematic thievery; it's grand larceny with scissors.

"Ladies and Gentlemen, please do not misunderstand: bad editing is indeed a horror," the director exhorted to the packed USC auditorium. "But there is one mercurial force that is the only power in the film universe capable of overcoming virtually any negative: *Cinematic Chemistry*.

"Film Chemistry is indefinable; it's the connection of personalities meshing magically in the camera lens. It was Tracy and Hepburn; Fred and Ginger; and Bogart and Ingrid Bergman. It's the most electric phantasm a picture may ever possess. How many movies can you name that boasted a glittering cast, fine screenplay, and the finest director at the peak of his game only to fall flat on its face a week after release? Chemistry is chance; it's a roll of the dice; all one can do as the filmmaker is to set the proper conditions for the seeds of chemistry to germinate—and even then one must pray very, very hard that it evolves at all. Ah, but when chemistry percolates and catches fire, the genie is in that legendary bottle. Never doubt it for a moment: when you have screen chemistry, you have cinematic Shangri-La."

The USC audience gave Seville a thunderous, standing ovation. My God, Deanna thought wearily, whether Jon knew it or not, he was talking about *Sea Breeze* and the other bombs I made at Vantage Pictures. As Deanna wiped her moist eyes, the applause from Seville's lecture on the tape faded and applause from another standing ovation rose up in its place. Suzanne Donahue stood alone in the hue of soft blue stage light after the University of Michigan's final performance of *A Streetcar Named Desire*. She appeared as Blanche Dubois in a production that stunned those who saw it. A bad actress could have never the pulled that off, she reasoned with pride. Jon's chemistry was palpable in that production. It existed from day one between Teddy McGuire, who played Stanley, and me. But cinematic chemistry at Vantage Pictures? The concept could never make it past the studio gates.

The night of the final performance of *Streetcar*, an elderly man approached Deanna as she left the theatre. "Ms. Donahue, may I say that was the most superb performance I've ever seen from anyone so young?" I have seen every major Blanche Dubois since Vivian Leigh appeared in the role on Broadway. I would place your Blanche at the very top. You were mesmerizing, Miss Donahue. When I speak to my son, I'm going to tell him I saw an astounding young actress tonight."

Three days later David Forbes called from Vantage Pictures in Culver City and asked her to send him a photographic portfolio. She raced around campus and nailed a photographer who took dozens of pictures. Deanna mailed the photographs to Forbes who called her as soon as he saw them. Two days later she flew to California and went through an afternoon of screen tests. That same evening she had dinner with Forbes.

"Vantage wants to offer you a contract, Suzanne. Suggestion: complete your university degree, get an agent, and re-locate here. We'd like you to start production on *Hollywood Castaway* end of June. But Vantage has another actress named Donahue. Can you suggest a surname you could live with?"

She answered the question immediately. "My mother's maiden name—*Deanna*."

Two days before she graduated from Michigan State, her mentor, Professor James Sterling, spoke his final, memorable words to her: "The screenplay you wrote for your degree, *Woman on the Edge*, is very, very impressive, Suzanne. In my opinion it equals your acting talent—which is sayng something. You have a gift for creating memorable characters and weaving an intriguing drama. As high above the clouds as you may be over this Hollywood contract you just signed, my advice is to concentrate on polishing the craft of writing."

The studio had her before the cameras a week after she received her degree. *Hollywood Castaway,* a film that offered her little dialogue and multiple scenes bordering on complete nudity, became Deanna's first link in a chain of losers. No sooner had she finished filming than she was handed the screenplay for *In Search of Camille.* A twinge of disappointment raced through her when she realized her character was that of another kewpie doll seducing the nearest man. But her agent, Terry Bequith, calmed her fears: "Suzanne, an actress rarely starts out her career in this town with a meaty Blanche DuBois role. You must view pictures like *Camille* as the marketing of Suzanne Deanna. Accept what you're offered for now and work hard. You'll shine through this phase like a gem and move up. I promise."

The limousine crept passed the security gate of the Seville mansion. It was a two story, 10 bedroom palace spread over seven secluded Malibu acres. It was the baby sister of The Hearst Castle,

Deanna often kidded herself. Game rooms, miniature theatre, Greecian pool, library, tennis courts, and lagoons with scores of koi always begged the same question when she entered: How did I ever graduate college, make 5 pictures in a hurry, marry a three-time Academy Award winning director, and land in this chateau? She stood in front of the spectacular vista of the Pacific that swept in through the sumptuous livingroom's wrap-around picture window. If I have one true source of peace in this citadel, it's the ocean, she told herself often.

Sliding back the glass door, she stepped out to the redwood deck looking for Seville. Chaise lounges, lavender umbrellas, and sitting chairs scattered about like deck furniture on a Princess cruise liner. Her husband was not at the glass table where he usually wrote from morning until early afternoon. She searched down the stairs which descended from the deck and lead to the private beach below. Returning to the house, she found Seville lying down in the bedroom, a warm towel applied to his forehead. "Joint pain, malaise, a little nausea," he smiled. "The perfect storm. I quit fighting it around two."

"Jon, you're *not* feeling better, are you? What can I do for you?"

"I think the point is: What can I do for *you*?"

"Watching that screening was like being in a haunted house: every scene had a different monster coming out of a different closet. When, oh, when will the chemistry be right for me, Jon?"

"Suze, if chemistry were sold in a bottle in this town, the stores would never be able to keep the shelves stocked with it."

"Right after the screening, I made an appointment to see David Forbes."

"For the purpose of....?"

"I want to clear the air concerning how I feel. And I intend to ask him, not demand, just ask, if the possibility exists to do a picture with someone like Stanley Cain, the one half-way decent director at Vantage. I just can't continue to waste my efforts rattling around inside tin cans like *Sea Breeze*. I have the right to ask that, don't I, Jon?"

"Yes, you have the right. But remember, Suze, your ambitions come way down the ladder on David Forbes's list of priorities. Producer's Rule number 100: A studio boss eats the same thing every morning for breakfast: pictures that gross profits. But you want to see the boss, go see him."

"Guess my insecurity level is off the charts at the moment."

"Understandable. But don't let it become an epidemic. This is not about you as an actress. Chemistry, remember? I will never patronize you, Suze; it's not in my genes; I'll repeat what I've said over and over: you have depth, but haven't scratched a tenth of it yet. Say what's in your heart to Forbes, be sincere, show strength, but don't whine. Above all, remember that one day a script will come along with your name on it and when it does, you'll skyrocket."

The next morning Deanna stepped into Forbes' office at Vantage Pictures. The producer was a Jeckyll and Hyde: a garrulous, happy-go-lucky tennis zealot on the courts; but a ruthless, silver-haired ice man in dark suit and turtleneck once he passed through the studio gates. Sitting behind his long mahogany desk flanked by walls of black and white glossies of the studio's actors and directors, Forbes smiled tightly at Deanna. "How is Jon? I know he has Lupus."

"Good and bad days. Mostly good right now."

Forbes raised his arms to the sky. "What we would do to have him here, but you know that. And I understand he's taking an extended studio leave to work on a major project."

"Yes, a screenplay he intends to write and direct. Quite an undertaking."

"How I'd like to be a fly on the wall overlooking his word processor."

"You wouldn't see much, David. He writes long hand and hates computers."

Deanna spilled her disappointment out immediately at the way *Sea Breeze* had been edited. She had not finished two paragraphs before Forbes came forward, put his hand up, and stopped her like a traffic cop.

"I'm aware of all this, Suzanne," he began. "And I don't want you to utter one more unnecessary breath. This is difficult for me, but here it is: I'm afraid Vantage is not going to renew your option. It's not you, per se, Suzanne; the studio is moving toward new streamlined, hi-tec productions. Corporate in New York wants to whittle down and stick with tried and true money-making box office winners. As you know, your pictures have lost money. This distresses me because I brought you in and saw—and still see—impressive depth in Suzanne Deanna."

The walls closed in on both sides of her. Forbes continued rattling off skyrocketing studio production costs, but Deanna heard none of what came from the executive's lips.

Forty minutes later, she was back in the Mercedes. "Mickey, get me out of here *now...*"

She did not call Seville. She did, however, call her agent.

"Forbes nixed me, Terry," she stated in a cracking voice. "Vantage is not going to renew my option. I'm out. Terry, be perfectly honest: Do I stay in this business?"

"Are you crazy? Of course you do, Suze. Give me some time to work up an approach; but let's not rush into anything we'll regret. What I'd like to do is re-position you completely. There are a couple things brewing for a television series too new to go into now, but don't worry, I'll have something soon," he promised. "You've got too much talent not to be working."

Shell-shocked, Deanna sank in the back seat of the limousine unable to believe that Vantage Pictures had flushed her into unemployment. A huge wave of anxiety and fear swept over her as she closed her eyes and tried breathing exercises. She craved the warm images of her Ann Arbor home life and four wonderful years at the university. She wished Professor Sterling were there to advise her. "Mickey," she said, "Drive me to Town Center. Drop me off, then take the car back to the house. Tell Jon I'll cab it back to Malibu later."

She dreaded telling Seville Vantage Pictures had released her. The potential for climbing on the back of a legendary movie director and coat-tailing off his reputation, ran contrary to Deanna's sensibilities. I may need a new studio; I may need a new agent; but I will steer my career on my own away from Jon.

Deanna threw on her wrap-around dark glasses, tied her hair back tightly, and pulled a Dodger baseball cap over the top of her head. Do movie fans recognize has-been actresses in shopping malls? As she watched Mickey drift off in the Mercedes, she wondered how she got trapped in the swinging hatchet of Hollywood.

The mall was an upscale shopping plaza between Santa Monica and Malibu. Strolling along its storefronts inconspicuously, gazing at her own alien image in the windows, she kept hearing Sterling's words about her writing. She went into a drugstore, bought a spiral notebook, walked to Coffee Cantata for an espresso, and found a secluded table in the cafe's back patio. Shaded under the table's umbrella, she opened the notebook and wrote, "The Elements of Screen Chemistry" at the top of the page and poured out every particle of truth she could think of from Seville's film lecture at USC. After she had written about 25 lines, she went on to describe everything she had learned about making bad movies at Vantage Pictures.

Deanna hadn't noticed the extremely lean teen-age girl who stepped out into the quiet patio toward her, but she suddenly appeared under the umbrella. "Would you by any chance be the actress Suzanne Deanna?" the girl asked delicately.

"I'm afraid I am."

"Oh, Miss Deanna!" she shrieked, "How awesome to actually meet you! May I have the sincerest pleasure to shake your hand?"

Deanna extended her hand and smiled politely. "I'm sorry to interrupt your writing, Miss Deanna, but if I didn't come up to you right now, I'd kill myself over and over for the rest of my life!"

"Oh, I think you'd live…"

"Miss Deanna, I've seen every one of your movies at least

twice starting with *Hollywood Castaway*. But my most favorite movie was *In Search of Camille*. I saw it five times!"

"You saw *In Search of Camille* five times?" Deanna repeated in disbelief.

"Oh, God, yes. In fact, I want to start a Suzanne Deanna fan club."

"You're—going to start a fan club for—*me*?"

"Oh, yes! We kept trying to email you about it, but the stars' email addresses are always bogus on the internet. Then we wrote to Vantage Pictures, but all we got was some form letter advertising their movies."

Deanna was incredulous. "May I ask, why in the world would you ever create a Suzanne Deanna fan club?"

"Why?" she asked as if the question were ridiculous. "Because you're so awesome and inspirational!"

"I'm *inspirational*?"

"Of course! Absolutely! When you were in *Casting Couch* there was that scene where you said, 'Stars are friends for the misbegotten.' I never forgot that line. Then in *In Search of Camille* you took Mitch over that rich guy who was a real player. I mean, what is that saying to young girls? We need to see those things, especially today. Your intelligence always stands out as the best quality trait in your movies. Young girls should be required to see all of Suzanne Deanna's movies at least twice..."

Deanna put the pen down and sat back to catch her breath. "I guess I didn't realize that I was *inspirational*. Honey, you're just about the nicest thing that has happened to me in a while—especially today."

"Oh, Miss Deanna, thank you! Would you ever consider appearing at a meeting of the Suzanne Deanna fan club once we form it?"

"Oh, I don't know," she groped. "I—"

"Oh, and I'm dying to see *Sea Breeze* which I know is coming out next week."

"*Sea Breeze*," Deanna repeated as if a loud foghorn had gone off in her face. "Melody, *Sea Breeze* may not be, well, it isn't quite…"

"Quite what?"

"*Sea Breeze* has been a bit disappointing for me, I'm afraid."

"It is? Why, Ms. Deanna?"

"Well," she laughed self-consciously, "I'm afraid the answer to that is a bit too complicated to go into at the moment."

"Miss Deanna, please don't get offended, but I think the producers should not be trying to make you into a sex symbol; you're not that at all. You're more on the level of a Deborah Kerr or Barbara Stanwyck. OK, OK, maybe your pictures aren't money-makers, but so what? It's what your fans want that's important, isn't it? Fans don't care about garbage like 'gross profits'. See, even in those scenes where your beauty seems to be the highlight, you still communicate subtle meaning in your acting."

The girl's words went straight through her.

"Would you please come to one of our fan club meetings?"

"Of course I'll come to your club. Go ahead and give me your cell number."

Deanna tore off some notepaper and handed it and a pen to the girl. That was when she noticed the girl's straw-thin legs and the tiniest waist she had ever seen. This child doesn't weigh more than 85 pounds, she guessed, the possibility of anorexia striking her.

"Do you mind if I ask your age?"

"Sixteen—well, I'm 15 and three quarters," she laughed.

"Honey, I would be honored to come and talk to your fan club."

"Awesome!"

The young girl handed Deanna her cell number.

"Miss Deanna, I don't care if *Sea Breeze* is the best picture of the year or the worst. I will see it at least three times before I decide," she laughed.

"Well, if you see the movie three times and if everybody else sees it three times, maybe…." She cut herself off before finishing the sentence with, "…*then maybe David Forbes at Vantage*

Pictures will call me and tell me he made a mistake not to renew my option..."

An hour later Deanna walked thoughtfully over the highway footbridge and headed down to the beach. She removed her shoes, then strolled over the warm, white sand drowning Forbes and Vantage Pictures in the crash of surf and screech of seagulls. She remembered her father telling her that shells and rocks rolling in from the sea had secretive markings that, if one knew how to read them, predicted the future. The words spoken by the young girl at Coffee Cantata buoyed her. Even that star-struck, 15 year-old child saw through the studio's efforts to make me something I wasn't. Out of the mouths of babes.

Deanna took a cab back to Malibu and found Seville writing at the glass table on the deck. Seville always wrote with pencil in long hand on a yellow legal pad and never typed on a computer keyboard which he believed stifled a writer's creative juices. His hair blowing in the soft wind, his finished pages stacked in front of him and anchored by a thick volume on cinema history, Seville looked up, smiled, and said:

"You didn't come back with Mickey. He indicated you wanted to go to the mall and said you'd take a cab."

"I needed space and thinking time, Jon."

"Did the need for that thinking time have to do with your summit with Forbes?"

"Well, let's just say they won't be putting my star on the Walk of Fame this year. Jon, Vantage isn't picking up my option. Forbes canned me."

Seville lifted an eyebrow. "He actually let you go? What reason did he give?"

"They want to stay with proven box office and Suzanne Deanna isn't proven box office, blah, blah, blah...."

"Certainly wasn't what I expected to hear when I got up this morning."

"Terry wants to 'reposition' me."

"Into what?"

She shrugged. "God only knows."

Seville put his pen down and studied his wife. "So—go right ahead and vent. I'm listening."

"At first, what you'd expect—feeling like a rug's been pulled out from under me. The sense of stepping on nothing. Anxiety, hyperventilation. Then, when the smoke cleared, I suppose I felt some relief knowing there won't be any more *Sea Breezes* and *Hollywood Castaways* to kick me down the stairs. At the moment, I'm numb, Jon."

"All perfectly understandable. A studio dropped you without a clue the end was coming. But my gut tells me there's more to it than whatever Forbes said there was."

"What's the difference, Jon? I asked Terry if he thought I should stay in this fruitcake business. He said he might have 'something soon.' I don't want 'something soon'; I want something *good*. I want to make my mark."

Seville smiled. "So betrayal on the one hand; pride on the other."

"What do you mean—'pride on the other'?"

Seville rested back and met his wife's bewildered, violet eyes. "Suzanne, let me ask you a question: what would you like to do? I mean *really* like to do? Think hard before you answer."

"Make good pictures. Get strong and memorable roles. Maybe one day rise to the top in this industry."

Seville chuckled. "How is that different from what every actor in the history of Hollywood ever wanted? Don't play with me, Suze. You need to dig a lot deeper."

She pulled a chair up to the glass table, folded her arms, and considered the question thoughtfully.

"Stop denying it. Go ahead, Suze: reach down with all you've got. Recognize what's lurking down there, catch it, and pull it up. Whatever it is, it's inside of you waiting to be actualized."

An image returned to her: Deanna flashed on the thrilling fulfillment she felt after Professor Sterling praised her screenplay, *Woman on the Edge*. Oddly, she had never regarded writing the three-act play as work. The entire effort was a euphoric, creative release that gave her a captivating sense of satisfaction.

"I would like—to *write* for the screen, Jon," she stated. "It's been simmering inside me even before college. But it has nothing to do with you; and it certainly isn't connected to a desire to bask in your shadow. Yes, to take the kernel idea of a script like *Sea Breeze*, re-write its weaknesses, and fashion it into a wonderful screenplay."

"Then do it. Dammit! Sit down and write. Forget about Jon Seville and his windmills. You're not in competition with anybody, certainly not me. Just plain write and write and write for God's sake."

"You make it sound as easy as putting on a pair of slacks. Just step into the study for a couple weeks and pound out *Citizen Kane*. Is that about it?"

"Don't be ridiculous. Does it take an act of congress for a woman whose been tagged a sex symbol to learn the craft of the screenplay and become a fine writer? Suzanne, this may sound out of kilter right now, but getting the boot from Vantage may have placed you squarely in the doorway of opportunity to re-invent and discover the latent talent within you. I won't go as far as to say you should be thanking Forbes, but he may have done you an unintentional favor. As a matter of fact, I'd hazard a very educated guess that he let you go because he, more than anyone, knew Vantage could not do Suzanne Deanna the justice she deserved."

"You think that's what really happened today, Jon?"

"Rule Number 10A of Corporate Downsizing: Management explains a heartless layoff to an employee as an 'economic, cost cutting decision.' In truth, the employee didn't fit the mold and his or her continued presence was a personal or financial thorn. Suze, from what I've heard, Vantage is in serious financial difficulty."

Deanna looked at Seville in amazement. "Well, this is quite a bombshell," she stated. "It's the first time you've shared *that* revelation with me, Jon. So I was a thorn?"

"You were under contract when we met. What would have

been the point of telling you I thought that Vantage Pictures was the Doggie Diner of studios? You were legally committed. But neither was your time at Vantage a totally negative experience. You had to start somewhere; just think of what that studio taught you about bad picture making. You were there because you needed to be, Suzanne. Now you're moving on. Care to discuss my humble beginnings writing and directing *Indigo Moon*, my first torpedo? I cringe even now when I see it among the cable TV listings and would pay a fortune to permanently erase that compost from the celluloid universe. Deanna, when you were at Michigan appearing in *Streetcar*, did you say, 'This is too bush league? I need to be at Vantage Pictures in Culver City making movies?'"

"Of course not."

"Right. Vantage was a next step up on the ladder you needed to climb. Yes, it's crushing to be let go, but I'll tell you this: the film making industry is filled with legendary actors, directors, and writers whose legs were cut out from under them early in their careers, but who picked themselves up off the sidewalk and literally went studio door to studio door and eventually found a fabulous niche in this business."

"Jon, before this goes one step further: there's something I need to ask of you. I want an agreement here, on this day, in stone right now, that you'll never use your influence or power behind my back to advance my career. I abhor nepotism, cronyism, and any other 'ism' that bleeds independence from me and props me up on stilts. Will you agree, John, that you won't light any Roman candles on my behalf?"

"Agreed, signed, and notarized," he stated flatly slapping the glass table top. "But on one condition: that you leave me room to rant and unleash the howling wind when I see fit. Yes, Suze, I'll commit to that. Seville will not be picking up any phones nor calling any heads of studios on behalf of Suzanne Deanna."

"In stone, then?"

"It is. In the meantime, stay away from the supermarket tabs and television talk shows, the worst thing you could look at right now. I heard they're running that tabloid piece again saying I was 'so overcome by your sexuality, I bought you as a sex pet'."

Deanna laughed out loud and shook her head.

"Of course, what those magazines will never know, and never want to know, is that most actresses would have manipulated their director husbands to use their influence with important heads of studios. I've always been aware that you're not that breed of cat, Suze. And I love you for it. Your inner core is made of bronze. As I've said repeatedly, there's a script with your name on it and when you find it you'll skyrocket."

"Oh, and how I want that skyrocket, Jon—as long as it is built and launched by Suzanne Deanna alone."

"It will be. And the day it touches off, I'll be in the grandstands watching it ascend as thrilled as the day I completed *Mt. St. Michel*."

She went over and wrapped her arms around her husband's neck in a burst of joy. "I shudder to think what I'd do without the pearl of Jon Seville in my life. God, I've been so preoccupied with my own melodrama, I neglected to ask you how you're feeling."

"Much, much Better."

But Seville was not better. He wrote for another hour, then went to bed feeling as if he had taken a two mile sprint down the beach. Deanna brought him cortisone for the arthritis, made him broth and green tea, and read excerpts to him from books on film history. In the morning, Seville was worse, could not get out of bed, and developed breathing problems. Deanna drove him to UCLA Medical Center in Malibu. His doctor examined him, then spoke privately to the actress.

"Ms. Deanna, as you know, your husband has Lupus. But he also has Hemolytic anemia. The symptoms include the extreme fatigue he's been feeling, but it can extend to shortness of breath, chills, and other debilitating conditions. You need to know his anemia is rather acute. Anemia can aggravate the heart and lungs. What we don't want is cardiovascular collapse."

The floor swayed beneath Deanna's feet. "*Collapse!*"

"I'm going to treat this with iron replacement and folic acid both of which I'll prescribe in substantial amounts."

"Doctor, when did all this develop? I had no idea Jon had severe anemia this serious on top of the Lupus that could affect his heart."

"Frankly, Miss Deanna, your husband asked me not to disclose it to you. But I'm going to have to override his wishes and tell you because I feel you're now an indispensable part of his care."

Trying to conceal her fear, she scolded Seville on the way home for not disclosing the severity of his anemia to her. Seville moved in and out of bed in the next two days, said little, and wrote little. On the third morning, he got up and said he felt so strong that he wanted to write until the sun went down, then spend the evening on the beach grilling steaks and sipping wine coolers.

The sunset was an unforgettable, spectacular Egyptian sky. Burnt orange streaks painted the corners of the setting sun as small waves tapped the shore noiselessly a few feet from Seville who poked at steaks on the smoking grill. "You smell that, Suze?" he asked her. "That light breeze carrying the sweet scent you're now detecting has drifted in from Bali just to grace us and say hello."

"This *is* Bali," she stated, closing her eyes, resting back in her sunken beach chair. She sprawled out in a black bikini bottom and halter-top, her shapely, copper-tanned legs stretching straight in front of her. Deanna could not help but think that this evening with her husband was more serenely composed than any evening since they were married.

"Suze, it should be against the law for anyone to look like you look right now. If a camera filmed you at this moment reflected against this Walt Disney sundown, you'd blow the lens away."

She laughed and tied her hair back with a scarf. "Oh, but if you put the scene into a film produced by Vantage Pictures, it would be edited with a bayonet."

"Quit whining. I predict Mr. Forbes will be stewing in his own juice sooner rather than later."

"Jon, I try to write, but all I do is shoot blanks. Question: does inspiration come all by itself when it feels like it or do you wish it to happen?"

"Neither. Don't believe in inspiration and never have. Writing comes from a muscle in the mind that one must train and exercise endlessly. You wanna' be a great shortstop in baseball, you have to get out there and field ground balls for hours every day, maybe years. Rule 100A in the craft of writing: you have to write, write, and write some more. And when you think you're written out, you sit down and *really* write. We put the stars' names up on the marquee; sometimes the director; sometimes the producer, but seldom the name of the screenwriter who hammered the nuts and bolts together that created the foundation. Why is writing an art most eschew? Because it's too damn lonely and too bloody hard. But as far as I'm concerned, writing is the most fundamental form of thinking. If I were king, no one would be allowed to graduate college until they wrote a full length novel or three-act play."

He prodded the steaks and painted them with his own customized tomato paste, then added, "But when in doubt, take the 81A, Suze."

"The *who*?"

"That was a bus I took to school as a kid in Albuquerque. The first bus came along, the 81 bus, for public school kids. I had to take the 81A that went a different direction to private school. After the kids sailed away, I'd always be left there standing alone at the stop waiting and wondering if the 81A were ever coming at all. But it would pull in, always a bit late, but arriving faithfully nevertheless. You're waiting for the 81A, Suze."

"Reminds me of a line of dialogue in *Streetcar*: 'They told me to take a street-car named Desire, and then transfer to one called Cemeteries and ride six blocks and get off at—Elysian Fields.'"

"The point is you have to be patient and catch the streetcar in the first place. If your ticket is destined for writing, then the commitment to writing must endure through the rainstorms that follow."

"Bus or streetcar, hope it rounds the corner soon, Jon. I just can't bear up under a career where a three-time Academy Award winner becomes my advertising."

"He has no intention of becoming your advertising. It's in stone, remember? But put the lid on your impatience. You think Lillian Hellman turned out *The Little Foxes* overnight? The craft of fine writing is nurtured through a million edited paragraphs."

They had steaks, a leafy cucumber-almond salad, and strawberry cheesecake. The ocean seemed to stop rolling in and turned to a placid, golden pond as they sat with wine coolers chair to chair holding hands. Seville recounted some meaningful experiences making *Mt. St. Michel* and cited a critic's ugly censure of the film a week after the picture's release. Then Deanna told Seville about the young girl at Coffee Cantata and how she had seen all of her pictures several times.

"Jon, that sweet thing didn't care that my movies were raspberries. She just liked *me*."

"Studios track ticket receipts and sales down to the penny, but nobody ever knows how many of those gross sales include people who have seen a film 3, 4 or more times."

A few minutes later a sudden, bitter wind rippled over the beach and kicked up a small sandstorm around them. Seville got up and stoked the dying coals on the grill. Then, with his back to his wife, said:

"Keeping our agreement about your independence front and center, would you indulge me for a moment and listen carefully to what I'm about to say? Afraid I'm going to rant."

"Please do."

"Suzanne, two Hollywoods have always existed side by side in two parallel worlds. The first world is the glamorous Hollywood of a galaxy of worshipped stars and their glittering careers in magical studios. This Hollywood serves as a dreamland for searchlights illuminating star-studded Academy Award red carpet nights. It's the tempest for the latest Hollywood gossip mill feeding fans with the rumors of who's marrying whom. It's the allure of Sunset Boulevard and groupies in Beverly Hills tour buses hungry to see the homes where Clark Gable and Elizabeth Taylor lived and loved. This Hollywood intoxicates the masses who get hooked on a life-long addiction to a mythology: a mythology that drapes Marilyn Monroe in diamonds and lavender brocade as she wiggles down a staircase; a mythology of Judy Garland and the scarecrow strolling toward Oz; a mythology of Gene Kelly dancing in the rain. As sure as I stand here, Suzanne, there is absolutely no cure for the addiction to this Hollywood."

"And the second Hollywood, Jon?"

"The second Hollywood peels the skin off the first one. This is the gruesome Hollywood that dwells in the shameless sadism of an innocent woman hacked to death in a bathtub. This Hollywood is a cinema of human debasement with accompanying dialogue straight out of the toilet. This is the cinematic world where murder and rape exist for the mere sake of its unthinkable sensationalism. The tragedy here is that box office receipts in this 'other' Hollywood keep breaking records empowering studios to go farther to push the envelope and grind out more sewage. And behind the cameras? It's a privileged culture where the lives of actors and executives manipulate power and spin webs of lust-ridden, cocaine-laced carnality. Suzanne, I see this second Hollywood as a chief cause of the moral corruption of our age. And it covers the culture like a thick coat of grease. Doesn't this second Hollywood prove to you the mighty power of motion pictures once and for all: that life imitates art?"

Seville's eyes suddenly narrowed in on his wife with an almost alien demeanor. "No need to say it, Suzanne: I'm the supreme anachronism in our era. I know it. Won't debate it. I should have been born decades before I actually came out of the womb. But I managed to slip through the jungle and attach myself to *Mt. St. Michel* which launched me very fortuitously in this industry. Had I never written and directed that picture, I'd have been known as a holy roller who ended up a second rate editor at some tin can studio. And," Seville laughed, "I certainly wouldn't be here now on this beach at Malibu married to the breathtaking Suzanne Deanna."

She looked puzzled and shook her head in bewilderment. "Jon, this is a little too much."

"Suzanne, no matter what happens, I want you to know I never once manipulated a single frame of celluloid in which sex and violence were created to make a movie sell."

"You don't need to prove anything to me, Jon," Deanna said with great concern. "No one in his right mind would ever question the genius of Jon Seville's body of work."

"Suzanne, please don't misunderstand: fine films are released every year. I'm not talking about good pictures with positive story lines. I'm referring to the writers and producers who control an orb of homicidal, misogynistic, violence-driven, sexually perverted cinema. Their cosmos crushes the very concept of *consequence.* And consequence is my point as I stand on this beach at this moment in time. *Consequence* is the sine qua non of my life, Suzanne. And I pray it becomes the same for you, too."

"Jon—when you say 'consequence' you mean—"

"I mean pictures that will live in the mind 100 years from now! I mean movies they'll be running at film festivals in the next century that pulsate with meaning and impact lives because they strike at the transendence of Man's human condition. Look, *Oedipus Rex* has horrific violence, but the bloodshed is committed off stage. Yet that tragedy is required for drama majors at the university level over 2,000 years after it first appeared in a Greek theatre.

"I'm saying I fear the day is coming when you may not be able to find any film that does not drown in themes of violence and sexual dysfunction. The parents are alcoholic, the children are almost always alcoholics; the father beats up the son, the son ends up beating *his* son; the mother's promiscuous, the daughter sleeps with every guy who buys her a cocktail."

The romantic beach interlude had dissolved. Not a trace of the weakness Seville had shown days ago was evident. Deanna was thrown by her husband's sudden reversal and rambling outburst. "I'm sorry, Jon. I'm at a loss here. You're saying—bad movie making makes bad people, right?"

Frustrated she still hadn't grasped his point, Seville's countenance became a foreboding silhouette hovering over his wife. Stern, wiry lines stood out in his face and flared eerily against the last threads of flames that crackled in the grill. Suddenly, another swift chill whipped over the beach and Deanna reached behind for her sweatshirt, slipped it over her head, and gazed up at her husband fearful that he might drain himself of his strength.

"What I'm trying hard to inject into your bloodstream is the need, the moral mandate, to make pictures with *consequence*. *Consequence* is the pottery of art produced on the filmmaker's lathe. I'm saying the mind behind the script has today embraced the horrors that spill out every night on the six o'clock news. And when that happens, degeneracy becomes the expected bedrock for the industry's craft. Then that, in turn, shapes the minds of audiences who end up swallowing this perversion in their livingrooms on Netflix.

"Suzanne, do you have any idea what *Stars of Gold* is really and truly about? What in God's name do you think I'm writing every day at that glass table out there—*The Forsyte Saga*? Do you seriously believe I sit on that deck 4-6 hours a day scribbling some mundane family dynasty? *Stars of Gold* has at its very heart the ramifications of the goodness of human transcendance told through film history, yes, but told in a way that I am fashioning for the ages. And I assure you, Suzanne, I will crawl on my hands and knees to fashion that portrait in the paint of *consequence* until my dying breath. My prayer is that *Stars of Gold* will be put up on screen 75 years from now and, for those who see it then, will experience nothing short of a spiritual transformation. If I fail in this effort and die first, well, so be it. But I will at least succumb with the satisfaction of knowing I pushed a peanut with my nose from California to New York trying."

"Jon, please, stop this! I don't want to hear any more about 'dying breaths.' One day you'll finish *Stars of Gold* and the world will see it produced. There's not one shred of doubt in my mind that it will be as brilliant as you envision it to be."

Seville laughed sardonically. "Suzanne, you know I love you more than I could possibly make you realize, but those are the obligatory words of an adoring director's wife. No matter how much you deny it, you could never be even remotely objective toward my work. But that is not a sin; you're incredibly supportive and loving and I thrive on that, believe me I do, but in truth, if I handed you the completed script of *Stars of Gold* this very minute and you read it tonight, I guarantee you'd say, 'Jon, how magnificent! It's your magnum opus!' It is simply impossible for mothers, daughters, wives to be objective about their loved one's art. But this is only half of what I wanted to say.

"The fact is, I've grown increasingly uncomfortable with my—our—lifestyle. And I'm uncomfortable with it because of the excess of all this." Seville waved his arms around in a complete circle to indicate the mansion sitting high on the hill above. "How many millions more does one need before it becomes obscene? How many yachts, tennis courts, swimming pools, and four star cruises to Paris and Cancun are enough? What does the Bible say, *'It is easier for a camel to go through the eye of a needle than for a rich man to enter the kingdom of God'*? I do get that, Suzanne; I really and truly do. And I pray you get it. Do advantaged folks like us believe they're spiritually redeemed by a 14-bedroom home with 6 toilets? Does the opulence on that hill up there not give you pause, Suzanne?"

"Yes, Jon, it does give me pause," she shot back coming forward. "But I didn't marry Jon Seville to live in a palace with koi ponds and tennis courts. You think I don't often wonder what separates me—my celebrity with you here in this fairy tale existence—from the lonely woman in her 80's who sits in a wheelchair alone in a rest home on Christmas Day? I think of that more than you know, Jon. But tell me, please, what is it that you'd like me to do about it?"

"*What is it you ought to do*?!" he shouted back at her loud enough for his voice to carry over the entire beach. "First, you can visit that lady in the rest home, read to her, pay for her care. And when you do it, please do it anonymously for God's sake without the trumpets and sirens that often accompany other Hollywood celebrities who make very, very sure the public is aware of every penny of their philanthropy. As for me, I intend to sit out there at that glass table at least six hours a day and use the artistic talent God lent me to get *Stars of Gold* written and one day produced and glorified in 70 millimeter. Suzanne, my life, my art is screaming more and more each day for the *consequence* that I have come to believe is the singular path left to me."

"Jon, I don't like this!" she yelled back at him. "Everything was so peaceful and romantic here minutes ago. Your mood is suddenly frantic. I've seen you passionate many times, but this is beyond the pale. Why are you so reckless and dark?"

"No matter what happens to me, Suzanne, I want you to keep your mind straight. Your professor at Michigan hit the nail on the head: you've got untapped, God-given depth and intelligence. Truly. It's obscene to try and mold you into a vacuous sex symbol— which is what that twisted Forbes wanted to do. Promise me you'll never buy the poison this industry of ours disguises as candy. Above all, remember that while film may be just light and celluloid flashing out of a projector and thrown up on a screen, it has the potential for *consequence* capable of transforming lives."

"You're scaring me, Jon! I don't plan on buying any 'poison.' Why are you lecturing me right now so harshly as if I'm a child who needs to be disciplined?"

"Just promise me, Suzanne, that as you move into your new phase you nurture your work in this industry with every fiber of your being; pledge to yourself that when you go back to pictures, and you will, that you become driven by *consequence*."

"I pledge that, Jon. Of course I do; but I can't pull a rabbit out of a hat. When I was with Vantage Pictures—"   '

"Godam Vantage Pictures!" he cursed. "There must never again be a Vantage Pictures in your life, Suzanne! Never mention that foul studio name again when you're in my presence! Studios like that are Hollywood vampires who don't care who they corrupt. Take proper steps now, Suzanne, and work very hard to assure that the rotten carrot a future studio holds out to you is rejected the instant it's offered. And you will reject it if you labor to understand that 'stardom' and 'multi-million dollar contracts' are often the ticket to moral oblivion."

A frightening premonition overwhelmed her. "Jon, I swear I will remain forever mindful of what you're saying here and I'll place it foremost in all that I ever do. But please stop stressing yourself like this. You need to build up your strength. Jon, I'm not the enemy!"

Seville went silent. He turned his back and gazed out at the sun's last orange arc sinking into the sea. Listening to her own racing heart, Deanna wondered if the outburst was coming from her husband's moments alone at the medical center when Seville lay reflecting on his own mortality. She wondered, with great dread, if the doctor gave Seville some secret diagnosis he may not have shared with her.

"Jon," she said, trying to inject a trace of lightness, "I often wonder if we have a marriage here or if I signed up for a lifetime course titled *Motion Pictures and Real Life 101*."

"One has to stand for something, Suzanne," he said softly. "Let others pour their work down the drain of plebeian temperance if that's their sorry plight, but those who care about good work in this industry must dedicate themselves to *consequence*. Jon Seville's Rule Number 1 of universal motion picture production: Filmmakers are morally obligated to dedicate themselves to *consequence*."

"Jon, so help me, if I ever work in this industry again, I assure you I will dedicate myself to—"

"*To consequence!*" he bellowed, raising his arms high, finishing the sentence in a sudden mood reversal, then wheeling around and laughing as if he had just uttered the funniest punchline of the year.

Vexed by it all, Deanna shook her head and tried to laugh. Seville walked toward her, knelt down beside her, and held her beautifully chiseled face in his hands. Then he took her into his arms and pushed her back against the sand and whispered, "Make no mistake about it, Suzanne; you signed up for a marriage extraordinare with Jon Seville."

II

In the next few days, Seville's strength improved. His joint pain was manageable and he wrote 5-6 hours a day at the glass table on the deck. Deanna marveled at the way in which his pencil moved from left to write with the rhythm of a typewriter carriage. "Today," he'd often say, "I couldn't write fast enough. I had to keep a second and sometimes third little note pad off to the side just to scribble down ideas that flashed at me for a scene twenty pages ahead of where I was."

Two hundred pages of *Stars of Gold* was finished when Sig Foreman, a good friend and independent producer and his wife, arrived one evening as guests. After dinner the two couples strolled along the beach, then went back up to the house for cocktails. Seville tossed out one hint after another describing his vision for *Stars of Gold*. Foreman joked about the soaring costs of the epic production which, he guessed, would escalate into the biggest budget in motion picture history.

"Jon, a script, my kingdom for a script," Foreman stated. "When do you think you'll grace me and let me be the first to read even a treatment?"

Seville teased him. "Sig, are you saying you'd want a crack at producing the most ambitious cinematic project of all time?"

"I'm saying I want to be first in line to read it. The budget, well, from what I gather from your hints, makes me dizzy; but I also know the mind behind the screenplay is the best there is in Hollywood."

After dinner, Seville began to grow faint and an attack of

painful arthritis returned. The Foreman's stayed for a while, then finally left around nine. Seville went to bed and suffered a general malaise that lasted for days. When it worsened, Deanna rushed her husband back to the Malibu medical Center.

"Miss Deanna," the doctor said, "I'm afraid your husband's heart has weakened. I want him to stay here indefinitely. Let's see how things progress and take it one step at a time."

She was at his bedside at the center for hours every day working hard to conceal her panic. Bryce and the Foreman's visited often, everyone conversed about Seville's plans to finish *Stars of Gold,* but Deanna grew frightened as she watched her husband's face grow pale and his voice trail off into a whisper.

Seville was in the medical center for three days when he finally looked up at his wife with exhausted, beleaguered eyes. "Suzanne, will you get me out of this crazy house right now?"

On the fourth day Deanna took Seville home. She attended to him as if he were her private patient making endless pots of green tea, broths, and steam-cooked holistic vegetables she had read could assuage the symptoms of Lupus. At night she read to her husband and, at one point, he returned to the deck's glass table to write. But soon he was in bed again drained of energy and complaining of pain.

Two nights later, Seville asked his wife to read to him from a chapter in a book on Hollywood history. She sat next to his bed narrating the collapse of the studio system of the 1950's and the sad tales of Hollywood legends who had been cut loose after decades living on sound stages. She read of the stars who were victimized by the corporate decisions that came down on their heads like a sledgehammer. But several pages into it, Deanna began to realize that the history lesson wasn't meant for Seville, but for her. At one point, she paused and caught her husband's pallid, sinking face gazing up at her as if to say, "Do you get the point of why I'm having you read this, Suze?" It took every ounce of strength Deanna had to continue reading.

When she finished the chapter, Seville whispered in a low

rasp: "Rule Number 75 of a Hollywood Actor's Career: Just when you think you're at the end of your tether, you suddenly find more tether. Suze, would you please boil me some green tea?"

Waiting in the kitchen for the water to boil, Deanna closed her eyes and felt the floor beneath her feet weaken. "Dear God, please bring this good man some merciful relief...."

She placed a small teapot and two cups on a wooden tray and carried it into the bedroom. Mustering all her strength, Deanna struggled to appear pleasant when she entered the bedroom. "Jon, tell me: when many of the stars went out on their own—"

The tray crashed to the floor. Seville was gone.

She walked to the phone and simply dialed Mel Bryce. "I just brought Jon some tea," she said blankly. "He left me, Mel."

Her parents and sister said they would fly out from Ann Arbor; Bryce and the Foreman's came to the house immediately; Mickey handled the calls to Seville's closest studio associates. Fighting the emotions swelling within her, Deanna handled people like a seasoned publicist. When Bryce thought the time was right, he met with Deanna in Seville's study.

"Suzanne, this must be said now: it was Jon's incontestable wish that I inform you of several particulars before you make any plans." The lawyer handed her a short, handwritten note signed and dated by Seville days after they were married stating that his express wish was to be cremated and that there be no memorial ceremony. "When you are feeling up to it, we can go over his trust, but it leaves his entire estate to you. Moreover, Jon makes clear that *Stars of Gold*, whether completed at the time of his death or not, the entire screenplay, its rights, all his research, become your sole property to do with as you see fit."

"He kept so much from me," Deanna said softly. "All he ever said was that Mel Bryce had a firm grip on our legal affairs and to not spend a moment worrying. But he made it clear you'd always be the compass, Mel. And I want you to continue being that."

"Jon Seville was an extraordinary human being, Suzanne. I'm a better man for knowing him. We all are."

Deanna took two steps, then her legs went out from under her. She fell into Bryce's arms and wept uncontrollably.

News of the director's death electrified Hollywood. Reporters and camera crews swarmed to the Malibu front gate less than an hour after Seville's passing.

"Mickey," Bryce said, "do what needs to be done: hire extra security, whatever. I don't want one paparazzi an inch inside the gate of Jon's estate."

The broadcast media spent much of the day and evening devoted to Jon Seville, running excerpts from his films on talk shows, and discussing the impact of the director's body of work. Shortly before 6 p.m., Deanna stood at the front gate before a throng of reporters and rolling network cameras. With Bryce at her side, she read a statement she had written herself.

"...Jon Seville, the pearl of my life, passed from all of us at one o'clock this afternoon. To the public, Jon was the consummate motion picture screenwriter and director; to me he was the consummate man. Jon's eternal wisdom and brilliant grasp of his medium were as complete an understanding of an art as it is possible for one man to possess. Even in the final shadows of his life, Jon was at work fashioning all he knew into a screenplay that he wished to be his greatest stamp upon the motion picture industry.

"Recently, Jon said to me that moviemakers must strive to make pictures with *consequence*. For Jon the human effort to create film meant nothing less than striving for universal transcendance. Whether he knew it or not, Jon was accurately describing his legacy.

"Jon will live in my heart every day for the rest of my life. But I am firmly convinced that the magnitude of Jon Seville's work remains light years from being truly appreciated. ..."

That evening Deanna gathered her parents, sister, the Foreman's, Roger Seville, and Mel Bryce into the living room and said to them: "Jon did not want a service. I'm having a very private ceremony on Monday in the ocean close to our home here. I want all of you to stay tonight. I am going to prepare a wonderful dinner and then I'd like to show *Mt. St. Michel.* The greatest tribute I could possibly give my husband is that all of us watch Jon's masterpiece."

On Monday, in waters a mile beyond Seville's private beach, Deanna tossed her husband's ashes into the ocean at dawn from a small yacht's starboard side. "Those who care about pictures must dedicate themselves to consequence." She made sure she enunciated his declaration with great care as she watched the ashes flutter about and dissolve upon the swaying, Pacific currents. In the afternoon, at Bryce's request, she drove to the attorney's Santa Monica office. The lawyer placed a large, black, leather briefcase on the desk in front her.

"Suzanne, for nearly 12 years, Jon asked me to maintain these records. After you were married, he added instructions that you would have these documents should he pre-decease you. What is contained herein will undoubtedly hit you hard. You will now know I was, in fact, Jon's interlocutor. I suggest that when you review the paperwork, Suzanne, you do it in a quiet place and give yourself quality time to reflect upon the contents."

Deanna followed Bryce's suggestion to the letter. She took the briefcase back to Malibu and, when she was ready, brought it to the glass table where Seville had written his last pages. Taking a deep breath, she gazed out at the ocean where earlier that morning she had cast her husband's ashes. Then she unfastened the briefcase's leather straps.

Sifting through the paperwork, she quickly realized she was looking at records documenting Seville's anonymous financial support of countless charitable causes. According to Bryce's spread sheets, well over $30 million in 12 years had gone to individuals, institutions, hospitals, and churches. Tears dropped from the sides of Deanna's face as she read through correspondence from recipients of Seville's philanthropy. There were letters from retired actors who had gone broke; the parents of children with leukemia; the spouses of those with terminal illness; priests who needed a church roof or donations to keep a parochial school solvent; and hospital administrators who built facilities and acquired medical equipment through Seville's generosity. Some of the correspondence contained photographs of small children with shaved heads, lucky emblems, prayer intentions, and pictures of Christ—and every envelope had been addressed to Bryce's Santa Monica office. Bryce maintained Seville's complete anonymity for years revealing only that financial assistance came from an unknown benefactor. Mel has carried out Seville's wishes beautifully, Deanna realized. Why didn't Jon confide any of this in me?

Combing through the correspondence, she began to perceive the message between the lines. It grew as unambiguously as if her husband had framed it in gold leaf. Jon did not instruct Mel to give me these records merely to impress me; this was Jon's way of communicating that he wanted his efforts to continue. And he wanted me to steer those efforts to completion.

She crept into the shadows of Seville's study, set the briefcase and its contents in the room's corner, and switched on the desk lamp. Thick, legal-sized handwritten pages collected inside a manila folder with *Stars of Gold* typed on the cover. A Bible lying on the desk's top left corner caught her eye. She picked it up and flipped to a ruler that marked a specific chapter and verse: *The Gospel Acording to St. Mathew.* Seville had underlined a passage in blue ink: "*...It is easier for a camel to go through the eye of a needle than for a rich man to enter the kingdom of God...*"

It was the first time she ever sat at Seville's desk, but she was glued to it for hours sifting through Seville's outline. As the scope of the story unfolded, Deanna began to truly discern what her husband meant by *consequence*. Spellbound, she spent the rest of the afternoon pouring through Seville's notes unravelling the immense landscape of *Stars of Gold.* Had this picture ever reached the screen, she thought, it would have been greater than *Mt. St. Michel.* That evening, Deanna called Bryce.

"Mel, please clarify something for me. Am I to understand

from John's trust that he wanted me to possess all rights to his screenplay?"

"He did. He copyrighted the work in his name and in yours. You retain full rights to it such as it is, to do with as you wish. When studios come calling and begin making offers and, rest assured, pay handsomely for the rights to have one of their screenwriters finish it, you have complete autonomy to negotiate."

"Mel, what if I finished it?"

At first Bryce said nothing. "Well, it's yours, Suzanne. All rights fall to you. You own the intellectual property, the whole kit and caboodle. But do you think you're up to it? Wouldn't that be an immense undertaking? Are you sure you want to try and tackle that skyscraper?"

"I think I do, Mel. Yes. It's what I think I truly want."

Seville's frenetic lecture on film *consequence* their last night on the beach returned. Jon knew then he would not live to see *Stars of Gold* produced. And he copyrighted the screenplay in my name and left me the rights to it in his trust. Why? Jon never said it nor implied it, but he wanted to give me the option of picking up the torch and seeing *Stars of Gold* brought to the screen one day.

She crept back into the study and switched on the desk's banker's lamp. All of it was there: the outline, the unfinished screenplay, and shelves that lined the room with books on Hollywood history. Deanna felt as if she were standing at the foot of Mt. Everest staring up at the mammoth peak 30,000 feet above her—a peak which stretched into the vault of infinite space.

III

After three days, Deanna had grown overwhelmed by Seville's vision. The brilliant scope of *Stars of Gold* led her to the painful conclusion that she was incapable of contributing significantly to the screenplay. What in God's name was I thinking when I seriously believed I could finish this masterpiece? Dropping her pen on the glass table dejectedly, Deanna told herself that completing the script was a ludicrous fantasy in the mind of a loyal, but very naive wife. The next morning she drove to Santa Monica and met with Bryce.

"I've made a tough decision, Mel: After really studying Jon's work and realizing the scope of what he was creating, I've come to the conclusion the project's over my head. The characters are too complex and the Hollywood history alone involves years of research. Jon was doing advanced calculus; my talents, at best, are limited to simple, grade school math. I tried, Mel, believe me. I'm so embarrassed."

"Then so be it, Suzanne," Bryce observed. "You don't owe anybody an apology. Why are you holding yourself accountable? This is crazy. For all you know, no one alive today in the movie industry is capable of completing the script the way Jon Seville envisioned it."

"I suppose I deluded myself foolishly into believing that somehow this was destined to be."

"Did Jon say that? I can tell you that never at any time did he ever indicate to me that he wanted you to add so much as a semicolon to that script. Stop beating yourself up over this, Suzanne."

That night Deanna curled up in the television room and watched *Mt. St. Michel*. Mesmerized again by the naked genius of Jon Seville, many images passed in front of her: her barren acting career, the sale of the estate, and her failure to contribute meaningfully to *Stars of Gold*. For weeks she lived in the cocoon of the mansion absorbed with her sorrows, fears, and a recurring nightmare in which a Pacific tsunami rose up and swallowed Malibu.

Days of lethargy passed as she sat on the deck staring at the ocean as if waiting for a huge sign to rise up with words that spelled out her future steps. She called Terry who told her to be patient; she called Bryce who said she needed to stop trying to be something she wasn't; she spoke with her parents daily who consoled her and wanted her to move back to Michigan. She jogged in the morning, paced the house restlessly at night, and finally decided she would fly back to Ann Arbor and find herself.

Late one night, Deanna's agent called. "Suze, exciting news: the Brightside Network is planning a medical series in the spring, *Manhattan General*, set in New York, a drama dripping with humor and serious overtones. Leonard Marsh wants you to read for the part of Mary Ann Driscoll, the hospital's head nurse."

"Television," she said with disappointment, thinking of a dozen different reactions to the opportunity. "Television..."

"And why not?" Terry shot back. "I'll tell you this, Suzanne: I just read the pilot and I think it has Emmy dripping from it."

Later that week Deanna met with Marsh and the show's director at the network's Culver City studios. They were ecstatic the actress was considering the series and explained the role as "substantive and witty." Rodney Chase, an aggressive, aging male model with years of television experience, was already cast opposite her as the hospital's chief of surgery. The director had the couple read their parts from portions of several episodes. In every scene, Deanna was in bed with Chase, seducing Chase in his office, manipulating Chase back to his Manhattan apartment for sex. Mary Ann Driscoll unfolded as a nymphomaniac thinly-disguised as an RN. Deanna labored through the reading, but more and more it became clear to her that Nurse Driscoll was the doctor's sex-obsessed, mealy-mouthed sex toy. By the time she reached the middle of the script, Deanna saw *Manhattan General* as a medical *Sea Breeze*.

Twenty minutes into the reading, a strange sensation overcame her. She felt as though she were not reading lines at all, but standing off to the side aloof, conscious of herself muddling through imbecilic words, aware of the senselessness of the entire effort. When Chase leaned over in a scene, kissed her neck a bit too passionately, and whispered, "Suzie, you're sexier than Marilyn Monroe. Drinks tonight?" Deanna winced, brushed him back, and let the script fall to her lap. Chagrined, she looked up at

Marsh. "This is the character who's 'substantive and witty?' Sorry, Leonard, I'm no Nurse Driscoll. Afraid this one's not for me."

"Oh, Suzanne," the director countered, trying to quell her fears, "But you are the quintessential Mary Ann Driscoll! You're she!"

His words cut straight through her. "'I'm *she*?' Think you just proved my point, Leonard. Thank you, Gentlemen, for the opportunity, but I think the woman you want is whoever's doing the foldout for Keyhole magazine this month because it sure ain't Suzanne Deanna. Excuse me, fellas, but I'm outta' here."

Hurrying down the hall frustrated and furious, she dialed her agent.

"How'd it go, Suze?"

"Terry, this is the drama you said had Emmy dripping from it? Those were your words, right?"

"Suze, yes, if you took the time to develop the character..."

"And you actually read the pilot, right?"

"Well—Leonard gave me a summary of the project and—"

"Terry, thanks for everything, it's been fun, but this is good-bye. We're done."

Smoldering over the day's pointlessness, she drove aimlessly through the streets of Culver City, picked up an espresso, and imagined a life back in Ann Arbor teaching high school drama. Suddenly, Deanna realized she was staring straight over the steering wheel at the gates of the old MGM studios on Washington Blvd. Idling there for a moment, she recalled that the last words she ever spoke to her husband described the history of this very place. She killed the engine, put on her dark glasses and Dodger baseball cap, and walked toward what had once been a magical portal for some of the greatest stars in the history of motion pictures. She ran her hand along the studio's iron gates noting the golden plaque acknowledging MGM which imbued the wall near the entrance. She thought of the legends who passed here every day on their way to sound stages: Katherine Hepburn, Fred Astaire, Clark Gable, and Judy Garland. But those were stars who made money for the studio and always worked. What about the actors and technicians

295

who had the rug yanked out from under them when the studio system collapsed?

That night Deanna called Bryce again. "Mel, how long do you think it would take to sell the mansion once it hit the market?"

"You're actually thinking of selling Malibu, Suze?"

"I don't know," she blurted out confused and agitated. "The question is: Does one unemployed, former actress need a 10,000 square foot mausoleum to tramp around in? I never felt like a woman who really belonged in Jon's palace, Mel; more like a tourist passing through it."

"Listen very carefully to me, Suze: the estate is as much yours as it was Jon's. You feel the way you do because the love of your life just left you. You need to draw a breath and take a very thoughtful step back. You're still grieving big time and on a mammoth rebound. If my advice carries any weight, don't make one serious decision now. May I suggest you take that respite back to Michigan; visit old haunts, and maybe see that professor you said inspired you to write? You're stepping into a new phase; let it unfold; let it play itself out. As legal advisor—and friend—I recommend that you not let your current state of mind lead you into one legal decision until more time passes and the dust clears."

That next morning Deanna took her usual jog along the beach before breakfast. Rough, uneven surf crashed in through the fog's curtain and a bitter chill swept across the deserted sands. After her half-mile run, she removed her shoes and strolled barefoot in the cold, shallow foam. The Jon Seville memory album began flipping its pages again with the words and pictures of their first dinner date. Deanna could hear his clear, intelligent voice describing his plans for *Stars of Gold;* she could see his passionate, driving eyes assuring her that one day the picture would come to the screen. She looked, like an outside observer might look, into their intimate moments together in the solitude of the Malibu house. Then she asked herself if it was her fate to negotiate her dead husband's legend for the rest of her life.

Deanna's eyes followed the current that rushed in over the

shells and tangled seaweed vines strewn over the beach. She compared the sea's destiny to life itself: an endless ebb and flow; life and death cast ashore, fixtures there, then not there, particles whisked away, swallowed, carried off, thrown up again upon distant shores.

...Just when you think you're at the end of your tether, you suddenly find more tether...

She was about to turn around and head back to the house when there, in the salty foam, a book floated in like a chunk of driftwood and landed 20 inches from her bare feet. A strange but pleasant golden glow circled the volume. Deanna reached down and lifted the book from the soggy sand. It looks brand new, she thought. How odd is this?

THE BOOK OF TIME

It was as dry as if it just rolled off a publisher's press. Glancing up and down the shoreline for a sign of life, she wondered if someone had just lost the book there at the beach. Then she turned back the cover and the lightning bolt exploded:

Stars of Gold Acclaimed
Greatest Motion Picture
April 2, 2034AD

The International Academy of World Wide Cinema in Paris, France, composed of 100 international actors, directors, and producers, named Stars of Gold the greatest motion picture in film history. Inspired by her late husband, director Jon Seville, the screenplay was written and produced by Seville's wife, actress Suzanne Deanna.

The mystifying words hit her so hard between the eyes that she dropped to her knees on the sand.

Stars of Gold traced the evolution of the motion picture industry through four generations of the Mansfield family beginning with Axle Mansfield in 1910 to his great grandson Michael Mansfield...

The book was without one drop of seawater. Scrambling through page after page, she was unable to find the author. Then she searched through the book for the source of the soft, golden halo. She blinked: this isn't possible.

Racing ahead over more pages, Deanna found details of the movie's gross receipts. Another portion described the film receiving the Academy of Motion Picture Arts and Sciences "Best Picture of the Year" award in Los Angeles in the year 2029. Deanna read the names of actors who appeared in the picture, only one of which she recognized. There were lengthy accounts from producers and directors describing how the picture had inspired them to create new techniques in filmaking. Her fumbling fingers turned other pages until yet another incredible line jumped out at her:

...Suzanne Deanna guided Stars of Gold into cinematic history...

Her widening violet eyes darted back to the foam-covered sand where the book had rolled in from the surf. It reached me the very moment I stopped here. I am having a nervous breakdown, she said to herself.

She flew back toward the house. She needed Bryce. She wanted him to see the miracle with his own eyes. She hadn't run twenty-five steps when a child, kneeling on the shore, called out to her as she raced passed.

"Miss Deanna! Hello! Remember me?"

A young girl knelt at the water's edge building an immense sand castle. From over her shoulder, the girl's question rang out clearly through the mist: "Did you find that book in the surf, Miss Deanna?"

The words stopped her cold. The girl hummed a strange little tune happily as she poked her forefinger into the top of the castle to create windows. It was the most spectacular sand castle Deanna had ever seen built on any beach.

"Pretty amazing, isn't it?"

Deanna caught her breath. "What did you say?"

"Remarkable things drift in from the sea, don't they?"

Taking slow steps toward the girl, she suddenly recognized her. "You're the one who was at Coffee Cantata that day, aren't you? The girl who said she saw all my pictures."

"Oh, yes. That was the day you thought your career ended."

"*What?!*"

"Don't be upset, Miss Deanna."

"When did—how did you know what happened to me at the studio that day? *How do you know that?*"

The girl popped a few more windows into the side of the castle, then she stood up on her boney legs that quickly disappeared under the incoming flow of salt water. Unfazed by the powerful current, she rubbed her hands to wash off the sand. "Suzanne, did you know that *one ripple in a pond leads to succeeding ripples?*"

"What in God's name are you talking about?" Deanna asked. "Who are you?"

"I'm a helper."

Deanna shook her head unable to believe the conversation was taking place.

"If you work hard on your God-given talents, Miss Deanna, you may one day build a castle the world will admire."

The question cracked out of her throat without one more moment's thought: "Did Jon—write this book and send it to me?"

"No." The girl stood back and admired the magnificent castle she created one last time. Then she smiled at Deanna. "*Discovery* points the way. *Discovery.*" The young girl stood up and sauntered off through the gushing current as if she were stepping away on a flat, wooden surface.

"*Wait a minute!*"

The sudden crash of surf pounded in like a raging bull and knocked Deanna flat. Clinging to *The Book of Time*, she got to her feet and stood in stunned, frozen panic as the young girl disappeared into a drizzily fog.

"*Hey!*"

Deanna's violet eyes searched for the girl in the Malibu mist. Terrified, she wanted no more of it. She turned and ran back down the beach toward the wooden staircase. Her heart pounding, she flew up the steps, shot across the deck, and threw the sliding glass door to one side. Two steps into the living room, her right foot tangled with the legs of a brass table supporting the collection of her silver wedding photographs. Deanna, the table, and the collection crashed to the floor. She grimaced at her bruised ankle, but got to her feet and hobbled into the kitchen in pulsating pain. Holding her churning stomach, Deanna closed her eyes, sipped water, and envisioned Mickey discovering her asphyxiated, lifeless body there on the kitchen floor. He'd call for medics, but she'd be dead by the time they arrived.

It took 15 minutes for Deanna to gain control of herself and creep back into the living room. She looked at cracked silver-frames and splintered glass scattered over the tile floor. In the midst of it all, *The Book of Time* lay pristine, face up in a golden halo's spray of light. Am I looking at a real object lying there on the tile? Did that thing actually float in to me from the surf? She lifted the book and opened to a random page.

...Under the aegis of Suzanne Deanna, The Hollywood motion picture industry established the 'Seville Award' on September 14, **2037AD** *presented to the actor, director, or producer contributing most humanely and selflessly to the scientific research of debilitating physical afflictions...*

The book slammed shut. Deanna placed it on the glass surface carefully and stared in awe at the strange, but pleasant golden halo. Then she hurried into her bedroom and grabed her cellphone on the nightstand. But her nauseousness seized her and, for a moment, she thought she would vomit. Sitting on the bed's edge with her eyes closed, she worked to control slow, rhythmic breaths. The girl's haunting words on the beach drifted back: *Did you know that one ripple in a pond leads to succeeding ripples?*

When she finally called Bryce, she said, "Mel, I need to see you as soon as possible."

"Suze, your voice is shaking. What's this about?"

"Yes, oh, yes, my voice *is* shaking. And I'm not sure I can guarantee whether I'm OK or not or who I am. Mel, I'm unhinged. I must see you..."

"All right. All right. It's now 7:45. Could you be at my office around 10?"

"I'll be there, Mel..."

Deanna flashed through a shower and change of clothes, then crossed in measured, cautious steps back into the living room. She froze in her tracks and her eyes opened in disbelief when she saw that the book was not on the picture table. She searched over the floor among the collection of framed photographs and broken glass. She shot out to the deck checking frantically to see if she had dropped it and never actually brought it into the house. Then she remembered she hadn't locked the gate at the bottom of the wooden stairs leading to the beach. Someone entered the house while I was in the shower! Did the girl on the beach follow me here? That book practically shot into my hands from the surf. How do I explain that to Mel? She imagined the lawyer's reaction: he'd listen to my story like a good friend, then he'd drive me to a psychiatrist.

The mirrored door of the bathroom medicine chest flew open. A shaking hand reached for a vial of valium. She swallowed two tablets quickly, then stood at the sink feeling the twinges of a nausea rise up again. A thought suddenly catapulted her into her bedroom's walk-in closet. She rifled through clothes searching for the bag she had with her the day she met the girl at Coffee Cantata. The bag—I put the piece of paper with the girl's phone number in my credit card billfold! Deanna dumped the purse's contents onto the bed. The billfold dropped out and her two fingers jammed inside the private slit behind the cards and removed the paper. She picked it up and studied the dim markings. The ghost of a telephone number, faint scrawls on the paper, had all but faded away. Deanna squinted hard at the writing, then raced into the study, pulled a magnifying glass out of the desk drawer, and, under the banker's lamp, copied the numbers that had nearly disappeared. She picked up her cell phone, punched in the number slowly, and listened breathlessly.

"The number you have reached is no longer in service. Please be sure you have dialed correctly..."

Deanna clicked off, then pressed the buttons again carefully. The message re-played. She went through it a third and fourth time. The number did not exist.

But the faded scrawl on the paper was there. The numbers prove the first encounter with the girl had been real. And that proves the second encounter, too. Deanna's eyes tightened into joyous thanksgiving: I'm *not* having a breakdown. No. No, I'm not.

IV

Deanna raced down to the Malibu beach and found the spot where the girl built her huge castle. She combed up and down the beach, but the icy current had washed the cool sands flat. In the distance, a man hurled a stick, his dog fetched it and raced it back to him obediently. Not far away, a fisherman stood guiding his taut line into the surf. The man thought he recognized Deanna and smiled flirtatiously. She watched the seawater roll in, then retreat as if yanked back by some colossal drawstring. *If you work hard on your God-given talents, you may one day build a castle the world will admire."*

When she got back to the house, she called Bryce to tell him she was all right and preferred to meet him for lunch on Wednesday as usual. Then she sat at the glass table on the deck trying to comprehend what had happened. Was the entire experience communication from Jon? Is he saying I should go forward on *Stars of Gold?*

The desk lamp clicked on in Seville's study. Sitting at her husband's desk, she perused the trappings of Seville's unfinished work. The screenplay, the endless notes, and half a dozen books sprawled out under the lamplight. A blank sheet of paper and Seville's ballpoint pen were in her hands. In clear, blue ink, she wrote the words on a new title page, then placed it on top of the script:

Stars of Gold
By Jon Seville and Suzanne Deanna

Deanna's hunger to absorb the fundamentals of screenwriting never diminished. Sig Foreman arranged private sessions with retired screen writer Leonard MacGuffin who schooled Deanna in three-act structure, character arc, and dialogue. The friendship with MaGuffin led to his referrals to new contacts who advised Deanna in pre and post film production. She hired Victoria Gunn, a USC graduate assistant, who came to the mansion twice a week and typed her handwritten pages. On her birthday, Gunn gave Deanna several books filled with screenwriting advice from celebrated directors and writers. She read every page in every book, but grew frustrated when one personality seemed to contradict the philosophy of another. Then she found a line from legendary director Alfred Hitchcock that expressed precisely what she thought she needed:

"Drama is life with the dull parts left out. Take chances. Avoid writing beautiful paragraphs to impress readers. You won't succeed...

Deanna took a red marker pen and printed the words in large letters on a piece of butcher paper, then taped the quotation to the outside window above the glass table on the deck.

Word quickly shot through the movie colony that Suzanne Deanna had picked up the torch from Jon Seville's work on an unfinished, epic screenplay. This forced her to assign Victoria to handle requests for interviews and field media phone calls. The more Deanna refused to grant an interview or commit to any studio or producer, the more it fed the media's fascination with the actress' efforts. Deanna had unintentionally created a mystique around *Stars of Gold* that began to take on a life of its own.

Every week she met Bryce in Santa Monica where she continued to oversee the lawyer's support for over 20 different charities. One afternoon, she walked into Bryce's office, sat down, and said with resignation: "You know, Mel, in the big picture, the

303

truth of it is, I'm a paper pusher here; I need to be called just what I am: Jon's charity clerk, nothing more."

"People in need are getting great help from you, Suzanne."

"Not from me, they're not. They're getting it from Jon. I'm simply spending my dead husband's money—from a nice, safe distance. It makes me uncomfortable. It leaves me unfulfilled."

"Well, if you feel that way, then do something about it."

That evening Deanna went on line and sifted through numerous websites until she stumbled upon "The Mother's Place," a special home for elderly women in Glendale. Identifying herself as Ms. Donahue, she spoke with an administrator, Mrs. Whaley, who described the home as one for the aged infirm, many of whom suffered from Alzheimer's Disease, Parkinson's, and other debilitating illnesses. The home sat on a financial precipice and was locked in a legal battle with the city over codes pertaining to its declining upkeep. The health department threatened to have the building closed and the residents moved to county hospitals.

The next day Deanna had Mickey drop her one block from the home. Dressed plainly, wearing dark glasses and no makeup, her hair tucked under a tweed kettle hat, she walked in and met the administrator. Down the hall from Whaley's modest office, dozens of aged women in their 80's and 90's sat stone-faced around a small television in a cramped living room. Yet the sound coming from the set wasn't audible; nor did it seem that any of the women cared. For a few moments she lingered in the corridor staring at the lonely women sheathed in gloom. Her heart sank: this is the depressing portrait of women waiting to die.

"The residents here have no families, or never really had families at all," explained Whaley. "Visitation amounts to volunteers who come once in a while; in fact, not one of the residents here now has had a family member to see them that I can ever remember."

"You see, I thought perhaps my mother might be here," Deanna lied. "She left our family in Michigan many years ago for another man. We had known they settled here in Glendale, but lost track of them years ago. My brother and I are hoping she might reside here. Her name would be Donahue."

The administrator shook her head. "There is no Donahue here, but would that be the name she'd be under?"

"I suppose the only way to know for certain would be if I could see the women. I'd be happy to make a generous donation if you'd allow me that."

The administrator led Deanna on a heart-wrenching tour. Women with the look of timeless resignation in their faces sat in wheel chairs and recliners in the living room. Some smiled at Deanna as she passed; others did not appear able or interested enough to raise their eyes and note the visitor in their midst.

Then Mrs. Whaley showed Deanna the small rooms where other women, too infirm to get out of bed, lay quietly. A few slept, others craned their necks in the hope that the stranger might be coming to see them.

At the end of the hall, a small room. In the far corner, a hunched woman in her late 80's sat in an old wooden wheelchair with her back to the door. She was staring out the window at an unkempt garden of pyracantha and tangled weeds.

"This is Mildred," Whaley whispered. "She was an elementary school teacher for over 40 years. She has no one."

Deanna went over to her, knelt down, and took the woman's arm. The elderly woman peered up, her face corniced with the grim wrinkles of time. A dim, lost expression sagged in her eyes, but she smiled warmly at her visitor.

"Mildred, this is Ms. Donahue."

"How are you, Mildred?"

The woman's smile broadened. She lifted a finger. "Are you here to see—*me*?"

"Oh, yes, I am, Mildred," Deanna said.

"Did—you know my daughter Kathleen? She was about your age and died very young."

"No. I'm just someone who's hoping you'll be my friend, Mildred. My name is Suzanne."

The woman's hand grasped Deanna by the wrist with surprising strength. "Will you stay and talk about Kathleen?"

"Of course I will."

When she got back to the car, Deanna picked up her cell phone. "Mel, have a pencil? The name of the home is 'The Mother's Place.' It's in Glendale, on Scott St. It's having some problem with the city; they're threatening to condemn the building. Listen carefully, Mel: I want you to do whatever needs to be done to take care of the home's issues so that the house remains solvent."

"What do you mean—take care of its issues?"

"Look into the legal side of what's going on with the city. The bottom line, Mel, is to provide the rest home with whatever funds it needs to survive."

"Suzanne, the legal entanglements may not be all that easy to deal with."

Deanna spoke to Bryce in a tone of voice she had never used to the lawyer before. "Mel, do you understand English? Do it. Whatever money it takes, spend it. And if it's not your area of law, get the best legal mind you know who *can* do it. Do you understand what I'm instructing you to do, Mel? This issue is number one with me. Your efforts are to begin the moment I hang up. I want a call on Wednesday to let me know the progress you've made. I'm clicking off, Mel. I've said all I can right now."

The black Mercedes pulled away, then suddenly glided back to the curb and idled. The glass window between the driver and its passenger slid back. Mickey looked over his shoulder. "Is something wrong, Miss Deanna?"

The writing of *Stars of Gold* grew like a living web in Deanna's life. After her jog along the beach, she worked in the early morning hours copying Seville's habits by writing long hand at the glass table on the deck. Submerging herself in the Mansfield saga until early afternoon, she would often spend evenings reading celebrated screenplays. She filled notebooks with insights into cinematography, set direction, and camera angles. But a week did not pass in which Deanna failed to watch at least a dozen films. Studying pictures such as *Citizen Kane,* she noted the strenghs that made those movies great. Or she'd make it a point to see inferior films and pick apart flaws in the direction or shallow character development and consider precisely how she would have re-written certain scenes to improve them.

But once a week, she returned to "The Mother's Place." Sitting with Mildred on Wednesdays, she read to her and assuaged the aged woman's need for companionship. No one ever connected Suzanne Donahue to the "anonymous benefactor" who was behind the lawyer's legal work that saved the home from closing and paid for complete restoration of the building.

Deanna's interest soon expanded to other homes. With Bryce carrying out her instructions to the letter and maintaining complete anonymity, she oversaw the purchase of furniture, equipment, and clothing for nearly a dozen rest homes. But she never failed to devote her Wednesdays to Mildred and the other women confined to "The Mother's Place" who began to look upon "Miss Donahue" as the shining star in their grim world of confinement.

Increasingly, Deanna succumbed to the desire to embellish *Stars of Gold* with her own personal vision. Plot insights took new directions; characters and scenes never envisioned by Seville were added. But never did she stray from her late husband's theme of the Mansfield family and its historic influence upon the history of the motion picture. Sometimes she'd take a break from writing and tried to convince herself that Seville was smiling his approval. Other times she'd glance down the Malibu shoreline trying to pinpoint the precise location where *The Book of Time* rolled in from the surf and where the young girl on the beach had built her formidable sandcastle. The same question always arose when her eyes found the location: Was everything that happened down there on that beach sent from Jon?

On a rain-washed September morning a year and a half after Seville's death, Deanna drove to see Mildred, then bedridden in a private room. As soon as the aged woman saw her loyal friend, she brightened and nearly jumped up with excitement. "I couldn't wait to see you today," Mildred said in a voice just above a whisper. "I had a wonderful dream about you."

Deanna brought a dozen red and yellow roses and began to arrange them into a vase near Mildred's nightstand. "Oh? I'd like to hear it, Mildred."

"It was a dream about a work of art that some man never finished. Might have been a painting or sculpture. But the man died. You knew this man and finished what he started. At first it seemed too hard to do. But after a long time, you did finish it. People all over the world saw it. They loved it."

When she heard Mildred describe her dream, the vase dropped from her hands. "I did that?" she asked weakly, staring down at the crumpled roses in a puddle of water on the floor. *The Book of Time* and the image of the girl on the beach flashed before her.

Mildred did not react to the broken vase at all. "You created art of lasting beauty, Suzanne."

Deanna couldn't move. "Do you know what this thing was I was working on?"

"No, I don't. Just that it took a very long time to finish. But that wasn't the part of the dream I loved the most. The best part was how people who saw your work were inspired to create great things on their own."

Deanna wasn't sure her legs could carry her across the room. "I think that was...a very nice dream, Mildred..."

Mildred's dream filled Deanna's thoughts as she drove back to Malibu. Overcome by all that Mildred's experience meant to her, she decided to pull off the highway. Drifting into Town Center, she parked in a lonely stall near the far end of the lot, put on her dark glasses and Dodger baseball cap, and went into a café for an expresso. She took it back to the car, still shaken by what Mildred had described. As she sat in solitude sipping the expresso, she removed one of Seville's CD's from a zippered, leather satchel on the passenger seat. Without looking, she inserted the disk randomly into the dash console. It was the sound track from *Finian's Rainbow,* a Broadway musical Seville loved more than any other. As the overture played, she picked up the back of the plastic case and read that in 1948 John Kennedy had been a young congressman who was listening to the cast album in his Washington, D.C. apartment when he learned that his beloved sister had been killed in a plane crash in France. The song "How are Things in Glocca Morra?" caused the future President to break down in tears, it said. Deanna's eyes moistened when she compared Kennedy's loss to her loss of Seville. Yet Kennedy's tragedy did not prevent him from running for senator and eventually becoming President, did it?

It led her to reflect on what she had learned about tragedy as a drama major at Michigan State. Professor Sterling often lectured how the Greeks believed in catharsis—purification of the emotions—as the most important element of Greek tragedy. "At the end of the play," Sterling taught, "the protagonist must have a catharsis. From that moment on, he learns how to live a better life until his soul is cleansed. Then he's whole again."

I'm not in a Greek play, Deanna reasoned. But the idea of becoming whole again—it will become my fate.

Later, when Deanna passed through the mansion, she imagined Seville to be at the glass table writing. Papers and notes would be blowing in the breeze, he'd be looking up smiling, and praising her for her commitment to *Stars of Gold.* "Then do it. Dammit! Sit down and write," he'd burst out all over again. "Forget about Jon Seville and his windmills. Just plain write and write and write for God's sake."

Deanna went into the study, picked up *Stars of Gold,* and brought it out to the deck. The screenplay had grown to nearly three inches of polished manuscript and a grand sense of fulfillment swept over her when she thought of the work she had done since Seville's last written lines. Knowing that scores of scenes lay ahead of her, Deanna also knew that if she wrote a thousand more pages, she would never stray an inch from what Seville worshipped: the essence of consequence.

Gazing out at the magnificent, cerulean Pacific, Deanna dreamed of the day when *Stars of Gold* would finally reach the screen.

I will write, John. But I will become far more than the woman even you envisioned.

Without giving it another moment's thought, she removed the old title page from the screenplay, crumpled it into a wad of paper, tossed it high in the air, and watched it sail away in the wind. The paper swirled to the left, whipped to the right, then blew off toward the ocean and disappeared.

Then she picked up the blue pen and re-wrote two lines on a brand new title page:

Stars Of Gold
By Suzanne Deanna and Jon Seville

October Time

The bags were loaded and it was the top of the 13th inning.

The Cardinal shortstop dug his spikes into the dirt around the left side of the plate, choked up on the bat, and peered at the Giant left-hander on the mound. The six-foot, six-inch relief pitcher, his shoulders shrunken, his arms dangling at his sides, looked like a cornfield scarecrow on a New England Halloween. He came set, glanced at the runner on third, kicked, and poured in a cut fastball straight down the middle of the plate.

The shortstop swung from his heels and snapped his wrists. The fat of the bat met the ball cleanly and a loud crack ripped through the cool evening air. An immense roar filled Oracle park as the baseball rocketed on a line drive toward deep left field. Three-hundred-fifty feet away, King Fontaine had locked onto the drive and was sprinting toward the left field line. Arching his back, he thrust his left arm toward the sinking rope as the ball disappeared into the leather webbing a foot off the outfield grass. At that same instant, the runner on third tagged up and broke for the plate.

It was as if the ball had been ejected from a machine, not a human arm, screaming in on a wire toward the infield. As the knock-kneed runner galloped like a racehorse for home, the Giant catcher crouched and waited pie-eyed for the ball to come in.

Whop!

It spanked the middle of the glove and the catcher reached down and applied the tag to the toes of the sliding runner's cleats in a cloud of dust. The umpire nearly dislocated his shoulder making the call.

"Out!"

311

A double-play. King Fontaine threaded his way through his joyous teammates in the Giant dugout as the announcers' voices boiled over into their microphones and press box keyboards pounded out descriptions of the impossible catch and throw. In the bottom of the 13th, the Giants pushed a run across to beat St. Louis in a scoring circus, 16-15.

With a week left in the season, the 29 year-old Fontaine had gone 8-9 in the game, boosted his batting average to .447, raised his runs batted in to 267, and had smashed his 79th home run. After the game, he stood shirtless in the clubhouse in the middle of a sea of reporters as pencils scribbled furiously, scores of recorders taped his words, and shrieks and cries barked out at the superstar from every direction.

"King, a major league record with 8 hits in a game. Did you—"

"Nope, did nothin' different. It's still a regulation baseball with a rubber core in wool yarn, ain't it? Did the regular season start yet?"

"You'll win the Triple Crown again this year, King. Why do you think there's so little competition in either league?"

Fontaine wiped his mouth with a towel. "Guess there's too many guys chasing highballs this year."

"Contract is up at the end of the season. What do you think you'll be asking?"

"All I know is that in football the fans take the goal posts; in baseball and horse racing the stars and the horses get the gate."

The reporters laughed, loved it, and recorded every word. Fontaine answered a few more questions, then wrapped the bath towel around his neck, the signal his audience was over. As he turned and ambled toward the showers, he told himself once again that if you boiled water, added a sports writer, you would get instant crap.

He stood six-foot two with muscularly rounded shoulders, abdomen rippling to a 34 "V" waist, a physique Fontaine enjoyed exhibiting often as he sauntered around the clubhouse nude. A few threads of natural white streaks peppered his thick, black head of hair which he kept short because he disdained the styles of shaved heads and dreadlocks. He was not a handsome man; the gilt of boyish good looks had faded; instead, rugged facial lines combined with a square jaw and firm cheekbones molded the taut face of a hardened Wyoming cattle wrestler. His dark eyes seldom gazed or roamed so much as they darted, often suspiciously as if sensing a fan or reporter was drawing near. But it was his arms with their body-builder biceps and brick-like wrists that often resulted in a flash of disbelief when fans saw the superstar up close for the first time. They were the might behind his lightning-like stroke into fastballs and sliders that slashed pitches high and deep over outfield fences. "Fontaine has a gorilla's arms," a reporter once wrote. "But he's trained those arms to swing with the bat speed of a cheetah."

An hour and a half after the game, Fontaine collapsed in the soft luxury of his gleaming, silver Jaguar as it drifted around the haunted house-like stillness of the VIP stadium drive path. A knot of kids exploded out of nowhere and chased the car after recognizing the infamous gold-plated brass batsman that crowned the Jag's hood. Fontaine scowled. "Punch it," he ordered.

Karyn floored the accelerator and the park's lights collapsed in the Jag's rear view mirror. Fontaine's thoughts shot ahead to the playoffs, the record book he knew he'd be re-writing, and his new contract—which he intended to have his agent fashion into the biggest in major league baseball history. As the Jag slipped onto the freeway, Fontaine picked up his cell phone and speed-dialed Arthur.

"Popeye here," he said in a whisper.

"A very nice day at the office," the husky voice replied. "I saw it all on satellite."

"All in a day's work. What's the scorecard?"

"Angels just lost 6-2."

Fontaine pinched the bridge of his nose. He had stepped up to the toilet, dumped thirty-five grand into the bowl, flushed.

"What's on the stove?"

313

"Braves 7-5 tomorrow over the Dodgers."

"Put five dimes on Atlanta. And give me New England Sunday in the NFL. Another five dimes."

"Interest you in Miss Santa Anita, Popeye?"

"Nope. Hate the nags. Screwed me to hell last year. I'm through shopping for the evening, Popeye; gotta' go." He flipped the cell shut, dropped it into his shirt pocket, and cursed the day he ever laid eyes on Arthur.

White needles flickered across the city's domino skyline as Fontaine imagined the bookie posting odds on the big Bay Area quake: "Give you 8-5 only 50,000 get done in," he could hear the bookie declaring seriously.

"Head for the office," Fontaine ordered again.

He fell back against the headrest, closed his eyes, and re-played the throw from left field. Over his right shoulder, a beeping horn honk drew close. "Lose that shit!"

Lightning went off in the restaurant's foyer when Fontaine and Karyn stepped into the dim, golden glow of Angelo's. The clink of glasses, the bubbling conversation, even the bustle of tuxedoed waiters came to a standstill when the pair walked across the plush black carpet. Light applause rang out, broad smiles beamed, and Jules, as always, showed the couple to Fontaine's secluded booth near the dining room's far corner. The private table was roped off and obscured from the rest of the restaurant by a wrap-around trellis filled with plastic yellow roses that thickened over the latticework. Every customer craned his neck to catch a glimpse of King Fontaine and his gorgeous lady friend, but once inside the restaurant, Fontaine never acknowledged anyone except Jules.

"Lasagne with salmon, oysters, and steamed vegetables as you know I like it, Jules. And two chilled bottles of that Domaine Chardonnay."

"Of course, Signore," Jules bowed, his long bony nose practically scraping the floor as he withdrew.

Karyn straightened the collars of her lavender blouse, then picked up the menu and pretended to read through the Italian dinners. Her outfit was skimpy, but Karyn possessed no outfits that weren't skimpy. She patted her speckled blonde hair as if to show Fontaine she had it arranged to one side precisely the way he liked it, then sprayed some perfume from a small bottle across her tanned neck. He noted that her brassiere-less breasts, always the evening's bill of fare, were featured a bit more conspicuously tonight. But Fontaine now saw Karyn's breasts as torpedoes—weapons that rammed his starboard side, slowly taking him down, slowly sinking him a little bit more each day and sending him to the bottom in defeat.

"Just for conversation, Karyn, how much of the game did you see?"

"That home run was so cool."

"I know, but did you actually see it? Every time I looked up at your box, it was empty."

"Oh, I was probly' getting a dog and a beer. But I heard it all on the broadcast."

"Mind tellin' me where you bought those Chinese pajamas?"

She zig-zagged a finger down the middle of her breastbone. "This happens to be a very sheik ensemble, you oughta' know, Babe. You ordered me to get it at Victoria's."

"I describe it as a very sheik prostitute's ensemble."

"How about a date tonight, Mr. Fontaine? How about playing 'What's underneath'? We haven't played that in a long time. The night we met: you said you were psychic about my underwear. Care to find out if you're still psychic?"

Jules brought the wine and Fontaine sampled it. "Good. Pour, Jules." Karyn took a sip of Chardonnay, ran her tongue over her lips, then set the glass down and folded her hands flat on the table. "Now for the big $64 question, Mr. F: How soon after the ball season ends do we make tracks for Nassau?"

It was useless. "That's the $64 question?" he asked annoyed. "Well, the answer is that Nassau or Maui or Paris couldn't be further from my mind right now. They might just as well be located on Mars. Do yourself a favor, Karyn, and erase those places from your Saturday wish list."

He had met her at Jack Tangler's pool party. She wore a bandage bodycon, sleeveless mini dress with no brassiere. Every male eye was pinned on her, but she clung to Fontaine like a backstage, rock star groupie. That evening they left together in the Jag and went to a secluded Mill Valley spa where they had animal sex in a hot tub. Three weeks later Karyn moved into the Hillsborough mansion.

But things were changing fast. In the beginning, Karyn's dull-witted small talk was coated over by the heat of her Playboy magazine persona—high cheekbones, thick, pouting lips, luscious thighs and hips. The saucy flare in her sapphire eyes and the sensual way she carried herself in skin-tight wardrobes once excited Fontaine, but the electricity was sparking out. Karyn's allure was diminishing with her hackneyed, vacuous small talk, feigned interest in his career, two-pack-a-day cigarette habit, and what he saw as her manipulation of sex to drain him of his possessions. Even her idioms had become painfully clichéd like sandpaper grating over a rotten piece of plywood. Moreover, he winced at her smoker's cough and the twinge of huskiness that had crept into her voice. Fontaine studied the woman sitting across from him and, for the very first time, began to plot a way in which he could simply eject the woman from his life forever.

"Let me ask you a question, Karyn: Do you actually know what a batting average is?"

"Babe, please, not another sports quiz. Hey, we headin' for the Caribbean soon or ain't we? Oh, King, I don't like that look," she warned a little uneasily. "Announcement: I'm going to the can. In the meantime, would you please think about Nassau seriously and just try to name a date? Can you do that for me, Baby?" she asked smacking her lips.

Jules appeared at the table holding a pen and one of Fontaine's rookie sports cards. He grimaced when the waiter held it out to him because the rule was that restaurant management would allow no fans and no autograph requests near his table.

"Signor Fontaine, pleesa' forgiva' me, but the father of ah little boy in-a-sist I ask you to sign-ah' this for his son. The child sits in-a wheelchair right-ah over there..."

Fontaine looked through the slit in the trellis and saw about half a dozen heads turned in his direction on the far side of the restaurant. The boy was about 11 and looked like he weighed 50 pounds. Vertical straps around his chest fastened him into his chair.

"Go ahead and leave it, Jules."

Fontaine felt his ears burning. Those people tip Jules for his little favor, then he gets his usual stipend from me; that kid gets a $200 investment off the trading card, and I sit here gettin' hosed."

Karyn walked out of the Ladies room humming an idiotic rock tune she heard on MTV. She was thinking that baseball was a much dumber sport than football. In football men destroyed each other like real men should always do. In baseball a guy stole a base and had to call time out to dust off his pretty pants; in football, the dude broke his pecker and still had to rush the quarterback by knocking down a 350-pound guy running with the ball. Is King Fontaine secretly gay? Karyn giggled to herself as she strode back to the booth.

But her giggles turned to ice when she saw he had left her there alone again. A pen and signed baseball card lay on his plate. She peeked under her napkin and found two $100 bills for dinner and carfare home. What a bastared lowlife, Karyn thought, clenching her teeth and cursing Fontaine. She removed a brass cigarette case in anger, popped a smoke into her mouth against restaurant rules, and put on her I-pod earphones. Fuck Italian, she thought, as she gazed over the menu searching for a thick, juicy cheeseburger with fries. And screw Fontaine. He's a King, all right—king of assholes..."

It was completely impulsive, but Fontaine was in the Jag flying down 101 south to see Janette. The thrill is gone, he told himself. Karyn's the faded polish on a pair of old spikes. As he sped toward Saratoga, he compared his ex-wife to his live-in girlfriend: Janette was a Parisian vacation; Karyn was a quick trip to Reno; Janette was a ballerina; Karyn was a plastic cheerleader who showed off her pink panties; Janette was a fine wine; Karyn was cheap vino. Fontaine cursed himself again for allowing his marriage to Janette to fail. Racing down the freeway at 80 miles per hour, he went over the gambling he had lied about; the pills Janette discovered that she said turned him into a rattlesnake on too many holidays; and the last straw: Marily. I kept her hidden in LA for three years until that bitch called Janette and sang her soap opera in all its filthy detail. When Janette confronted Fontaine with the affair, he denied it and swore Marily was a woman he had scorned years before. Three days later Janette did what Fontaine never thought possible: she served him with papers. Janette was the only woman he had known who refused to worship at the altar of King Fontaine. Slamming the steering wheel with his fist, punching the Jag's accelerator to 90, Fontaine reasoned that Karyn had to be eliminated yesterday. Once she was ejected, he would win his ex-wife back on a road he would personally pave with gold.

The Jag circled the neighborhood streets three times because Janette demanded he must never be followed. The home was a two-story, Victorian gingerbread house that sat at the end of a private road in the Saratoga hills. Enclosed by the finest security system Fontaine could buy, he punched in the codes at the front gate and deflected thoughts of a cold, gray day when he pulled in and found Janette with another man. The gate slid to the side and the Jag crept into the driveway. As the iron bars closed behind him, Fontaine swore he'd crush the balls of any man he ever found moving in on his ex-wife.

Marcus was on the living room floor surrounded by toy airplanes. The five-year old looked at his father completely startled, then held up a plastic jet fighter as if to say, "Look at this one, Dad?"

"Where's your mother?"

"Washing clothes."

Janette stood at the top of the staircase glaring at her

ex-husband. Then she turned and headed down the hall toward the laundry room.

"Thanks for calling ahead," she stated sarcastically, folding Marcus' underwear and socks on the dryer. "But I'm glad you're here. I need to talk to you."

"How's Marcus?"

"'How's Marcus?' you ask after just walking by him; when you haven't seen your son or so much as asked about him in how many weeks?"

"Janette. It's been a very long, very stressful day."

"Yes, we know. They ran the throw and catch you made over and over on ESPN. Marcus was mesmerized. Tough day at the ballpark, eh, King? You know, right after the game Marcus asked me if divorce goes on forever."

He watched her put on a pot of coffee and marveled again at how incredible she looked even when performing simple household tasks. The night they met he called her a "blonde Cleopatra" which Fontaine still believed. Janette could do the laundry in faded jeans, sweatshirt, and worn out running shoes, but her sensuality never diminished one degree, he mused. He loved her disheveled, dirty blonde hair and the springs of curls that draped down around her ears. Even now her sleek, leggy figure moved through the house with a sort of unintentional, modelish glide that still lit fires within him. As Janette set down two cups of coffee, he considered that Karyn spent hours every day fine-tuning her buttocks and thighs on a Stairmaster, dressed like a rock star, yet looked cheaper than Janette did when she took out the garbage.

She slid the cream toward him across the table and the powerful desire rose up and nearly overcame him to take her by the waist and pull her in. But that, he knew, was the ultimate non-negotiable. Breaking that rule would get him thrown out and this night inside the house could be his last.

"So what did you want to talk about, Janette?"

"King, I'm seeing a very nice guy. His name is Stewart. We're making an agreement here and now that you always call ahead before you come here. This won't be a debate, King, and it begins now. This is the last time you appear here at the house without letting me now ahead of time. I'm changing the gate codes tomorrow."

Fontaine was speechless.

"And you also need to know it's moving in a serious direction, King."

"*Damn, Janette! What is this cock and bullshit you're telling me?! What are you saying here, Janette?!*"

"Is the 'damn' because of Stewart or because you'll have to call ahead?"

"Does this guy know who you are?"

"Of course he knows."

"Has this bum actually been here?"

"Don't ever call Stewart a bum again, King. Of course he's been here. But so what? It's none of your concern. This is in stone, King. From now on you'll call before you come. And if you do call and get my voice mail, you're to stay away. You may control your harem of women and the San Francisco Giants, but that control ends with me. I'm not kidding: the next time you try to go through the security fence without letting me know, I will call the police and file a restraining order. You want all that in the papers?"

The bars of a cage had dropped down around him. "And Marcus: has he laid eyes on this gold digger you're seeing?"

"I've been dating Stew long enough for that to be appropriate. And Stewart's no gold digger."

"*Appropriate?!*" Fontaine yelled, jumping up and stomping around the kitchen with clenched fists. "We've been divorced for a litle over a year and now some scum bucket casually passes through this house on his way to your bedroom to screw you—and you call that 'appropriate!?'"

"Stop it! For you to comment on what's appropriate is the pot calling the kettle black, don't you think? I'll see anyone I want any *time* I want. We're divorced, remember?"

"I can't believe I'm hearing this! Really, Janette, I can't. I'm in the middle of the greatest season a ballplayer ever had, the press is on my back like a 10,000 pound gorilla every time I take a piss, the goddam pressure hasn't let me sleep decently in weeks, and now you tell me you want me to call you before you jump into bed with some freeloading asshole?! *How long have you been sleeping with this trash bag, Janette? Tell me, how long*?!" Fontaine pounded the kitchen table with his fist so hard that the force of the blow nearly smashed the surface in half.

Their heads turned. Marcus was standing in the kitchen doorway paralyzed. He was holding a toy airplane. His lips quivered and he looked terrified.

"That's it, King! I'm telling you to leave *now!*"

Fontaine flew back to Hillsborough with murder behind his eyes. The image of Janette's new boyfriend rose up before him like a salivating vampire. Fontaine was weaving in and out of traffic, needling cars in his path, and racing close to 100 miles per hour. Cockroach! Undress my wife in the very bedroom of the house I bought and paid for?! Not one dime of money that goes from me to Janette and Marcus will ever get to him, he vowed. What am I now—the goddam Welfare Department? Fontaine's bare hands were at Stewart's throat as he gasped on his knees for air and took his last breaths. Then Fontaine watched in satisfaction as the man dropped to his death. *That tarantula will never, never, take my wife away from me!*

The Hillsborough mansion was a regal, 12-room edifice standing in a plateau under a canopy of eucalyptus and redwood trees. An imperious main gate composed of seven-foot spiked points stood at the property's entrance, though the mansion could not be seen from even there. Fontaine shouted his codes to the modem angrily, the gates swung back, then the Jag bolted forward and skidded into one of the stalls in Fontaine's 6 car garage.

Karyn was in the mansion's spacious living room watching *The Wizard of Oz* blazing across the huge wall screen. "Hi, Baby," she called out from the couch behind a cloud of cigarette smoke.

"You left poor little Karyn all alone at the restaurant. I got lonely and had to take one of those smelly Iranian cabs."

He walked right passed her. "I'll be alone tonight," he announced sternly.

Still breathing fire, Fontaine swam 50 laps in the pool nude, wrapped a towel around his waist, and poured himself a glass of Chardonnay. Taking the white wine into his private bathroom and opening the door of the medicine chest, he removed the hypodermic needle and the steroid bottle hidden in the chest's side pocket. He drew the steroid into the needle and injected the units into his thigh. Tomorrow, the San Diego Padres and their garbage pitching staff crawls into Oracle Park, he thought. I should go 5-5 against that southern California muck. After putting the paraphernalia back into the side pocket, he took a capsule off the medicine chest shelf and dropped two pills into the wine glass. Then he put on his silk Japanese bathrobe and headed for his study. It was the one place in the world Fontaine found peace of mind where he could read about his favorite subject: General George S. Patton and World War II. But in between the lines of Patton's African campaign, "Stewart" poked his head up several times and wormed his foul way into Fontaine's thoughts.

Around midnight Fontaine slid into his satin sheets in the mirrored bedroom Karyn was forbidden from entering. He grimaced as he lay back thinking about Janette's ultimatum and the scum behind it. Jannette won't come back into my life as long as Karyn exists in it, he reasoned. A strategy had to be concocted that would eliminate Karyn and open the door for Janette's return. Running through several scenarios, Fontaine closed his heavy lids and dreamed the dream again.

All he knew was that the game was tied, runners were at second and third, and he had replaced Lindeman at the corner bag. The pitcher delivered, and an instant later a line shot shoulder-high rifled straight at him. He back-handed it, stepped on the bag to double the runner, then saw the man at second had stumbled. He ran him down and tagged him out five feet from second base.

An unassisted triple play. The umpire signaled the third out, the crowd went berserk, but the dream began to bleed as if it were an open wound. Muscle and nerve tore away and blood oozed out on the infield. The stadium lights poured down on him and thousands witnessed him falling to the ground, lying prone, writhing in pain.

Fontaine opened his eyes and jumped up in panic heaving like a race horse. The satin sheets and pillow cases were drenched in sweat. Dazed, his heart hammering, he sensed an immanent, unseen monster was pressing down upon his chest. He threw his legs over the sides of the bed, got up, but stumbled and had to grip a chair for support. The dream wasn't a dream. It was real. Whatever the menace was, it was out there breathing in the stadium like a fiendish gorgon waiting to strike. And every time he dreamed the dream, it seemed to come closer to the moment when the gorgon would finally reach him and destroy him once and for all.

II

The superstar stood in left center gazing up at the light tower that reigned like a galaxy of electric suns pouring white streams down upon the cool October playing field. A bat shattered at home plate and broke his trance. The ball lined down the right field line and he chuckled as he watched Ogilvie hustling over into the corner, his big rear-end poking out high behind him like a sack of potatoes. The runner skidded in to second standing up well ahead of the outfielder's throw.

He rested his glove on one knee, spat, then ruminated over what really lay at the heart of baseball. Baseball was waiting. Baseball was anticipation. It was second-guesswork, righty-against-lefty, watching, and more waiting. In baseball you had to outthink the pitcher's next offering hoping to crash his belt-high fastball into the left field seats. He tried to guess just how many hours he had spent waiting in the outfield, waiting to come to bat in the dugout, waiting for something to happen. He guessed the time totaled tens of thousands of wasted, meaningless hours which translated into months or even years hoping for significant action on the field. Would anyone mind if I had a glass of Chardonnay out here? Fontaine wisecracked to himself. He formed a huge glob of saliva and spat it out on the grass. I should have played professional football when the Seahawks offered me a contract, he mused. In football you don't have to wait long for something to happen. Every play's a train wreck.

The batter popped an off-speed pitch straight up to the infield. Lindemann called everybody off, tapped his glove, and squeezed it.

Janette's new non-negotiable about calling before coming down continued to gnaw at Fontaine. It was an issue he had to close the lid on before it ever kicked into second gear. An entirely new approach toward his ex-wife needed to be created. Karyn's days are numbered; she needs to be history—and before the playoffs, he promised himself. An unbelievable body, a face that splits granite, performs incredible sex, but a woman who does coke, smokes too many cigarettes, fills her head with nothing but Walt Disney movies, secretly hates baseball and probably thinks I'm shit. Karyn's a cloud of steam floating over my life. And steam does one and only one thing—it dissolves.

A soft fly ball lifted directly toward him. He circled under it and tapped his glove. Suddenly, the ball carried, drifted higher, farther. He was on his horse peddling backward quickly and wasn't sure it was going to stay in the park. Five feet from the fence, he leapt, stabbed at it, twisted, and made a spectacular over the shoulder catch.

Forty-two thousand fans roared in ecstasy. Fontaine tossed the ball back, spat, and resumed his place in medium deep left. But it was an act. Pain was pounding below his right knee like a wild fire. For a moment he thought it would split through muscle and fiber and send him cringing to the ground. He rested his hands on his thighs, closed his eyes tightly, and knew that if a ball was lined to left, he wouldn't be able to get to it. But the batter kept fouling off pitches. Two minutes later, the hammering was gone. He watched Lindeman glove a slow roller to third and gun it to first to end the inning. Fontaine trotted back to the dugout and wondered if Foxworthy caught any sign of his reaction to the pain.

The Giants' manager went right over to him with hard lines in his face. Foxworthy's chubby pink hands were clasped behind his back and the skipper's paunch spread out over his belt like a sack of oats. "What is it, King?"

"A little twinge in the hamstring," he lied.

"You're through for the night. I want you with the trainer, then stay in the tub."

After the game Fontaine rested back in the whirlpool with a coke and held court with reporters. He joked about the little twinge that Foxworthy had overreacted to, recounted a George S. Patton anecdote, and told the writers he was excited about the playoffs. That's what he wanted to say and that's what the press reported. Two huge bags of fan mail had been placed on the floor of his dressing stall. Just before leaving the clubhouse, he made sure no one saw him dump the bags into the trash.

He was in the Jag again bolting down the peninsula toward Hillsborough. He reached for the little bottle in the glove compartment and popped a pill. Karyn's time was up, he knew. He began to construct a plan for her ejection. When the security gate swung back, he cursed himself for ever allowing such a gold digger to soil his home and personal life in the first place.

Karyn glided around the house like a princess in one of his skimpy, thigh-length Japanese robes decorated with red and purple dragons. "Baby, the whole world's talking about your hamstring thingy. Where is the hamstring anyway? And what's the big deal about it?"

"It's nothing," he answered, flipping through a pile of bills. "Forget you ever heard about it."

She started in on her ex-husband's custody fight over her little girl and how low he had stooped to win the battle. Then she switched to her schizophrenic mother who had just run off with a Reno blackjack dealer named Andy Farcas. She may be a red-hot Playboy goddess, he thought, as she continued rambling on, but the

325

head on her shoulders will always be filled with sulfur dioxide. If a contest were held for the finest, Class A female with sawdust for brains, Karyn would win hands down.

He went into his library and tried to collect his thoughts over a glass of Chardonnay. Dozens of books on military history lined the shelves and, as he pulled out the volume he had been reading on General Patton's war exploits, the television exploded in the living room with the monotonous sounds of *The Wizard of Oz*. He pinched the bridge of his nose, gulped some wine, and listened in hateful silence at the dwarfs' asinine, shrill sing-song. Fontaine put the wineglass down and reached into his bottom desk drawer for the .38 wrapped in a white handkerchief. Scowling with increased anger at the ungodly sounds coming through the room's walls, he checked to see if the cylinder had bullets. Then he threw the door open and marched down the hall toward the living room.

She was sitting on the couch, a bare leg up, painting her toenails purple. A cigarette dangled from her lips and a thick circle of smoke formed in the air around her. He grimaced at the odor of a huge bowl of corn chips mixing with plates of deviled eggs on the coffee table. For a moment Fontaine stood behind her in nauseous silence asking himself how he let such a creature slither into his life. This is a child who watches children's movies, reasons like a twelve-year old, and talks baby talk. The fact is I let an adolescent female sap me of my hard-earned financial resources and physical well-being. As soon as I figure out a way to eject her, that two bit gold digger on my couch will be history.

Completely unaware he was standing behind her, Karyn giggled witlessly as Dorothy and the scarecrow went down the yellow brick road. How can somebody laugh at something they've seen 10,000 times? The barrel of the pistol drew to within an inch of the back of her head. Fontaine wondered if he could beat a murder rap like O.J. Simpson.

He cocked the trigger. The .38 held in place for a murderous moment, then he turned the barrel toward the scarecrow on the screen. He fired straight into the television, paused, and fired again. Glass and debris exploded through the living room as Karyn cringed in horror and desperately covered her head with a sofa pillow. Fontaine took her by the hair and slammed her back down on the couch. The hot barrel of the .38 pressed against the bridge of her nose.

"First, never ever play that goddam movie again. Second, when I'm in my study, you are invisible, get it? I'm reading in there. People need quiet when they read. Got that? Third, clean up the mess in this livingroom, then get out of my sight. If I see you again anytime tonight, I swear I'll put a bullet up your—"

Karyn bolted off the couch in complete terror and disappeared into the mansion's hollows.

Fontaine returned to his study and settled into a pleasant evening sipping Chardonnay and reading about General George S. Patton's 1943 tank victory at the Battle of El Guettar.

Just beyond the patio, the pool's waterfall filled the house's interior with the soothing splashes of cascading water.

The Giants would close out the regular season with the hapless Chicago Cubs. With three games left, San Francisco stood 14 games ahead of the Dodgers. Yet those games loomed as consummate Americana for millions anxious to see how high the king could soar. The Fontaine litany: 81 home runs, 179 RBI's, and a .429 batting average. Any other superstar might have been rested for the playoffs, but King Fontaine demanded that Foxworthy play him in every remaining game. And the sports world applauded his passion.

A special "Fontaine Watch" was published daily in the San Francisco Chronicle. Columns, contests, and features analyzed the King's historic season. The city's hotels spilled over with sportswriters from all over the world who came to witness the dramatic climax of the superstar's rendezvous with baseball history.

When he jogged out of the dugout toward left field to start the game, the sell-out crowd rose to its feet screaming in delirium.

The Fontaine chant erupted immediately as the superstar took his place in left field.

"Fontaine! Fontaine! FON-TAINE!"

In his first at bat, he drove a slider to deep center field. The ballpark rocked as if it were on casters, but the Cubs center fielder raced to the warning track and squeezed it routinely.

In his next trip to the plate, Fontaine stroked a frozen rope to left field. Ogilvie was at second and rounded third coming in for another Fontaine RBI. In the sixth inning, Fontaine lined a double up the alley in right-centerfield sending Fredricks home. The bases were loaded when Fontaine moved toward the plate in the bottom of the eighth. The Cubs' manager went to the mound, gave the pitcher the hook, and signaled for reliever Richard W. Rightmire. Rightmire was well-regarded for his wicked screwball, but he was infamous for his confrontation with the superstar that occurred earlier in the season.

In April Fontaine had belted a three-run blast off Rightmire at Wrigley Field. The next time up, Rightmire brushed Fontaine back with a high inside fastball. Fontaine shook it off, but on the very next pitch Rightmire cut loose with a second straight fastball that poured in at Fontaine's head. The superstar twisted, but it nailed him in the shoulder blades. The dugouts emptied and it took 25 minutes for the umpires to restore order. A few weeks later, the two faced off again. Fontaine cracked Rightmire's first pitch up the alley in left center field for a two-run triple. When he got to third, Fontaine stood on the bag glaring at Rightmire, pointing and clapping. Rightmire went to the showers soon after, but the relief pitcher seethed over Fontaine's antics. Now the Cubs bullpen ace was striding in to face his antagonist again. Fontaine said hello with a prolonged, sardonic smile. Rightmire's neck turned red: the pitcher knew he would retire from baseball before he'd ever become a footnote to Fontaine's storied season.

A fastball came in low and away. Fontaine backed out of the box, tapped his cleats with the fat of the bat, spat, stepped back in, and assumed his feared stance: bat cocked jaw-high, slow practice swings moving over the center of the plate, nasty facial grimace.

The Cubs' right-hander glanced at the runner on third, kicked and poured in another fastball directed at Fontaine's head. The left fielder hit the deck in a cloud of dust as the bat flung off behind him. The dugouts unloaded and stadium security did all it could to prevent fans from rushing onto the playing field and murdering Rightmire.

But Fontaine had already reached the mound. The Cubs' pitcher timed his arrival perfectly and threw an uppercut squarely to Fontaine's jaw. The superstar's knees buckled, the stadium lights swirled in front of his eyes, Fontaine staggered, then passed out and dropped.

After the game, the clubhouse crammed with reporters. Fontaine couldn't wait to cut loose:

"I will only say Mr. Rightmire was ejected and the league will correctly fine him. The Giants are going to the playoffs, the Cubs are in the basement, and Rightmire's one of the major reasons. But I'm a forgiving man: I'm sending Richard a World Series ticket for a nice seat—in the left field bleachers. And I promise to hit a line drive right at him; but I doubt he has the athleticism—or brains—to duck."

Two hours later Fontaine was in the Jag picking up his cell phone. "It's Popeye," he stated. "Let's play professional football this weekend..."

"A fine American pastime if ever there was one, Popeye."

"Put five dimes down on the Pats."

"In the stove. Done. Wanna' talk playoffs?"

"No deal. I'm in bed with a naked lady at the moment and can't talk."

"I'm wise," Arthur said. "Have fun."

He punched Arthur out, then punched in Karyn at the mansion. Soon she'd be gone, he knew, but thought it might be nice to have one last trip around the block. After four rings, she picked up the phone. Fontaine was boiling: the house phone was never to ring more than three times.

"Karyn, what took so long to answer?"

"I was outside vacuuming the pool. Did it go to five rings?"

"It's not supposed to go to three! What are you wearing?"

"Your favorite French bikini bottom."

"No top, right?"

"None."

"What color is it?

"Black."

"String?

"Naturally, Baby. For you..."

"What do you want to do as soon as I get there?"

"As soon as you walk in, Baby? You mean once I get through vacuuming the pool?"

He fought his temptation to let her have it right there, but bit his lip and said, "Yeah, when you're through with your goddam chores."

"That's easy, Baby: I want to do whatever you want to do."

It was the wrong answer. He wanted to drive straight to the mansion where he'd physically kick her out of the house once and for all for failing to repeat the script she was supposed to act out.

"Of course, Baby, you have to find me first. I'll be hiding. But once you find me, it will be soooooo exciting because I'll be wearing your favorite mini-skirt. I will try to run away, but it won't be any good because you always catch me and get what you want."

"And then what will happen?"

"You mean after you catch me?"

"Yes, after I catch you, for Cri'sake!"

"Well, I will have no control if you rip off my skirt. You always get your way because I'm too weak to defend myself, Baby."

There was no doubt: Karyn was a four-star, lying prick tease. He knew she wasn't standing there topless. He knew she was probably dressed in the same Japanese Komono she wore around the house 24 hours a day with a smoke and its sagging ash pasted to the corner of her mouth. The stench of her toenail polish and corn chips breath was doubtless filling the living room air around her; and he knew she had probably turned off *the The Wizard of Oz* on the newly installed high definition television the moment the phone rang.

It was time for the other shoe to fall.

"I'm going into the city to see my agent," he lied. "I won't be back at the mansion till later tonight. Be sure at least two bottles of Chardonnay are chilled; and be sure you're scalding hot and ready for action when I arrive, understand?"

"OK, Baby," she said with a catch in her throat. "I'm already hotter than a fire poker on a stormy night...."

The cell phone slammed shut. Her stupid cliches made his foot press down even harder on the accelerator as he headed straight for Hillsborough. Speeding down the peninsula, Fontaine began to speculate on the amount of time Karyn had spent alone at the mansion when he was on the road with the Giants. A typical day for Karyn was watching one Walt Disney movie after another, smoking cigarettes, or blowing the serious money he gave her on clothes and salon appointments. But what did she do with the rest of her time? Had scores of men been marching through my house like lemmings? Godalmighty, has Karyn given me AIDS?

The Jag brushed up quickly to the mansion's electronic fence. Fontaine punched his codes, then watched the gate swing back as he drifted in quietly and parked out of sight of the front windows. Except for the pool's cascading waters, the house's interior was silent when he slipped in. She wasn't watching television, nor was she in the game room or in the workout room. But a faint trail of cigarette smoke clung to the air and he followed its threads to where she was never to be: his study. The door was ajar. Fontaine stared at her through the crack in stunned disbelief. It was the smoking gun he needed. Now Fontaine's fury could be real: Karyn was sitting in his fine leather chair at his desk sniffing coke.

"Godamn," he swore murderously, nearly kicking the door off its hinges. "*I don't believe what I'm actually seeing!*"

331

She looked up in panic. "Baby," she said, as the blood drained from her face, "this is really no big deal."

His mouth went dry. His fists were clenched. *"Woman, be out of my house now...."*

"No, no, no, Baby! Please!"

"Everything—your clothes, your drugs, your bullet brassiers—*outa' here now!"*

"Oh, Baby," she whined with pleading, desperate eyes, "this was just the tail end of some stuff that I needed to get rid of. You know I love you, Baby..."

"Do you understand English, Whore? I want you gone yesterday! And here's the scorecard: you pull one of those 'Lady Tells All' routines to Spy magazine or CNN, so help me I'll blow your drug cover, name names, put people in jail, all of it. And if you ever hoped to see that daughter of yours again, forget it. By the time my lawyers are through with you, the judge won't give you custody of a rabid dog." It was all Fontaine could do not to take her kicking and screaming out to the hot tub and hold her head underwater until her face turned purple. Instead, he pulled out the desk drawer enraged and reached for the .38. When Karyn saw it, she sprang from the room as if her two feet were on fire.

She was out of the mansion in two and a half hours. The one time he peeked through a slit in the curtains, he saw that she was crying as she piled clothes into the trunk of her car. A tiny ache opened up inside him, but he rationalized that ejecting Karyn was necessary groundwork to pave the way for his reconciliation with Janette.

He changed the codes on the security gate, clamped the front windows, and called the police and spoke to the captain of the Hillsborough Police Department. "This is King Fontaine. Could you apply extra security in my neighborhood pronto? Somebody tried to break in last night. Anyone found on my property is to be arrested. Nobody should have their ass inside the gate of my home. Just flat cuff 'em and throw their rearends in the can. Then call me and I'll sign papers and press charges right there."

That evening Fontaine went straight to the bathroom medicine chest, removed the hypodermic needle and the anabolic steroid, and injected the substance into his thigh. Then he dropped two pills into a glass of Chardonnay and, as he sipped the wine, slipped into the pool's hot tub nude and thought how great his leg felt. He chalked the pain up to a psychosomatic reaction caused by Karyn's parasitic presence. Today I executed a triple play: I got rid of an abscess, opened the door for Janette's return, and took the first step toward blowing Stewart away. Thank God my mind will be crystal clear for the playoffs.

That night he dreamed the dream again.

"King, I want you in for Lindemann. He's through for the day..."

Fontaine trotted out to the infield. The game was tight, runners were at second and third. Suddenly, the pitcher was into his delivery. A line shot came at him shoulder high. He gloved it, stepped on third for a double play, then looked at second and saw the runner had stumbled. He ran him down and tagged him out a few feet from the bag. An unassisted triple play.

He jumped up in bed gasping for breath. His sheets and pillows were soaked with sweat. Panicked, Fontaine rushed into the kitchen, dropped two pills into a glass of water, slurped them down, and braced himself against the sink as the mansion swayed. That goddam woman nearly killed me, he reasoned. Had Karyn stayed another day, the Giants would lose the playoffs because I'd be dead.

The last game of the regular season was one of the most watched in baseball history. How high could King Fontaine go?

In the bottom of the first, Lindemann walked, and Fontaine strode up to the plate. Oracle Park shook to its rafters:

"*Fon-TAINE! Fon-TAINE! FON-TAINE!*

Nearly oblivious to the pandemonium, he took his practice cuts a few feet from the batter's box, then stepped in at the right side of the plate.

Orville McCracken stood perspiring on the mound for the

Cubs. He was a journeyman, 37-year-old left hander who had gone 4-10 during the season. He sent in two sliders, both nearly wild pitches. The veteran stood in courageously, fighting off, as best he could, the hellish sound that reined down upon him. Rubbing up the baseball, McCracken wished he could walk Fontaine, but that would put runners at first and second. McCracken took the sign, glanced at the runner on first, and sent in a cut fastball intended to hand-cuff the batter. Fontaine's powerful wrists snapped in a micro-second and the pitch was belted so high and so cleanly it sickened McCracken the instant his offering made contact with the wood of the bat. Fontaine's line shot landed 10 rows over the left field fence. King Fontaine had crashed home run number 82. Oracle Park rocked with a sound heard in Oakland.

In the fourth inning, Fontaine came up again with the Giants leading 5-1. McCracken was still on the mound and the Cubs' pitcher served up a slider as his first offering. The ball soared high and deep to the center field warning track. It was a heart-stopping moment as the entire world watched the outfielder streaking along the warning track, reaching up, and putting the fly ball away easily.

Wallace Shorts came in to face Fontaine with the bases empty in the seventh. After brushing back Fontaine lightly on the first pitch, he then delivered a change-up that was smacked up the center of the diamond. The Chicago second baseman snagged it and retired Fontaine by two steps.

In the ninth, Fontaine took his last at bat of the regular season. Millions of screens around the world filled with the image of King Fontaine striding toward the plate. The crowd rose to its feet and showered the man with a din of praise for what most thought was the greatest season in the history of sports.

Bryan Schrath, a tall, young left-hander, was now on the mound. Appearing unfazed, he stood in digging his cleats into the dirt around the rubber. Schrath wanted nothing more than to one day brag to his grandchildren that he had retired King Fontaine in his last at bat of the season.

Fontaine grimaced in the box as his dark eyes studied Schrath's body language. But the left-hander made the mistake of trying to paint the outside corner with a fastball. The pitch got away from him and poured in belt high. Fontaine's eyes opened like saucers when he saw it riding in. The fat of the bat simply connected with the pitch in a moment of supreme grandeur.

As the baseball's flight pattern began its historic trajectory toward the center field seats— the players on the field, the fans on their feet clamoring madly, the entire baseball world beyond Oracle park—every eye savored the timeless frames that followed: one man taking a casual jog around a baseball infield performing a ritual that had remained changeless for over one-hundred years. Rounding the bag at third, it occurred to Fontaine that he had just circled the bases 23 more times than the Babe did in his finest season.

It was now official: King Fontaine was the greatest who ever played the game of baseball.

III

Fontaine became convinced Janette was using Stewart as a wedge against him. That's what women did: they played one man off against another to force the hand of the man they really wanted. Erasing Stewart—if there really was a Stewart—had become Fontaine's obsession. The fact that Janette agreed to meet me today away from the house on neutral ground speaks volumes, he believed. As he pulled in to meet his ex-wife, Fontaine's spirits soared.

The couple sat down at 8 a.m. inside a secluded café in Saratoga. Fontaine gave the owner $1,500 to open early and keep the "Closed" sign out in front until they had left.

"Janette, I'm a new man," he began by lying. "I've been in treatment you know nothing about. This has been going on for months."

"How's it been kept quiet?" she asked skeptically. "King, you couldn't tie your shoe laces without it finding its way into the press. How could anything that big remain unknown?"

"The Giants have worked very hard on this to keep it confidential, Honey. But that's not why I asked you to meet me here. Janette, I want reconciliation between us more than I want a World Series ring or another 500 homeruns. I will do whatever it takes, whatever you ask, just to hear you say 'yes.' We would need time to—"

"It's not going to happen, King," she said just above a whisper. "Reconciliation is impossible."

She said it softly and sweetly, yet it came at him like a swinging axe. Her tender words and tone in that one sentence were more devastating than if she had gotten up, pointed at him, and laughed out loud at the imbecilic suggestion.

"King, when you're at your best, you're a pretty decent guy, but together we're oil and water; a square peg in a round hole. I do care for you in a way—you *are* Marcus' father. Right now the relationship you need most is with him."

Fontaine had trouble remaining seated. Her tender, serene demeanor without a strain of acrimony or harshness tore him apart with kind, gentle hands. He wanted to lift up the cafe table, crash it through the window, and bolt out to the car to get his pills. But he struggled hard against the pressure to do it and tried to convince himself Janette was still oozing hurt from his cheating on her when they were married.

"You don't understand. I'm re-born," he pleaded, using every bit of self-control he could muster. "I'm a brand new man, Jeanette. I've reformed. I even started going to church."

"Are you really saying that with a straight face, King? I know you," she said gently. "Only a transformation of the highest kind could ever change you and that isn't happening now. But I repeat that I do care—to a point. Yet I know precisely where that point begins and ends. What you want, King, is a relationship fix. In your mind, our being together provides that fix—but falsely so. I'm not your fix, King, and never will be."

"You're wrong, Janette," he argued, his neck turning red. "I don't consider you my fix. Look, that woman I was living with—did you know she's now history? She's out. Gone. She was a showpiece playgirl, nothing more. I want you and Marcus to move into the mansion. You're the one I truly care about."

"Is that why you walked by your son the other night and ignored him completely? I was the one who had to console him when he cried himself to sleep. That boy is desperate for love from his father who can't or won't give him affection. That's not the behavior of a man who's reborn; a man who claims he's going to church."

Her caring tones squeezed him on all sides like a vice: Janette, the woman he loved and needed; Marcus, the son who was a thorn in his side, a distant stranger. Both entities pushed against the sides of his head for different reasons and, for a few moments, Fontaine thought his skull would smash together and his brains would spill out all over the floor in an ungodly, slithering mess.

"King, listen carefully to me: Your women, your compulsive gambling, whatever drugs you're addicted to now, eat away at you a little more every day of your life. What amazes me more than anything is that your athletic performance isn't affected by these poisons—right now. But it can't last, King. It never does. You can only live the way you're living for so long. Then one day it will come crashing down on you. It's inevitable.

"King Fontaine needs to calm the storm within him before he can effect the storm without. If it helps, I'll use a baseball analogy to try and get through to you: you need to swing at a ball harder than you've ever swung at a ball. And the home run you'll hit will be the greatest one of your life. If you smash one-hundred homers for the San Francisco Giants this season, it will still leave that one that must go farther and higher than all the others. But *that* home run needs to be hit outside the stadium, outside the game of baseball. And the day you do hit it, it will be your true October Time, your *real* October Time, and the greatest blessing of your life."

It was as if a wrecking ball crashed into the side of the café. Janette hadn't intended her words to be a wrecking ball, but they were mighty smashes from a ball that slammed into him as surely as they might have slammed into the side of a condemned, 90 year-old brick façade in the middle of downtown San Francisco. Janette was in complete control; and Fontaine, a weak little boy, was overpowered, hating himself for mewling like a baby, yet helpless, growing tinier with every whine he was driven to make.

He continued pleading. He promised sacrifices and lied about his transformation. Janette listened like a good, loyal friend, then finally observed, "I've learned too much from our broken marriage, King. And those hard lessons taught me volumes. We don't always get what we want, but we usually always do get what we need. And what King Fontaine needs more than anything now is to face his corruptions and destroy them. No father can have a true relationship with his son until he conquers the demons that plague him."

"Janette, please, give it one more chance," Fontaine begged. "Consider the new man I've become, *please....*"

"You need to swing and hit that home run outside the park, King. Only then will the afflictions controlling you be exorcised. I say all this because I do care: devote your efforts to quelling the storm inside you—that's the tempest damaging you, not reconciliation with an ex-wife just to get a superficial fix."

Fifteen minutes later he watched Janette drive off along the road that snaked out of sight and into the Saratoga hills. Leaning against the Jag for support, Fontaine felt as if he were falling through the center of the Earth. He thought he was losing his mind and was probably moments from suffering a fatal heart attack and dropping to the lonely dirt road behind the cafe. For the first time in his life, Fontaine seriously considered suicide.

The Giants coasted over the New York Mets in the playoffs first round sweeping them in four straight games. King Fontaine at the plate was simply a clinic in the art of hitting a baseball.

In 22 at bats, he collected five homers, two triples, a double, and three singles. He drove in 12 runs, batted .500, and unleashed two comets from deep left field to throw runners out at second and third. Fredricks, Ogilvie, and Lindemann always seemed to be on base when Fontaine came to the plate. And that forced the Mets to pitch to the clean-up hitter which ultimately led to New York's doom.

Janette, however, never left his mind. The morning of the first Mets' game he called her and left a voice mail message that he was dedicating his entire playoff efforts to her. Tickets would be left at the park's Will Call and he was counting on her to be there. From 11 a.m. until the third inning, he had a team aide check for him, but the tickets were never claimed. She has scar tissue from my lousy behavior when we were married, he was certain. Now I'm too needy and I've tried rushing her back into a relationship too fast. But all wounds heal in time. It's a law of nature. They *have* to heal. I'll make them heal.

That night Fontaine, morose and sullen, sat in front of his huge slate fireplace. Wearing only his favorite Japanese bathrobe, he roasted marshmallows, drank a few glasses of Chardonnay and analyzed Karyn's compliant exit. The image of the woman moving out of the mansion in complete acquiescence had begun to trouble him. Was she planning retaliation? Will she try to hurt me? He saw Karyn seething in fury, crying on the shoulder of one of her cocaine dragons who might be willing to offer her revenge. Fontaine imagined himself at the plate during the coming World Series with the Yankees while somewhere in the stadium's upper deck a hit-man with a high powered rifle was focusing him into the telescopic crosshairs.

His anger over Karyn's manipulation of him for over two years boiled over. How can a woman with nothing going for her except a world-class body get the upper hand over me, a sports icon, and force me to flush a fortune down the toilet? Why do men sell their souls for a pair of beautiful tits and thighs? A female pelvis is still a female pelvis; thighs will always be thighs. What really was the

339

difference between a man and a woman anyway? It ain't physical, he reminded himself. We got the same parts, just in different arrangements. You give a man estrogen, his voice gets high and he grows breasts; you give a woman testosterone, her voice deepens and she grows a beard and hair on her chest. Has to be hormones. Testosterone is what makes a man like George Patton an aggressor. Estrogen is what makes a woman manipulative and a user. Yeah, hormones are the difference. They're built into the glands."

One by one, the females in his past paraded before him. Fontaine went through every woman he had ever chased and realized it was like flipping through a Cheerleaders' Hall of Fame. They were all cheerleaders, every one of them, with a cheerleader's mentality, cheerleader's bodies, every one a coquettish, prick-teasing, gold digging Barbie doll. That kind of woman has cost me millions since I became a celebrity. The fact is, brainless tarts manipulated me all my life and sapped me of my precious resources. He dropped two pills into another glass of Chardonnay, then drank the wine vowing once and for all that a gold digger would never rule him again.

As he browned another marshmallow in the fire, he could see that Janette, the jewel in his life, was clearly the antithesis of the cheerleaders who had forever dragged him down the road to perdition. And that's why she is so very right for me, he reasoned. I have to commit to using mind over matter and throw myself into the complete effort to convince Janette I'm a new man. If I can hit 80 home runs for the San Francisco Giants, I can sure win back the finest, most decent woman I have ever known. And I need her now more than ever.

The wine and the pills continued to pull Fontaine down into the stupor of a maudlin reverie. Whenever he fell into this nadir, a high school teammate loomed up before him: Tommy Boggs. He had watched Boggs struggling at the plate during his junior year of high school and remembered the kid striking out repeatedly in practice. Boggs was completely lost and Fontaine remembered thinking, "What's this guy's problem? Why can't he just whack the goddam thing and line one to left?" One day after practice, the coach called for Boggs. Fontaine's locker was just below the coach's open office window. Every word of the pathetic encounter drifted down to him.

"Tommy, you're not going to make the team. Maybe baseball isn't for you. Afraid I'm going to have to ask you to turn in your equipment."

Boggs walked out of the coach's office, sat down in front of his locker, and cried his eyes out. That's when it struck Fontaine for the first time that what he took for granted was an uphill battle for most players. Three days later, Boggs took his father's shotgun and blew his brains out. As Fontaine moved sullenly through Boggs' funeral, he realized how easy it was for him to bat .350 with one hand, yet Tommy Boggs had destroyed himself because he couldn't so much as ground a seeing-eye single through the middle of the diamond.

Time went on, players like Boggs dissolved, and in their place came others who could hit balls a little farther and whip the ball around the diamond faster. Though the caliber of player improved, Fontaine still remained light years ahead of them all. No matter where they put him—third, first, or left field—Fontaine played in his own league and filled in his own box scores.

The fire burned with an intense, crackling melancholy as Fontaine wiped away tears rolling down his cheeks. Poor, poor Tommy Boggs, he sobbed. Then, in a moment of ghostly detachment, he sensed the spirit of Boggs had actually materialized there in his living room at the mansion. Tommy's here now, Fontaine was certain; I can feel his comforting hand on my shoulder. He's speaking to me. I can really and truly hear Tommy's voice!

"There, there, King, don't fret. It's not so bad. I'm happy now where I am. Don't worry about me, just go out and have a great World Series. You'll win Janette back. If anybody can do it, King, you can."

IV

The Giants had a tough opener against the Cardinals in the NLCS, but after dropping the first game, they took four straight from St. Louis. Fontaine smashed 3 home runs, 4 doubles, and 3 singles. The New York Yankees would now bring the best pitching staff in baseball to San Francisco for the World Series.

None of the tickets Fontaine left for Janette at Will Call were ever collected. He called his ex-wife repeatedly, sometimes from inside the clubhouse, but when her voicemail went off, he slammed his cell phone shut. He wanted her there at the park; and he wanted to wine and dine her and win her over forever. But with each successive voicemail, the ugly nightmare of Janette and Stewart alone in a quiet hotel suite in Acapulco ate away at him. She can't continue to ignore my calls, he told himself that evening as he slipped the loaded .38 into the Jag's glovebox. If she does avoid me, I'll have no choice but to crash that security gate at the house and rip the front door off its hinges. And if that scumbag Stewart is there in bed with her, I'll blow his balls off.

The night before the World Series opener, Fontaine sat in the Jag parked in the shadows behind a San Mateo elementary school. He was poised to rocket south once he reached Jeanette and got permission to drive down to the house. Speed-dialing every five minutes, he listened to her agonizing recorded message over and over and swore bitterly every time it played. Then, as he sat at the wheel, a horrible scenario loomed up: what if Janette had married Stewart? His stomach was in knots just thinking about the possibility. As he pictured the image of the two of them in bed having sex, his cell went off. Fontaine cursed when he heard Arthur's scratchy, filthy voice.

"Hello, Popeye. I hate to be a spoil sport, but you're about 3 dimes light after last weekend."

"You know I'm good for it," Fontaine stated, wishing the bookie would choke to death on the food he could hear Arthur chewing.

'Oh, yeah, I know. But I got a hole and it don't pay the rent."

"I'll have it by the end of the big four."

"Now that does bring up a point I wanted to get to..."

He knew where Arthur was going. The bookie wanted clubhouse intelligence, inside information, anything that could give him an edge."

"What's that?"

"I could lighten the load some if Popeye had some intrestin' news bulletins."

Fontaine bit his lip. He had always drawn the line at giving Arthur anything confidential about the Giants, players in slumps, or health issues that even the press knew nothing about.

"How much of a load could you lighten?" he asked cautiously.

"Say—half..."

Fontaine weighed it. It was a generous offer too good to pass up. He had lost more than $200,000 in the last two months and needed breathing room until his next pay check.

"...The guy on the hill tonight for orange had a stomach virus two nights ago that's left him weak," he lied.

"Very nice, Popeye, but I'd need a little more dope that hits closer to home..."

Arthur was cornering Fontaine into his own private world. Fontaine thought very hard, then said, "The King wants his lady back bad. He's dedicated everything to her. He's putting it all down for his former queen."

"I like that, but he'll need to prove it, Popeye. How can he do that?"

Fontaine was now in too deep to pull back. "Popeye wants to put two hundred and one-half dimes down on orange."

"Now that I really do like! Can do, Popeye. Can and *will* do. Let's say half the tag is paid."

Fontaine gripped the wheel of the Jag tightly and stared straight ahead with intense, fiery eyes. He had just placed a quarter of a million dollar bet on the Giants to win the World Series.

The Series opener in San Francisco saw Fontaine go 4-4 leading the Giants to an 8-5 win over the Yankees. In game two, New York's pitching staff turned off the spigot and shut the Giants out, 3-0. The Yankees took the first game in New York in 10 innings, 7-6. In game four, Fontaine hit a grand slam home run to straightaway centerfield estimated at 572 feet highlighting the Giants 6-3 win. The Series evened out, 2-2. But it would be the fifth game in New York, however, that would send an ominous chill through the major league baseball universe.

Angling into the left field corner for a high, twisting foul ball, Fontaine missed the fly completely and cracked up against the fence. It was his right shin, just under the knee, that began to hammer. Too painful to ignore, he lied to Foxworthy that it was his hamstring. The skipper pulled him from the lineup and within minutes the superstar was in the clubhouse with two trainers working over him. New York went on to win on a two-run double in the bottom of the ninth and went up in the series 3-2 with the Series moving to San Francisco. After the game, the press caved in on Fontaine.

"Guys, it's just that hamstring twitch again. A little pinch. I'm feeling 100 percent right now, and I'll be out there whacking that thing around Oracle Park day after tomorrow. You know Fox: if I had a hang nail, he'd carry me into the tub. Take it to the bank: I could run the Boston Marathon an hour from now and not break a sweat."

But the pain below his right knee felt, at times, like a sledgehammer was swinging away at it. Fontaine refused all requests for television interviews and tried to relax that night in his hotel bathtub sipping his usual Chardonnay cocktail. The next morning the pain was gone, but just before boarding the plane back to the bay area, he tried calling Janette. When he heard the message saying her phone had been disconnected, Fontaine exploded in the passenger lounge at JFK. He threw the cell against the wall, kicked over chairs, and had to be restrained by teammates. The press reported the incident, but Fontaine laughed it off later and explained that he had been frustrated when he lost the key to his valuable briefcase.

Once on the plane, he went into the bathroom where he tossed three pills into a glass of orange juice and slurped the drink down in two gulps. His inability to cope with Janette's bullheadedness had run its course. She's costing me my piece of mind during the series, he told himself wearily on the flight back to San Francisco. The issue has to be dealt with now. As soon as I'm back in the Bay Area, I will take action that settles this shit once and for all.

On the morning of the sixth game in San Francisco, Fontaine met with Foxworthy behind closed doors in the Giants clubhouse.

"Fox," he said, lying back in the whirlpool, "I'm 95 percent. I'll be 100 by game time. No worries."

But Foxworthy was very worried. Fontaine looked pale. The lines in his face were taut and the skipper detected a hint of slurred speech. The manager sensed his superstar was lying about his hamstring; moreover, Foxworthy had learned he was having serious problems with his ex-wife. But he had to remain focused on the Series. If Fontaine's hamstring was less than 100 percent, chasing line drives into the left field corner could prove disastrous. King's not right, Foxworthy concluded. The Giants skipper made the toughest decision of his 20-year coaching career.

"King, I'm starting Endicott in left. Let's see how it goes and do everything we can to rest that hammie for game seven. Don't fight me on it, OK? My decision's made."

If there *was* a game seven. One more New York win and Fontaine's health would be academic. Foxworthy knew better than anyone in the baseball world that if he kept Fontaine out of game six and the Yankees won the Series, he'd be crucified.

The sixth game of the World Series was a pitcher's chess match for eight and a half- innings with only a few medium-deep flies leaving the infield. The Familiar *"Fontaine!! Fontaine!!"* chant erupted from time to time, but the superstar could only pace restlessly in the dugout and peer out at the field. His shin felt fine, but whenever he glanced at Endicott in left field, a strange foreboding overtook him. Is that 24 year-old farmhand the future after me?

Gloom set in as one ground ball and pop-up followed another in a scoreless tie. By the sixth inning, the thrill of seeing Fontaine appear in the on-deck circle grew into a thunderous *"Fontaine! Fontaine!"* roar. Foxworthy, however, stood like a sphynx on the dugout steps and never once glanced at his superstar.

With one out in the bottom of the ninth, the Giants loaded the bases. Fontaine, assuming he'd hit for the young left fielder, was incredulous when Foxworthy let Endicott bat. The kid wasted nothing and stroked a fast ball over second base for a clean single. The Yankee outfielder charged in hard to field it, but the ball sailed just under his glove and rolled to the warning track. Not only did all three runners score, Endicott rounded third and slid home safely just under the tag. The San Francisco Giants' cosmos tilted as the Giants won 4-0. But as Endicott was buried in team love, Fontaine stood alone in the dugout and watched the jubilation like a man viewing his own wake.

In the post-game clubhouse, Fontaine held court. "No doubt about it, I'll play tomorrow, guys. Physically, I feel like I'm in spring training. Fox and I have agreed: I'll start." He threw the towel around his neck indicating the audience was over. But Fontaine and the Giants manager had agreed on nothing. Foxworthy would not make a decision until he talked to Fontaine and worked him out the next morning.

Three trainers attended to Fontaine's leg in the post-game clubhouse, then the superstar spent over an hour in the whirlpool. Soon after leaving the park, Fontaine picked up several cars of fanatics who followed him down 101 south and tailgated the Jag into Burlingame. Honking and screaming behind him, Fontaine wished he could press a button and blow the cars to pieces. Circling the San Francisco Airport twice, he finally lost the tail and got back onto 101 south. His cell went off. It was Arthur.

"I need to know just how healthy that hamstring's doing, Popeye..."

"Hamstring's perfect. Like new," Fontaine lied. "As a matter of fact, Popeye took outfield this morning and the skipper said Popeye never looked better. Just one more day to be sure. Popeye stubbed his toe. Forget about it."

"So Popeye's starting tomorrow for sure?"

"Who told you he wasn't?"

"I'm very relieved to hear that, Popeye. And I know your word is your bond. I'm puttin' everything down on orange, understand?"

"A smart move."

"And the lady friend Popeye's devoting everything to...?"

"She can't live without him."

Arthur is a human pus bag, thought Fontaine, slapping the cell phone shut. And as long as he breathes air, he'll remain a role model pus bag for every bookie in the business."

The cell went off again. The softness of the woman's voice made Fontaine's heart race.

"Hello, King. This is Janette..."

Fontaine nearly careened off the road. *"Do you have any idea how many calls I made to you in the last week, Janette?!* Why wouldn't you answer me? Why'd you disconnect your phone and throw me to the wolves?"

"Because I didn't want to be a distraction, King."

"A *distraction*?! The greatest distraction you could make was to ignore me!"

"If I came to the park, you'd have taken it as a signal. And I will not give you a false signal, King. You need to rid your mind of any idea our relationship can be as it once was because it's not possible. But, yes, Marcus and I have been watching every moment of the series. How is your injury?"

He ignored the question and begged her again. "Please, Jeanette, please see me. Let me drive down now. *See me tonight...*"

"What about your son? Will you see him? My son is part of me, King; and he's part of you. Why will you not accept him?"

347

"Yes...Yes, I'll do that, but after we straighten things out between *us*, Janette. You and I come first, don't we?"

"King, I debated about calling you, but I decided to go ahead because it just came over the news less than a minute ago; and I thought that if you heard it right away, it might prepare you: Your girlfriend Karyn has given a tell-all interview. I saw it live on ESPN. She tried to destroy you, King. It was disgusting."

"*Huh*?!"

"She says you did drugs, have a gambling addiction, shot up the television one night in the living room with a gun, threatened to kill her, and took steroid injections the whole time she lived with you."

"*That scum-bag bitch! She's a dead woman!*"

"King," Janette said softly, "I don't know how much of it is fact, but we both know you have a gambling addiction and mix valium and God knows what other drugs with alcohol. If even half of the rest of what she says is true, you need treatment. I'm very, very concerned about you King. Truly I am."

It was as if she had peeled off an inch of his skin. "*You call me with the Series on the line tomorrow and shove this dagger up my ass? You actually believe that witch whore I kicked out is telling the truth? Who you kidding, Janette? You called to destroy me, that's all. You don't return my calls and then say it's not wanting to distract me?! Deep down you always wanted me to fail, didn't you? Hey, is this guy 'Stewart' a Yankee fan? Lemme' give you the real newsflash, Lady: tomorrow I'm gonna' hit 'em all out of the park—and what I said about devoting everything to you—you can goddam shove that up your sweet ass, too! This time I'm out for me! Everything's for me! King Fontaine!*"

He fired the cell phone against the side passenger door, then ripped into the glove box for the bottle of pills. As he swallowed two tablets fast, he lost control of the wheel, then swerved back into the middle lane safely. Fontaine came within two feet of ramming the side of a school bus.

The next morning, the day of game seven of the World Series, Fontaine sat in owner Bob DeRiguer's office at 8 a.m. Foxworthy, Al Blanch, the team's legal counsel, the general manager, two of the team's vice-presidents, and Fontaine and his agent were present. Karyn's disclosures on ESPN had been one of the most watched interviews in sports history.

"Bob, the whole thing's a pig in a poke. That woman lived with me, yes," the superstar explained matter of factly. "But I aced her last week when I caught her doing coke. She's gone ballistic. My take is she's tryin' to get a big time book deal out of this. The story's bogus. Look at the timing: the day before Game Seven of the series? Gimme' a break, Guys. She's blowing smoke and wants a pile of dough. You'll probably be seeing her next on Oprah Winfrey bawling her eyes out. The woman's a field goal wide to the right."

"We've got a World Series to win today, King," DeRiguer said firmly. "Right now that remains the issue for all of us here. In the meantime, we're going to place a moratorium on interviews. I don't want to see you worn down by the press over this. We'll keep reporters away. Now let's talk about your hamstring."

"Bob, it feels like I went to Walgreen's and bought a new one. All I want is to get into the starting lineup. May I quote General George Patton? 'A good plan violently executed right now is far better than a perfect plan executed next week.' Bob, you're right on: we've got a World Series to win so let me go out and win it."

Fontaine left DeRiguer's office and headed toward the clubhouse. Everyone at the meeting was alarmed at Fontaine's run-down, physical appearance. The superstar smiled, even joked, but his voice was husky and his face had an almost waxen texture to it. His red eyes squinted at times as if a bright light were pointing straight into them. DeRiguer also thought he detected slurred speech when Fontaine quoted Patton.

Twenty-five minutes later coaches and management watched keenly as Fontaine went out to left field and took a dozen fly balls. He fielded well until a bullet cracked into the left field corner. The

349

superstar pulled up short and grimaced in obvious pain trying to reach the sinking liner. The Yankees were loaded with right-handed batters and if a tough shot went down that same line into the corner again, the skipper doubted Fontaine would be able to get to it which could mean Yankee runs. The superstar's haggard image also gnawed at Foxworthy no end. Was the hamstring all that was wrong with Fontaine? The skipper had no doubt there was a great deal of conflict happening in Fontaine's personal life. But his baseball reasoning ruled. He wished it did not have to be done, but Foxworthy had no choice: he penciled in Endicott's name on the starting lineup card again.

A crazed standing ovation poured down on Fontaine when he took pre-game batting practice. Nothing had changed inside the cage: a few lazy swings and balls tapped to medium deep centerfield followed by one towering drive after another that left the park. A phalanx of security officers surrounded the batting cage and held back the reporters and television crews that surged in.

Fon-TAINE! Fon-TAINE! Fon-TAINE!

The fans' excitement drained, however, when they realized Endicott would be starting in left field.

A Yankee home run in the top of the first gave New York a 1-0 lead. The next six innings were a carbon copy of the sixth game: one ground ball after another, quiet Giants and New York bats. Then in the bottom of the seventh, Endicott got hold of a change up and sent it beyond the right field fence to tie the score at 1-1. Fontaine stood in the dugout watching Endicott circling the bases as if he were watching Janette going down the church aisle with Stewart. It wouldn't be until the top of the ninth, however, that one of the greatest milestones in the history of baseball would unfold.

A Yankee batter slashed a liner to third. Lindemann stepped in front of it nicely, but the ball took a wicked hop and skidded into the infielder's left temple. He was on the ground holding his hands in agony over his face a few feet from the bag. Foxworthy and the trainers rushed out as a deathly silence gripped the park. "I think his orbital bone is broken," the trainer told Foxworthy as they walked off the field with a grim Lindeman holding an ice pack over the side of this face.

The superstar knew exactly what was coming. Foxworthy was already moving toward him. Fontaine could have recited the words that were about to be spoken.

"King, go in for Lindemann. He's through for the day…"

The warm-up jacket flew off. Fontaine picked up his glove and trotted out to the diamond.

The dream was unfolding.

It was as if the entire stadium lifted toward the heavens when Fontaine jogged out to third. As he took his allowed practice ground balls for the injured Lindemann, the ballpark unleashed the familiar din:

FON-TAINE! FON-TAINE! FON-TAINE!

With a runner at first, Giants pitcher Dale Leonnetti got the Yankee batter to ground out moving the runner to second. The next Yankee batter singled up the alley in right center field and the run scored. New York went ahead 2-1 and Oracle Park was in the vice of an ugly, gut-wrenching stillness.

Leonetti notched a strike out, then, after going 0-2 on the next Yankee, sent in a cut fastball that was whacked high and deep to left field. Endicott took it off the wall and uncorked a great throw to third. The runner slid cleats up into Fontaine as the throw landed on the money. Fontaine applied the tag easily in a little whiff of dust.

"Out!" The side was retired.

The ballpark rocked with a joyous howling as the Giants jogged into the dugout for the bottom of the ninth.

But no one, not even Foxworthy, could have guessed the agony Fontaine was in. The base runner's cleats had brushed the shin under his right knee, though even Fontaine didn't think it was bad enough to cause the pain he was enduring. The superstar sat on the dugout bench with his head down praying for the miserable, vicious hammaring to stop.

Endicott led off with a walk. Then Ogilvie also walked. Rowes followed with a seeing-eye single between first and second and the stadium's mighty roar could be heard across the bay in San Lorenzo. The bases were loaded with no outs and King Fontaine was striding toward the plate.

FON-TAINE! FON-TAINE! FON-TAINE!

The pain in his leg had waned. Yet, in the midst of the madness that rained down upon him, Fontaine saw only Janette. He knew she was watching him at that very moment. He wanted to step out of the batter's box, walk up to the camera, and ask her before millions of viewers why she had disconnected her phone and unloaded on him at the worst moment of his life.

Fontaine took his first slow practice swings, the handle of the bat up near his jaw, and tried to stare down the pitcher with the same familiar grimace that had stared down countless pitchers since the first day he manufactured the routine in the minor leagues.

The runners took their leads. The pitcher looked in for the sign, came set, delivered. Not a fan in attendance at Oracle Park was seated.

Fontaine connected on an inside pitch and fouled it deep to left field against a roar that shook the park to its foundation.

Janette, why wouldn't you return my calls? And then when you did call, it had to be to tell me about Karyn—why did you try to hurt me, Janette?

The next pitch came in below the knees. The count went to 1-1.

Fontaine stepped out of the box and tapped his cleats with the fat of the bat. As he glanced at the third base coach for the sign, he caught something strange along the left field foul line. His eyes squinted in hard at it. It was the ghostly, chilling image of a 17 year-old boy in a dazzling white suit standing completely alone and nodding at Fontaine in a mist of bright light. It was Tommy Boggs. He was there in the first row just behind third base. He was looking straight at the superstar, yet he appeared sad and defeated. Fontaine was transfixed. Foxworthy saw it in the dugout and knew at that moment something was very wrong with his superstar.

Tommy! I can see you! Can you hear me, Tom? Can you hear what I'm thinking? This is for you, Tommy.

The umpire told Fontaine to step back into the batter's box. Fontaine wiped his moist eyes. Then he stepped toward the plate.

"...King, you need to swing at a ball harder than you have ever swung at a ball...And that will be your true October time..."

The pitcher glanced at Endicott and his generous lead at third. The other runners took their leads. Fontaine waited. The park waited. Arthur waited. Foxworthy waited. And Janette and Marcus, holding hands tightly in their living room, stopped breathing and waited...

You need to swing and hit that home run, King. And then the demons that have had a hold of you for so long will be exorcised. We don't always get what we want, King; but we usually do get what we need...

It happened in less than 20 seconds, but it was destined to be the most re-played tape in World Series history.

Ogilvie misinterpreted the sign and thought the hit and run was on and exploded toward second with the pitch. Fontaine wrists snapped to protect the runner and he skied a monstrous pop-up straight up to the middle of the diamond. The entire Yankee infield rushed together uncertain as to just where it was and who would take it. The fly was twisting, cork-screwing higher than any pop fly had ever risen in the history of Oracle Park.

The infield fly rule was called: Fontaine was out.

Ogilvie pulled up too late and passed Endicott at second. Ogilvie was out.

Endicott stumbled at shortstop and froze when he realized Ogilvie had gone by him. The ball came down untouched and struck Endicott on the shoulder. Endicott was out.

The announcer's voice went horse screaming the words into his network microphone:

"...It's a triple play! Nobody touched the ball! An unassisted triple play! The World Series is over! Has this ever happened before?!...It's the most unbelievable finale ever! The New York

Yankees are the new world champions after the most impossible of finishes! It happened here in San Francisco—the unimaginable, the most inconceivable World Series ninth inning of all time! The New York Yankees win the game 2-1 in a game they'll be talking about when the players on this field today have great grandchildren!..."

Arguments erupted, protests raged, fist-fights broke out on the diamond, but the Yankees were champs.

No one seemed to notice that King Fontaine had collapsed at home plate and lay flat on his back writhing in agony.

Dr. Hazlit stared down at Fontaine lying anxiously on the examination table. He held X-rays and looked grim. A second doctor entered the room, said nothing, and closed the door quietly.

"King, this is Dr. Shoffner who I've asked to assist in consultation. He's one of the finest oncologists I know of. Are you in pain now?"

"Not as much as before," Fontaine said thickly.

Hazlitt's hand dropped to Fontaine's shoulder comfortingly. "King, I'm afraid you're going to have to brace yourself..."

Fontaine's eyes widened. His heart raced.

"It's something called Ewing's Sarcoma. Cancer, I'm afraid, King. It's in the bone just below your knee. Dr. Shoffner and I agree that it *can* be checked successfully and the spread eliminated. But I'm very sorry to have to tell you that the leg from the knee down will have to be amputated..."

In the sterile, white medical examining room, the horror exploded everywhere at once and the superstar's bowels turned to ice. King Fontaine rode a rocket straight to hell.

V

The mansion's security gate swung open, Maria's Toyota drifted away noiselessly, and the gate closed behind her and snapped shut. The Hillsborough house was a deserted chasm, a silent edifice, an auditorium where voices echoed and winds whistled.

Without Maria, movements that were part of common home life—crossing into rooms, fixing meals, climbing stairs and washing clothes—would now require patience and anticipation. Better get used to it, King, he told himself months ago. You'll be living this way for the rest of your life.

Near the front door, three huge bags of mail forwarded from the Giants sat unopened and untouched. He knew the contents: Hallmark cards with advice from amputees; drawings and poems signed by elementary school children, prayers, and letters. Fontaine asked himself if he'd soon be crocheting an Afghan blanket to keep his one leg warm like his grandmother used to do in her living room.

The sliding glass door slid to the left. He gazed out at his gorgeous two acres: redwood deck curving around the pool with chase lounges; at the pool's far end, the waterfall cascading over the grotto of lava rocks spilling evenly and serenely into the Tahoe blue surface; and the lush plants and shrubs none of which he could name—a technicolor rainbow of rich pinks, dark blues, and bright reds blooming around the meandering koi pond and rolling green lawns manicured to postage stamp sharpness. In the distance, sagging eucalyptus and redwoods hovered like sentinels against the far ends of his property. And all of it landscaped to Sunset Magazine perfection by the Japanese gardeners paid well to maintain it.

Stepping out on to the deck in the April sunshine, Fontaine pictured the endless laps he swam in the pool when he had two healthy legs. Now I'll have to wade and tread water there like a child. His doctor's words were in his ears: *Post operative loss tempts you to throw a never-ending pity party. Don't RSVP, King...*

Erased forever were batting cages, scrambling after outfield fly balls, and running pre-game wind sprints along a ballpark's warning track and foul lines. Now his daily routine consisted of 10 obligatory morning laps limping on a prosthetic limb around his own swimming pool. As he lapped the pool a second time, it occurred to him he had never really appreciated the landscaped gardens that bloomed here. Nor had he ever spoken one word to the Japanese men who maintained the beautifully lush grounds. He pictured the Giants who were still in spring training and about to start a new season. Against a soundtrack of bats cracking flies to the warning track and pitches slapping into catcher's gloves up and down the foul lines, he saw Ogilvie heading into the right field corner tracking down a liner; Foxworthy squatting on the dugout steps like a sphinx; and a kid named Endicott. Endicott, the team's starting left-fielder whose young, hopeful image sent a spray of something he couldn't quite describe through his veins. Then Endicott dissolved and Fontaine was a lonely, washed-up superstar hobbling around a swimming pool like Peg Leg Bates. On the fourth lap, he pulled up behind the cascading waterfall and considered calling Maria. He would tell her she needed to be there more than three times a week.

As he wiped the sweat from his brow, Fontaine wondered why an odd golden glow was shining near the base of the birdbath. He limped over and looked down at the top half of a book rising from the dirt and emitting a pleasant halo of light. Reaching down with one hand, he lifted the volume and read the title:

THE BOOK OF TIME

The Japanese gardeners left this damn thing behind, he thought. He ran his fingers over the cover's smooth surface: firm, yet oddly supple. Why is it glowing? He turned back the cover.

T-99 Asteroid Threat To Earth
February 07, 2057AD

Dr. Ryan Shorer, director of the moon's Schofield orbiting telescope, reported on Februray 07, 2057 AD, 6:49 PM Universal

Time, that an asteroid 2.7602 kilometers in diameter had escaped the Edgeworth-Kuiper Belt, 91.9 Astronomical Units from Earth.

The International Science Bureau classified the body as 2057-T99 and calculated the asteroid would strike the Earth at Punjar, India in 27 hours, 41 minutes, and 37 seconds from the time of the director's announcement.

My gardeners must love science fiction, Fontaine mused. Carrying the book to one of the chairs on the redwood deck, he sat down and tried to find the source of the book's golden light. Leafing through pages, his eyes arrived at a second headline:

The Launch Of The Des Moines
February 07, 2057AD

The nuclear powered space interceptor Des Moines launched into Earth orbit on February 07, 2057 AD at 10:05 AM Universal Time from the Ronald Reagan Space Flight Center in Broom Lake, Nevada. The interceptor's mission was to rendezvous with 2057-T-99 and destroy the asteroid by nuclear beam bombardment.

Mission commander Colonel Marcus Fontaine, United States Air Force, led a crew of 7 scientists, engineers, and military personnel...

Colonel Marcus Fontaine?!

He jumped up. His incredulous eyes read the sentence again:

Mission Commander Colonel Marcus Fontaine, United States Air Force...

Fontaine's crazed fingers flipped ahead until he read the next sub-title:

Destruction of Asteroid T-99
February 07, 2057AD

The Des Moines interceptor rendezvoused with asteroid T-99 at 11:21PM Universal Time and launched two successive nuclear detonations striking the core of the asteroid.

The disintegrated ejecta from T-99 particles damaged the fuel housing units of the Des Moines and threatened its safe return to Earth. Commander Fontaine guided the spacecraft into geosynchronous earth orbit and repaired the units in space.

Dumbstruck, Fontaine negotiated his prosthetic limb as quickly as he could and hobbled back into the house. Once in the living room, he dived for his cell phone. His cold fingers speed-dialed the company that landscaped his property.

"Kiko," he stated, leaving a voicemail message, "I need to have you ask every worker who has ever been at my home if they ever lost or misplaced a book that I just found in my yard titled *The Book of Time*. This is very important, Kiko. Please call me back the minute you get this....."

Fontaine read through the account again:

The interceptor landed at the Ronald Reagan Spaceflight Center on February 8, 2057 9:57 Am Universal Time. Science General Secretary Sundeep Jabar awarded the "Science Badge of Merit" to Colonel Fontaine who cited the courage and inspiration of his mission: his father, legendary baseball hero Richard "King" Fontaine...

What kind of two-bit bullshit is this? A whacko wrote this thing and slipped through my security gate and planted it. But why—what's the point?

He turned to the passage on Colonel Marcus Fontaine and read that he had attended the Air Force Academy at Colorado Spings, graduated a second lieutenant, and became a decorated Air Force pilot flying advanced aircraft all over the world. Then his cell went off.

"No, Mr. Fontaine," Kiko explained, "the workers assigned to your home say they never lost any book of any kind on your property."

"Are you absolutely sure, Kiko?"

"Mr. Fontaine. I spoke to every man—there are three—who have landscaped at your home since we contracted with you."

"Are you *positive* about that?"

"Yes."

Fontaine picked up the book and read the chilling words again.

As a result of the global crisis, the World Security Council directed the International Science Bureau to create a permanent asteroid interceptor team at the Ronald Reagan Space Flight Center in Broom Lake, Nevada under the direction of Colonel Marcus Fontaine...

He set the book down on the long mahogany table in front of him and stared at it as if it were a human jaw bone found on Mars. Then he ran his fingers over the volume's fine texture comparing the smoothness of the cover to his silk bed sheets. Yet it's firm, nothing like silk at all, he thought. Taking the book back to his study, he placed the volume under a magnifying glass and analyzed the cover and the sentences more closely. Fontaine drew the blinds and cloaked the room in darkness. The book continued to glow pleasantly as if illumined by an invisible candle flame burning at its center. He thumbed fitfully through the pages and re-read one haunting line:

... His father, legendary baseball hero, Richard King Fontaine...

Hobbling back into the living room, Fontaine remembered the countless times he had seen Marcus playing with model airplanes and rockets. Insanity, he reasoned, reaching for his cell phone and quickly tapping out Janette's number. It's a nasty prank dreamed up by a Fontaine hater who wants me to lose my mind. Karyn? No way. That woman couldn't put two coherent sentences together and knew nothing about Marcus.

When Janette's voicemail went off, Fontaine said, "Call me ASAP, Janette!" He slammed the phone down and went out to the birdbath again, inspected the dirt hole, scoured the shrubs and plants around it, and pushed back limbs and branches hunting for evidence that might lead to an answer. Then his eyes roamed over the grounds searching for an intruder who might be stalking him near the eucalyptus trees at the far end of his acreage. Hastening back inside the house, he collapsed on the sofa mystified.

Fontaine's eyes bulged. The book was gone.

He turned over the table, then searched the entire living room. Faint, cascading splashes from the pool's waterfall drifted through the house's quiet interior as Fontaine wondered if he were hallucinating. The only rational explanation rose up before him: the poisons he fed his body for years were now taking their toll. I'm finally having delusions, he thought. This may be my future—the fog of dementia.

No, I found that book and read it. The hole near the birdbath is proof...

His cell phone went off.

"King? Everything OK?"

"Janette, I wouldn't ask this if it wasn't important, but I need you to get to the mansion as soon as possible. I won't go into it now. Please, just be here."

No matter how he explained it to her, he knew she was going to believe he had fallen back into the drugs and alcohol. Scrambling out to the birdbath again, Fontane studied the hole and searched through the shrubs and bushes furiously. When he returned to the living room, he sank to the couch exhausted and bewildered. Then he closed his eyes and thought how his relationship with Janette had been transformed since his surgery.

During the agonizing months following his amputation, through his brutally honest public admissions to the baseball world, and in the hundreds of hours spent in rehabilitation thereafter, Janette had become his part-time caretaker and closest friend. The more that sobriety and treatment replaced his addictions, the more stable their relationship became. The old Fontaine, the Fontaine who flashed in his Jaguar down 101 chasing his demons and his infantile need to control his environment, *that* Fontaine was excised when his right leg was amputated. It was no more possible for that man to return to life now than it was for his severed limb to be sewn back on and enable his legs to race along the base paths for the San Francisco Giants.

She was there within the hour. He described finding *The Book of Time,* the accounts in it, and the book's physical properties. He told her that he had called the Japanese landscaper who said the workers had nothing to do with it. "When I came back into the house," he continued, "that damn thing flat disappeared off this table.

"Now before you ask, Janette, I haven't had a drop of alcohol and haven't touched a pill in seven months. I may not be cured, but I *am* clean. I know what I'm saying is making you fight very hard against believing that I'm addicted again."

They went out to the birdbath. Janette stared at the hole in the ground.

"I brought that book back into the house, Janette," Fontaine stated, gritting his teeth. "And I read it turning pages with these hands. Then it wasn't there. That's it. That's all I can tell you."

"King, what's going on here?"

"That's the point: What *is* going on here?"

"And you say this book referred to Marcus?"

"Yes! And I read the lines several times to be sure I wasn't dreaming. The book was specific. *Scary* specific." Fontaine repeated the details with passionate, unrelenting insistence.

"King, I wish I could get the handle on this. What about the gardners?"

"Called them. The head guy said they had nothing to do with it. Look, I don't expect you to swallow all this, Janette. If my mind is going, I will have to accept it."

She knelt down and placed a finger at the edge of the hole. "You know, in the last year Marcus has said at least three or four times he wants to grow up and fly rockets in outer space. This is so—

"Irrational? You're being very tactful about saying I'm suffering brain damage caused by the steroids and drugs. But who could blame you?"

"King, what I do know is that since the surgery, I've watched one courageous man grow stronger and rise taller with each day.

What I see now is more of a man with one leg than he ever was with two."

"Funny thing is I actually want this to be a delusion," he stated. "But then, there's that hole in the ground. Who dug it? I know I didn't. Janette, finding that book and reading the words in it were as real as the two of us standing face to face right now."

They went back into the house and Fontaine pointed at the mahogany table. "That's exactly where I left it." He ran his hand along the smooth surface. "Right here. Didn't touch it once after I set it down."

"Things have gone sideways," she observed in amazement.

"Janette, my whole life has been sideways."

Fontaine stood at the sliding glass door peering out as if focusing on some distant point. "I've been wrestling with a decision, Janette. Maybe what happened here today screwed the lid on it. Fact is, maneuvering around in this place on one leg is like hiking through the Grand Canyon. Too many ghosts haunt these rooms. I've decided to sell the house and head back to my roots in Seattle. I may come back. I may not.

"Janette, you've been the rock in my life that every man oughta' be lucky enough to have in the first row rootin' for him. Especially after what I did to you and Marcus. But the truth hits me harder every day and night in this 12 room mausoleum: the memories of the foul balls I hit in all the years I played. Then every morning I limp around the pool 12 times on doctor's orders. Later, the mail comes and I stare at bags the Giants forward to me stuffed with pity for a peg-legged ballplayer. Then I limp around the pool some more. Meanwhile, I stare at this:" He pointed down to his prosthetic leg. "This kind of life just don't cut it for me."

Janette's eyes filled with tears. "If going back to your roots is what you have to do, then neither I nor anyone else should persuade you otherwise. I won't say deserting Marcus is right, but I will pray you'll come back to him one day, King. I once told you that your greatest home run is yet to happen. I still believe you're going to hit that big one and it will be the mightiest one of your life. And

I'm telling you that when you do hit it, no stadium in the world will keep it within its walls."

VI

The cool autumn air drifted across the school's lush grasses and into a classroom where the children sat transfixed in front of their storyteller. The young teacher stood before her class speaking in a softly dramatic tone that, for the children, filled the room like hypnotic wind chimes. Not a head moved as the magic of the tale of the Greek father and son captivated every young mind.

"'And so Daedalus plotted his escape from prison, but could not leave the island by the sea as the king kept strict watch on all the vessels...

"'Daedalus began to fabricate wings for himself and his son Icarus. He wrought feathers together, beginning with the smallest and adding larger ones so as to form an increasing surface. The larger ones he secured with thread and the smaller with wax, and gave the whole a gentle curvature like the winds of a bird...'[4]

The spellbinding style in which the teacher narrated the story stirred the children's imagination. A few of the students gazed out the classroom's window as if to search over the cloud-flecked sky for the characters that were being described. None of them, however, saw the lone figure moving along the narrow cement path just beyond the cyclone fence that circled the elementary school buildings.

He limped passed the open classroom windows stepping determinedly, trying to make each step improve upon the previous one. The teacher's soft words floated out the window to him and he could clearly make out the tops of the children's heads. They reminded him of his own grammar school days at this very school. He remembered Mrs. Pryor, a wonderful third grade teacher who played the piano like Brahms.

"'They passed Samos and Demos and Labynthos when the

363

boy, exulted in his flight, began to leave the guidance of his father and soared upward as if to reach heaven…

"'The nearness of the blazing sun softened the wax which held the feathers together and they came off. He fluttered with his arms, but no feathers remained to hold the air.

"'While he uttered cries to his father, he was submerged in the blue waters of the sea. His father cried, "Icarus, where are you?" At last he saw the feather floating on the water and was very sorry he had ever created the wax wings.'"

The teacher's voice trailed off. "All right, class, what do you think is the lesson of Icarus? The man who flew too close to the sun?"

Fontaine pulled up when he reached the end of the cyclone fence. Leaning against the wire, a flood of nostalgia swept over him as he studied the broken-down backstop and weed-strewn outline of the baseball diamond. I caught my first flies over there in the fourth grade; I hit my first home run there, too. Taking in the vista of the entire elementary school, he noted all the old wooden classroom buildings and recalled how he struggled with long division and fractions. Beyond the baseball diamond, the old auditorium stood haggard and detached from the rest of the school. He remembered how everyone had called it 'the barn' and how he had once been an elf in a Christmas play one rainy December afternoon inside that very building. He was trying to recall the name of some of his classmates when he noted a thread of white smoke pop out from a small open window above the auditorium's back service entrance. A moment later, a second puff released. When a blob of ugly black smoke ejected into the air, Fontaine cupped his mouth with his hands:

"Anybody here?! Hey—Fire!"

Fontaine's hands groped for the top of the fence. His powerful wrists and biceps lifted him to the rim, but when he tried to throw his prosthetic leg over the top, the shoe caught on one of the jagged edges. He rattled the limb frantically, then tried working it again and again until it finally pulled free. Finally, in one motion, he whipped the entire prosthetic around and braced himself with his hands and forearms as he dropped down to the dirt on the school's side of the fence.

Hobbling over the playing field, he reached the auditorium, opened the service door a crack, and peered into an empty pantry. It was a tiny room with a metal sink and faucet and a second door next to it. He looked up and winced: a sheet of light orange flame was curdling silently across the ceiling from left to right. He was about to turn and race out to shout for help again when he thought he heard a child's whimper.

Fontaine placed his palm against the inner door. Feeling the warm surface, he pulled the handle back gently. Thick smoke filled the space in front of the door, but he could make out a small knot of children standing on an auditorium stage paralyzed with fear. He limped inside quickly and headed toward the wooden stairs and skittered across the stage. Half a dozen children, seven or eight years old, huddled in front of black, smoking curtains, moaning, frozen in panic. Their eyes were fixed on a woman's body that lay on the floor of the stage next to an upright piano.

The teacher either passed out or she's dead. Christ Almighty!

The sound of flames crackled everywhere inside the building, smoke was thickening, and the bottom curtains had caught fire. It would be simple: he would carry the woman out and lead the children back through the pantry. Fontaine tore off his shirt, crumpled it into a ball, and placed it over his mouth. "I want you to do this," he ordered, showing them. "Your shirt or your blouses. *Do it now!*"

The woman emitted an agonal breath. She's alive, he realized. Suddenly, he heard a tearing sound like that of a splitting forest branch ripping off in the hollows behind him.

"Keep your eyes and your mouths covered!" he hollered. "We'll be fine! Just do what I tell you to do!"

Where's help? Where's the fire alarm in this place? Fire is silent, he thought in agony. Fire purrs like a cat. No one hears it until it's too late...

365

He hobbled back to the pantry door and opened a slit. The ceiling draped over the door in a blaze of flame. Even through the crack, the intense heat burned hard against his face. The pantry was blocked. Fontaine closed the door tightly and raced back to the children who moaned through the shirts and blouses pressed to their mouths.

Through the white mass, he could see orange waves eating their way across the auditorium ceiling. The stage curtains were beginning to torch like crepe paper. He pushed his face into his shirt; his muffled voice screamed through it: "We're going to go another way! Hold your shirts to your mouths! Hold hands and don't let go!"

Fontaine tore his shirt apart, wrapped half the material over the woman's head, then he slung the body over his shoulder. One arm braced the woman against himself; with his other free hand, he pressed his shirt material over his mouth and nose.

"This way!" he shouted. "Follow me!"

The ceiling above him suddenly ignited into a sheet of fire, the proscenium walls had caught, too, and flames were coiling up the curtains. But he led the children down the stairs through the smoke and along what he thought was the side of the auditorium. Carving through the haze, he groped forward leading the terrified children wailing and coughing behind him in a tight chain of linked arms and hands. Another splitting sound, like that of cardboard tearing apart, ripped somewhere above his head. "*Squeeze in tighter!*" he screamed back over his shoulder. The roof was ready to collapse at any moment. "*Keep your eyes and mouths covered!*" Suddenly, one of the little girls behind him broke from the line and bolted for Fontaine in horror. She was screaming hysterically at the ceiling embers that had dropped onto her hair. Fontaine took the shirt from his mouth and suffocated the orange sprinkles on her head. Her tiny arms clung to his waist. "Don't stop! We have to keep moving! We'll get there!" he hollered.

Gray smoke threaded with ugly black bands cloaked the human chain as it made its way down the aisle. "Clasp hands!"

he screamed. "Breathe through your shirts!" All at once another ominous crash exploded somewhere up ahead. Smoke and debris swept over them, the line halted, and two of the little girls wailed in horror. Fontaine closed his eyes and wrenched in the wind of heat that blasted his naked torso as he took the brunt of it. But he grasped the body slung over his shoulder firmly, inched forward, and peered with burning eyes through the thick carpet of grey.

"Hold on to the person next to you!" he cried. *"Make a chain of people!"*

He had reached a row of seats and felt their backs to be sure they *were* seats. They had crept down the stairs to the left of the auditorium stage, and an exit door had to be somewhere along the aisle, he reasoned. "This way!" he shouted as he led the line forward.

For the first time Fontaine became conscious of his prosthetic limb. In the breath of a moment, it occurred to him that he had climbed a cyclone fence, carried an unconscious woman, and led 6 traumatized children through an inferno, yet his artificial leg hadn't slowed or hindered him at all.

A wall!

He felt it with the tips of his fingers. It meant that between the seats and the wall he had to be in the auditorium aisle. And where there was an aisle, there had to be an exit at the end of it.

"This way!" he shouted again. "We're going down this way!"

The children coughed, whimpered, and tightened the line behind him.

Where is the fire alarm?! Where is help?! Doesn't anyone see smoke?

He pressed the mangled shirt against his mouth and nose. But his eyes, watering against the white, stinging smoke, searched frantically for the exit that had to exist in the stretch of space through which he moved. Then he raised his eyes again and glimpsed the horror above and to his right: a huge sagging portion of the roof's sheath was ablaze and seconds from caving in. Turning away quickly, cowering and shielding the children from the storm of flame, the sheath peeled downward slowly in an awful, curving arc of fire and debris. The heat washed over his spine, but not all of the roof had collapsed; the rest of it, he knew, would have to fall soon. Unable to see more than a foot or two in front of him, he spat into the shirt material that had covered his face and rubbed his eyes with the mositure. Then he looked hard into the mass of smoke ahead. Above him another huge portion of the roof writhed in flame. The human line was blocked in all directions.

Fontaine could carry the woman no longer. Setting her down on the floor, he huddled the children together into a tight ball. "The firemen are coming! They're outside now! Breathe through your shirts!"

Leaning back resignedly against a portion of wall, he listened to the children's miserable weeping as they grasped one another, clung to him, sensed the end was near. His liquid eyes studied the bits of roof raining down like orange hail. But he knew what they would say if they could speak. He could practically hear their anguished voices through the surrealism of it, crying out and asking how this horror could swallow them so fast, and how could it engulf them so cruelly.

He felt the urge to scream, not so much for himself, but for them. A few years of life measured against his 29 years balanced in the twisted, blazing holocaust into which a one-legged stranger had been cast to lead children into damnation. What is my connection to all this? What made me come back to this school on this day?

Somewhere on the far side of the auditorium, another huge portion of roof finally gave way in a shredding of material and burning rot. He knew that the roof over his head was minutes from burying all of them. He pulled the children in tighter and got them to face away from the inevitable. He listened to the horrible shearing sound, as one would listen to the first strains of an avalanche straight above his head moments before Armageddon opened its mouth and swallowed its victims into eternity.

Why did I go through that pantry door? Why did I hear that child's whimper leading me to where I am now? Why did the vault close so fast behind me?

...Rehabilitation.

...Physical therapy...

Was the point of the last 7 months simply to bring me into this hell? It would have been better to die in surgery when they cut off my leg than to have worked so hard for so long to come to this. A ray of bright sunshine promises heaven, then a blackjack to the back of the neck hits you while you whistle passed a playground. You're emperor of the universe one minute, they slice off your leg the next. But what in God's name did these children do wrong?

He gazed up at the ceiling again. Through the thick smoke he could see a huge slice of roof beginning to peel off directly above his head. The heat's intensity ached against his shirtless shoulders and sternum and he wondered if he'd suffocate first or fry. But Fontaine was breathing through remorse, not terror. It surprised even him to think of it, but if he could, he would gladly trade himself for these children's lives. I lived. I possessed. I wasted. They will never have a chance to choose.....

He crouched down as best he could against the wall and tried to rein in the little bodies behind him that were screaming. *"Everybody get in tight!"* he yelled. *"The fireman are almost here!"*

As the children formed a moaning, human ball within his grasp, it occurred to Fontaine that of the thousands of kids he had been around throughout his baseball career, the card shows, fan appreciation days, spring training, he had never actually put his arm around one child. Worse than that, he cringed thinking that he had abandoned Marcus, his own five year-old son. But now, trapped in a malestrom, Fontaine decided that his final act of life would be to shield these nameless innocents. And in that act he'd think of Janette, the only woman in his life that he ever truly loved.

Flames began to lick their way down the wall. Embers tossed about in beads of fire. Let it be quick, he prayed. Just let it happen fast.

His eyes roamed in misery over the top of the torn shirt through which he breathed. *I grew up in this auditorium; now I will die here...*

A thick pole broke off and collapsed away from the wall above his head and nearly speared him. It was the American flag, flames crackling through the cloth, yet he saw that it was still attached to a bar that had the thickness of a baseball bat. Clutching at it wildly through the dense smoke, he tore the flag from its hinges by stomping it on the floor with his good leg and ripping the pole away from the smoking cloth. Then he felt the wall. Flames were snaking their way down and he knew the ceiling would go when the support from the wall weakened.

...You're going to hit that big one and it will be the mightiest one of your life...

His naked upper torso hammered with heat. He knew he had only a few breaths left, but he shouted at the top of his lungs:

"I want all of you to turn away from me! Turn away now and keep your eyes closed and the shirts over your mouths and eyes. Do it now!"

The children were paralyzed.

"I said turn away now!"

The crackle of death was everywhere around them, the children screamed, moaned in agony, and finally turned in terror.

"...And the day you do hit it, it will be your true October Time, your real October Time..."

"Close your eyes and keep them closed!" he screamed. "Do it!"

The wall next to him pulsed with the crackle of flame. Taking the shirt that had covered his mouth, he wrapped it around the base of the bar. He steadied his hands over the material, a grip he had formed tens of thousands of times at home plates in scores of major league ballparks. Clenching his hands as tightly as he was able, he turned one last time to the children and roared at the top of his lungs, *"No matter what happens, keep your back to me! Keep your eyes closed!"*

Lifting the bar high above his head, he brought it back at an angle over his shoulder. Then he took in all the air that was left in the space around him, closed his eyes, and unleashed the mightiest swing of his life.

A vortex of wall, smoke, and boiling red embers crashed in an explosion of debris and flame. Stumbling and choking in the aftermath, his eyes burning with smoke, Fontaine detected a crack of space forming a narrow opening leading to miraculous white light. He squinted through watery eyes. He saw what he thought were two human figures breaking through a wall in the distance.

"*Go! Run through it!*" he screamed. "*Get oughta' here!*"

Six little bodies bolted through the hole.

In the craze of the holocaust, rationality and delirium finally fused. I'm on fire now while I'm thinking this. I'm burning up at this very moment, he thought, as the stab of phantom pains had returned to the leg that wasn't there. Patton knew glory was illusion. But no one knows anything because everything is sand in your fist. You're leading 6-1 in the seventh, you blow it in the ninth. A fastball is timed beautifully, then it twists like a cobra and passes through a hole in your bat. One minute you're Ruth, the next minute you're Tiny Tim. A forty-million dollar contract buys air and a Jaguar is tomorrow's scrap metal. Screwing cheerleaders in the heat of lust is like penetrating a frigid chasm without meaning.

Is the woman I'm carrying through this hole dead yet? Did I die in the pantry or was it a dream? Am I still back there under that roof? It's October. The World Series is here and it's a rainbow of nightmare balloons with painted, ugly faces beguiling me into hell...

The trawler's knotty planks squeaked as the little vessel plowed ahead like a miniature Victorian house at sea. Rust-covered steel and aged wooden beams creaked disjointedly as the ship cut sharply through Puget Sound's choppy, silver waters. Overhead, a dome of gray was breaking up into streaks of blue as geese, guided by the instinct of life, moved determinedly in a "V" formation across the patch.

He set the butt of the fishing pole into the rail cup, flipped the automatic gear, and watched the line tighten in the silver water. The waves lapped against the vessel's hull as he jammed his bandaged hands into the flak jacket's pockets. Raising his eyes to the bright blue patch above, Fontaine breathed fresh air and marveled how some places on earth smelled naturally cleaner than others.

A San Francisco ballpark suddenly filled in the blue sky between the clouds. He saw a thrilling, electric day in the warm sun, a wonderful afternoon in a universe where nothing went wrong. Spikes thumped across canvass bags, seeds from outfield arms were sucked-up in a leaping catcher's leather. Bats whacked against wicked sinkers and line drives bulleted over wooden advertisements.

Batting averages, slick double plays, and twenty game seasons swelled in the dreams of a franchise hoping to find a howitzer arm like Clemente's; legs like the Sey Hey Kid; a swing like Fontaine's.

Grown men ought to be punching time clocks or shoveling cement, not rubbing up baseballs for a living. Adult men are supposed to fight commuter gridlock and wear suits and ties. When they get home, they should fall asleep on the couch during the evening movie because they had a long, hard day. Men weren't intended to report to a stadium clubhouse at 10 a.m., put on sliding pants and cleats, then spend quality time learning how to play a ball's carom off a right field wall. How did the game of baseball ever reach the point where a 29 year-old man not only got paid for playing the game, he got paid more money than it took to start an automobile manufacturing plant?

He saw Ogilvie trotting out to right field and Lindemann backhanding a line shot at third nicely. There was Jack Tangler's picturesque delivery and his wicked screwball under Foxworthy's watchful eye. There was the smell of a brand new glove's cowhide and a faint aroma of dogs and fries and yelps from peanut vendors climbing the stairs at Oracle Park.

And, of course, Fontaine saw Endicott. A kid working overtime taking his licks in the batting cage with stars in his eyes. Endicott was an asterisk to a circumstance; a footnote to a milestone. In the orchestra of life Endicott was an oboe in a long row of oboes. Endicott: Zeus' pinch-hitter in the candlelight flicker of an inning. You take the helm, Endicott. And God Bless you for taking it, but I hope you never travel down the road I knew.

On balance: all debts, relationships paid and stamped. The record set straight, the truth told, reporters satisfied, millions of words written, books published, and the league declaring it would take no action against the greatest home run king in baseball history who saved six children's lives—respectful bows of sympathy for a one-legged former superstar with second degree burns over his bandaged body.

And a book that was there, then not there.

During the winter, Giants' management proposed a "King Fontaine Appreciation Day" for next season. They guaranteed an "unforgettable experience." The celebration would include the children whose lives he saved. Fontaine declined.

All my life I played for October. Now it's time to be a father to my son.

The Gift of Time

Brouwer passed through the Avon Theatre lobby and, as he exited the front doors, paused and admired the poster of "Laura" in the glass display case next to the ticket booth. Taut, brilliant script. Raksin's timeless musical score and theme song. And Gene Tierney: screen goddess. Quintessential film noir. Does a motion picture get any better than this?

He reached into his shirt pocket and pulled a cigarette from a pack of Camels. Leaning in to read the movie's credits at the bottom of the poster, Brouwer caught his reflection in the glass and winced. His husky frame pushed tightly against his wrinkled salt and pepper sport coat; a spare tire sagged over his belt; thinning, curly hair hung over his ears like worn out black threads; a sad mouth seemed cemented in place and tired eyes squinted above puffy bags. Wishing he had a whiskey sour right there at that moment, Brouwer lit a Camel. Then he headed down the sidewalk toward his car wondering if he really wanted to endure his mother again tonight.

Brouwer drove over to Benefit St., parked, and climbed the stairs to his mother's townhouse thinking she had probably divined his presence the moment he turned the engine off at the curb. When he reached the left end unit along a row of shoebox front doors, he considered turning around and heading back down the stairs again. But he pressed the doorbell, slipped his house key into the lock, and entered.

"Ma!"

"Is that you, Steven?" Mrs. Brouwer called from the bedroom.

"None other."

The living room was small, but immaculately kept. Retain

furniture, tropical couch, teakwood end tables, cherub lamps, and several oil landscapes of Cape Cod sand dunes on the walls. A cozy fireplace supported a mantel crowded with framed family photos on either side of a porcelain swan clock. Brouwer noticed the clock in the center of the swan's stomach had stopped at 5:01. He checked the plug, then tapped and shook the swan to try and get it to start.

An electric wheelchair rolled into the room with its passenger, Mrs. Adora Brouwer. She regarded her son with obvious disappointment. "I thought you'd be earlier, Steven. I fixed some meatloaf. But it's cold now."

"Caught a film at the Avon, Ma. Then had a sandwich downtown," he lied.

"Was it "Laura"? Saw they were running it."

"How'd you guess?" he asked sarcastically.

"Gene Tierney. Clifton Webb. The shotgun in the grandfather clock. How many times have you actually seen that movie, Steven?"

"A few times. Lost count. Mentioning clocks, Ma, did you know the swan on the mantel's broken?"

"Yes. It stopped running Sunday."

"You need a new clock, Ma. I'll get you one."

"That's not necessary, Steven."

"You have to know the time, Ma. Just don't count on the clock being another porcelain swan."

His mother looked suddenly older. Her grey hair had turned white; her shoulders and arms were more sunken and hunched than the last time he was at the townhouse. Arthritic hands seemed to be twigs of fingers folded on her lap with blue veins protruding like crooked threads Brouwer did not want to see. The lower half of her body was an irregular lump hidden under a woolen blanket. Though his mother's face appeared pale, her blue eyes remained steely sharp and clear, more like that of a woman in her 30's. All his life those eyes reminded Brouwer of an intensely keen awareness like that of a bald eagle enabling it to swoop down and clutch its prey before it realized what hit it.

"Well, the year's over at Brown, Steven. How would you rate it?"

"On a one to ten scale, I'd give it a two. Obtuse, undisciplined students with the critical thinking skills of a high school sophomore."

"Sorry to hear you have such a negative opinion," observed Mrs. Brouwer.

"Ma, college kids today are lethargic twenty year-olds who sit on their asses waiting for success to drop into their laps. They want the moon, but won't unplug their earphones long enough to absorb two chapters in the text."

"Do most of your colleagues share the same assessment?"

Brouwer shrugged. "I have no idea."

He decided to tell her: "Ma, I need to let you know that I'm taking off the next two weeks for R and R beginning day after tomorrow. I'm going to meet with my department chair, Joan Mercer, then head up to the lakes area."

"The lakes?" Mrs. Brouwer repeated shooting against the backrest of her chair very surprised. "Precisely where?"

"Lake Winnipesaukee. I want to do some writing and I need complete solitude to do it."

"Of all places," she commented. "Lake Winnipesaukee?"

"I'll talk to Ruthie tonight and let her know you might need her."

"What's this writing you're doing, Son?"

"Major course overhaul for the department," he lied. "Mercer asked me to oversee it. And while I'm up at the lake, I'll get you a new clock."

"Lake Winnipesaukee," she repeated. "A nice vacation from me, no doubt."

"Ma, I need a change of scenery. Need to re-charge the batteries. I think I'm entitled."

"You wouldn't by any chance be planning on staying at the Oak Birch Inn, would you?"

"As a matter of fact—yes. Didn't make a reservation. Just shooting straight up after I see Mercer."

Mrs. Brouwer was about to say something, but stopped short and adjusted herself in her chair. "Steven, do you ever see or have contact with Jillian?"

"You segued into that nicely. Ma, Jillian dissolved during the late Jurassic."

"I always thought of her as a wonderful girl."

"Well, she exited a long time ago and ain't comin' back. Could we please drop Jillian from all future discussions?"

"Was disappointed the two of you couldn't make a go of it."

"Yeah, I'm aware, Ma. With a little time you thought we'd stay together; then with a little more time we'd get married, have kids, and would be over here on Sundays for dinner so you could drum medicine into their heads."

"Is that such a horrible thought?" Mrs. Brouwer asked.

Brouwer glared at his mother and reached for a Camel without thinking. Then he remembered that he was forbidden from smoking in the townhouse. The cigarette was stuffed back into the pack reluctantly.

"Ma, let's put this to bed: life with Jillian would have been a science fiction. So could we please bring down the curtain on that little drama?"

"I'm just a mother confined to a wheelchair who would like to see her son settle down with a nice girl."

"C'mon, Ma, you may be in a wheelchair, but you're not 'just another mother.' Your intelligence gathering faculties are as acute today as when you controlled Providence General."

"Such an exaggeration, Steven. An RN doesn't control a hospital."

"You did. You controlled every doctor and nurse in that building for 25 years."

"Is that why you hated Providence?"

"I hated the stench of ether, mercurochrome, and the smell of surgery."

"Did you now? Are you absolutely sure that was it?"

"Ma," Brouwer asked with rising irritation, "is this our argument du jour?"

"We're not having an argument, just a discussion. Son, I have to make an observation here: you snap at everything I say. I can smell your cigarette breath from here. I can't remember the last time I saw you smile or laugh. And that coat: it's all you ever wear. I'd love to see you discard it. Something's going on with you, Steven. Care to provide your mother some insight?"

"Look, Ma, I had a long, stressful year at Brown. I need some serious R and R up at the lake."

"Are you sure there's nothing more that's causing the agitation I detect?"

"Once I get up to the lake and spend a few days breathing clean air in peace and quiet, I'll be fine."

Mrs. Brouwer tightened the wool blanket around her legs. "Children never discern the connection mothers have with their sons. Never. So—you saw "Laura" again tonight?"

"Correct."

"Funny how you're so mathematically and scientifically oriented, yet you possess such a love of film, a creative art. "Laura" resides in the center of your world, doesn't it?"

"Well, I made it to Dartmouth," he stated. "And, if I'm not mistaken, graduated with honors. Film's my escape. Nothing more."

"You not only made it to Dartmouth and graduated Summa Cum Laude, you became a fine professor at Brown."

Brouwer's attention turned to the family photos on the mantel. His eyes fastened on the framed, color shot of Caesar, the family dog. "Caesar was one hell of a canine," Brouwer observed. "The greatest dog on Earth."

The photo of the dog always sent Brouwer back to the Norman Rockwell summers at the lake when the family would take a room at the Oak Birch Inn. Brouwer and his father would fish or swim during the day, then later in the afternoon Mrs. Brouwer would spread a red checkered tablecloth over a picnic table and serve cold chicken, corn on the cob, and apple cobbler. In the evening they'd all play canasta or Brouwer and his father would have chess matches till midnight along the inn's screened-in porch. But the last year at the lake, the summer after Brouwer graduated from high school, Caesar chased a raccoon across the highway below the inn and was hit head-on by a pick-up truck and killed. The family came home early that year. The station wagon back to Providence seemed like a hearse to Brouwer who did all he could to hold back tears.

"Curious that you're going up to Lake Winnipesaukee, Son. When exactly was the last time you actually drove up there?"

"Couple Labor Days ago, I think."

"Odd you didn't mention it. Did you go up with Jillian?"

Brouwer cursed under his breath. "God Almighty, Ma, every time I come over here I feel like we play Truth or Consequences. Can we play something else for a change?"

"Son, it makes no difference to me if you stay at the Oak Birch Inn or at the Waldorf Astoria, but I think we both know that since Jillian you've been—unhappy. Then seeing the film "Laura" again today. That movie represents something to you, doesn't it, Son?"

"Jesus. Can't a film be just a film?"

"Not when you've see it a hundred times."

"A hundred, a thousand, what's the difference?"

"I suppose a mother's connection to her children stretches to eternity. She never stops being concerned about her children's interests and challenges no matter what their age. It's genetic. Guess mothers have a permanent, psychic attachment to the children they bear."

"And mothers always see their grown sons as little boys in need of having their noses wiped. Psychically attached? A euphemism women use to convince themselves of the omnipotence of their maternalism. Ma, never understood why you didn't go all the way and became an M.D. You would have been surgeon general of the United States. Adora Brouwer, the queen of diagnosticians. Physical *and* psychological."

379

"I do resent you saying I controlled everyone at Providence General, Steven. That was not even remotely true."

"Ma, you were J. Edgar Hoover at Providence Hosptal for over 25 years. Period. You had intelligence on every doctor and nurse in the building who ever touched a stethoscope. Not a blade of grass ever grew under your feet. And you used what you knew to its maximum effect."

"I was always concerned, yes, about the staff's welfare. But to call me J. Edgar Hoover is a bit offensive."

Brouwer rubbed his face in frustration. "I'm tired, Ma. I just need to get up to the lake."

"Be honest, Steven. You're tired of me."

"Jesus! Ma, do you ever quit? Can I at least score some points for coming over here and letting you know I'm taking a couple weeks R and R and offering to replace the broken clock?"

"And missing a dinner it pained me to prepare?"

Brouwer quoted a line in frustration: "'In the quiet bliss alone seemed I'...'"

"Steven," Mrs. Brouwer said without batting an eye, "go on up to the lake. Rest, cogitate, and write. Find whatever you need to find. Let the lake be your therapy. And, since you made the offer, I'd love a new clock."

II

Joan Mercer tended caringly to dozens of African violets in her small backyard greenhouse. Admiring the 50 or so flower pots spread in rows over several redwood tables, she decided the violets were prettier and far more robust since she began to use a new plant food suggested by one of her colleagues at Brown.

Mercer was a petite woman in her early 40's with blonde hair clipped back behind her head in a tight bun. A pair of bifocals always perched at the tip of her nose and combined with small ears and a swan-like neck and small shoulders that lent to an almost impish countenance. But Mercer's bantam features belied her status at Brown as not only a brilliant professor of calculus, but a formidable faculty union representative who never lost a battle. She was about to pour some soil into a new clay pot, when a man she knew very well suddenly appeared in the greenhouse doorway.

"Thank you for seeing me, Joan," Brouwer said.

"Oh! Hi, Steven!" Mercer slowly removed her garden gloves and glanced at her watch. "A little early? Thought you'd be here around 10."

"Joan, I need a sabbatical."

Mercer was thrown off guard. "You do?" she asked surprised.

"Yes, Joan, I do. Beginning in September."

"Well," Mercer groped trying to get the handle, "this calls for some serious green tea. Let's go inside, Steven."

As Brouwer sat down at Mercer's kitchen table, she noted her colleague's obvious anxiety and disheveled appearance. She remembered how run-down he looked at the department's end-of-the-year luncheon a week earlier. When Mercer poured Brouwer his tea, she had the chance to study the man. His fingers were trembling and his red eyes looked like he was sleep-deprived.

"Joan, I'm aware this puts you between a rock and a hard place, but I need a sabbatical. Jump through hoops if you have to, but please get it done."

"Steven, is this decision a definite?"

"It is."

"And the reason?"

Brouwer exhaled and rested back against the chair. "You know I respect you, Joan. More than anyone at Brown. Which is why I'm going to ask you for your trust and confidence because when I give you the reason you're going to think I've gone off the deep end."

Mercer folded her arms. "All right," she said. "I'm listening."

"Your graduate thesis was on Hermann Minkowski, wasn't it?"

"That's right," she said. "Hermann Minkowski, the creator of the science of numbers. Einstein's teacher who once called old Albert 'a lazy dog.'"

"Correct. Joan, about a year ago I locked into something in

381

Minkowski's work. And I took what I found to the moon. Now I want your assurance you'll keep what I'm about to tell you in the strictest confidence. But no matter what your personal opinion may be, I'm asking that you keep an open mind."

"All right. My mind is open. I'm listening."

"Strap your hat on, Joan, but I think I've discovered the mechanics for negotiating time."

Mercer's eyebrows shot up. "I beg your pardon?" She shook her head. "Steven, what are you talking about?"

"I have about 285 pages of a manuscript which I intend to publish. I need six months to finish it—which would constitute the sabbatical. I've worked like a dog 12-14 hours a day since extrapolating on a keystone in Minkowski's theories. Just get me that sabbatical, will you, Joan?"

"You can't possibly be serious, Steven."

"Dead serious," he emphasized.

Mercer shook her head. "Do you have any idea—"

"I'm talking about travel back in time, Joan," he repeated. "Not one scintilla of ambiguity here: *travel back in time*. I'm not going into any more specifics right now; let's just say Minkowski laid out the apples and I made apple pie. Notice I said 'back in time' not forward. I think I can prove traveling forward is impossible."

Mercer looked at Brouwer as if he had told her he just came from having cocktails with Hermann Minkowski himself.

"Steven, I don't know whether to laugh or cry at what you're telling me."

"Joan, tomorrow I'm heading up to Lake Winnipesaukee for two weeks to work on the final leg of the book. I'm also going up there to get away from my oppressive mother. The woman's a world class manipulator. I can't be within 50 miles of her without feeling her suffocating presence. I need to breathe healthy air away from Providence to have clear thinking. I need peace and quiet, Joan." Brouwer rubbed his tired face. "Clear thinking, peace, and quiet is the RX that will allow me to finish the book."

Mercer flashed back over 10 years of her friendship with

Brouwer. Her colleague had been an exemplary professor of Algebraic Geometry with his feet solidly on the ground from the day she first met him. Though a bit moody at times, Brouwer had never exhibited a shred of eccentricity or an idiosyncrasy that seemed odd or questionable. The department chair sipped some green tea, then leaned forward and chose her words carefully:

"Steven," she began, "Minkowski used geometric methods to solve problems in the theory of relativity. But the idea of time—"

"Don't even think of going there, Joan," Brouwer interrupted. "You'd never be able to connect the dots I connected. But I would like to offer you the opportunity to become the first person to read my manuscript and, if you so desire, write the introduction. All I ask is that you keep an open mind until you read my book."

"Steven, may I level with you? What you're saying concerns me. Greatly. Twelve to 14 hours a day with little sleep? Time travel? Frankly, I find what you're telling me to be implausible and inconceivable. I say this as a friend, Steven: this isn't healthy."

Brouwer waved her off. "Doesn't matter to me at all, Joan. All I want is that sabbatical beginning in the fall. Use any reason that works: I need to care for my disabled mother or time needed to write a textbook. Anything. I don't care. If we have ever had any friendship at all, just get me the sabbatical beginning in September, Joan."

Mercer studied Brouwer carefully as he sipped his tea. The cup seemed to shake a bit as it came to his lips. A wimsical notion flickered in the department chair's mind: Am I sitting across the table from the next Albert Einstein? But the idea was quickly smothered by Mercer's common sense and rationality.

Stephen Brouwer's having an emotional breakdown, she concluded. The question is: What do I do about it?

III

Light traffic moved in either direction on Highway 93 from Providence to Concord, New Hampshire. A talk show was on the radio and Brouwer listened to an an author of a book describing how President John Kennedy had been killed by a conspiracy. The book maintained that the President's head wounds had been altered to coincide with shots being fired from the rear. Tearing cellophane from a new pack of Camels, he popped a cigarette into his mouth and heard the writer say that the official casket that arrived at Bethesda Hospital in Maryland for the autopsy on the night of the assassination was empty. Another plain casket carrying the body of the President arrived at the back of the hospital in secret after the head had surgery. What is truth? Brouwer smirked cynically to himself.

As the dashboard lighter went to the tip of the smoke, Jillian rose up before him. She was sitting across from him at their usuable table at The Equinox, the restaurant they often frequented on weekends. Brouwer watched her purple fingernails poking into her lobster bisque. Finally, she pushed her plate to the side and said, "I'm stuffed." It was the same line that punctuated the end of all her dinners. "You barely touched your lobster, Steven."

"Wasn't that hungry," he said reaching for a Camel.

"Wish you'd stop smoking. Those cigarettes don't even have filters."

"Can't," he stated putting a match to the tip of the Camel and inhaling to his toes. "If I quit smoking, I wouldn't have an addiction to keep me happy."

"I don't keep you happy?"

"You're not a cigarette."

Jillian was modestly pretty. Her short brown hair was softened into a shag style which Brouwer rather liked because it complimented her oval face, smooth skin, and high, dimpled cheeks. She had an attractive, girlish shape and the low-cut ruffled blouses she often wore teased the neckline effectively. Tight blue jeans fitted snugly against her slim figure which Brouwer found puzzling given Jillian's voracious appetite for sweets.

"How goes it at the university, Steven?" Jillian asked, picking up her white wine and smacking her lips.

Brouwer exhaled a long train of smoke. "Nothing changes. The acned faces come; the acned faces go. Most sleep with their eyes open. Ivy League punks who take my course as a necessary evil. Nevertheless, Steven Brouwer stands dedicated at his post teaching his ass off, dispensing geometric wisdom to the minds of Johnny and Jane Doe who demonstrate the critical thinking skills of a greasy spoon dishwasher. And the whole time I keep wondering how these morons earned a high school diploma in the first place. By the end of the day, I ask myself if I'm being paid enough to endure this horse shit.

"Last week during finals I went into the faculty bathroom. While I was sitting there, I overheard a conversation between two of my sweet little girls who were in the quad just below my open window. I know who they were. One called me a geometry vampire. The other one said she'd need $20 million to fuck me for an A. Well, they're both flunking and I can't describe the pleasure I'll get from giving them F's. They're Daddy's girls living off Daddy's credit cards; they're gold digging, prick teasers: leeches treading water till Prince Charming swings by in his Mercedes. What they need is a couple years living in public housing, eating bologna sandwiches for dinner and cleaning toilets to earn their tuition."

"Steven, you're so cynical," Jillian stated coming forward. "I've never seen you this dark. Your students couldn't possibly be that bad."

"They are, trust me. Every day at Brown is pretty much an academic shit hole."

The waiter appeared and set down Jillian's blueberry cheesecake with creamed bananas.

"If I had to do it over, Jillian, I think I'd open a one screen theatre that showed nothing but film noir."

"Let me guess: opening night you'd show "Laura." But you'd go broke," Jillian cracked. "Only a tiny minority of moviegoers like those old black and white romance pictures. Hey, how's your Mom?"

385

Brouwer let out a draft of cigarette smoke. "My mother: seer of all things unseen. The only difference between Mom and the Oracle at Delphi is the wheelchair."

"Well, I just think it's wonderful of you to give her the care you do."

"Tell me, Jillian: where does care end and guilt begin? When I'm away, I'm guilty. When I'm there, I put on armor and go to war with her and hate myself for showing up at all."

"I offered a Mass for her on Sunday," Jillian announced shoving a forkful of cheesecake into her mouth.

Brouwer grimaced. "I'm sure it will empower her to jump up miraculously and be cured of her arthritis. Please, not one more spec of that crap, Jillian."

She leaned forward. "Yes, Steven, I did offer a Mass for her and I'm glad I did. Which leads me to something I've debated about asking you, but which I will ask anyway: What would it take for you to go to Mass with me this Sunday?"

Brouwer looked as if he had just swallowed cyanide. "Jillian, I'd jump into a barrel of tarantulas before I'd do that. Tell me, what is it that you see in that wooden man hanging from that cross up there on that stage or altar or whatever it is you call it? All those tales of this guy curing the blind and walking on water that you accept at face value? Do you ever tax your intelligence and see the holes and inconsistencies in those imbecilic accounts? Jesus, the man who rose from the dead, but couldn't keep 6 million Jews from being barbecued by the Nazis?"

"Man-made evils, Steven."

"And children's leukemia? That, too, is a man-made evil?"

"No one ever said the world was perfect."

"The world's not perfect," he repeated cynically. "Is that it? Is that all you've got, Jillian? Your Jesus turning water into wine: ever apply your cognitive skills to these superstitious 'miracles' and question them? The mother of three children is told she has cancer. The entire family prays for a cure, but your God ignores it and looks the other way from his heavenly throne and lets her die. Does that not give you a scintilla of pause, Jillian?"

Jillian put her fork down. "Steven, why are you so grim? Not a positive word exists in anything you say. Let me tell you, I'd rather believe in a God and find there isn't one, than not believe in God and find out there is."

That did it. That was the cliché that broke the floodgates open. Brouwer knew that his relationship with Jillian died right there at that dinner table at that very moment. Jillian's a dictionary of vacuous clichés, he said to himself. She knows nothing beyond the superficial romance novels she reads or the propaganda her religion jams down her throat. Brouwer considered cancelling the rest of the date right there at that moment and forego the motel-spa tryst where they usually ended their Saturday nights. But he ordered two whiskey sours and loosened himself up so that he could go through the motions of the next few hours. Later, his relations with Jillian became what he feared they would be: obligatory and mechanical. It was as if he were having sex with a plastic blow-up doll. Neither of them said a word as they drove back to Jillian's apartment around 1 a.m. Just before jumping out of the car, Jillian asked, "Call me, will you?"

"Sure," he lied.

She gave him a dry peck on the check and he watched her go up the stairs and disappear into her apartment building. Brouwer sped off with a throbbing headache. Good-bye, Jillian, he whispered to himself. And may you find a compliant Charley McCarthy dummy-man who kneels beside you adoringly under your asinine wooden Christ.

Highway 93 was in front of him again. Jillian and I: oil and water. We *were* oil and water philosophically and therefore incompatible, weren't we? For the next few miles he played with the proposition and concluded that had they married, he and Jillian would engage in endless warfare and be divorced within a year.

The car drifted across a short bridge over a meandering pond that could have been a page in a New England chamber of commerce calendar. Just below, the heads of two beavers moved through the still water carrying gnawed tree branches in their teeth toward a lodge under construction. A flock of loons swooped down overhead and disappeared into the endless birch forest beyond. Driving up here was very wise, he thought. The Oak Birch Inn will be my balm and the eyes of Adora Brouwer will not prevail against it.

Deciding on ham and eggs, strong coffee and apple pie, he pulled off 93 and into Concord a little before noon. Drifting along South Main, Brouwer found a café, pulled in quickly, parked, stepped to the sidewalk, and reached for a Camel. He was about to light the smoke when his eyes caught a pretty blue awning strung over a shop window across the street:

NESTER'S CLOCKS
"Give the gift of time."
Nester I. Leabnit, Owner

Perfect, Brouwer thought. I'll buy Mom's clock right there and be done with it.

What appeared to be a modest clock shop from the outside opened up to a universe of clocks expanding outward to shelves, walls, and glass showcases. Thousands of clocks were everywhere representing every conceivable style and motif: wall and desk clocks, digital clocks, clocks for businesses, alarm clocks, and Swiss cuckoo clocks. There were barometer clocks for sailing vessels; grandfather clocks, radio clocks and children's clocks with cartoonish hands over Donald Duck faces. Brouwer had never seen so many different styles of clocks collected in one place.

At the far end of the shop, pretty, gingham curtains parted. A man who looked to be in his 80's stepped out smoking a glistening, calabash pipe.

"Hello," Brouwer said. "You're the owner?"

"Yes. I'm Nester. How may I help you?"

He was a small, slim man in a loose fitting sweatshirt that

said 'Princeton'. A mop of white hair was streaked with threads of black. A thick moustache nearly covered his mouth from which hung a calabash pipe forming a perfect 'J'. Bags sagged under the man's droopy eyes. Smoke from the pipe sent a pleasant bourbon tobacco aroma into the air.

But Brouwer's attention had turned to an oddity: all of the clocks in the shop seemed timed not only to the minute, but also to be running in harmony to the second. "Am I seeing things? Brouwer asked in disbelief. "Are the second hands on all the clocks here timed perfectly together?"

"The clocks with second hands are synchronized precisely," Leabnit replied.

"I never would have thought that possible," Brouwer stated in amazement. "How'd you do it?"

The owner smiled and released a puff of smoke. "Seeing is believing, isn't it?"

"How many clocks are in this store?"

"There are exactly 2000 clocks for sale here. Every clock is guaranteed to run without ever losing a second of time."

Brouwer moved from clock to clock with fascination trying to verify the owner's claim. "Utterly amazing. I just don't believe I'm seeing this."

Leabnit stood behind the glass counter observing Brouwer with his hands clasped behind him. "What particular style of clock were you looking for?"

"I'd like to get a clock for my mother's living room mantel."

"Very fine." The owner walked over to a shelf of clocks along the far right wall. He reached for one clock in particular, examined it, and brought it back to the counter.

Brouwer started back to the man when he suddenly caught sight of a grandfather clock standing against the wall on the opposite side of the shop. It was a carbon copy of the grandfather clock in the movie "Laura."

"What a coincidence," Brouwer remarked. "This is a clock that is just like a clock in a very famous movie I've seen many times. A shotgun was hidden in its door panel." Brouwer reached down and ran the palm of his hand over the surface of the door, then clicked the door open and looked inside.

"That's a German made Hensmyer clock and costs $500," Leabnit stated. "But I assure you, Sir, there's no shotgun in there. Please take a look at this nice mantel clock for your mother. Octagonal shape, gold Roman numerals, pretty walnut wood frame, and a long cord that will reach to almost all wall circuits below. It's $22 and comes with a 100 percent guarantee."

Brouwer closed the door of the grandfather clock. "It seems nice," Brouwer said. "Will it be dependable?"

"Sir," the owner promised, "if this clock stops running within five years of purchase, I will personally drive over to your mother's house and hand her 10 times what you paid for it. Plus, if you buy it today, I'll give you 15 percent off."

"Well, you can't beat that," Brouwer smiled. "So that'd be—$3.30 discount? Which makes the clock $18.70, not including tax, right?"

"Exactly," the owner agreed. "You're very fast with numbers, Sir. What do you do for a living?"

"I'm a professor of Algebraic Geometry at Brown University."

"Sounds complicated," Leabnit commented. "Did you say your name?"

"Steven Brouwer. Yes, I will definitely take this clock, Mr. Leabnit."

The owner pulled out a cardboard box and a sheet of brown wrapping paper from behind the counter. "Very good, Professor."

"Mr. Leabnit, how long have you been selling clocks?"

"Over 60 years."

"Here in Concord?"

"No. I was born in Germany, came to America, and had my first clock store in New Jersey. Years later I moved to Concord."

"Would I be correct if I said you're obsessed with time, Mr. Leabnit?"

"No, I'm not obsessed with time, Professor; I'm obsessed with movement."

A light switched on in Brouwer's head. "Well, what's the difference, if I may ask?"

"Movement is the true arbiter of the physical world. Time is wires, springs, and dials."

"So you don't believe in time then?"

"Time is the fog God gives us to stumble around in for as long as we live in this paradoxical universe."

The remark smacked at Brouwer, but he bit his lip and watched the owner set the clock into a box and stuff protective tissue around it. "Here we stand in June, 1990, in the midst of all these clocks telling time. The big joke, of course, is that there is no time."

"Then why have a clock at all," Brouwer asked coyly.

Leabnit patted down the tissue around the clock with the care of a mother coddling a newborn infant in its crib. "You know very well why, Professor. Because time systematizes civilization: time to get up; time to go to work; time to start a football game or begin a new calendar year. Time to sign an armistice ending a war. Civilization would collapse without clocks and timepieces. The irony is that whether it's midnight or 9 a.m., time is movement based on the earth turning on its axis and rotating around the sun."

Brouwer regarded Leabnit curiously. "You certainly do have very precise ideas about time, don't you?"

"Listening to millions of ticks for over 60 years has given me the opportunity to reflect on time. As I say, we exist here in 1990 in Concord, New Hampshire foolishly believing we're standing still. The moon circles the earth at 2,280 miles per hour. The Earth orbits the sun at about 67,000 miles per hour; the sun moves through our local galaxy at 450,000 miles per hour; our solar system moves at a speed of 514,000 miles per hour; and the entire Milky Way galaxy is shooting through the cosmos at 2.2 million miles per hour. Everything in our universe is movement, Professor. A still pond turns stagnant, the fish die. The wind blows; the oceans roll, waves crash, clouds drift, houses settle, electrons spin."

"An array of cosmic movement," Brouwer observed. "I certainly won't argue with any of that, Mr. Leabnit."

"Prehistoric man did not need clocks to populate the Earth, migrate over sheets of ice and across the African plains. He didn't sit in his cave and chit chat about the weather. The second hand sweeps around the dial and moves the minute hand which in turn moves the hour hand. Movement on movement on movement."

"Mr. Leabnit, I have to say you're the most philosophical shop owner I ever met."

Leabnit folded the corners of the wrapping paper over the box, pressed them down hard, and scotch-taped the corner into a perfect seal. "That will be $18.80 including tax, Professor."

"Yes, of course," Brouwer said handing Leabnit a $20 bill. The owner's face had nearly disappeared in a cloud of pipe smoke as he rang up the sale on the cash register and returned the change. Suddenly, Brouwer's desire to get up to Lake Winnipesaukee took second to hearing the next gem proceed from the mouth of Nester I. Leabnit.

"Sounds to me like you've read and studied a great deal about astronomy and related subjects, Mr. Leabnit."

"I studied out of my own needs by reading books I needed to read and not swallowing academic propaganda. Most truth never makes it into the history books. Oh," he added quickly, "Did not mean to offend. Forgot you were a professor at Brown."

"No apology necessary," Brouwer said. "There is a lot taught in the academic world that I myself have trouble with. But I'd like to hear an example of what you call 'academic propaganda'."

"Well, you can start with biology. Specifically, evolution. If evolution is everything we've been taught, Eskimos would have hair to keep warm. Conversely, lions living at the equator have fur, but have no need for it. The equatorial bear, a terrifying beast which lives on the African contenent, has fur, too. Why didn't evolution cause these animals to lose all that unnecessary hair? They thought the coelacanth fish became extinct around 66 million years ago with the dinosaurs, but one was caught in 1938. It was found not to have undergone any physical changes in over 300 million years. Why didn't it evolve? Then there's the archaeopteryx, a creature half bird, half reptile which lived in the late Jurassic about 150 million years ago. They said it pre-dated birds and supposedly provides a link between dinosaurs and birds. But in 1977 the fossil of a bird was discovered in west Colorado that came from the lower Jurrrassic well before the archaeopteryx. Out of millions of discovered bird fossils, not one transitional form has been found proving what the evolutionists tell us occurred."

"You certainly are a thinking business man," Brouwer observed.

"Another example, Professor: Darwin himself admitted it was absurd to think the human eye was the result of natural selection. Yet evolution and natural selection are taught as law on the same par as English grammar. The point is that time, no matter how much of it we think collects through the eons, does not make a thing so because scientists want it to be so. For example, the Earth is 4,567,000,000 years old. Yet we think we've pigeonholed every event step by step and know just what creatures existed and precisely how they evolved into a more sophisticated species.

"Evolution is loaded with contradictions. All those epochs separated by periods called the Jurassic or the Cretaceous. Or take the Cambrian, 540 million years ago when animal life exploded. Life which has no fossil record suddenly 'appears' and explodes out of nowhere. Darwin knew it and admitted he couldn't explain it. But the biggest question glossed over goes beyond physical matter. For me it's: How did consciousness come from chemicals? Of course, none of these matters concerns the modern biologist. They pass over these inconsistencies like they pass on a sour bottle of milk."

Who was this man!?

Nester I. Leabnit, an obscure clock shop owner in Concord, New Hampshire who expounded on inconsistencies in evolution as easily as if he were describing one of his cuckoo clocks. Brouwer looked down at the packaged clock he just purchased. The ironic parallel between the clock on the counter and the manuscript lying on the back seat of his car was not lost on him.

"I'm sure your mother will get great pleasure from this clock as it sits on her mantel," Leabnit observed. "Please come again, Professor."

"If I'm ever in the area again, I promise I will do just that," Brouwer replied. "But I'm starting to wonder just who the real professor was here."

"You are," Leabnit said with a gentle smile as he released a whiff of pipe smoke. "*You* are the professor."

Driving the last leg of his trip to the lake, Brouwer thought about how much of modern American curriculum was propaganda. The talk show he heard earlier about the Kennedy assassination came back to him. How many fairy tales in science and history masquerade as fact? He shifted uncomfortably, slipped a Camel to his lips, and brought the dash lighter to the tip of the cigarette. Why *did* lions in Africa have fur? Newsom laughed to himself. And how did intelligent, human consciousness derive from chemicals? But mathematics, though, is a different breed of cat, isn't it? Mathematics was concrete, immune from subjectivity. Mathematics, geometry, algebra, and calculus were incontrovertible subjects. But what about history, sociology, psychology, and other liberal arts whose cores change as the wind blows? No, mathematics and geometry will always be the jewel of eternal logic. Isn't that why I chose the discipline of Algebraic Geometry in the first place?

Brouwer reached Alton Bay, the southern tip of Lake Winnipesaukee. A small strip of beach ran under the winding, two lane roadway. Several senior women played cards and sat in folding chairs on the sand under colorful umbrellas. Not far from them, children drifted lazily on the water in inner tubes soaking in the warm sun. A bit farther up, an angler stood on a smooth face of a large boulder and whipped his line into the water. In the distance, a speed boat raced over the glistening lake towing a water skier who performed perfect twirls on one leg.

The narrow roadway swerved to the left. Brouwer remembered running down below at the water's edge with Caesar and teaching him how to retrieve a rubber ball at the snap of his fingers. Two story homes with screened-in porches set well back up the hill on the right. The Oak Birch Inn, built in 1903, he mused, with tales of it being haunted by the original owner and guests reporting seeing a man roaming the hallways in a tuxedo. In the early years, the inn was a retreat for the well-to-do who arrived in carriages and steamboats. Now, over 80 years later, the old, wooden landmark had probably served tens of thousands in its time. The sharp right turn was just up ahead. He knew he'd drift up the foot of the slope that led to the inn's dirt parking lot. At last, Brouwer thought, I'm finally here. Maybe I'll take one of the old rooms that—

Brouwer hit the brakes. The car froze at the foot of the dirt incline at the parking lot's entrance as Decker's eyes widened in disbelief. Above him, blackened lumber, scorched wiring, and twisted plumbing fixtures piled in ugly heaps across his field of vision. Did I miss the turn? It has to be the next one. No, this is it! My God, where's the inn?

The car crackled up over gravel and dirt clods. Brouwer cut the engine, got out, and stood dumbfounded in front of the ruins. Off to his left, the inn's lone remnant stood in senseless post mortem: 50 wide, wooden steps rose to nothing. It's gone. The inn burned down! Why in the name of Christ didn't I know about this?

Brouwer poured through the charred debris as if sifting through the artifacts of an antediluvian city. Did these burned particle boards once form the walls of rooms where I slept? Were these chunks of granite part of the fireplace where Mom, Dad, and I sat on cool summer nights browning marshmallows? Buried under a huge tangle of electrical wiring, the backrest of a seat lay burnt and split in half. This is from one of the chairs in the inn's little movie theatre built in the 1940's. I sat in one of these seats the first summer we came up here and saw "Laura" for the first time.

395

The old wooden inn probably went up like tissue paper. This is all that's left of my childhood summers, Brouwer thought mournfully.

He walked to the steps that once reached the inn's grand, front doors. How many times did Caesar and I race down here with my fishing tackle and bag lunch? Looking out at the roadway below, Brouwer pinpointed the precise spot where Caesar had been hit and killed. Just beyond, the remnant of the old boathouse, its doors torn off, shaded the lake's waters which sloshed to and fro inside the ghost of a hull.

He crept back to the charred debris spread over the inn's parking lot. Sinking sorrowfully to a log that lay in front of a mound of scorched tables and particle boards, Brouwer detected a faint, burned, charcoal scent. The fire must have occurred recently, he guessed. The locals must have been heartbroken when they stood here and watched the landmark go up in flames. Brouwer's right hand was about to reach for a Camel when his eye caught a pleasant golden glow shining through the cracks of blackened two-by-fours a few feet away. Kicking some boards aside, he stared at a document lying face up. The title page was pristine and showed no signs of soot or ash.

THE BOOK OF TIME

Puzzled, Brouwer brought the book up out of the pile. He turned back the cover:

Aldous Dassler's Paradigm Principle
November 20, 2065AD

English physicist Aldous Dassler proved the impossibility of time travel in his treatise The Paradigm Principle published in London, England, November 20, 2065AD.

Using the space-time theories of Albert Einstein and the physics of Charles Genet, Dassler negated irrefutably that movement

forward or backward in time could be achieved in the material,
physical world.

Brouwer's hands went cold. Grasping the edges of the book in
a spasm of incredulity, he raced through the pages ahead filled with
biographical material of the life of a man named Dassler followed
by page after page of mathematical formulae and geometric
constructs. Some of it Brouwer understood; the rest of it might just
as well have been printed in Chinese. Reading various sentences
and paragrahs, he wondered why all the verbs were written in past
tense: *Proved* the *possibility*? Dassler *negated*? Then he flashed
through the so-called Paradigm Principle. The concepts dazzled
him. This doesn't make sense, Brouwer thought. Flipping pages,
he turned to the book's last line:

"To my grandfather who taught me faith in the face of
failure, a thirst for more knowledge when all knowledge seemed
exhausted, and courage when even my closest colleagues rejected
my theories." Aldous Dassler, 2065AD.

The book fell to the ground as if it had turned into a diseased
animal. You could read this thing in complete darkness, he thought.
What is it? Where did it come from?

2065? Who in hell is Aldous Dassler?

The light tapping of shoes on pavement reached his ears from
the roadway. Brouwer looked down and saw a woman in running
shorts and T-shirt coming into view. Pulling up alongside the slope
leading up to the lot, she rested her hands on her knees and was
trying to catch her breath.

"Say—Hello, there!"

The jogger glanced up, sweat pouring down the sides of her
face. She had a shaved head and her face was streaked with dark,
crimson spots. Her thighs were muscular and she appeared to be
an experienced marathon runner.

"Could I talk to you?" Brouwer called out creeping down the
dirt path toward her.

When he reached the bottom of the slope, the woman said out

of breath, "Oh, the fire? Yeah. The inn burned down a year ago April. Terrible. Many think it was arson."

"I just found something amazing up there in the debris. Would you please take a look at it and tell me what you think?"

"As soon as I catch my breath," she said.

Brouwer led the woman back up the short hill. When he reached the spot where he had dropped the book, his bewildered eyes widened in disbelief."

"What's wrong?" the woman asked.

Brouwer fumbled furiously through the burnt two-by-fours. "It's gone!" he exclaimed. "I dropped it right here! I held it in my hands!" Throwing pieces of clutter left and right in a maddening attempt to find the book, he cried, "I'm not crazy, believe me! It was right here!" Brouwer lifted a huge section of blackened plywood and shoved it back over the top of the pile. "Mam, I found a book no more than 10 minutes ago and dropped it right on the ground here. This is crazy!"

"I know it's gone," the woman stated softly.

Brouwer froze. Suddenly, the woman was not out of breath. Her face contained no beads of sweat or crimson patches. A wry smile crossed her mouth.

"Huh? What did you—"

"Believe me. It isn't there, Steven."

"*What*?!"

"Steven, did you not read about a man named Dassler who will one day prove time travel an impossibility?"

Brouwer stepped back in disbelief and nearly tripped over a thick wad of burnt wiring. "How do you know my name?"

"Are you absolutely sure you want to publish your book, Steven?"

Brouwer could barely speak the words: "*How do you know about my book?*"

"Steven, I'm a helper who wants to point you in the right direction."

"What do you mean 'a helper'? What direction?" Brouwer's voice cracked.

"The manuscript you're writing rests upon a fiction, Steven. Publish it and you will suffer embarrassment and humiliation for the rest of your life."

Brouwer could only stare at the unbelievable figure of a bald-headed woman standing before him who could not possibly know what she knew.

"Open your heart and mind to *Discovery*, Steven. That is the key. *Discovery.*"

The woman smiled, nodded, and began inching down the slope backwards without even looking. Brouwer couldn't believe he was seeing it, but in what seemed like a portion of a strip of film in which frames were instantly spliced, the jogger was sprinting again over the roadway below.

"Wait!" He called, hurrying after the woman breathlessly. All at once Brouwer's left foot caught on a tangled ball of copper mesh. He fell hard and only his flat palms prevented his face from slamming into the ground and breaking his front teeth. An awful ache shot through his legs and spine. *"Ehhhhh..."*

He sprawled out over dirt and gravel and could only listen to his miserable, wheezing breath. A sportscar careened at high speed, shifted into third gear, then raced away on the roadway below. A flock of loons flew overhead and squawked indifferently. The purr of a motor boat on the lake sputtered like a distant leaf blower, then faded. Bouwer got to his feet in pain, limped down the slope, and searched in all directions for the woman. But the jogger had disappeared around the roadway's curve. He crept up the dirt lot again and picked wearily in vain through the burnt ruins hoping that he might still find the book. Exhausted, he sank to the long log and wiped the sweat from his forehead and neck. Suddenly, his mother's wheelchair rolled out in front of him. Mrs. Brouwer was shaking her head at her son's sorry predicament. "What's the matter with you, Stephen? Don't you ever learn?"

Brouwer's head sagged in his hands. The name Aldous Dassler echoed between his ears. And the year 2065? And the jogger—
Wait!

Brouwer's eyes expanded in a sudden, blast of realization. I had a student named Dassler! Yes! I'm positive a Dassler was enrolled in one of my classes this past year. Or was it the year before?

Brouwer stared out at the summery blue waters of Lake Winnipesaukee and tried to connect the name Dassler to a first name and face. Unable to picture anyone, he was certain a young man named Dassler had been in his lecture hall at Brown. But what was that student's first name? He asked himself again and again. The image of his grade book popped into his head. It contained computerized grade sheets now lying under papers on the left side of his desk at home. Brouwer was convinced that somewhere on those sheets the name Dassler was listed in a recent class. And with it, the student's first name, grades, and contact numbers. Was that Dassler connected in some way to the Aldous Dassler described in the book I found? Brouwer's mind whirled with ideas, but only one thought seemed clear to him at that moment: get the grade book and find out if Dassler's first name was Aldous.

Frantic to fly back to his townhouse in Providence, Brouwer threw the key into the car's ignition, backed out of the dirt lot in a cloud of dust, then exploded away from the demolished remains of the Oak Birch Inn.

IV

The Book of Time? It had that strange glow, Brouwer kept thinking. And a man named Aldous Dassler—a physicist who wrote something called the Paradigm Principle? And that woman who knew I found the book and knew of my own book? Joan Mercer's words returned: *Steven, this isn't healthy.* Brouwer wondered if he had gone off the deep end the moment he discovered the ruins of

The Oak Birch Inn. But what if it turns out I actually had a student named Aldous Dassler?

He smoked half a dozen Camels on his race back to Providence. Casting aside every one of his prejudices against the supernatural, Brouwer began to rifle through the possibilities. A 20 year-old Aldous Dassler living today would be in his 90's in 2065. But what if that Dassler was the father or grandfather of the Aldous Dassler described in the book? The second Dassler, if born when his father was, say, 25, would be in his late 60's or early 70's in 2065. But I know a Dassler was in one of my classes as sure as I am in this car now. I *am* at the steering wheel of my car, aren't I? Brouwer crushed another cigarette in the dashboard ash tray, then pushed his foot down on the accelerator. And just what would I do if an Aldous Dassler did turn out to be a student of mine? When the odometer inched passed 80, Brouwer reminded himself he'd never find out anything if he wrapped his car around a tree.

The front door of Brouwer's townhouse blew open and slammed against the wall. Breathing through his nose, he dashed into his study and rifled through the pile of papers on the top left of his desk. Yanking out the spiral notebook from the bottom, he began flipping through the computerized grade sheets beginning with the spring quarter. A nervous finger ran down the column of alphabetized names. Spring, Section One—nothing. Sections two and three—nothing. Winter Quarter, Section One—nothing. Section Two—

Brouwer's face went white. The name "Dassler, Evan" jumped off the page. Evan Dassler, senior, had received one of the few A's Brouwer had given out in the winter quarter. Unable to put a face to the name, Brouwer glared at Dassler's telephone number clearly printed on the computer sheet's far right column. Collapsing into his leather chair, he drew a breath. He had gone over the rough numbers in his head driving back from New Hampshire, but now he took a pencil and put them to paper:

If Evan Dassler of Brown University were now 21 years old and fathered a child when he was 25 in 1995, that son would be

70 in 2065. Brouwer knew that Einstein was in his mid-twenties when he published "On the Electrodynamics of Moving Bodies"— the theory of Specific Relativity. Seventy was probably too old to do one's groundbreaking work, he reasoned. Then Brouwer remembered the dedication at the end of "The Paradigm Principle." Aldous Dassler had referred to his grandfather as inspiration. Yes! Was that grandfather the Evan Dassler who was my student last winter and the one who graduated from Brown three weeks ago? If the son of Evan Dassler had a son in 2020, he'd be 45 in 2065. My age now, Brouwer thought with irony. Of course, brothers, nephews, and cousins of any future Dassler complicate the picture. But could an Aldous Dassler exist in the future family tree of the current Evan Dassler?

Brouwer threw his pencil down and caught himself. He was amazed he had fallen into such twisted reasoning. He rubbed his face with his hands thinking that what happened to him at the lake had to be an elaborate hallucination caused by his exhausted, sleep-deprived mind. Yet I held that book in my hands, didn't I? And I read words which led me to Evan Dassler, a very real person enrolled in one of my classes, didn't I? The jogger was real, wasn't she? Brouwer reminded himself that the unconscious was a very powerful force. Did my mind weave all the necessary parts of *The Book of Time* into a believeable illusion?

Glaring at Evan Dassler's telephone number printed on the far right column of the computer spread sheet, Brouwer asked himself what reason he'd give if he did call Dassler. Then again, what if that kid told me he had a cousin, nephew, or brother whose first name was Aldous? And for all I know, Evan Dassler may have a son right now named Aldous.

He stared at the phone as if picking up the receiver would be like taking a dangerous step forward along a 500 foot precipice. How did I get to this point? Brouwer asked himself. Have my beliefs about supernatural explanations evaporated? But I want to find out about Aldous Dassler, don't I? And there was an Evan

Dassler in my class, wasn't there? What possible harm is there in a simple call to a former student?

His left hand lifted the receiver slowly. Brouwer's heart raced as he considered the implications of speaking to someone related to Aldous Dassler who might rank with the likes of Albert Einstein. The kid got an A from me, didn't he? I give A's to outstanding intellects only. Evan Dassler had to be a superior mentality. Does that prove something right there?

Put the damn phone down now, a little voice inside him warned. This whole thing goes against rational thought.

Brouwer dialed the number.

"Hello, this is Professor Brouwer at Brown University. I'm trying to reach Evan Dassler, a student who was in my class this last year."

"Oh, hello, Professor," the woman said reacting with surprise. "This is Evan's mother. He just stepped out the door. Let me see if I can catch him."

If only I had gotten to know my studens better, Brouwer thought with great regret.

"Hello?"

"Yes, Hello, Evan," Brouwer tried to say cheerfully as he heart beat faster. "This is Professor Brouwer at Brown. I know this phone call is out in left field, but I was very impressed with your work this past year. Evan, the student who was to be my graduate assistant for this coming term is moving out of state. And you came to mind immediately. Would you consider taking the position?"

"Well," said Dassler, "I'm flattered you'd consider me, Professor, but I hadn't planned on graduate school in the fall. In fact, I thought I'd be leaving Brown and do some traveling this summer."

"I understand. OK. But may I point out some of the benefits of being a grad assistant. I hope you won't say no just yet."

"Well…"

"How about meeting and talking it over? Costs nothing to

just discuss, right?" Brouwer chuckled awkwardly. "You're free to decline, Evan."

"All right, sounds good," Dassler agreed.

"Say tomorrow? Why not hop on over to my place. How about one O'clock?"

"That would be fine. I'd like that. Why don't you give me directions, Professor?"

Brouwer was sweating like a race horse when he set the receiver down. This is idiotic! What possible line of questioning could be asked of a 22 year-old college graduate that would shed light on events 75 years into the future? He was fighting hard against what he had experienced at the burned remains of the Oak Birch Inn. A book from the future reveals a future scientific proof negating all I've worked for, then suddenly disappears. And that is followed by a woman jogger who taps into my conscious thoughts, then also disappears. Am I having a cerebral infarction? Brouwer wondered, closing his eyes wearily, regretting calling Dassler and wishing he had never gone up to Lake Winnepesaukee at all.

He spent a long night smoking, drinking whiskey sours, and watching the movie "Laura" on his VHS. When he finally passed out, he dreamed of a drained Lake Winnipesaukee. It was a huge basin of rock, sunken ships, and the bones of dead whales. At the bottom of the lake, a clock ticked away like a booming canon.

Minutes before 1 p.m. the next day, Brouwer watched through a slit in the living room curtains as a dented, yellow volkswagon pulled into the visitor's parking stall across from the townhouse complex. How asinine this is. I should have called Dassler and cancelled.

When he opened the door, Brouwer found a large, freckled hand extended toward him. Dassler was a tall, very lean young man with dirty blonde hair covering his ears. Dressed in jeans, t-shirt, and sleeveless windbreaker, Dassler's closely set brown eyes held a curious, impish twinkle. Flakes of a blonde moustache curled over his upper lip and his pleasant mouth was set in an easy smile. Brouwer now remembered: Dassler had been a nondescript student who always sat quietly near the back of the hall and never asked a question nor did he comment during any of Brouwer's lectures.

"Thank you for coming over, Evan. Why don't we go into my office? Coffee? A beer?"

"A beer would be nice, Professor."

Dassler sat in the cushioned easy chair across from Brouwer's desk. The young man's intense brown eyes settled in on him without the slightest self-consciousness.

"Did I forget to congratulate you on your graduation, Evan? Apologies."

"Thank you. So ironic that you called me, Professor. I was thinking of contacting you, actually." Dassler popped the tab on the can of beer.

"You were?" Brouwer pulled out a Camel and struck a match. "What about?"

"I'm working on a math theory relating to predictability."

The match halted in mid-air. "Is that—right?"

"It's crude and you'll undoubtedly see the holes in it right away, but I'd like you to look it over. I've always been fascinated by John Nash's game theories. When I was a kid I used to count the number of waves that would hit the beach in a specific period of time."

"Perhaps there's a future paper there," Brouwer observed, clinging to every word and syllable Dassler uttered.

"My problem is that I'm interested in too much," the young man laughed. "I'm all over the place."

"Not a problem," Brouwer observed. "Diverse interests expand horizons."

"Guess I'm everywhere, yet nowhere."

Brouwer lit his cigarette. "You just graduated with a degree, Evan. You're young. You'll find your niche and pursue it. Now you said you hadn't planned on graduate school. Is that decision in stone?"

"Right. See, I just became engaged."

"Congratulations."

"Thank you. Susie and I won't tie the knot for a couple years, though. We're planning on moving to England and settling there."

Brouwer froze. "To England?" he breathed, remembering that Aldous Dassler was described as an English physicist.

"Guess we'll live with Susie's parents till we get on our feet. After that we'll probably start a family."

Brouwer looked at Dassler with great intensity. "You could get a Master's at Brown before you go over, you know."

"A possibility. I won't rule that out."

"May I be frank, Evan? I think it would be a shame if someone with your potential didn't get a Master's in mathematics or a related discipline. You have all the tools to rise to that level. Later, perhaps, a PhD."

Dassler smiled. "With a specialty in Algebraic Geometry, Professor?"

"Yes. A possibility, I suppose." Brouwer laughed weakly.

"Not to collect brownie points here, Professor, but your class was something that influenced me greatly. I really enjoyed it. You were always so prepared. Never a minute wasted. Never any down time. And always such fantastic concepts."

Brouwer leaned forward and worded what he wanted to say very delicately.

"Evan, if I could segue for just a moment and ask a question. Years ago I had an old college buddy at Dartmouth who might possibly be related to your family on your father's side."

"Oh? Who's that?"

"His name was—*Aldous Dassler.*"

The young man shook his head. "No, that name doesn't register, Professor. My Dad has no brothers. Weird, though, that you mention the name 'Aldous'. It's Susie's Dad's name. But he's Aldous McBride and he's never been to the United States."

Brouwer's flat, trembling palms pressed down on the top of his desk. "You mean Susie's Dad, the one in England? He's Aldous McBride? And he has no brothers?"

"No. None."

"What about a son? Does your fiancé have a brother?"

"No, Susie is an only child," Dassler laughed. "She made me promise, though, that if we have a son we'll name him after her Dad. So he'd be Aldous Dassler."

The sky fell. The walls imploded. The floor beneath Brouwer's feet dropped away into the abyss of space.

Aldous Dassler, author of The Paradigm Principle who cited his grandfather in *The Book of Time* referred to the young man now sitting in the chair on the other side of Brouwer's desk.

The Book of Time had been as real as Lake Winnipesaukee.

In 2065 Aldous Dassler, the grandson of Evan Dassler, would prove forever that time travel was impossible. And in that crazed, electrifying explosion of a moment, Steven Brouwer's work concerning time and its effects disintegrated within the dominion of an unassuming, humble, townhouse study in Providence, Rhode Island.

But most of all, Brouwer had to accept that an omniscient intelligence existed in the cosmos.

"Professor Brouwer?" Dassler asked coming forward with concern. "Professor? Are you all right, Sir?"

V

The packaged clock was under Brouwer's arm as he climbed the stairs to his mother's townhouse. He pressed the bell, inserted the key into the lock, and stepped into the quiet living room. Tearing off the brown wrapping paper, he lifted the clock out of its box. After removing the porcelain swan from the mantel, he carefully set the new clock in its place and plugged the cord into the side wall socket.

"Mom!"

"Be right out, Steven."

Brouwer watched the second hand beginning to move around

the dial. He thought of Mr. Leabnit's Concord clock haven and all of the second hands timed to impossibly perfect synchronization.

The wheelchair rounded the hallway corner and Mrs. Brouwer appeared smiling.

"Take a look at your new clock, Ma."

"How handsome," she observed, rolling her wheelchair over to inspect it."

"Gold Roman numerals, octagon walnut frame, fluorescent dials. I'll throw the swan out."

"Very nice, son. It really makes the room, doesn't it? Back from the lake a little early, aren't you?

"I am. Ma, I've got some bad news, though. Better brace yourself for this. The Oak Birch Inn burned down."

Mrs. Brouwer turned her wheelchair back toward him.

"Burned to a crisp, Ma. Except for the front steps that lead nowhere. It's a scrap heap. Nothing but burnt remains. The inn where we spent many memorable summers is history."

She said it softly. "Yes, I know."

"*...Huh?*"

"It burned down a year ago last April."

Brouwer froze. "You knew? You knew the inn burned down? You knew when I told you I was headed up to the lake the other day? Yet you said nothing? You let me go up there like a damn jackass? Why in Christ did you do that, Ma?"

"Because I wanted you to see it destroyed for yourself. With your own eyes. You needed closure with the inn, Son. You needed to release the grip it has had on you for years."

"*Closure?!* You took it upon yourself to manipulate my *closure?*"

"Son, I regret a fire destroyed the inn. I have memories there, too, you know. But I felt it was imperative you see the remains first hand. I toyed with the idea of telling you when I first heard about what happened, but I knew you were taking periodic trips up there and not telling me. I decided to wait and let you go up there to see for yourself."

Brouwer looked at his mother in utter disbelief. "So you knew all along. What you did was punish me for not telling you I was going up to the lake..."

"Steven, I've always been aware of your overpowering nostalgia for the inn and the summers we shared at Lake Winnipesaukee. The fact is, you've never been able to extricate yourself from Alton Bay and the maudlin sentimentality attached to it. Memories are fine, Son, but you have lived in them and allowed past experiences to rule even your personal relationships as a grown man. And they do, Steven. We both know they do."

Brouwer said it with controlled, boiling anger: "Ma, this has to be the most insidious act of control you ever perpetrated upon me."

"Stephen, could we put the inn aside for a moment? Because it's not the crux of the issue here."

"The crux of *what* issue?"

"I spoke to Joan Mercer." Mrs. Brouwer folded her hands on her lap as if to say, 'There. I said it.'

"Brouwer's face tightened into a hard, red grimace. *"You did what?!"*

"Yes, I did speak to her. Stephen, you looked awful when you left here the other day. I was very concerned. You mentioned you'd be meeting with your department chair before going up to the lake. I debated, but I called the math department at Brown and got Joan's number. I had to pry it out of her with a crowbar. She finally admitted to me she's as concerned about you as I am."

"Concerned about what?"

"This disturbing manuscript you're writing. Stephen—time travel?" Mrs. Brouwer shook her head sorrowfully. "My God, Son, you can't possibly be serious, can you? And taking a sabbatical to finish this inane book? Stephen, I would really like you to see a professional person about this."

Brouwer felt like picking up the new mantel clock he bought and hurling it into his mother's face. "Jesus Christ, Ma! Is there anything in this fuckin' world you do not control or manipulate? Do I ever stop becoming the laboratory rat in your labyrinth?

409

And please, don't lean on that tired wheelchair routine because it doesn't fly anymore. You haven't changed one bit from your days at Providence General when you were J. Edgar Hoover terrifying the entire staff with the shit you had on them. You were J. Edgar Hoover then, and even in that wheelchair, you're J. Edgar Hoover now!"

Mrs. Brouwer closed her eyes as if she felt a sharp stab of pain. "That's utterly ridiculous, Steven."

"Is it? Since the day I was born I haven't been able to go to the toilet without you looking through the bathroom window to see if I was zipping my pants up straight. And Dad? At least I talked back to you and stood up to you; but poor old Dad was an emasculated bowl of mush. Dad wasn't your husband, Ma; he was your son."

"Oh, you're so blind, Steven. You're completely blind to the terror I endure in this chair which grows worse every day. Did you know I can barely dress myself now? To me this chair is a prison. You, Steven, are my sole lifeline. Don't you see that if you're not mentally well, I'm panic-stricken at what might happen? Son, I'm holding on for dear life in this townhouse and more than ever I need you to be mentally healthy. I cannot have you trapped in your past and unable to function in the real world. I won't permit it!"

"Stop it, Ma! You're still manipulating me! I need a professional person? That's the pot calling the kettle black, isn't it? You're exhibit A for a therapist. Manipulation is pathological with you. What is it exactly that feeds your need to control everyone who comes close to you?"

She rolled her chair closer to him. Brouwer turned away from his mother in disgust.

"Stephen, I'm going to make a speech I've been wanting to make for years. I may regret making it later, but it's a speech you need to hear...

"Am I a 'soft' woman? No. Chalk it up to my genes. I know my career as a nurse was an arctic, frigid world to you. You hated Providence Hospital, but not because it smelled of ether and mercurachrome. You hated it because it was Adora Brouwer incarnate—a cold house of horror where masked surgeons amputated limbs and sliced open chest cavaties. In the eyes of Steven Brouwer, Adora Brouwer never took off her uniform when she got home. I was always Dr. Frankenstein to you, wasn't I? How tragic it is that you never saw the greater good of medicine: the blood transfusions that kept people alive; the hip replacements that let people walk; the heart pacemakers that gave people years.

"I think something inside you came unhinged the day you and your father surprised me on my birthday one year at Providence. You were 10 years old and ran down the hall looking for me. You opened the wrong door and stood there paralyzed watching me place a screaming child into an iron lung. You ran away horrified. An hour later we found you cringing in the back of the station wagon in the hospital parking lot. Something snapped inside you that day, Steven. You never saw me the same way again, did you?"

"Ma, you're Rembrandt when it comes to painting a straw man."

"Let me finish, Son. I intend to go all the way here because saying what needs to be said is long overdue.

"I don't think it was an accident you chose mathematics and geometry as your life's work. There's no sensibility connected to mathematics. Finding the square root of 100 or the hypontenuse of a triangle—it's mental gymnastics. When your work is sociology, psychology, medicine, you deal with humanity: conflict, loss, and, yes, pain, the essence of life. But you picked a discipline with no emotional matrix; one that has no flesh and blood. Steven, you ran away from real life and into the arms of sterile numbers which gave you asylum from humankind. Just like the boy in the iron lung you ran away from; just like Jillian, the woman you ejected who was in love with you. You hid, Son, from real life and took refuge inside the shelter of sterile numbers."

Brouwer gritted his teeth. "Finished with my autopsy yet?"

"No. So you go up to The Oak Birch Inn ostensibly to write about time travel, for God's sake. And I don't care how impressive your manuscript is and how complex the mathematics and geometry. You've used this 'discovery' you've made as a doorway to time to recapture the summers you knew with your father playing chess till midnight on the inn's screened-in porch; the warm sand on the lake where you and Caesar ran like pals together; the drives we'd take for a day in Cape Cod and picnic along the shores of Orleans. But I think the cherry on the banana split is your obsession with the movie "Laura." For years I used to think Gene Tierney simply represented the ideal woman to you. Son, the hard truth is: take away Raksin's beautiful theme music and "Laura" becomes just another run of the mill 1940's detective picture. It didn't hit me until a few years ago that the first time you ever saw "Laura" was in the little theatre at the Oak Birch Inn the very first summer we ever went up to Lake Winnipesaukee. "Laura" and Lake Winnipesaukee are one in the same to you, aren't they, Steven? They're the emblem of the tender, nostalgic past which you desperately crave. So what do you do? As intelligent, as educated as you are, you let your mind convince you that you discovered a means of time travel that you wish might take you back to all of that. I find that so very troubling. And so very unhealthy."

"Amazing how the heart is capable of burying the mind, its intelligence, and its advanced education. In your case, you succumbed to an inner need to recapture idyllic summers at The Oak Birch Inn. Maybe a psychologist is the only one who can help you see it, but the lake and the inn never let you escape our family's magical August's. That's why I didn't tell you about the fire. I wanted you to go up there and see the inn's corpse first hand with your own eyes so you could come to grips with it and bury it once and for all."

The living room went silent. Brouwer stood reeling from the exhaustion of decades of fighting his mother. He wanted to storm out of the townhouse at that moment and vow he'd never lay eyes on the woman in the wheelchair again. But he was left staring at the fireplace mantel with its framed photos of his father, Frank Brouwer, sitting on the inn's screened-in porch playing chess. He was wearing a corny sea captain's hat cocked to one side as his boney finger reached for a bishop. Why didn't you fight her, Dad?

She wasn't your wife; she was the mother you never had. Then his eyes fell on the new clock a few inches to the right of his father's photo. The second hand was ticking its way around the octagonal timepiece. Time, the past, Brouwer thought. What in God's name is its essence?

"Well, Ma," he finally said. "When you clean house you really do make sure you scrub every inch of the attic, garage, and crawl space, don't you? Now I'm going to tell *you* what's what.

"Despite everything else, I used to think you were the most intelligent woman I ever met; but for you to say that mathematics and geometry are sterile actually reveals your stunning ignorance. Geometry is used in mapping and is critical in surveying, navigation, astronomy, and the construction of civilization. But that's academic. And it's subordinate to the larger issue you hit me with.

"Hate to tell you this, but your two bit psychology falls flat, Ma. I ended it with Jillian because we were incompatible, period. People *are* incompatible, you know. Had we married, it wouldn't have lasted six months. And that you could never see because you never took the time to know the woman. Jillian and I were oil and water, pure and simple. End of story.

"Ma," Brouwer continued, coming close to her with red, fiery eyes, "You wanted me to go up to the Oak Birch Inn and get whacked hard because to you pain equals truth. Eliciting pain from others is what empowers you. That was true at Providence and it's still true today. You think I don't know you got people fired at that hospital because you couldn't manipulate them? Dad told me everything. But he was too weak to ever confront the dictator he married. I am the one man in your entire life who didn't bow down to Adora Brouwer and kiss her ass. You've never been able to deal with that before or after the wheelchair. My independence and self-reliance always throttled you, didn't it? The fact is you worked overtime for 40 years trying to turn me into the little boy you couldn't manipulate. You tried to turn me into Dad and you failed."

413

Brouwer backed off. Mrs. Brouwer adjusted the blankets over her legs and seemed unable to add any more to what she had said.

"As for my time travel adventure," he continued, "breathe easy, Ma. It's over. Buried. Went up in flames with the Oak Birch Inn, if you like. No, I'm not having a breakdown and I'm not schizo. So take it to the bank: there won't be any sabbatical. I'll show up at Brown in September, walk into the lecture hall in my two-bit sport coat and tie, call the role, and teach my bloody geometry ass off till the day I retire.

"Last, think you need to know my trip up to Lake Winnipesaukee wasn't for naught. Something incredible happened up there. And it's far more significant than discovering the inn burned down. In fact, it's light years beyond that. But what it was will stay right here with me forever." Brouwer thumped his chest with his fist and smiled at his mother with great satisfaction. "The experience is probably going to be the greatest one of my life. But sorry, Ma: it's one you'll never have a chance to manipulate."

Mrs. Brouwer watched her son pull out a cigarette blatantly, light it, inhale, and proudly release the smoke through his nose and into the living room air.

"We've said a lot here, Steven. I suppose it's like all meetings of the minds: some truth, some words coming from deeply-held anger. I just hope that whatever it was that you experienced at the lake will make you a better man for it, Son."

"Oh, I most assuredly will be a better man," he stated. "Count on it."

Mrs. Brouwer folded her arthritic hands on her lap and managed a faint smile. "May I say again, Son, that I love the clock. I really do."

VI

(Laura turns off the living room lights and goes into the bedroom. The apartment's front door opens and Waldo enters stealthily. He steps to the grandfather clock, quietly opens the bottom door panel, and removes the shotgun. In her bedroom Laura goes to the radio console on the wall and turns on Waldo's previously recorded Sunday night program)

Waldo's voice: And thus as history has proved, love is eternal. It has been the strongest motivation for human actions throughout centuries. Love is stronger than life. It reaches beyond the dark shadows of death. I close this evening's broadcast with some favorite lines from Dowson: 'Brief life, they are not long, the weaping and the laughter, love, desire, and hate. I think they have no portion in us after we pass this gate.'

(Standing next to the grandfather clock, Waldo slips two shells into the shotgun. Out in the hall Mark speaks to a detective)

Mark: Who's tailing Lydecker?

Detective: I was going to when he came out.

Mark: He left five minutes ago.

Detective: He didn't come out this way.

Mark: Must have gone out the back way. C'mon, let's check.

(Laura goes to the bedroom vanity, sits down, and begins brushing her hair in front of the mirror. She continues to listen to Waldo's program)

Waldo's voice: And they are not long, the days of wine and roses. Out of a misty dream our path emerges for a while then closes within a dream.

(Waldo enters Laura's bedroom and stands ominously in the doorway only inches from her. He is holding the shotgun)

415

Waldo: And that's the way it is, isn't it, Laura?

(Laura turns startled)

Laura: What?!

Radio voice: You have heard the voice of Waldo Lydecker by electronic transmission.

Laura: (breathlessly) Waldo, you've taken one life. Isn't that enough?

Waldo: The best part of myself. That's what you are. Do you think I'm going to leave it to the vulgar pawing of a second rate detective who thinks you're a dame? You think I could bear the thought of him holding you in his arms, kissisng you, loving you?

(Waldo raises the shotgun and points it at Laura. Out in the hall Mark tries desperately to get into the apartment, but the door is locked)

Mark: Laura! It's Mark! Open the door!

Waldo: There he is now.

Mark: Laura!

Waldo: He'll find us together as we always have been, as we always will be.

(Laura shoves the shotgun barrel upward and it goes off. She runs past Waldo and out of the bedroom. Mark breaks down the door. He and the detective rush into the apartment. Laura falls sobbing into Mark's arms, Waldo right behind her. The detective steps out with a .38 and fires it at Waldo point blank and stops him cold.

The shotgun goes off and hits the grandfather clock behind Mark and Laura. Waldo is hit and drops to a knee mortally wounded.)

Waldo: (whispering) Good-bye, Laura.

(Laura and Mark go to Waldo, but all we see is the broken face of the grandfather clock struck by the shotgun blast, its glass shattered, and Roman numerals partially destroyed. Waldo's dying words are the last sounds he utters)

Waldo: Good-bye, my love.

(The camera fades in slowly on the face of the shattered, grandfather clock)[5]

The credits rolled over the screen as the theatre's house lights came up. The audience began filing out, but Brouwer remained in his seat waiting for the auditorium to empty. When he was the last person in the theatre and the screen had finally faded to black, he rose, walked up the carpeted aisle, and exited through the lobby. Once outside, he stopped for a moment to look at the 1944 poster of "Laura" in the glass display. He popped a Camel to his lips, lit it, turned, and walked toward his car.

Forty-five minutes later, Brouwer stepped into his townhouse and went down the hall to his office. The manuscript sat on top of his desk blotter as he studied the title page one last time:

The Boundaries of Time
By Steven Brouwer
Brown University, 1990

He brought the manuscript into the living room and set it down on the brick ledge next to the fireplace. Removing the protective gold screen, he began stuffing wads of newspaper and wooden twigs on top of the interior grate. Then he lit the paper and watched the tiny flames grow until they spread to the kindling.

When the fire reached its peak, Brouwer took the manuscript and tossed it into the flames. He stared at the fire curiously as it ate its way across the corners of the pages and eventually burned through the rest of it.

Two books, he thought. One real, one fantasy.

A Camel came to his lips. Watching the manuscript devoured in a burst of flame, Brouwer wondered if Nester Leabnit's clocks were still running in perfect synchronization up in Concord, New Hampshire.

Beyond Space And Time

At last the day had come.

Duran Roh entered the side chamber of the Grand Hall preparing himself for his historic presentation to the General Body. Thousands of voices buzzed under the dome as a palpable sense of destiny began reaching a crescendo. Scores of other members on Martian and Moon colonies, in space stations orbiting the earth and ships sailing at the edge of the Solar System were also watching their screens anticipating Duran Roh's long-awaited report on *The Book of Time.*

Though his words would be instantly translated into every world language, Roh decided to deliver his speech in English because it reflected the nuances and inflections most suited to the meaning and content of what he wanted to convey. But that won't be the problem, he knew. Will members explode into chaotic revolt here in The Great Hall when they hear my conclusions?

Roh was a 41-year-old journeyman researcher who rose through the ranks in the modest research centers along the Mediterranean complex. Devoting his life to the service of the Super Computers with a patient, iron-clad resolve, he was an imposing figure towering a little over six-foot-five. A shock of fire-red hair combed straight back over his head; strong, curved shoulders; long, muscular legs and large, deft hands always caught the immediate attention of those meeting Roh for the first time. The signet of Roh's demeanor, however, was his voice: the melifluous sounds issuing precise words and their correct inflections stamped him with a wisdom that gained universal respect as a wise and fastidious philosopher-analyst.

But Roh's crowning achievement was the creation of The Human

Analogue. The ultra-computer rendered all previous generations of computers obsolete. He had coordinated the Analogue's complex web of databases and engineered their universal integration with impeccable facility. Three months after The Human Analogue had been perfected, President Mott awarded Roh the highest honor attainable for a private citizen, the Medal of Research.

But the Master Researcher also knew great tragedy. His entire family—wife, three children, mother and father—had perished on the Moon's colony of Sirinia when a relatively tiny asteroid struck the colony's helium power center. Radiation leaked into the living quarters and all were lost. When informed of the news, Roh collapsed and spent a year under medical guidance. *I should have been with them and perished, too,* he told himself nearly every day.

The tragedy transformed Roh's ambitions. Losing all desire to climb higher in the state, he dreamed of one day settling upon the island of Acrylia in Micronesia where he would, for the rest of his life, engage his true passion: undersea exploration. The sea, Roh believed, possessed far greater secrets than the stars.

The implant in Roh's wrist flashed to emerald green. The moment had come. He took a long breath, exited the chamber, and scaled the steps to the Great Hall. The podium stood on a tiny island platform in the center of the auditorium facing a sea of faces that rose tier upon tier to the top of the octagonal, transparent dome. When the throng detected his presence, spirited applause rang out. Striding across the stage and placing his notes down on the lectern, Roh wondered if these same members applauding now would later demand his resignation and curse his name forever.

A moment before he spoke, Roh's family flashed before him. *At least Cassandra, the children, and my mother and father will not be present today,* Roh thought. *For if my efforts go up in the flames of outrage, they won't witness their husband, father, and son committing intellectual suicide before the entire solar community.*

"President Mott, members of the Governing Congress, colony citizens: I salute you and wish you good graces. I acknowledge profound gratitude to all for honoring me with the profound task at hand. Truly, I stand accountable to you on this day."

Roh paused and looked up at the rows upon rows of expectant faces climbing one level upon another into the blur of the vast upper reaches of the governing dome.

"Nearly a year ago, you, the Governing Congress, in consultation with President Mott, entrusted me with the greatest mission of any researcher in history: to determine the two most insoluble riddles underlying *The Book of Time*: One: the book's origin; Two: the book's purpose. I asasure you that not a shred of data went unexamined in forging our conclusions. First, however, it behooves me to establish indispensable background.

"The evolution of simple computers in the Twentieth Century was the first step toward complete amalgamation of human knowledge. Even superior generations of computers remained well below data acquired through traditional forms of linkage. Then we discovered the greatest technical enlightenment breakthrough in history: the wonders of RTSM—*Referred Time Synchronized Matrix*. RTSM gave birth to The Human Analogue, the most advanced computer Mankind has known. For the first time, researchers could ascertain knowledge dating back to the beginning of recorded history. Through The Human Analogue, we mastered Earthly knowledge on a scale undreamed of in the history of civilization.

"But when The Analogue stood as the most powerful force on Earth, its vast potential to transform civilization demanded that only one of its kind could be allowed to exist. For the consequences resulting from an unscrupulous individual or clandestine group accessing data from their own private Analogue might prove catastrophic to civilization. Therefore, all research submitted to the Analogue could only be incorporated into statute passed by you, the members of the Governing Congress. Acknowledging these precepts, I will proceed with the research team's findings...

"From 1963 to 2101, *The Book of Time* appeared to 99 subjects predicting a future event. The Human Analogue examined every strand in the lives of those subjects and amassed over one-hundred thousand hours of scrutiny penetrating the subjects' personal histories.

"It was learned that the first subjects who experienced *The Book of Time* were John Decker and his future wife, Jeanne McClelland on November 21, 1963AD. Both discovered the book in separate geographical regions in the Midwest, USA, on the same day. Both met one another seemingly by chance that same day also. The Human Analogue concluded that the probability of this occurring randomly was one in 1,897,557.

"These two subjects received identical versions of *The Book of Time*: the assassination of their contemporary President, John F. Kennedy, to occur the following day, November 22, 1963AD. We know all there is to know about these two subjects and John Decker's courageous but fruitless attempts to prevent the death of his President. And we know all there is to know about the next 98 subjects to whom *The Book of Time* appeared thereafter, spanning a total of 138 years.

"The protocol for the appearance of *The Book of Time* has been curiously random. Each subject receives the book in a mundane location: thoroughfares, libraries, mountainous terrain, tropical forests, waste centers, and polar outposts. The subjects absorb a dramatic future forecast, undergo some degree of psychological trauma, then experience the sudden and distressing disappearance of the book. The physical properties of the book itself are extraordinary: its condition is pristine; it contains a source of unknown illumination; and it cannot be modified physically in any way.

"The subjects are farmers, doctors, adolescents, politicians, military leaders, and athletes. They have no common denominator by age, sex, geography, economic or social status. Soon after a subject discovers *The Book of Time,* an individual appears who identifies himself as a 'helper'. Some subjects experience more than one helper; in other instances, a helper appears twice to the same subject. These helpers are always benign figures—males, females, maintenance workers, law enforcement officials, aged persons, and children—but they possess the ability to know the subject's central concern. Their time with the subject is brief, but their role is certain: to assuage the subject's fears.

"It is critical that I now address the *Paradigm Principle* proven by Aldous Dassler in 2077AD.

"As we know, Dassler proved the impossibility of travel through time and established the immutability of history. Is *The Book of Time* attempting to motivate the subjects to alter history which would invalidate Dassler? *The research team concludes with 100 percent certainty that the answer is emphatically in the negative.* A paramount question then looms: If history is immutable, why are the subjects being exposed to future history at all?

"Fellow members, all of this necessary background and foundation leads us now to the research team's specific conclusion with respect to the first principal line of inquiry: the origin of *The Book of Time...*"

"Since the first Homo sapiens stalked the plains of sub-Saharan Africa 200,000 years ago, Man has been driven by a passion to comprehend the mysteries riddling his world. It is not an exaggeration to say that with the creation of The Human Analogue many believe that we reached the pinnacle of scientific and historical understanding in our era. But what I and the research team concluded demonstrated that though we have indeed scaled grandiose peaks of knowledge, we remain far below the heights of earthy erudition.

"Fellow Members, our exhaustive efforts to discover the answer to the first insoluble riddle of *The Book of Time* struck an impenetrable wall. I will not waste another breath: For the research team, assisted by the Human Analogue, failed to determine the origin of *The Book of Time.*"

Voices in the Great Hall rumbled and called out their disbelief. Many turned in confusion, but Roh expected it and assumed an emotional detachment. Waiting patiently for the clamor to subside, the Master Researcher maintained his composure. Finally, the disturbance in the Great Hall waned and Roh began to speak again:

"Precisely why was the team unable to determine the book's origin? It is because the realm in which The Human Analogue dwells is the material, physical universe. And, as I will later elucidate, *The Book of Time* is not a physical phenomenon. It is a physical nothing. And a physical something is, in fact, incapable of analyzing that which is non-physical. There is, however, one unquestionable certainty concerning the origin of *The Book of Time*: it appears from outside our physical, material cosmos."

This time the members in the Great Hall burst out into greater shock. Heads shook. Colonists on Mars, the Moon, and those in ships watching Roh on screens well beyond the Jovian planets studied the face of the master researcher with fascination and bewilderment. It was as if a collective question had been shouted back to the researcher: *"How can this be, Dr. Roh?! Why has The Human Analogue rendered such a vague and imprecise conclusion regarding the origin of The Book of Time?"*

After several moments, a hush eventually settled in again among the sea of faces before the Master Researcher. When the tumult subsided, Roh continued.

"However, Fellow Members, I now acknowledge that the research team will deliver a definitive finding to the second line of inquiry: The purpose of *The Book of Time*.

"As the team began to probe deeply into every case study, one irrefutable common denominator stood above all others: for after finding the book, every subject experienced an 'epiphany', a sudden, intuitive perception into his or her life. And that transformative perception in turn became a current that extended outward affecting countless other lives in succeeding generations. The irrefutable fact is *The Book of Time* never appeared to alter or modify history in the least. It appeared to a subject to forge the epiphany just described and to ultimately become a ripple in the pond of time. And that ripple would ultimately stream outward to achieve the purpose which I will now describe.

"Fellow Members, it is the research team's conclusion to a 100 percent certainty that the purpose of The Book of Time was to enable Man to ultimately mold humanity's invincible future."

Voices erupted again. Roh's findings were simply not close to anything that had been anticipated. But the researcher endured, stared down at his notes and waited. Yet even this, he knew, was not the end of it. For now would come the time bomb he must, in conscience, deliver to the solar community. Again Roh remained composed through the chaos and used the interruption to collect his last bit of strength. When the dome had calmed, he spoke.

"Fellow Members on Earth and beyond, what you have heard thus far are generalized findings from complex research. But it now behooves me to go beyond these findings and present my personal observations. All of that which I now express concerning *The Book of Time* is unknown even to the team. For the conclusions that follow are mine alone.

"As I re-explored *The Book of Time's* impact on all of the subject's, I wrestled with a great perplexity: Why was it that *The Book of Time* first appeared in 1963AD? Why did the book not appear earlier in history during the Roman Empire, The Renaissance, or before any of the world's great wars? That signal year, 1963AD, we recognize as the beginning of the Second Modern Age. Man took his first steps into space; education, technology, social mores and culture were undergoing historic revolutions at this precise point. Most of all, Man crept to within a breath of his own nuclear annihilation. *The Book of Time's* arrival had to be a nexus. I then pondered this critical juncture to The Human Analogue's failure to discover the book's origin. Though the Analogue defined the book as "non-physical," the book did indeed appear in some form in our physical world and forecast very real future events. How was this contradiction possible?

"I was led inexorably to one hypothesis: that since *The Book of Time* was not physical matter and since human subjects received it in a physical plane, it had to be a hallucination. But let me be clear: this hallucination bore no resemblance whatsoever to the hallucination of a 'mirage of water' a man believes he sees in a scorching desert. No, this apparition was completely distinct from that phenomenon. For *The Book of Time* left unmistakable, physical traces. And a desert mirage leaves nothing in its aftermath because it is a phantasm. As to the 'helpers' who appeared to the subjects after discovering the book? They, too, were hallucinations; facilitators, if you will, designed to communicate concepts intended to fulfill *The Book of Time's* purpose."

The vast audience in the dome was enveloped in stunned silence. Most all of the members were paralyzed in disbelief and wondered where Roh was heading next. Nevertheless, Roh's impressive stature stood unflinchingly at the platform's pulpit to let the effect of his hypothesis settle. The Master Researcher consoled himself with the words of his favorite Twentieth Century poet: "I have miles to go before I sleep..."

"Therefore, I conclude what The Human Analogue was unable to conclude: *The Book of Time* derives from a Master Intelligence. And this intelligence is a teacher who teaches us that though Man will glean much from the discoveries of Einstein, Dassler, and all great scientific minds yet to come, he will never know what enlightens such great mentalities to intuit their wisdom. That while we believe we have reached the highest levels of earthly knowledge, that knowledge is not the singular jewel in Mankind's crown. That while our spaceships may travel to distant suns, we will never discern the pure essence of starlight.

"Fellow Members, we exist today as more profound world citizens because of *The Book of Time's* appearance to 99 heroic subjects. Let me be clear: we are indebted to these subjects and owe them more than we may comprehend; for they negotiated the book's apocalyptic forecasts, endured personal trauma, and turned fear into decisive action that affected countless others.

"Finally, I, Duran Roh, conclude without the slightest embellishment whatsoever that the Master Intelligence which sent Mankind *The Book of Time* bequeths a daunting gift to us all—that of *Discovery*. For Discovery leads to discernment. And discernment shepherds human progress and fashions civilization toward grandiose progress."

Roh drew a final breath of immense relief. His mission was complete. The researcher simply walked off the platform accompanied by a stunned, reflective silence. He wanted to be gone from the dome; he wanted to be out of the city; he wanted to be alone racing over the Pacific toward Acrylia, his beloved, blissful sanctuary. He had nearly reached the side chamber when a slow ovation began to build behind him in the Great Hall. As he entered the interior, the ovation had grown into a din of approval. For members were also applauding in Martian and Moon colonies, in orbiting space stations, and in ships beyond Neptune. The master researcher could not believe his ears. Is it possible they actually sympathize and agree? Roh asked himself in disbelief. Are they actually validating *me*?

Miramar, one of the hall's adjutants, stood waiting in the reception concourse as Roh wiped his perspiring forehead with a cloth. "Your presentation was inspiring, Dr. Roh," he observed. "I believe it will become historic."

"The project is finished," he whispered. "I would just like to leave for my holiday."

Roh walked out of the Great Dome breathing fresh air and feeling as if iron weights had been lifted from his shoulders. He had taken only a few steps into the spray of the city's bright sunlight when a blue light flashed on his wrist implant. He pulsed the sender and his heart ticked into a quickened pace. President Mott was requesting his presence at once.

"Duran, I have read your report several times since receiving it this morning. Nothing short of awe-inspiring." The President's grey eyebrows furrowed. "Needless to say, I found your personal conclusions to be— shocking."

"I understand, Mr. President."

"Of course, it is regrettable you could not give a definitive answer to the first area: the specific origin of the book. But there's an ancient saying, 'You can't get blood out of a stone.' As for me, those personal conclusions were generally electrifying on a number of levels."

Roh was incredulous. He had expected censure for including his personal opinions.

"I am reacting to all your conclusions somewhere between stupefaction and awe. Perhaps you are right, Duran: *The Human Analogue* may not be the crown jewels of human knowledge we think it to be."

"Then—you approve of the report?"

"Approve and respect, Duran."

An enormous sense of relief swept over the Master Researcher. "I won't lie, Mr. President. I felt as if I were stepping up to the precipice of intellectual suicide. I expected the complete opposite from you."

"Hogwash. Roh, you possess one major shortcoming: you suffer from the unfortunate malady of the humble perfectionist. Rest assured, your contribution to this effort will be recognized for generations. Now take your deserved holiday to Micronesia and spend as much time as you need to recharge your energies for a job well done."

"Thank you, Mr. President. I am eternally grateful," Roh said, as he started to turn and leave.

"Oh —just one more thing, Duran...."

"Yes, Mr. President?"

A forefinger tapped the President lip. "After many years in government, I have learned one compelling lesson: that reports and investigations never tell the entire story—*publicly*...."

Roh looked worried. "Sir?"

"You know what I'm getting at, don't you, Duran? Tell me the rest of it."

"I'm not sure I know what you're referring to, Mr. President," Roh stated anxiously. "Could you be more specific?"

"I will. Call me a fuss-budget, but I think I detected something in the last part of your presentation when you offered your personal opinion and ostensibly gave the impression of 'baring it all from the heart.' Call it intuition, a gut sense, or just plain cynicism born of too many years in office, but it was palpable. What is it you're holding back, Duran?"

"With all due respect, Mr. President—"

"Come now, Roh. We both know there's more. Out with it."

"More, President Mott?"

"Surely you didn't reveal everything you and the research team found; everything you imparted in the Grand Hall today. Tell me, in the strictest confidence, Duran, and without any fear of recrimination whatsoever, privately, now, in this room between you and me, what that hidden secret was that you perhaps discovered late one night burning the midnight oil; perhaps some revelation you kept from even your closest associates. What is it, Duran? Lower your guard; spill it out. You may disclose it safely here..."

In the few moments that elapsed there in the President's quarters standing before the highest authority on the continent, Roh considered revealing the unrevealed. He weighed the loyal support and approval Mott had shown toward his efforts. How could he, Duran Roh, disrespect such a humane political leader nearly 110 years old, a man who had invested so much faith in him? Now that the President had correctly guessed he had not told all, how could he refuse to disclose at least some of the truth he kept hidden?

"Mr. President, Sir, your perceptive powers are too keen. Yes, in fact, there is more."

Mott was thoroughly intrigued. "Go on, Duran. I'm listening with great interest."

Roh took a long breath and felt as if he had returned to the lectern in the Great Hall with the anxieties and a sense of foreboding rising up all over again. His final revelation may now be before an audience of one, but that one was the most powerful leader on Earth.

"Mr. President," he began, "you may know that I lost my family in a moon base catastrophe several years ago."

429

"Yes, I do know that. I and everyone else are well aware of the devastating tragedy you endured."

"After my loss, the extensive therapy I underwent, I left for the solitude of Acrylia, in Micronesia, a place that for me is the most tranquil oasis on Earth. It was there, while walking along the mountainous peaks that *The Book of Time* appeared to Duran Roh..."

The President was stupefied. His hand came to his forehead and he sank to a chair.

"*No...*"

"It did, Mr. President. It most assuredly did. I am the 100th subject to receive the book."

"I can barely believe my ears." Mott was breathless. "And— what may I ask was its forecast?"

Roh paused and chose his words carefully.

"It forecast the greatest period of extra-terrestrial colonization to distant stars ever dreamed."

Mott was flabbergasted. "Irony of ironies," was all he could muster. "And how much into the future until this colonization unfolds, Duran?"

"I'm afraid not until long after your term, President Mott. Please understand why I did not disclose all this in my report today. For I am sure you can appreciate how such a revelation could be interpreted as self-serving. After all, who could disprove it? And for that matter, who could disprove anything I claimed to have read in *The Book of Time*?"

An ironic smile broke out over Mott's face. His head shook from side to side in disbelief. "Yes, I do see that. There could have been members who might view the disclosure as political; your own bias to help the prediction unfold. Divisions and controversies might have erupted. How utterly wise of you to omit it."

Roh was emphatic. "Controversy would have been the least of it, Mr. President. It could have had a cataclysmic reaction. Certain factions could have interpreted that I was lying and manipulating history. A split could have gone straight through the Congress.

That could have led to a breach in *The Analogue's* security to obtain what some believed was the 'real' truth. Rest assured, I labored back and forth on this matter, but finally concluded I had the ethical obligation to remove my personal experience of discovering the book from the report. And, Mr. President, really, what is the difference? Why would the future need to be disclosed if it is destined to be anyway?"

Mott sat back pondering the ramifications of Duran's disclosure. "Duran, I must congratulate myself for selecting you to lead this great research project in the first place. It may have been the finest decision I ever made. A lesser man might have revealed what you kept private. Yet you chose not to succumb to that temptation; you avoided a potential disaster for the sake of world security. Thank you, Duran. I have not the slightest doubt that your family would be very proud of you today." A light went on in Mott's head. "Duran, I hesitate to ask this next question: Did a 'helper' also appear to you?"

"No. It is my belief that my complete acceptance of *The Book of Time* required no need for a 'helper.'"

Mott was in awe. "Wonder of wonders. Well, perhaps one day the book's origins will be known, but probably not to our generation. Congratulations, Duran. Now please go and take your well-deserved holiday."

Roh turned and left the President's private quarters feeling as if a great weight had been lifted from him. Just before passing through the outer hall, he paused and regarded the glimmering array of holographs that lined the curving corridor walls. Near the middle, one in particular was of a man who seemed to look straight at Roh with an uncanny sense of irony. Roh read the inscription under the holograph: *President John F. Kennedy, 35th President of the USA, 1917—1963AD.*

Roh's study of the first subject to discover *The Book of Time*, John Decker, and his attempt to save his President from assassination, came back to him as he read the quotation under the holograph: "History is a relentless master. It has no present, only the past rushing into the future. To try to hold fast is to be swept aside."

The Master Researcher carried the day's weight with him on his journey to Micronesia. As his ocean bus bolted over the Pacific, he rested back, closed his eyes, and listened with curious detachment to reports acclaiming Duran Roh as the greatest research scientist in history. One observer hailed him as, 'a man of the highest principle incapable of taking one scintilla of a self-serving road.'

Gazing out the window at the blue Pacific waters, Roh recalled the night a few months before when the research team collected in the auditorium's main complex to finally present the unstained strand known as **RTSM-λφα1** to the *Analogue*. Standing alone in his research quarters, he gave the signal for the chief project engineer to insert over a year's synthesized data into *The Analogue's* headface. The master researcher faced his screen and waited breathlessly as he reflected upon 138 years of *The Book of Time's* interface with Man. Now that century and a half was about to climax with one grand, dramatic conclusion.

The maroon diamond light switched on indicating the *Analogue* understood and accepted the strand. Not a sound could be heard anywhere in the center's labyrinthine halls as the research team pinned their eyes on the master screen above their heads.

Precisely thirty-seconds of time passed before the headface's maroon light switched off. All at once the response appeared on screens throughout the complex. The words were shockingly brief:

...Response 1 to problem RTSM-λφα1:
Origin of The Book Of Time:
ORIGIN IS INTRINSIC TO THAT
WHICH IS NON-PHYSICAL
EXISTING BEYOND PHYSICAL REALM.
NO FURTHER EXPLICATION POSSIBLE.

Response 2 to problem RTSM-λφα1:
Purpose of The Book Of Time:
HUMAN SELF-DISCOVERY TO ASSIST HISTORICAL CONTINUUM OF CIVILIZATION

—End of 2 Responses—

Gasps exploded from members of the research team when the electrifying sentences lit up. Roh stood frozen at his desk and immediately projected the negative reaction that would rain down upon him the day he reported these findings. He wondered what words he would use to the governing body to disclose that the book's source was not only beyond the present time, it was beyond the physical universe and emanated from the metaphysical realm. It was proof that a Master Intelligence existed outside physical matter.

Racing through the final leg of his trip, Roh listened to his praises with an aloof, heavy heart. How I wish Cassandra and the children were with me now. Life's greatest achievements are empty when one experiences them alone. Celebrity never replaces family bonds, the harsh lesson he learned through the prolonged pain of loss.

Roh stepped off the space bus at the tranquil docking port near the beautiful coral sands of Acrylia. He had decided to pass through the island's majestic gardens on foot and then ascend the hill toward his retreat house in solitude. His tall frame and strong legs climbed the arches of blooming orchids, plumeria, white hibiscus, and endless beds of red and yellow roses covering the slanting face of the hill like a magnificently spun quilt. The warm, tropical winds rushed in from the sea blowing Roh's burnt red hair askew. Yes, *The Book of Time* did indeed appear to me, Mr. President. But out of deep respect, I disclosed to you only half of what it forecast. And I am comfortable with the decision to keep the rest with me and me alone.

Reaching the hill's crest, Roh paused and drank in the vista of the curve of the terrain as the ocean swept around Acrylia's irregular, jagged shores. The surf below, the swirl of gulls against the white face of rocks, the interior of lush tropical forests, reminded him that among all the Eden-like paradises on Earth, this island sanctuary was, for him now, his private paradise.

The two-storied structure rose like a silver citadel from the top of the crest. The home's elliptical walls reflected the sun's rays and mirrored a poignant glint of white light out to the sea.

You see, Mr. President, *The Book of Time*, this *100th* book, has never left me.

Roh reached the summit and hiked over the private footpath lined with orchids and blooming ironwood. Finally arriving at the silver facade, he raised his palm and watched as the opening rose. The house's interior atmospherics—the fresh scent of an evergreen forest—had been programmed by Roh hours before in his ocean bus. The walls of the narrow entrance way shimmered with pictures of his family. A circular couch, lined with comfortable mauve and sea-blue pillows, swept around the elliptical curve of the room.

He descended to his leisure quarters below. Wall screens filled with a myriad of squares flashing instantaneous data from the world and from space. Weary of information, he turned off the screens. Roh's gaze then turned to the opposite side of the room. He walked toward the alabaster cabinet and its crystalline, glistening panes. Then he raised his palm and watched as the center cabinet door slid back. A soft light sprayed out filling the room pleasantly with its golden glow. The volume lay on the shelf.

THE BOOK OF TIME

Roh lifted it and regarded the book's cover with great awe. Then he opened to the first page and read the words once again:

The Presidency of Duran Roh
2120—2130AD

...*The Presidency of Duran Roh to the Federal Governing Body of the International State in New York City was announced*

434

upon the death of President Cyrus Mott on July 1, 2120AD
after an emergency election in which 2,000 members of the
General Membership Congress cast unanimous votes for Master
Researcher Roh...

How in the world could I possibly disclose your own death to you in four years, Mr. President? Even more, how could I become so foolish to also disclose that I would be the one to succeed you?

Roh's fingers explored the book's firm, yet satin-like golden pages. Do I hold in my hands, this one-hundredth book, yet another hallucination? Whatever its true essence, I will accept the mystery of *The Book of Time* and its presence in my life as a gift. Then he placed the volume back upon the cabinet's shelf, raised his hand, and watched the glistening, oval pane slide shut. *Discovery.*

An hour later, Roh waded through Acrylia's gentle, bath-like surf. Inspecting a piece of white corral that had washed up to the sand, he reflected upon its origins. I will secret *The Book of Time* through my Presidency and for the rest of my life. Perhaps some day I will reach for it and it will have vanished as it vanished from 99 others who came before me. The last thing to worry about, he smiled. For *The Book of Time* forges its own destiny. And Duran Roh knew that better than any man on Earth.

Swimming out to sea, an image returned to him, one of the more distant subjects, a woman named Suzanne Deanna in the early 21st Century. She, too, discovered *The Book of Time* rolling in from the ocean current. He remembered studying her life and how she met her challenges with new-found courage. And that courage became her greatest collaborator strengthening her to create a work of art which led to great consequence for others in succeeding generations.

President Duran Roh, he thought again with overwhelmingly mixed emotions. But I have miles to go before I sleep. Roh had, at last, accepted his place in the destiny of Man and recognized the good work he did for his own generation and for future generations.

And the source of his discovery had been gleaned from the wondrous book that came from beyond space and time.

References

[1] CASABLANCA. 1942. Screenwriters: Julius and Phillip Epstein; Howard Koch. Warner Bro.

[2] MATTHEW 7:15.

[3] MARK 10:25.

[4] THE MYTH OF DAEDALUS AND ICARUS. Van Bryan. In Classical Wisdom Weekly. May, 2013. (classicalwisdom.com/the-myth-of-Daedalus-and-Icarus/)

[5] LAURA. 1944. Screenwriters: Jay Dratler, Samuel Hoffenstein, and Elizabeth Reinhardt. 20th Century Fox

Made in the USA
Las Vegas, NV
27 February 2021